Drive

A Novel

by

Don Tassone

Golden Antelope Press
715 E. McPherson
Kirksville, Missouri 63501
2017

ISBN   978-1-936135-41-7 (1-936135-41-8)

Library of Congress Control Number:

Published by:
Golden Antelope Press
715 E. McPherson
Kirksville, Missouri 63501

Available at:
Golden Antelope Press
715 E. McPherson
Kirksville, Missouri, 63501
Phone: (660) 665-0273
http://www.goldenantelope.com
Email: ndelmoni@gmail.com

"The only journey is the one within."

— Rainer Maria Rilke

For Liz, my love

Acknowledgements

This is my first novel. I want to thank those who have given me guidance and encouragement: Christine Sneed, Kathy Kennedy, Christine des Garennes, Dale Brown, Tom Millikin, Dan Mersch, Mike Moore, Erin Bailey, Andi Rogers, Bob Becker, Pete Smith, Sandy Weiskittel, Ray Rytel, Jake Adams, Ryssa Kemper, Tom Steele, Eileen Levesque, Greg Icenhower, Dominic Vaiana — and especially my wife, Liz, to whom this book is dedicated.

I also want to extend my appreciation to Edward Lewis Wallant, whose first novel, *The Human Season*, has inspired mine.

Finally, I want to thank Neal and Betsy Delmonico, who own and operate Golden Antelope Press, for being such wonderful partners.

Don Tassone
August 2017

Chapter One

Nick Reynolds, his neck reddening, his eyes narrowing, his jaw clenching, leaned forward and stared down the length of his conference table like a hunter peering down the barrel of his gun.

"Is that all?" the president of the world's largest snack cake company huffed.

A woman sitting to his right forced a smile and touched his sleeve with her fingertips. "Maybe I should lead off."

He shot her a withering look.

"No, Jennifer," he said, pulling his arm away. "I'll handle this."

"Mr. Reynolds," said a man at the other end of the table. "We would be happy to provide more detail on any part of our proposal."

Nick appeared to be looking at the man who was speaking. But he was looking past him. He was looking out the large window behind him at the sleek, black exterior and tinted, bronze windows of the Willis Tower shimmering in the afternoon sun.

Willis Tower. Nick could hardly bring himself to put those two words together, even in his head. It's Sears Tower, and it always will be, he thought. The very idea that anyone would have the audacity to rename such an iconic building pissed him off, as so many things did these days.

"Mr. Reynolds?" asked the man sitting at the other end of the table.

"What?" Nick said with a scowl.

"I said we would be happy to provide more detail on any part of our proposal."

Nick now fixed his gaze on the man. Leaning toward him, he stretched his arms out and slapped his palms down on the table. His head, which was the size of a bowling ball, began to vibrate. His face was blood red. A vein stood out on his neck. He was breathing hard. He looked like a volcano ready to blow.

"Oh, really?" he growled. "Well, guess what, Tom? That won't be necessary."

"It won't?"

"No, it won't. Your proposal doesn't need any more detail."

"It doesn't?"

"No, Tom. What your proposal needs, what it really needs, is to be shredded and started over!"

Tom and his teammates cast their eyes down. They had worked at Elgin long enough to have a sense of what was coming next.

"Nick, easy," Jennifer, his vice president, said.

This time, he didn't even spare her a glance.

"I gave you six weeks to come up with a marketing plan for our most important new product launch in years. I gave you full access to our experts and our best ad agency. I approved your creative brief. I gave you fifty-thousand dollars to develop a proposal. Let me ask you something, Tom. Given all that, how is that you and your team could have come up with such a piece of crap?"

"Mr. Reynolds, in fairness, I think our team has done some excellent work."

Tom stuttered over his last few words. He knew he'd made a terrible mistake.

"Tom!" Nick Reynolds bellowed, slamming the palm of his meaty hand down on the table. "I don't think you heard me! I said your plan is a piece of crap!"

"I heard you, Mr. Reynolds."

"Well, if you're still listening, then take a note."

Nick picked up his notepad and slipped on his reading glasses. He stood up and began pacing around the conference table, staring everyone down, like a drill sergeant reviewing his platoon.

Everyone picked up their pens, as if to record instruction from God.

"I'm going to make three points."

Of course. Nick always made three points.

"First, get a strategy. Does anybody here know what a strategy is?"

No one moved or said a word. Nick kept pacing around the table, glaring at each member of the team as they hunched over their note pads and tried to avoid making eye contact.

"Strategy, folks, is about choosing. It's about sacrifice. It's a narrow bridge between your goals and your tactics. Your plan is all over the place because it lacks a clear strategy."

Then, bending down over Tom until he was almost in his face, he said, "Work on your damn strategy. Whittle it down. Then build your plan accordingly. And keep it tight."

Except for the sound of scribbling, the room was silent. Nick continued pacing around the table.

"Second, timing. Everything depends on this new line hitting stores like wildfire next June. That's less than a year away. Don't give me any of this pre-market conditioning crap. All our research shows people are going to love these new low-cal snack cakes. So don't give me any garbage about a test market. And forget influencers. We're already late. Your plan needs to make these new products fly off store shelves by June! Focus on that and quit screwing around."

By now, Nick had circled the table twice and was back at his black leather chair, which was so tall, wide and heavily padded that it looked more like a throne.

"Third," he said, crunching into the chair and pausing for effect.

Everyone knew Nick always saved a real zinger for last. Their pens were at the ready.

"I want a fresh team on this project in the morning. You can keep one person for continuity. Otherwise, you're all reassigned."

Pens down.

Finally, he turned to Jennifer.

"I want our best people on this project. I don't care what they're working on now. If anybody pushes back, let me know. I want you to pull an 'A' team together, and I want to meet back here in two weeks to hear their proposal."

"Two weeks isn't much time, Nick," Jennifer said. "Let me work with Tom and his team to improve their plan in line with your direction. We'll still come back in two weeks. I think you'll see a big difference."

Nick had had enough. He reached out and pounded the table with his right fist, making coffee cups, water glasses and a silver platter of snack cakes rattle. Then he stood up with such force that his chair shot back and hit the wall behind him. The tip of his tie dangled two inches above his belt buckle, revealing the bottom button of his shirt, which was straining to hold back his colossal belly, which hung over the edge of the table. He was a hulking figure, at least seventy-five pounds overweight.

"This meeting is over! Jennifer, I will see you, one of you," he said nodding toward the other end of the conference table, "and a new team back here in two weeks."

With that, Tom and his team quietly gathered their things and left.

"Nick, that wasn't necessary," Jennifer said.

"Jennifer, you're my best vice president," he said, picking up his notepad and slipping his pen into the inside pocket of his suit coat. "But you coddle people. That was one of the worst proposals I've ever seen. Imagine what customers would say if we showed them something like that. We'd be laughed out of the room."

"I admit it needs work, Nick. It clearly wasn't ready for you today. But we need good people on this project, and that's no way to motivate people."

"See, Jennifer? That's what I'm talking about it. You still don't get it. I don't want to motivate these people. I want to fire them. I want new people, people who are going to put together a plan that will smash the competition and take us to glory."

"You mean take you to glory."

He shot her a stare as cold as the North wind.

"Two weeks," he said, getting up and walking to the door.

#

Nick walked down the hall to his corner office. It was nearly twice the size of the office of any other president in the company. At work, Nick gauged a man's power by the number of ceiling tiles in his office. Whenever he entered someone's office, his eyes would drift upward. During meetings, he would count the number of tiles along the length and width of the ceiling and multiply in his head. To Nick, every tile mattered.

The first thing he did when he moved into his current office was to have it expanded. In the process, he displaced several people in the adjoining offices. But he didn't care. Far from it. During the reconstruction, he hosted as many meetings there as he could. He boasted to all his guests that two other offices had to be cut in half to make room for his new space — which, he was quick to add, would require eighty more ceiling tiles.

Most days, Nick was the last one to leave the office. But it was Friday afternoon, the Friday of Memorial Day weekend, no less. It had been a tough week, and Nick was ready for a drink, especially after that disaster of a meeting. He decided to leave a little early.

He was stuffing a few file folders and his laptop into his lambskin briefcase when his secretary, Pam, appeared at his door. He looked up without acknowledging her.

"Mr. Reynolds, Mr. Bradford would like to see you."

"Crap," he muttered. There's nothing worse than ending your week in the CEO's office, he thought.

He pulled his notepad back out of his briefcase and reached behind his door for his suit coat. No one else in the office wore suits or ties any more. Nick never gave up either.

"Would you like me to stick around?" Pam asked.

"No," he said, brushing past her.

"Have a good weekend," he grumbled.
"You too, Mr. Reynolds."

#

"Go right in, Mr. Reynolds," Louis Bradford's secretary, Helen, said. She had worked for Bradford for at least two decades. She reminded Nick of Mrs. Seltzer, his high school principal's ancient secretary. Nick thought Helen looked like a cross between Grandma Moses and a Rottweiler. Helen never seemed to like Nick, and he was always a little intimidated by her. Seeing her always made him feel like he was going to the principal's office.

Today, though, Helen gave Nick a big smile. This made him especially nervous.

"Come in, Nick," Bradford said. "Shut the door."

This was not a good sign.

Nick had known Bradford his whole career. They started with the company at the same time, thirty-one years earlier. Bradford's career took off faster. But a decade later, Nick had caught up. There was a lot of speculation that either of them might become CEO one day. A few loyalists even began identifying themselves as "Nick's guys" or "Lou's guys." They were both ambitious and no doubt saw each other as rivals. But they remained friends.

Over time, Bradford began to distinguish himself as a stronger all-around CEO candidate. Nick's numbers were slightly better. But Bradford had a much better track record in developing the organization. He was an inspiring leader. He cared about people. He connected with people. Nick thought of employees strictly as either helping or hurting his sales and profits, and he rewarded or punished them accordingly. He knew, of course, that, as a CEO contender, treating people this way would put him at a disadvantage. But he didn't care enough to change.

Now, by all counts, it was clear that the previous CEO and the board had made an enlightened choice in putting Bradford in charge. In five years, he'd doubled Elgin's sales and tripled its profits. Investors were thrilled, and employees, with the notable exception of many of those working for Nick, were happy.

But like everyone, Bradford had a weakness. As good as he was at making business decisions and motivating employees, he was reluctant to tackle tough personnel issues, especially when they involved people he knew well.

Now in walked his old friend, his top producer and his biggest personnel headache.

"Hi, Lou."

"Hello, Nick. Sit down."

Nick had been in this office hundreds of times. This time, though, it felt different.

As Nick sat down, Bradford stood up. He walked over to his window and looked out.

"Nick, we need to talk."

"Someone complained?"

"Yeah."

"I should have known. It was that—"

"Nick, shut up."

Bradford had never been so blunt with Nick.

"I have something to tell you," he said, stepping back over to his desk and sitting down. "And I want you to listen."

"All right."

"I want you to take some time off."

Nick laughed. Bradford sat stone-faced.

"Lou? You're kidding?"

"I'm not kidding, Nick. I want you to take the summer. I want you to decide whether you want to continue to work here."

Nick stopped smiling and shifted his considerable weight in his chair.

"Are you letting me go?"

"No, Nick. I'm not letting you go. But I'm telling you there will be no more days like today here, no more meetings like the one you had this afternoon."

"Lou, you should have seen this proposal. It was awful."

"A piece of crap, I heard."

"Okay. I lost my temper. But I gave Tom and his team every chance. They blew it. Lou, this is our biggest launch in years. If it flops, how in the hell are we going to explain that to the board?"

Bradford gave him an icy stare.

"You know, Nick, the last time I checked, I was the one responsible for working with the board around here."

Bradford never pulled rank. Nick knew he was on thin ice.

"Look, Nick. Your business results are unmatched. But when it comes to the organization, you're a human wrecking ball."

"Lou, I'll change."

"Nick, you've told me you're going to change the last ten times we've had this conversation. But you're getting worse, not better. So here's the deal. You're going to take a sabbatical. Go away with Jean. Relax. Get help. Do whatever you need to do to sort yourself out, then decide what you really want to do. But know that, if you come back here, you're going to need to treat people well. If you decide to come back, I'll be glad to have you. If not, I'll understand."

At last, Nick's situation was becoming clear to him. He realized there would be no negotiating his way out of this one.

"What will we tell the organization?" he asked, sounding resigned.

"We'll tell them you're working on a special project."

"And who will take charge while I'm gone?"

"I'll ask Jennifer to fill in for you."

This was all sounding very definitive.

"And so that's it?"

"Nick, I want you to succeed here, on my team. But whether you do that is your choice."

They sat there for a moment, eye to eye, saying nothing. Then Bradford stood up and extended his hand. Nick stood up and took it.

"I'm in your corner, Nick."

"Thanks, Lou."

Bradford came around his desk and walked Nick to the door. He opened it with one hand and put the other on Nick's back.

"Take care, Nick."

"I'll see you, Lou."

Helen was sitting at her desk, still smiling.

"Goodbye, Mr. Reynolds."

"Goodbye, Helen."

He walked out, wondering if he would ever see her or anyone there again.

#

Nick took the elevator to the tenth floor. He swiped his ID across the card reader, pulled open the large glass door and waded through a sea of cubicles to his office. Pam was gone. Good, he thought. No need to explain.

For a moment, he did think about leaving Pam a note. But then he figured Bradford would cover her and no doubt find a new role for her too. He was good at the soft stuff.

He looked around his office at the framed Food Marketing Institute and American Marketing Association awards for best new products and ad campaigns of the year; at photographs of him teeing off with Tiger Woods, shooting hoops with Michael Jordan, playing guitar with Carlos Santana; at a small battalion of gold-plated statuettes perched atop a tall glass table in the corner. This was the center of his world. From here, he had built an empire. This was his place, and now he was being told to get out.

Where would he go? It was too much to think about right now. At that moment, as he looked around his office, all he could do was ask himself what, if anything, he should take with him.

Nick liked to make decisions fast. He grabbed his laptop. It was all he needed. It contained all his active files and gave him access to the company's email and intranet systems. Surely, he thought, people would start reaching out to him within a few days, when they began to comprehend his indispensability.

He walked to the door and flipped the light switch. It was late May. The late-afternoon sun shone brightly through the huge windows that were his office walls. Turning the lights off at this hour hardly made a difference. It seemed an odd thing to think about at the moment. But Nick was always thinking about cutting costs. He made a mental note to issue a directive to start turning lights off in the summer.

By the time he made his way through the maze of cubicles again, just about everyone had cleared out. Nick did spot one guy at his desk. He looked familiar, but he didn't know his name.

"Good night, Mr. Reynolds," he said as Nick passed by. "Have a good holiday."

Holiday? What did he mean by that? Had word already gotten out about his sabbatical? Then he remembered it was indeed a holiday weekend.

"Yeah," Nick said, as he kept walking and avoided eye contact. "You too."

He pushed open the glass door to the atrium and pressed the button for the elevator. He hoped he wouldn't run into anyone he knew on the way out. He was in no mood for small talk.

The doors opened at ground level. The lobby was awash with sunlight. Nick decided to stop here rather than keep going down to the garage because he needed a drink. Besides, I-94 would be packed, and he couldn't stand the idea of telling Jean what had happened just yet.

He slipped on his sunglasses, stepped outside and headed to his favorite downtown pub, a place called Tony's on East Wacker, just two blocks from his office.

"Good evening, Mr. Reynolds," said the pretty hostess. "Would you like a table tonight?"

"No, thanks. I think I'll grab a bite at the bar."

Nick had seen this hostess many times. But he didn't call her by name because he'd never taken the time to introduce himself. But she knew his name. That's all that mattered.

He laid his laptop on the bar and sat down.

"Good evening, Mr. Reynolds," the bartender said.

"Good evening, Eric." This guy he knew by name.

"The usual?"

"Yeah."

Eric eyed the laptop as he reached for a bottle of Absolut. "Bringing your work home over the holiday?"

"What's that?"

"Your computer."

"Oh, yeah. It never stops."

"That's the way it is when you're the top dog, I guess."

"Yeah."

Eric prepared a drink with the precise hand movements of a tailor.

"Here you go, Mr. Reynolds," he said, sliding a napkin in front of him and setting a vodka martini on top of it. "Can I get you anything else?"

"Actually, yes. Bring me your best steak, medium well. And a baked potato with sour cream."

"You got it. Anything else?"

"Another martini, when you get a chance."

Nick took a long drink then looked down the bar. At the end sat Tom and two other guys who'd made the presentation to him less than two hours earlier.

He hadn't seen them when he came in. But they had seen him. Now they were looking his way. They were saying something to each other and gesturing wildly, as if they were acting in a play. One of them was shaking his finger at Tom. The other raised his thumb above his fist and extended his index finger, like a gun, then "shot" Tom. Tom put his hands over his heart and slumped down over the bar. His faux assailants laughed. They all grabbed their beers, raised a toast and drank them down.

Tom laid a couple of bills on the bar, and the three of them got up. Rather than walk by Nick, they walked around the other side of the bar and left. Just as well, Nick thought.

He gulped down the rest of his martini and stared at his reflection in the mirror behind several shelves lined with a colorful array of bottles. He didn't like being fifty-three years old. And yet whenever he came upon a mirror, he always stopped and stared. He might no longer be considered handsome in the eyes of the world, but there was no face Nick loved to look at more than his own.

"Here you go, Mr. Reynolds," Eric said, setting down a fresh martini with one hand and removing the empty glass with the other. "Your dinner will be right out."

Dinner, Nick thought. He'd better let Jean know he would not be home for dinner.

He reached inside his suit coat. He pulled his readers out of the vest pocket and slipped them on. Then he pulled his iPhone out of his breast pocket and sent Jean a text. *Working late. Will grab dinner. Don't wait for me.* He laid his phone on the bar.

A few minutes later, his phone vibrated. He put his readers back on and looked at Jean's response. *Heading out soon for dinner and a movie with Sarah and Diane. Don't wait up.*

Oh, yeah. She'd told him that last night. He had had a few beers at that point. These days, he tended to forget little things like that, especially after he'd been drinking.

Now he was glad he remembered because he felt relieved that Jean would not be waiting for him at home. He could relax. He had a lot to think about.

Eric sat Nick's dinner down in front of him.

"May I get you anything else?"

"How about a glass of cab?"

"Certainly. House okay?"

"No. Give me the best cab you have."

"Very good."

Nick downed the last of his martini and dug into his steak. He took big bites between swigs of wine. When he finished his glass, he motioned to Eric to bring him another.

Three months is a very long time, Nick thought. For twenty

years, his idea of a vacation had been a long weekend. What in the world was he going to do for a whole summer?

For a moment, he thought about staying home. Then he winced, imagining playing house with Jean, and put the idea out of his mind.

He opened his laptop and slipped on his readers. Between his business trips and golf trips over the years, he'd been in just about every major city in the country and stayed at some of the best resorts. He needed a change of scenery, a place far enough away to clear his mind, a place where he would be invisible.

But where had he not been? He typed in "map of the US." The weather forecasters were predicting a hot summer, so he scanned the northern states. Washington? Too liberal. Idaho? Too nutty. Montana? Too rugged. Wyoming? Too conservative. North Dakota? Too boring. Minnesota? Too buggy. Wisconsin? Too close. Michigan? Still too close, and he might run into Jean's people. New York? Too depressed. Vermont? Too socialist. Maine? Maine? Hmmm, Maine.

It was one place he had never been. He enlarged the New England portion of the map. His eyes followed the coastline north to Bar Harbor.

Bah Habah. It sounded nice but seemed awfully far away. He typed in "distance from Winnetka to Bar Harbor." Twelve hundred and seventy-five miles, twenty hours driving. He could do that.

Bar Harbor it was.

#

Nick lived only twenty miles north of the city, but it took him more than an hour to get home. Not that traffic was heavy. He just drove slowly, staying in the right lane, knowing the cops were on the lookout for drunks on a holiday weekend. Plus, he had to pull off twice to pee.

Of course, he shouldn't have been driving at all. But over the years, he had convinced himself that he could handle his alcohol and that, if he just drove slowly, he'd be fine. Indeed, he had never had an accident.

He did, though, have contempt for every other driver on the road.

"See those cars?" he would say to his kids when they were little. "They're being driven by idiots. Good thing you're with me."

Nick routinely drove drunk. It was a miracle that he'd never hurt anyone. Once, after a particularly boozy night, he'd had the good sense to call a cab. As soon as he stumbled in the front door, though, he regretted it.

"You're an alcoholic!" Jean screamed, using the taxi as her latest proof.

Nick learned his lesson that night. He never called a cab to go home again.

#

When he got home, he went upstairs and changed into a golf shirt, shorts and deck shoes. Then he went downstairs to his den. In the corner stood his old Fender Stratocaster. He was tempted to pick it up and, with Jean not around, crank it up. But that night he just didn't have the strength.

Instead, he grabbed a fat Cuban and a small box of wooden matches from his humidor and went to the kitchen to pour himself a glass of bourbon.

He slid the patio door open and stepped out on the deck. It was a warm night. There was a party going on next door. The smallest lots in his neighborhood were three acres. Nick's was five. There was plenty of privacy. Still, through the trees, he could see people sitting on the patio and standing in the grass. He could hear music and laughter. He could smell smoke from the fire pit.

He loved parties, but that night he was glad to be alone. By the light of the moon, he clipped his cigar. He bit down hard on the end to flatten it and licked the sweet, rough tobacco leaves for a slower burn. Holding the stogie in his teeth, he pulled out a match, struck it and lit the end, cupping it with his hand. There was no breeze. But he cupped the end anyway, a reflex hard-wired in his muscle memory from lighting thousands of cigarettes years ago, before Jean made him give them up.

Nick sat down in his favorite Adirondack chair. Spotlights were trained on a few trees in his back yard. Landscape lights illuminated a stone path around the back of his house. It was too dark to see much. But in the moonlight, he could make out the silhouette of the tall trees in the woods at the edge of his property and beyond. The treetops were swaying. With all the alcohol and now an extra buzz from his cigar, Nick felt a little dizzy.

He closed his eyes. In his mind, he could see Bradford. He could see the stern look on his face. "You're a human wrecking ball," he could hear him say.

In his heart, Nick knew his boss was right. He did chew people up. His strong business results had given him cover for years. But he knew the way he treated people would catch up with him eventually. In fact, in a corporate world now ruled as much by HR as Finance, he was surprised it had taken Bradford so long to do something about it.

But he didn't want to think about that any more tonight. He finished his bourbon and decided to have a nightcap. That meant he would have to get up, and getting out of this low-slung chair was tough even when he was sober. He stuck his cigar between his front teeth, pressed his elbows and forearms down on the flat arms of the Adirondack and pried himself up. But just as he began to lean forward, the chair wobbled. His empty glass, which was resting on the left arm of the chair, toppled off. It hit the deck and shattered.

"Crap!" he grunted, still clutching the cigar in his teeth. "Crap!"

He pushed down hard on the arms of the chair and at last extricated himself. But in the process, his cigar ashes crumbled and fell onto his bare thigh.

"God damn it!" he cried out, brushing the hot ashes away. He pulled the cigar from his mouth and tossed it underhand into the back yard.

He trudged into the house and grabbed a broom and dustpan from the pantry. He flipped on the outside light, stumbled back out on the deck and swept up the broken glass.

At first, he was going to dump it into the trash can under the kitchen sink. But then he realized Jean would see it and ask him about it. So he went out to the garage and dumped it into the recycling bin, concealing the shards of glass with a cereal box.

He was about to pour himself another glass of bourbon when he noticed he had two text messages waiting on his phone, which was sitting on the counter.

The first was a conciliatory message from his boss. *Sorry to be so rough today. Take care and stay in touch. See you soon. Lou*

The second was from Jean. *Grabbing drinks. Be home in about an hour.*

Nick poured himself a tall glass of bourbon, turned off the outside light and staggered back out on the deck. This time, he decided not to risk getting stuck in the Adirondack chair. Instead, he leaned against the railing. The party next door was still going strong.

He took a long drink. How did it get to this point, he wondered. How could he and Jean have become so distant, so cagey toward one another? How in the hell could Lou have asked him to leave?

Maybe I'll go away and not come back, he thought. Maybe then they'll appreciate me.

He finished his drink. Jean would be home soon. He didn't want to face her that night. He went inside and locked up.

Nick and Jean had slept in separate bedrooms for years. He went into his bathroom, peed, then climbed into bed. He lay on his back and closed his eyes.

The room was spinning. He opened his eyes and tried to focus on a spot where the moonlight through the windows hit the ceiling. But the room kept spinning. He felt sick. He slid out of bed and made his way to the bathroom. Falling to his knees, he reached the toilet just in time.

He got up slowly and flushed, then staggered over to the sink and turned on the faucet. He splashed his face, cupped his hands, slurped in a mouthful of water and spit it out.

He wiped his mouth on his shirt and caught a glimpse of himself in the mirror. His face looked ghastly, especially in the pale glow from the nightlight. His eyes were sunken, his face was bloated and his thin gray hair splayed out from his head, like spines on a desert cactus.

He stumbled back to bed. He felt chilled. He pulled the covers up over his face, shivering. He lay on his side, drawing his knees toward his chest as far as his big belly would allow, and passed out.

Chapter Two

Nick awoke to the aroma of strong coffee wafting up from the kitchen. His tongue felt as thick as a cow's tongue, the inside of his mouth as dry as cardboard. His head was pounding. He opened his eyes, then shut them tight to block the sunlight streaming in through his blinds.

It took him a minute to recollect what had happened the previous afternoon and night and to realize Jean was awake. He pulled back his blanket. He was still wearing his golf shirt and shorts. He couldn't go downstairs this way because Jean would then know he'd slept in his clothes and begin grilling him. So he changed into a T-shirt and flannel pajama bottoms and headed downstairs.

"Good morning," she said, looking up.

She was sitting on the sofa, drinking coffee, with her laptop resting on her legs.

"Morning," he said, glancing away from her. "How was the movie?" he asked from the kitchen.

"Oh, it was okay."

"What'd you see?" he asked, feigning interest as he poured himself a cup of coffee.

"It was a chick flick. You wouldn't have liked it. What did you do last night?"

"Well," he said, stepping into the family room and sitting down in his favorite chair, a leather recliner. "I stayed at the office longer than I was expecting and decided to have dinner at

Tony's. I got home about nine."

"Sounds like you had a quiet night."

"Yeah."

"How was work?"

"I had a tough meeting with Lou yesterday afternoon."

"What do you mean?" she asked, looking up from her computer.

"He wants me to take some time off."

"What?" she asked, setting her laptop on the coffee table. She tucked her feet under her on the sofa.

"He wants me to take a sabbatical."

"A sabbatical?"

"Yeah. He wants me to take the summer off."

"Why?"

"He thinks I've been too hard on the organization."

"Nick, what did you do this time?"

He knew this would happen.

"I heard a presentation yesterday afternoon by the team that's working on the marketing plan for our new low-cal line. It was a piece of crap."

"And you said that?"

"Yeah."

"Oh, Nick."

"What? I was just being honest."

"What else?"

"I reassigned most of the members of the team."

"You've got to be kidding me. In the meeting?"

"Yeah."

"And someone told Lou?"

"Yeah, I guess."

"Well, you deserved it. What did he say to you specifically?"

"He told me to take the summer off."

"Take the summer off?"

"Yeah, a sabbatical."

"Nick," she said, shaking her head. "Lou wasn't telling you to take a sabbatical."

"What do you mean?"

"He was giving you an out. Lou wants to fire you, but he's too kind. Don't you see? He's cutting you loose."

"He said he wants me back by Labor Day."

"That's ridiculous. He wants you to leave."

"Why do you say that?"

"Who's he putting in charge while you're gone?"

"Jennifer."

"I rest my case. Lou's been looking for a way to promote Jennifer for years. You've just given him his chance. She'll step in and do a great job. When you come back, Lou will put you on a special assignment, and you'll be gone in a month. He's probably already got Helen organizing your retirement party."

"Gee, Jean. I thought you might be a little more sympathetic."

"Nick, you should have seen this coming. But you don't see how harsh you've become with people. You act like a pit bull. I'm surprised it's taken Lou so long to move you out."

"Lou may not like the way I treat people, but he sure likes my business results."

"Nick, you've got to be kidding me. You actually believe that?"

"Believe what?"

"That good numbers mean you can treat people any way you want?"

"Jean, this team made a proposal that was all over the place. It was an embarrassment."

"Okay. Maybe their proposal needs work. Did you ever think about giving them another chance?"

"Now you sound like Jennifer."

"Jennifer is a leader. No wonder Lou wants to put her in charge."

"Jesus, Jean."

"So what are you going to do, Nick?"

"Well, I've been thinking about that. I think I'm going to spend the summer in Bar Harbor."

"What?"

"Yeah. I've always wanted to go to Maine. I'm thinking about renting a little cabin there for the summer."

She rolled her eyes.

"I'm serious."

"Nick, you're telling me that you, the guy who's barely taken a weekend off in twenty years, are going away to Bar Harbor for an entire summer?"

"That's right. I need a break, Jean."

"Yeah, you need a break. You need to retire. You need to go see Lou next Tuesday and tell him you've thought about this a little more and you're going to retire."

"Why are you doing this, Jean?"

"Doing what?"

"Why are you always so hard on me? I'm telling you I've decided to go away for a while, and your response is to argue with me. Would it kill you to be supportive for a change?"

"How are you going to get to Bar Harbor?"

"I'm going to drive."

"By yourself?"

"Yeah."

"How long will it take?"

"Twenty hours. But I plan to break it up and stop along the way."

"You've got this whole thing planned out, don't you?"

"Not really. I just looked at a map last night. I haven't planned anything. I thought I'd tell you first."

"When do you plan to leave?"

"Tomorrow morning."

"Tomorrow morning?"

"Yeah."

"Nick, I think you need to think this thing through."

"I've already decided. I'm leaving in the morning."

"Fine. And what am I supposed to do all summer?"

"Jean, you'll have plenty to keep you busy. You have that big project for school. Maybe the kids can come visit. You don't need me hanging around anyway. You'll be fine."

"So," she said, getting up. "That's the deal?"

"Yeah," he said, getting up too. He couldn't stand to have Jean looking down on him. "That's the deal."

Nick knew Jean was pissed. She had long ago given up any hope of controlling him. But she'd always been in charge of their social life, and now Nick had just ripped three months out of their calendar.

"Well, if you're going to leave tomorrow and drive all that way, you'd better get your car tuned up. You're overdue for service."

You can say that again, Nick thought.

"I'll call Mike and see if I can get in this afternoon."

"Good luck with that on Memorial Day weekend."

Jean grabbed her laptop from the coffee table, sat back on the sofa and opened it. Nick took this as a sign she was finished with their conversation.

He went back into the kitchen and made himself a piece of toast. Then he walked down the hall to his den and called Mike, the service manager at the local Mercedes dealership, where Nick had bought his cars and had them serviced for years.

"Let me see what I can do, Mr. Reynolds," Mike said. "Okay if I put you on hold for just a minute?"

"Sure, Mike."

Nick was just starting to listen to a recorded pitch for the newest S-Class sedan when Mike broke back in.

"Good news!"

"What's that?"

"We've just had a cancellation. Can you make it in at noon?"

"Yeah. That'll work great, Mike. See you then."

Sitting down at his desk, Nick opened his laptop, logged on and typed in Bar Harbor. He looked for a place on the water. He found a one-bedroom cabin overlooking Frenchman Bay and booked it for the summer.

He also thought about going ahead and lining up places to stay along the way. But what's the rush, he thought. He decided he would drive for as long as he wanted each day and get a room wherever he chose to stop for the night.

The idea of going on a trip with so little planning felt strange to Nick. His calendar at work was scheduled in fifteen-minute increments and, for him, nearly every day was a work day. He'd grown accustomed to living his life according to a plan. The idea of getting in his car the next morning and simply driving east, with no destination in mind or hotel reservations, was like deciding he would begin speaking Mandarin. This was going to take some getting used to.

Nick padded down the hall to his bathroom. He looked in the mirror. His eyes were sunken with dark circles under them. His nose was bright red. His skin looked pasty. He had the jowls of a bulldog and at least two chins. His thinning hair splayed out from his head like tiny wires. Sometimes when he looked in the mirror, he glimpsed the alcoholic that Jean claimed he had become.

He showered, got dressed and went downstairs.

"Can Mike fit you in today?"

"Yep. I have an appointment at noon."

"How long will it take?"

"He said a couple of hours."

"What do you want to do tonight?"

"Nothing. In fact, I think I'll get to bed early. I want to get an early start tomorrow."

"Do you want me to fix dinner?"

"No. I'm going to run a few errands after my tune-up. I'll just grab something while I'm out."

"Well, in that case, I might go out with the girls."

"Fine," he said, heading to the garage. "See you tonight."

#

The lounge at the dealership looked like a country club. It was spacious and elegant, with comfortable furniture, a gas fireplace, a widescreen TV and a full buffet. There was a fitness center and a movie theater upstairs. Each customer was greeted by name at the door.

The place was always busy on Saturday. It was especially crowded that afternoon. Nick usually brought his car in for service or a free wash on Saturdays. He often ran into someone he knew. As he looked around that day, he was relieved not to recognize anyone. He was in no mood for small talk.

He fixed himself a plate of food and a cup of coffee and sat down at a tall table near the fireplace. Two guys in their early 30s strutted in. Their hair was wet, they smelled of cologne and they had gym bags slung over their shoulders.

The receptionist, tall and blond, walked in to check on the buffet. She was wearing tight, black leather pants and a white, V-neck sweater, revealing ample cleavage. For Nick, seeing her there on Saturdays was always a treat. Watching her bend down to restock the mini-fridge was a particular highlight.

"Hi, guys," she said in a sing-song voice. "Getting a workout in today?"

"Yeah," said one, not even trying not to stare at her chest. "You've got a great facility here."

"Thank you. I'm so glad you like it. Is there anything I can get you guys?"

"Do you have any sparkling water?"

Oh, for God's sake, Nick thought. Sparkling water? Grow a pair, man.

"Yes, I think I might have one sparkling water left!" she chirped.

She opened the fridge, bent over, got down on her hands and her knees, reached way in and pulled out a bottle of Perrier.

Son of a bitch, Nick thought. That guy's a lot smarter than I thought.

She smiled and turned toward everyone sitting in the lounge.

"May I get any of you anything?"

She stood perfectly straight, with her hands folded in front of her. Nick could not take his eyes off her chest.

A couple of people murmured, "No, thanks." Nick hoped she would look his way. If she makes eye contact, he thought, I'll engage her. But she didn't. Instead, she sighed, shrugged her shoulders and walked out.

When did I become invisible to women, Nick wondered.

He had eaten two small sandwiches but still felt hungry. He waddled back over to the buffet for a giant chocolate chip cookie.

#

Nick and Mike settled up. As Mike handed him the key, Nick slipped him a twenty.

"Thanks for taking me on such short notice."

"Glad to be of service, Mr. Reynolds. It's always good to see you."

Nick knew Bar Harbor could be cool and rainy this time of year. He decided to stop at Dick's Sporting Goods to buy a lined, waterproof jacket.

On his way to the checkout, he spotted a big display of Chicago Cubs gear. Nick loved baseball. He was also sensitive about his thinning hair. For the sake of his hometown team and his vanity, he bought a Cubs hat, extra large.

On the sidewalk outside the store, Nick pulled his new hat out of the bag. He curled the bill, pulled it down on his outsized head and walked to his car, a little swagger in his step. I wish that receptionist could see me now, he thought.

By now, his hangover was almost gone, but he wasn't interested in a drink. Nor was he hungry. He didn't have any more shopping to do. He couldn't get any work done because he hadn't brought his laptop. But he didn't want to go home yet. He knew Jean would still be there.

So he decided to see a movie. He drove to the theater, a few blocks away. The only thing showing at that hour was a new "Transformers" movie. Nick took his seat midway through the previews, which were all about comic book figures or kids hooking up at summer camp.

As the movie ended and the lights came up, Nick realized the place was filled with teenagers. He slipped down in his seat, snugged his cap and waited until everyone cleared out before he got up, fearing some parent might work for him and recognize him.

Then he was hungry again. He decided to stop for an early dinner at Parker's, one of his favorite restaurants, just a few miles from his house.

He ordered a cheeseburger, french fries and a beer at the bar. He'd just begun digging into his cheeseburger when he spotted Jean in the adjoining dining room. She was sitting at a table with three other women. She was facing away from him. For a moment, he thought about going over to say hello. But he knew they'd want him to join them, and all he wanted was to be alone.

"Can I get a box for this?" he asked the bartender.

He paid cash so Jean wouldn't see the charge on their credit card statement and know he'd been there. He slipped out without her seeing him and finished his burger and fries on the way home.

When he got home, he went downstairs and grabbed a suitcase and a duffel bag. He lugged them upstairs and packed. Then he set his alarm for 5:30 and popped an Ambien.

He schlepped his luggage out to the garage and tossed it into the trunk. Then he grabbed a beer from the fridge and stepped out onto the deck.

It was just getting dark. He decided to tempt fate and relax in his Adirondack chair. Tonight, though, he would keep his drinking light. He knew the combination of a couple of beers and the Ambien would knock him out. He wanted to be in bed by the time Jean got home.

In the distance, beyond the woods, he could hear a party going on. He thought of the party next door last night. He hardly went to parties any more.

Maybe Lou was right, he thought. Maybe he needed to go away

and sort his life out. Or maybe he needed to just go away. Maybe he would go to Bar Harbor and not come back.

Maybe he would end it all there.

Once in a while, usually when he was drinking, Nick had given passing thought to taking his own life. But he always dismissed the idea. Not because he thought it was wrong. But because he was too egotistical.

Nick had come to believe that his purpose on earth was to gain as much power and wealth as he could for as long as he could. He had convinced himself it was his destiny. There was no rightful place for anything that got in the way. Nick didn't think he'd burn in hell for committing suicide. But he knew it would keep him from his destiny, and he couldn't allow that.

But one day after Lou had told him to take the summer off, Nick realized he might have peaked. For the first time, he was forced to pause and look over an edge he had convinced himself existed for other men, lesser men, but not for him.

He was only fifty-three. If he retired so young, and so close to the top at Elgin, no one would believe it was his choice. He'd be seen as a failure. If he chose to stay, one way or another, he'd be let go. Then he would be seen as not just a failure, but a disgrace too.

Or he could change. But that would mean becoming something other than who he was. He would be seen as giving in to his critics, the HR types who were always lecturing him about getting along with everyone. To hell with them, he thought. I didn't get here by being a nice guy. I'm not changing.

Nick was not keen on taking his own life. But if he couldn't fulfill his destiny, if he couldn't complete the Nick Reynolds he had worked so hard to build, why go on?

And so this is how it must end, he thought. There was no other way forward.

The Ambien was kicking in. He knew he needed to get to bed or risk falling asleep in his chair.

He heard someone inside the house. Jean was home. Damn.

"Nick?"

"Yeah. I'm out here."

Jean slid the screen door open and stepped out on the deck. She walked over to the railing and leaned against it, facing Nick. The moon was behind her. He could see the silhouette of her trim body. But the porch light was off, and he couldn't see her face.

"How long have you been out here?"

"Not long. I just got home and finished packing."

He was slurring his words.

"Are you drunk?"

"No. This is only my second beer."

"Did you eat?"

"Yeah."

"Where'd you go?"

Nick paused. Had Jean seen him at Parker's? He didn't want to take a chance.

"I stopped at Parker's for a burger."

"Really? We ate there tonight too. I'm surprised I didn't see you."

Nick sensed she was bluffing, that she had in fact seen him at Parker's and was simply testing him. With Jean, Nick always felt like he was under suspicion, like every question was loaded, like she was always trying to trip him up. It was like being married to a prosecutor. The constant head games wore him out.

"So, are you all ready for your trip?"

"Yep. I'm going to get to bed early and leave by 6:00."

"Did you get your car tuned up?"

"Yeah."

"I see you got a new baseball cap."

"Yeah, I bought it at Dick's."

"Nick, are you sure you still want to go through with this? I've been thinking about it. We could go away together this summer. Or do some things around here."

I'd *definitely* rather kill myself, he thought.

"No, Jean. I'm going. I've rented a place in Bar Harbor."

"Will you let me know when you get there?"

"Yeah. And you can track me on your phone along the way."

"Where are you staying tomorrow night?"

"I don't know. Toledo. Cleveland maybe. It all depends on how far I decide to drive."

"Oh, Nick. Are you sure?"

"Yeah."

"All right," she sighed. "I'm going to read in bed. So I'll say good night now."

She walked over to him in his chair, bent down and kissed him on the cheek. He turned to kiss her, but she had already stood up.

"Good night," she said, walking away.

"Good night."

Jean went inside and slid the patio door shut behind her.

Nick sat there for a few minutes, listening to the party in the distance. He was glad Jean was gone because, between his low center of gravity, the beer and the Ambien, it took him a good five minutes to get out of that chair.

Chapter Three

March 1964

"Turn around and let me look at you," his mother said, tugging at the lapels of his blazer. She was kneeling on the floor in front of him. She leaned back until she was at eye level with her six-year-old son.

"That's still not the right shade of blue," she said, peering up at the clerk.

"Lighter? Darker?"

"Maybe something a little darker."

"Navy?"

"No, not that dark. Something in between. And a tie to match, please."

"Let me see what I can find," said the weary clerk.

Nick hated this. This was their third store that morning, and all they'd bought were pants and a shirt. They would be shopping all day. He imagined his friends gathering for a game of baseball in the empty lot in his neighborhood.

His mother could see he wasn't happy.

"Cheer up, Nicky," she said, licking the palm of her hand and smoothing down his cowlick. Nick winced. "This won't take much longer. And just think of how handsome you'll look at Easter."

They were in the children's department of Burg's, a men's clothing store in downtown Cedar Rapids. Nick's family lived modestly. But his mother insisted on buying him only the best clothes. His closet was filled with pants, shirts, ties, belts and blazers. He had black and brown dress shoes, both loafers and with laces, and a dresser drawer packed with socks.

Every evening, his mother would pick out his clothes for the next day. She varied the combinations, making sure he never wore the same outfit two days in a row. She would hang his shirt, pants, belt and even his socks on a little rack in the corner of his room and set out a pair shoes. Brown shoes with blue pants. Solids with stripes. Always well coordinated.

Nick once asked his mother why she did all this.

"People judge us based on what they see, Nicky," she said. "People are watching you. Always look good. Everyone will love you."

Sometimes he would tell his mother he didn't want her to lay his clothes out or argue with her about what he wanted to wear the next day. But it was no use. She would always prevail.

Eventually, he stopped resisting. Not just because his mother always got her way. But because he didn't want her to stop loving him.

Chapter Four

Nick pulled out of his driveway just before six o'clock, without waking Jean to say goodbye.

He was eager to get on the road. He was an impatient man. Taking a sabbatical was certainly not his idea. But now that he'd signed up for it, he wanted to get on with it.

He'd thought about waking Jean to say goodbye. He'd gone to her bedroom door and almost opened it. But he didn't because he was afraid she might try to talk him out of going.

Nick didn't like the idea of not saying goodbye to his wife. But he liked the prospect of getting into a fight with her on his way out even less.

He decided to stop for breakfast at a cafe in downtown Chicago called the "Over Easy." He hadn't been there in years. Early in his career, he used to meet colleagues there for breakfast. Now he considered breakfast meetings a waste of time.

It was Sunday, and traffic was light. He made it downtown in thirty minutes and found a parking space on the street less than a block from the restaurant.

The hostess seated him at a table near a window overlooking the Chicago River. A mist covered the river this morning. It was so thick he had trouble seeing the water.

Nick was famished. He ordered steak, eggs, toast, pancakes, hash browns and a Bloody Mary. As he waited for his drink, Nick opened his laptop and logged on. He wanted to get a sense of his drive that day and where he might stop for the night.

Cleveland looked like a good goal. It was five and half hours away, about a quarter of the way to Bar Harbor. Years ago, he would have driven twice that far in a day. But he no longer drove for long stretches. These days, he flew just about everywhere. When he did, he always had a driver to take him to and from the airport. Nowadays, his drive to the office seemed long.

The waitress brought his Bloody.

"Your food will be out in a minute, sir."

When he looked up, he caught her staring at his head. Nick considered losing his hair a weakness, an imperfection. He'd developed an uncanny sense of when people were looking at his head. It put him on edge. Now he wished he hadn't left his new hat in the car.

Two men sat down at the next table. One looked to be in his 30s, the other in his 40s. They were wearing business casual clothes and carrying notebooks.

Nick didn't mean to eavesdrop. But he could hear every word they were saying. He quickly determined the older guy was interviewing the younger one for a job.

Some interview, Nick thought. The older guy never stopped talking.

"Here you are, sir," the waitress said, setting down three plates of food.

If his breakfast had been featured in a weight-loss ad, it would have had a big, red X over it. His food made his Bloody Mary look healthy. No wonder Nick was seventy-five pounds overweight.

Sir. Nick wondered at what point women started calling him sir. At what point did he get old?

Meanwhile, the older guy kept jabbering away.

"The most important thing you need to know," he said, "is that we take our core values very seriously."

He droned on about "core values." He talked about things like integrity, sacrifice and service. But not a word about the job.

If the young guy doesn't ask about the job soon, I'm going to jump in, Nick thought. Either that or strangle this dude so he'll shut up.

Core values. What bullshit. He'd heard that term his whole career, mainly from HR types. It sounded good. But Nick considered it fluff. He knew what was really important: selling things. That's what paid the bills and got you promoted. How you did it was your business unless you were stupid enough to get into real trouble.

Nick knew he was right, and his thirty years at Elgin Foods bore it out. The nice guys were all gone. They'd talked a good game, made everybody feel good. But they couldn't cut it. Only Nick remained, and all he cared about were the numbers.

The notable exception was Lou Bradford. Somehow, he made the soft stuff work.

"Can I get you anything else, sir?" the waitress asked.

"Yeah, I'll have another Bloody Mary."

What he really wanted was a different table, far away from this kook who was prattling on.

Nick admired Lou. After all, he had made it to the top. But he also felt Lou was too deferential, too polite, that he listened too much.

Nick wondered who Lou had been listening to lately. Jennifer? Nick was aware that she'd had more direct contact with Lou recently. He'd forbidden everyone who worked for him from ever going over his head. Jennifer followed that order. But Nick knew that Lou had been reaching out to her more and more on things related to Nick's business. These were interactions he couldn't stop.

Then there was that HR guy, Leonard. What a jerk. He was always in Nick's office any more, with some silly employee complaint.

His interactions with Leonard had grown increasingly contentious. Once the two of them landed in Lou's office. Nick wanted to move someone out of his organization for no good reason. Leonard — Nick called him Lenny, which seemed to get

under his skin — objected. He felt they should "escalate the issue." Nick called him a weasel but went with him to see Lou. As
usual, Lou sided with Nick.

Afterwards, though, privately, Lou told Nick to stop calling
Leonard names.

Nick knew his strong numbers had earned him a very long
leash at Elgin. At a time when growth rates in the food industry
were anemic and margins razor-thin, under Nick's leadership, the
company's snack cake business had become its shining star.

And Nick made it happen without caring a whit about so-
called core values.

He knew he created headaches for Lou. But Lou knew he
was ultimately accountable to shareholders and the board. And
when it came time to report earnings, shareholders and the board
weren't thinking about personnel issues.

"Would you care for anything else, sir?" the waitress asked,
check in hand.

"Yeah, I'd like another Bloody Mary for the road."

"For the road?" she asked, smiling.

"Yeah."

"I assume you're kidding."

"No, I'm not. Do you have a problem with that?"

His rough tone took her off guard.

"I'm sorry, sir. It's just that I'm not sure it's a good idea——"

"You're covering your ass, aren't you?"

"Pardon me?"

"That's what you're doing. You're just like the rest of them.
You'll take my money all day long. But the minute you see any
risk in it for yourself, you don't want any part of it."

"Excuse me," she said, flustered. "I'll be right back."

Nick looked over at the table next to him. Both men were staring at him.

"What are you looking at?" he sneered.

Neither of them said a word.

"By the way," Nick said, looking at the older guy, "why don't you let that poor guy get a word in? He might have something to say, you know."

"Pardon me?"

A man approached Nick's table.

"Good morning, sir. I'm John, the manager. Nicole tells me there might be an issue."

"Yeah, John. There's an issue all right. Your waitress thinks she's my babysitter."

"Sir, Nicole tells me you've already had two drinks and you're driving."

"Well, then she's telling you the truth. She's a person of integrity," he said loudly.

"Sir, I think it would be a good idea for us not to serve you another drink right now."

"Oh, yeah? Well, guess what, John? Me too. I'll take the check."

"Here you are."

Nick looked at the bill. It was for $34. He pulled $35 out of his wallet and laid it on the table.

"Thank you," John said, picking up the money.

"Screw you," Nick said, standing up. He was a hulking figure. He stood six-two. He had at least five inches and a hundred pounds on John. Nick had used his size to his advantage countless times over the years. John backed off, as most people did.

Nick looked down at the older guy at the next table.

"Drive safe," the man said.

"Screw you."

#

Outside, a few people were walking down the sidewalk. Nick spotted a young guy with spiky blond hair and tattoos heading his way and deliberately ran into him.

"Watch it, buddy," the kid said.

Nick stopped and stared at him. Looking up, the kid snarled his upper lip, like Billy Idol.

Nick took a step toward him. The kid backed off and walked away.

"Punk," Nick grumbled.

He got into his car and headed toward the Dan Ryan Expressway. But he hadn't even gotten to the freeway before he ran into standstill traffic.

"God damn it!" he yelled, slapping the steering wheel.

When he finally reached the highway, traffic was moving at a glacial pace.

"God damn it!"

Inching forward, it took him thirty minutes to get to a point where he could get even a glimpse of what was happening. Several cars had collided and were clogging the left two lanes. There were cop cars and emergency vehicles everywhere.

Nick stayed in the right lane. Whenever a car to his left would signal and try to cut in, he would creep up and block them out. He never let anyone in.

"Idiots," he muttered as he finally passed the wreck, not even pausing to check it out.

As soon as Nick was in the clear, he punched it, passing everyone. But not for long. Less than a mile down the road, white steam started billowing out from beneath his hood. It was so thick that Nick had a hard time seeing the road. The engine was knocking loudly and started losing power. He had to pull over.

"Crap!"

Nick turned off his car. He decided to get out and take a look under the hood. He tried to open his door. But it hit the concrete barricade and would open only a few inches, not nearly enough room for him to squeeze through. He would have to get out on the other side.

He grabbed the steering wheel with his left hand, gripped the console between the seats with his right and tried to hoist himself over. He almost made it. But he slipped off the console and fell backward. His head came down hard on the armrest of his door.

"Shit!"

He lay there for a minute, rubbing the back of his head. Then he grabbed the steering wheel and pulled himself back up. This time, he swung his legs up and extended them over the console. Straining so hard that his arms shook, he finally managed to drag himself over to the passenger seat.

There was so much steam pouring out from under his hood that it looked like his car was on fire. Other cars were slowing down to gawk. At least he wouldn't get mowed down trying to get out of his car.

He slipped out and stepped around to the front of his car. He bent down to open the hood, then remembered he'd forgotten to pop it from the inside.

"God damn it!"

Fortunately, his cell phone was in his pocket. He stepped over to the concrete barricade, leaned against it and dialed Mike, his guy at the Mercedes dealer.

"Hi, you've reached Mercedes of Winnetka," said a woman's voice. "We are closed Sunday and Monday for the Memorial Day holiday, but your call is important to us. Please leave a message, and we'll get back to you on Tuesday. Thank you and have a nice weekend."

It was the last thing he wanted to hear right now. Even worse, the recording was the voice of the woman who had ignored him in the lounge yesterday.

He would have to call AAA. Some sabbatical.

#

Nick was a "gold card" member of AAA. This meant he was entitled to roadside assistance anywhere in the country 24/7. In the city, AAA would be there within thirty minutes. But this morning, it took "Bob's Towing" more than an hour.

"Sorry it took so long," said the driver, as he jumped down from his truck. "I'm Bob," he said, extending his blackened hand.

Nick kept his hands in his pockets.

"What took you so long?"

"Traffic is a mess this morning. Wrecks everywhere. It's a holiday weekend. The drunks are out already."

Nick hoped Bob couldn't smell the vodka on his breath.

"What's the plan?"

Bob looked at Nick's car. Wisps of steam were still curling up from under the front of the hood.

"Was that steam a lot heavier before?"

"Yeah. It looked like smoke."

"Bummer. Could be serious."

"How serious?"

"Well, we won't know for sure until we get it into a shop."

"Is anything open today?"

"Oh, yeah. Two or three places around here. Of course, on a holiday, it'll cost ya."

"Let's just get to the closest one."

"Okay. You can hop in my truck while I hook 'er up. Can I have the key?"

Nick handed him his key fob and climbed up into the truck. The cab smelled like grease, and the seat felt like hard plastic. He tried not to touch anything. He was glad he was wearing jeans.

#

They got to Henry's Auto Repair in about twenty minutes. There were two garage bays. The doors were open on both. A man was working on a car in one. The other was empty. Bob suggested Nick hop out and wait in the customer lounge while he backed his car into the open bay.

"Do we need to settle up?"

"No, you're all set through triple A."

"Okay," Nick said, slipping him a twenty. "Thanks for coming out on a holiday weekend."

"Thank you, sir. And good luck with your car!"

Yeah, Nick thought. I need some good luck.

The man in the garage stopped working and stepped into the lounge. He was wearing dark blue work clothes and black boots. He was short and stocky, with flecks of grey in his curly brown hair. A cigarette drooped from the corner of his mouth.

"I'm Henry," he said, wiping his hands with a dirty rag. "I'd shake your hand, but …"

"No problem. I'm Nick Reynolds."

"Why don't you give me a few minutes to look under the hood?" he asked, the cigarette bouncing as he spoke. "Have a seat, and I'll come get you when I have a handle on the problem."

"Okay. How long do you think this might take?"

"No idea," said Henry, sounding a little irritated. "As you can see, I'm on my own today. And with that steam coming out from under your hood, I want to make sure we know what we're dealing with and fix it right."

"Yes, of course," said Nick, backing off. "Take your time."

#

Nick was the only customer in the lounge. One wall was lined with vending machines. A water cooler stood in one corner and a gum ball machine in another. A bright green rug, which looked like astroturf, covered most of the white linoleum floor. Several red plastic chairs ran along one edge of the rug. A bleacher of five blue plastic seats ran along the opposite edge, snug against a cinderblock wall covered by layers of light yellow paint so thick that it looked like rubber. Magazines were scattered across the top of an aluminum table in the middle of the rug. A large, olive green bass, its mouth open wide, was mounted on a wooden plaque above the door. It was a far cry from the Mercedes dealership.

After a torturous ride in the tow truck, Nick's back was killing him. He knew he couldn't take sitting in one of the plastic chairs, especially since he didn't know how long he might be waiting. So he sat down in the center of the bleacher.

A wave of fatigue washed over him. He leaned his head back against the rubbery wall. The next thing he knew, he was waking up, stretched out on the bleacher.

He looked up at the clock, whose face was the logo of Fram oil filters. It was almost noon. He had been asleep for an hour.

Nick heard a little rustling sound. He tilted his head back. A woman was sitting in one of the plastic chairs, turning the pages of a magazine. She appeared to be reading, but he sensed she had been staring at his head.

Henry stepped through the doorway.

"Mr. Reynolds?"

"Yeah," Nick grunted, as he sat up.

"I have your estimate ready."

"What was the problem?"

"You blew a gasket."

"Damn. I just had my car tuned up yesterday."

"Did they replace any gaskets?"

"No, I don't think so."

"Well, I can tell you this one was shot. But it's an easy thing to miss."

"What's the damage?"

"Let me show you what I think we should do."

Son of a bitch, Nick thought as he stood up. His back was throbbing, and he felt like the top of his head was going to blow off.

#

By the time Nick got back on the road, it was almost four o'clock. He hadn't eaten since breakfast. He was starving. Just before he got back on the freeway, he drove through McDonald's. He ordered a couple of quarter pounders, large fries and a large Coke to tide him over until dinner.

At this rate, he wouldn't get to Cleveland until well into the evening, even if he drove straight through. He began thinking about a plan B.

But what in the hell was between Chicago and Cleveland, someplace he could still get to at a decent hour tonight? Once he got his food, he pulled into a parking space and opened his laptop.

Gary, South Bend and Toledo were all on the way. But Gary was too close, and Toledo was too far. So South Bend was it.

It was two hours away. After the day he'd had, that's about as far as Nick could go.

#

South Bend. Notre Dame. Nick had led recruiting trips there over the years. The university's people had always put him up in a VIP suite at the Morris Inn, the best hotel on campus.

But now he was on his own. He booked a room at the Comfort Inn, about three miles off campus. He got there just before seven. It had been a long day, and he was ripe. He decided to shower before heading out for dinner.

He got dressed and looked at himself in the full-length wall mirror. He could see why people might stare at his head. His hair was getting very thin. Over the years, he'd tried all kinds of hair-loss treatments. None of them worked. There was only one sure bet. He grabbed his hat.

Nick was craving a good steak. He stopped at the front desk and asked the young lady working there for a recommendation.

"Sizzler," she said with a smile. "Best steaks in town. Are you driving?"

"Yes."

"Here," she said, grabbing a map. "Let me show you where it is."

She traced the route for him with a red magic marker.

"Thank you," he said.

She reminded him of Ashley, his daughter. Soft-spoken, upbeat, polite. With her blond hair, slender face and athletic build, she even looked a little like Ashley.

He hadn't seen Ashley, or his son Josh, in almost a year and a half. They hadn't come home last Christmas. They said they were busy.

Nick missed his children.

#

The steakhouse was nearly empty. Nick guessed it was be-cause it was a holiday weekend and most students had gone home for the summer.

He looked around for a bar but didn't see one.

"Do you serve beer?" he asked the hostess.

"Yes, sir."

He was relieved.

She seated him at a high-top table for two.

"Can I start you with a drink?"

"Absolutely."

"Would you like to see a drink menu?"

"What kind of beer do you have on tap?"

"We have several craft beers and Budweiser."

Nick loved craft beer. But after driving through the Rust Belt and the Corn Belt, a Bud felt right.

In all, he had four Buds to wash down his 18-ounce T-bone steak. Walking to the bathroom, he began to feel a little tipsy. And yet, thinking about his car trouble that morning, he had an urge to drink even more.

"Where can I get some good bourbon?" he asked the waitress.

"On campus?"

"Yeah."

"The Shamrock."

She gave him directions. He settled up. As he got up to leave, he had to grab the edge of the table to steady himself.

As he pulled his car key out of his pocket, he could feel the hostess staring at him. He glared back. Even drunk, he thought, I'm the best driver on the road.

The Shamrock was less than a mile away. But it took him fif-teen minutes because he never went over ten miles an hour.

The place was packed. This is more like it, Nick thought as he bellied up to the bar. He eyeballed the liquor bottles like a kid checking out flavors in an ice cream shop.

"Knob Creek on the rocks," he said to the bartender, a young hipster with long sideburns and a soul patch.

"You got it, man."

Nick looked around. He was surprised to see so many young people.

"There are a lot of kids in here tonight," he said to the hipster. "I thought school was out for the summer."

"Not if you're a perpetual student," he grinned.

The bar stool next to him was open. He noticed a woman sitting two stools over. She was plain but not unattractive, with a round face and short, brown hair. He guessed she was in her early 30s.

Nick was a man of bad habits. But cheating on his wife was not one of them. He loved to look at beautiful women. And from the time he was a teenager, he had deluded himself into thinking they all wanted him.

As a powerful man who traveled a lot, he had many opportunities, and he was often tempted. But he never gave in.

That he didn't give in was a surprise even to Nick. He was a man used to indulging his appetites — for power, expensive things, food and drink. But when it came to sex, he paid attention to boundaries and restrained himself.

Jean had watched Nick flirt with waitresses for years. At first, she thought it was amusing and even charming. Over time, though, especially as Nick began traveling more, she grew concerned about how far he might take it when she wasn't around.

She had no idea that, in this one way, she had no grounds for concern.

Now Nick glanced over at the woman two stools over. She was alone, and he was feeling very much alone.

He took a gulp of bourbon, turned and said, "Hello."

"Hello," she said, looking up at his hat. "You play for the Cubs?"

"No," he said, smiling. "But I get that a lot."

"I'll bet," she said playfully.

"Do you go to school here?"

"Well, in a way. I'm a grad student."

"What are you studying?"

"Business. I'm going for my MBA."

"Are you close to getting it?"

"No, I'm just starting. I got an undergraduate degree in English ten years ago. I've taught and had a bunch of small jobs. But I decided it's time to make some money."

"You think you need an MBA to make money?"

"Yeah. Don't you?"

"Not necessarily."

"Do you have an MBA?"

"Nope."

"A graduate degree?"

"No."

"An undergraduate degree?"

She was looking a little nervous.

"Yeah."

"What's it in?"

"English," he said, with a smile.

"And what do you do?"

"I'm in the food business."

She looked unimpressed.

"I see. What do you do in the food business?"

"I'm the president of a global food company."

She perked up.

"Marian," she said, extending her hand.

"Nick," he said, taking it.

#

Over copious amounts of bourbon and wine, they talked for several hours. Maybe it was because they figured they would never see each other again. Maybe it was the alcohol. Or maybe it was because neither of them had anyone in their lives who really listened to them anymore. But they talked openly.

Nick told Marian about his sabbatical, how Lou had made him take it and how he resented being told what to do, especially when it came to his work. He told her how strained his relationship was with Jean and just about everyone these days. He told her about how unhappy he was and that he wasn't sure if he could ever be happy again.

Marian told Nick she loved teaching but she was nearly broke. She told him she didn't have a mind for business and wasn't sure she could really get an MBA. She told him she was worried she would never find true love.

As they were talking, Marian moved to the bar stool next to Nick. She seemed to hang on his every word. She interrupted him once, though. When he was telling her how cold and distant Jean had become, she put her hand on his and gushed, "Oh! That woman doesn't realize how lucky she is!"

Maybe Nick shouldn't have been surprised when Marian asked him to go back to her place.

"I'm flattered," he said. "But I can't."

"Why?" she asked, wrapping both her hands around one of his.

Her warm, soft touch felt wonderful. But he pulled his hand away.

"Marian, I'm married."

"I know. But lots of married men sleep around. I mean, if you want, we can just sleep together. I mean really sleep."

"Marian, I can't give you what you need. I wish I could. But I can't."

"All right, Nick," she said, sitting up straight. "Then I guess I'll say good night."

She opened her purse and pulled out her billfold.

"Let me get this," he said.

"Okay," she said, sliding off her stool and steadying herself. "It was good to meet you, Nick. Good luck to you."

"Good luck to you too, Marian."

Then she left.

Nick sat there, his hands cupped around his empty glass on the bar.

Lots of married men sleep around. Why not me, Nick wondered. Some women still want me. Hell, a grad student just asked me to sleep with her. She's probably a tiger in the sack, he thought. He hadn't had sex in three years — and he was passing this up? Why? When had he become such a Puritan?

"We're going to be closing up pretty soon, buddy," said the hipster. "Would you like a night cap?"

Nick looked up. He was so loaded he could barely make eye contact.

"No," he said, slurring his words. "But would you call me a cab?"

Nick thought of Jean. He had an overwhelming urge to call her. He took out his cell phone but was having a hard time even entering the passcode. He knew he was in no condition to talk.

He slipped his phone back in his pocket.

#

Back at his hotel, on the way to his room, Nick tripped. He fell against the wall in the hallway. His shoulder hit hard, and he dropped to the floor. He lay there for a minute, dazed and moaning.

He tried to stand but couldn't. So he got on his hands and knees and crawled to his door. Still on his knees, he fished his key out of his pocket. He kept inserting it in the slot under the door handle the wrong way.

Finally, he heard a click. He pushed down on the handle. The door swung open, and he fell into his room. The door snapped back. It hit him in the shoulder, the same place he'd hit the wall in the hallway. He groaned but was too wasted to cry out.

Nick crawled over to his bed and tried to pull himself up. But he had neither the strength nor the balance to do it. He passed out on the floor.

Chapter Five

August 1965

"Nick, get up," someone said in a loud whisper.

Nick felt a hand shaking him.

"Get up."

It was dark. He looked up from his bed. In the moonlight through the window, he could see the outline of a man.

"Dad?"

"Yeah. Time to get up."

"But it's still nighttime," Nick said, rubbing his eyes.

"It's five in the morning."

"What's going on?"

"We're going out this morning."

"Where?" he said, pulling his covers back and swinging his legs out of the bed.

"I'll show you. Now get dressed. And don't wake your brother."

Nick took off his pajamas, tossed them on his bed and fumbled in the dark for his clothes. He slipped on a pair of jeans, a T-shirt and tennis shoes. He found his dad in the kitchen, scribbling a note, which he left on the counter.

"Ready?" he asked, looking up.

"Where are we going?"

"I'll tell you in the car," he said, turning off the overhead light. He grabbed a brown paper lunch bag, filled with something, and headed for the garage. Nick followed him.

In the beams from the car's headlights, Nick watched his father close the garage door. He was a big man, tall, not fat, but certainly not thin. His hair was dark and, in the bright light, Nick could see a small bald spot on the top of his head.

His dad got back in the car, and they backed out of the driveway and headed down the street.

"We're going shooting," his father said, preempting the question Nick was about to ask again.

"Shooting?"

"Have you ever shot a gun?"

"No."

"Well, it's about time you learned."

"What kind of a gun?"

"A shotgun."

"A shotgun?"

"Yeah."

"Whose?"

"Mine."

"Where is it?" Nick asked, looking in the back seat.

"It's in the trunk."

"In the trunk."

"Yeah. That's where I keep it."

Nick and his friends played with toy guns. But he'd never seen a real gun. Now he was having a hard time imagining his dad kept a gun — a real gun — in the trunk of his car.

"You keep a gun in your trunk?"

"Yeah. Does that surprise you?"

"Yeah. I mean, why do you keep it there?"

"Because nobody would expect it there. Only your mother and I have the keys to my car. I know that you kids would never find it there. But I also know it's close by, if I ever need it."

Nick sat there and didn't say anything for a minute. He was trying to wrap his mind around the idea that his father had been keeping a shotgun in the trunk of a car that he parked in their garage every night. He had never heard his father mention a gun. But he had heard his mother express her strong opinions about guns many times. "We'll never have a gun in our house," she would say. Certainly she must know his father kept a gun in his trunk. Then he smiled, realizing that, technically, their garage is not in their house.

Nick was about to ask his father something else when they pulled into the small parking lot of a donut shop, Bonnie's Bakery. Nick had been there with his mother, but not with his father.

"Let's grab a donut and something to drink," he father said, getting out.

The sun was beginning to rise. But as they walked into the bakery, the light inside was so bright that Nick had to blink.

"Morning, Jim!" chirped a heavyset woman from behind the counter. She was dressed in white, like a nurse. A paper cap rested on top of her gray, curly hair. She rested her hands, formed into loose fists, on the stainless steel top of a glass-enclosed case, in which waxed-paper-lined trays were filled with dozens of donuts.

"Who's this?" she asked cheerfully.

"This is my son, Nick."

"Well, of course it's your son," she smiled broadly. "It looks like you spit him out!"

"Good morning," Nick said quietly.

"Good morning, young man. I'm Bonnie. It's a pleasure to meet you. I see your dad in here almost every morning, but I don't think we've met."

"No, I guess not," he said.

"Well, what can I get you boys this morning?"

Nick looked at his father.

"Pick out anything you like."

Then his father turned to Bonnie and said, "I'll have the usual."

Bonnie grabbed a piece of waxed paper, picked out two glazed donuts and placed them into a white paper bag. In the meantime, his father turned around, stepped over to a coffee pot on a tall table against a wall and poured himself a cup of coffee.

"What'll you have, young man?" Bonnie asked.

Nick eyed all the donuts.

"One of those," he said, pointing to the ones with chocolate icing and chocolate sprinkles.

"Only one?"

His dad stepped back over with his coffee.

"Go ahead and get two, Nick."

"Really?" he said, looking up.

"Yeah," his father answered, nodding at Bonnie.

She placed Nick's donuts in the bag.

"What else?"

"Would you like something to drink?" Nick's father asked.

"Yeah," Nick said.

"Drinks are in the dairy case, sweetie," Bonnie said, tilting her head toward the corner of the bakery.

Nick stepped over, pulled the door open and picked out a small carton of chocolate milk. He let the door slam and sat the carton on the donut case in front of Bonnie.

"I see someone really likes chocolate," she smiled.

Walking to the car, Nick thought again about the gun in the trunk. As he got in, he glanced into the back seat and spotted the brown paper bag he had seen his father pick up in the kitchen.

"What's in the bag, dad?"

"Shells."

Shells?" Nick asked, imagining seashells.

"For my shotgun."

"Oh," Nick said, feeling stupid.

"I keep them in the house, away from my gun, in a place where you and your brother and sister will never find them. So don't even look. And don't tell your brother and sister, or anyone, about the gun I keep in the trunk."

"I won't," Nick said, suddenly feeling special.

The transmission in Nick's father's car created a hump that ran up the center of the interior. A plastic tray, rounded at both ends, straddled the hump in the front, just below the dashboard. Molded into the tray were two cup holders. Nick's father put his coffee cup into one of them. Nick sat his milk carton in the other. It make him feel so grown-up.

They drove for about half an hour, down country roads. Neither of them said a word. Then his father slowed down and pulled off the road, parking alongside it.

"We're here," he said.

Next to the road was a meadow. About a hundred yards into it was a long, split rail fence. Just beyond that were dozens of apple trees.

"Have you been here before?"

"Yeah. I used to come here all the time when I was a kid."

"Why?"

"To shoot."

Nick remembered the gun in the trunk.

They got out. Nick's father opened his back door, reached in and grabbed the paper bag. Then he went to the back of the car and unlocked the trunk. The lid popped up. Nick looked inside. The only thing he could see was a blanket. His father reached in a pulled the blanket back, revealing a gun, about three feet long, with a brown wooden stock and dark blue metal barrel. To Nick, it seemed a thing of dangerous beauty.

"Here," his father said, handing Nick the brown paper bag. "You carry these."

Nick took the bag from his dad. It was heavy. Carrying it made him feel important.

His father grabbed the gun at the base of the barrel and pulled it out of the trunk, then slammed the lid shut.

"Let's go," he said.

"Where are we going?" asked Nick.

"We're going to shoot apples."

"Apples?"

"Yeah," said his father, kicking his way through the knee-high grass.

Nick still wasn't sure exactly what his father had in mind. But he followed close behind.

When they got to the fence, his father leaned his gun up against it and pulled himself up and over.

"Come on," he said. "Set that bag down and climb over."

Nick did as he was told and followed his father over the fence.

"Now let's get a dozen apples and set them up along the top of the fence," his father said.

Nick followed his father. When they got to the trees, Nick looked up and saw the branches were loaded with red and green apples. There were dozens of apples on the ground too. Nick's father began picking them up, and Nick did the same. They each grabbed as many apples as they could cradle in their arms and headed back to the fence.

"Set them up about a foot apart," his father said, carefully placing the apples one by one along the flat spots across the top rails of the fence. Nick reached up and placed the four apples he was carrying along the fence.

"Good job," said his father. "Now let's shoot."

His father grabbed the gun, and Nick grabbed the brown paper bag. His father walked back into the meadow, toward the road. When he was about fifty yards from the fence, he stopped.

"Okay, Nick. Hand me that box of shells."

Nick opened the bag. Inside was a cardboard box. He reached in, with both hands, pulled it out. It was heavy. He handed it to his father.

His father pressed a lever on the top of his gun, on the stock, near the barrel, and the barrel folded down, exposing two empty chambers. He opened the box of shells and slipped one into each of the chambers. Then, in a motion Nick had seen only in westerns, gripping the stock in his right hand, his father swung the gun upward, and the barrel snapped into place. It was the most impressive thing he had ever seen.

"Now watch me," his father said. "I'm only going to show you this once."

He gripped the barrel of the gun in his left hand and lifted it, the stock resting against his right shoulder. He closed his left eye and peered through the sight on the top of the barrel with his right. With his thumb, he deftly flipped a switch near the trigger. Then he laid his right index finger next to the trigger and held the gun still, aiming at one of the apples on the fence. Nick wasn't sure whether to look at his father or the fence. At the last minute, he looked at the fence.

Boom!

Nick saw one of the apples explode into the air.

"Wow!" he exclaimed. "Good shot, dad!"

"Thanks," his father said, without smiling. "Now it's your turn."

"Me?" Nick asked, sounding nervous.

"Are you up for it?"

"Yeah," he answered, trying to sound brave.

His father handed him the gun.

"There's another shot in there. Just do what I did."

Nick could feel his heart beating hard. He almost couldn't believe this was happening. Oh, if his friends could see him now, he thought. He took the gun from his father. It was even heavier than he imagined.

"Can you handle it?" his father asked.

"Yeah," Nick said, using all his strength to lift the gun and try to hold it steady.

"Now line up an apple in your sight and pull the trigger. Don't think it. Once you have an apple in your sight, just shoot."

Nick held the gun as still as he could. He closed his left eye and could see an apple through the sight with his right. He reached for the trigger with his index finger and pulled it.

Boom!

The kick of the gun was so great that Nick fell backwards, onto the ground. He dropped the gun into the grass.

To his surprise, his father began laughing.

"I knew you couldn't handle that gun," he said, grinning. "I knew you were too young."

"Did I hit the apple?" Nick asked, rubbing his shoulder.

"Not even close!"

His father laughed again.

"Maybe next year," he said, reaching past Nick to retrieve the gun. "Hand me a couple more shells."

Nick got up and stepped over the open box of shells. He reached in, pulled out two shells and handed them to his father.

"Now watch this," he said.

One by one, his father proceeded to shoot each of the remaining eleven apples off the fence. Eleven shots in the row. He didn't miss one.

Between shots, his father would look down at Nick and let out a little laugh. At first, Nick thought his father was laughing out of a sense of satisfaction. But the more he looked at Nick and laughed, and the more apples he shot, the more Nick felt his father was laughing at him.

Nick wanted to try again. But he was too intimidated to ask.

On the way home, his father said, "I left a note for your mother this morning, telling her we're going shooting. She's not going to be happy. When we get home, don't say anything. I'll handle it."

"Okay."

When they got home, Nick's mother was waiting in kitchen. Nick let his father walk ahead, into the kitchen. He sat down on the sofa in the family room.

"You took him shooting?" he heard his mother say.

"Yeah. I thought he was old enough."

"Old enough? Jim, he's seven years old! What in the world were you thinking?"

The level of both their voices rose from there. Nick had heard his parents fight many times. Usually, his dad won. This time, though, his mother clearly had the upper hand.

"You will never take our kids shooting again!" she shouted.

Nick was just about to try to escape outside when his father emerged from the kitchen, walking briskly down the hallway toward the bedrooms. He caught a glimpse of Nick but didn't say a word. Then he saw his mother hurtle out of the kitchen and take off behind her husband down the hall. Her face was red, and she didn't seem to see Nick.

Nick heard a bedroom door slam and his parents yelling at each other. He hated it when his parents fought.

Nick was hungry. He went out to the garage and opened the front passenger door. He reached in and retrieved the white paper bag, which still contained one of his donuts and one of his father's. He grabbed the bag and his milk carton and slipped out the back door of the garage. He sat on a metal glider on the patio. His house was not air-conditioned, and he could hear his parents fighting through their open bedroom window.

Nick ate both donuts and drank the rest of his milk. He guessed his little brother, David, was playing down the street and set out to find him.

Nick's father never asked him to go shooting again, and Nick never again touched a gun. Even seeing a gun conjured disturbing thoughts for Nick.

Chapter Six

Nick woke up, lying on his back, with the bedspread wrapped around him loosely, part of it still clinging to the bed. He lay there, looking up at the white, stippled ceiling, his head throbbing, his shoulder aching, trying to figure out where he was and why he was on the floor. Then he remembered The Shamrock, taking a cab back to the hotel and crawling into his room.

Waking up hung over was not new for Nick. But waking up somewhere he had not expected to be was foreign to him.

Nick was a planner. He took great pride in having clear goals and priorities and well-defined plans. He scheduled his work life, and sometimes his personal life, with precision. He was rigorous in managing his time and ruthless in saying no to anything that wasn't on his priority list. Except for this trip, he hadn't had an unplanned day in twenty years.

He hadn't always been a planner, though. Growing up, he was quite disorganized. In fact, he had an aversion to planning. He liked spontaneity. He enjoyed dealing with the unexpected. He liked being agile. As a boy, he was happiest when he woke up and had no idea what he'd be doing that day.

The Jesuits fixed that.

First, in high school, where Nick was forced to keep and carry a day planner, and under the threat of demerits for being late, had learned to wear a watch.

Then at Loyola University Chicago, where all his courses, but especially philosophy, served to discipline and organize his mind. It would take Nick years, decades really, to begin to see and appreciate the irony that it was the Jesuits, men who took vows of poverty and obedience, who would teach him the skills that would ultimately enable him to achieve great wealth and power.

At first, away from the watchful eyes of his parents, Nick was lax. He skipped classes, blew off homework and didn't worry about his grades. In high school, he'd always gotten As and Bs. In college, for the most part, his introductory courses seemed like extensions of what he already knew, so he figured he could breeze through them.

He was mistaken. He was slow to realize that, although the titles of most of his courses sounded familiar, the content was not. He also assumed that if he missed a few classes, he could easily catch up. He didn't realize the pace would be so much faster and the volume of work so much greater.

Not that he had never fallen behind in a class. But in high school, the Jesuit priests and brothers were always there to give him either a gentle nudge or a swift kick. At Loyola, their counterparts seemed hell-bent on moving forward. Tough luck to anybody who couldn't keep up.

Nick's single biggest challenge was philosophy. Unlike English, math and science, here was something totally new, where he had no prior knowledge he could bank on. Even worse, philosophy was not so much about what he knew, but how he thought — about his critical thinking skills. Up until then, school had essentially been about memorization and knowing "the answers." Now, with philosophy, there was little to memorize and a premium on the questions, not the answers.

During his first semester, Nick was required to take a philosophy course called Logic. At mid-term, his grade in Logic was a D, and his GPA was a C-.

At Loyola, in those days, parents received their children's report cards at about the same time the students themselves were seeing them. The day after he got his mid-term grades, his phone rang. It was his mother.

"Nick, I'm concerned," she said. "Your scholarship requires a B average. We can't afford your tuition without your scholarship. Can't you bring up your grades?"

It was all she needed to say.

"Yes, Mom. I will."

After that, Nick buckled down and got serious about Logic and all his other courses. He studied every day. He made sure he understood the course material and asked for help when he didn't. He even joined a study group. By the end of the semester, he'd pulled his GPA up to a B.

Nick kept his scholarship. More important, though, he began to understand the value of planning and organization. His more disciplined approach to all his courses taught him this. But it was his philosophy courses in particular that forced him to think deeply.

He began to consider what he really wanted in life. What was most important to him? What were his goals?

As a teenager, Nick had a vague, if growing, desire for much more than the life he had known growing up in Cedar Rapids. By the time he started college, "power and wealth" had begun to emerge as the objects of his desire. These ideas were appealing to Nick. Yet he hadn't given much thought to what they really meant.

Then, one weekend, he took a bike trip with a few buddies to the North Shore. He was blown away by the mansions along the lake, with expensive cars parked in cobblestone driveways and sprawling, impeccably manicured lawns. To Nick, it looked like paradise.

In the back of his mind, he might have always known he wanted more than his parents were able to afford. But until that weekend, he had never seen where rich people lived. Now, riding his bike past their magnificent homes, Nick decided he wanted to live this way too.

But he also knew he needed a plan.

He had enrolled at Loyola as an English major. During his sophomore year, when a lot of kids were changing majors and most of his friends were majoring in business, he decided to stick with English but declare business as his minor. It might have seemed a bit counter-intuitive for someone who wanted to get rich. But he figured the unique combination would make him stand out at graduation time.

By his junior year, Nick decided he wanted to work for a big company and become CEO, even though he wasn't exactly sure what that meant. That winter, he made a list of all the big companies in Chicago. He created a resume, based mainly on his experience as a reporter for his college newspaper, and mailed it to dozens of companies, seeking an internship. He followed up each letter with a phone call. That alone distinguished him. By April, he'd lined up four interviews.

He got two offers. He picked the one that paid the most, with Elgin Foods, which was based downtown. It was a marketing internship in the fall semester of his senior year.

Nick performed well. The people at Elgin were so impressed that they offered Nick an entry-level position in marketing upon graduation.

His planning had paid off. Nick never forgot the lesson. He never left much to chance again. He approached projects with the intellectual rigor he'd developed and honed in his philosophy classes.

But in his bones, Nick longed for spontaneity. And now, as he lay on the floor, in an unfamiliar place at an unscheduled stop, not knowing exactly where he would end up that day, even though his head and shoulder were pounding and his back was aching, Nick Reynolds smiled, the way he used to on summer mornings when he was a boy.

#

Nick felt queasy. He knew he should get something on his stomach. He went downstairs to the dining area off the lobby.

It was almost ten, but the free breakfast bar was still open.

He walked over and dropped two slices of wheat bread into the toaster. As he waited, he poured hot water into a white, ceramic mug and picked out a sachet of black tea.

His toast popped up. He stepped over to a table in the corner and sat down. He took a bite of dry toast, then tore open the sachet and dropped the tea bag into the hot water.

He began thinking about Marian and his decision not to go back to her place last night. That was a good call, he thought. He couldn't remember if he'd given her his business card or even told her his last name. He hoped he hadn't. She would only want something from him.

He dunked his tea bag up and down. Small, light brown puffs billowed out, turning the water the color of apple cider.

He knew how this tea bag must feel, giving itself away in the water that surrounded it. From the moment he woke up in the morning until the moment he fell asleep at night, someone was asking him for something. People came to him because he was a powerful man, a man who could make things happen.

Power is what Nick wanted. But now that he had it, he felt constantly put upon, sucked dry by the people around him, bled out, used up, like a tea bag.

#

Nick showered, gathered his things andchecked out. The desk clerk called him a taxi. He took it to his car, which was still parked in the gravel lot behind The Shamrock.

With his tea at breakfast, hehad taken four Tylenol. He knew that was only adding to the destruction of his liver. But his headache was nearly gone now, and the pain in his shoulder was down to a low throb. Nick would worry about his liver some other time.

He followed the signs for I-90 east, which would take him all the way to Toledo. He could stop there for lunch.

Nick wondered if he'd ever been to Toledo. He couldn't recall it. But now that he was thinking about it, all he could think of was the big, red Toledo scale in the back room of the post office where his father worked.

One Saturday, when Nick was a boy, his father had brought him to work. Nick remembered stepping up on the big scale and watching the needle arm of the dial bounce around, then stop and point at sixty pounds.

"Wow!" one of his father's co-workers exclaimed. "Pretty soon, we're going to need a bigger scale for you, young man!"

Everyone laughed. Nick remembered how fun it was to weigh himself as a boy, how excited he felt to be getting bigger.

These days, he avoided scales. He didn't like to be reminded of his weight. But at this moment, thanks to Toledo, that's all he could think about.

#

As Nick drove on, he noticed that much of the land between South Bend and Toledo, along the northern edge of Indiana, was covered with soybeans and corn. Dark green leaves and sturdy stalks grew in neat rows across squared-up fields, like great patches sewn together in an endless quilt.

Nick knew that many of the ingredients in his company's snack cakes came from crops grown around here. Years before, when he was a lot closer to the "operational side" of his business, he knew which ingredients came from where. He visited suppliers. And even though Elgin didn't buy directly from farmers, Nick found out which farms his suppliers bought from.

On several occasions, he personally reached out to these farmers to ask if he could come visit them. All said yes, even though they'd never had anyone from one of the big food companies ask to come visit. But Nick showed up in his suit (without his tie) and walked their fields with them, learning all about soybeans, corn and wheat and all the planning, hard work and care they required.

Now he had teams of people who took care of raw materials. To Nick, the ingredients in his products had become simply a line item in his budget. He got involved only if there were issues, usually to put the hammer down on some price-pinched supplier.

This morning, though, everywhere he looked reminded him of a world he had once known well, long before he had begun working and moved to Chicago.

He had spent much of the past thirty years in an office. Now, as he drove through the open land, watching a crow fly across the cloudless, powder-blue sky, Nick rolled his window down, drew a deep breath of fresh, warm air and tried to remember what his life was like when his mornings were slow and simple and smelled sweet and earthy, like this.

#

About twenty miles southwest of Toledo, the farmland faded, and factories and warehouses emerged. The landscape of Nick's youth receded, and more familiar urban contours took shape.

It was almost noon, and Nick was famished. He was thinking about driving into downtown Toledo for lunch. But then he saw a sign for the Maumee River. For some reason, he felt drawn to the water. So instead of veering north, into downtown, he kept driving east. He took a bridge over the river, turned off and followed the water into East Toledo.

He had no idea where he was going, and he loved it. He knew he was heading east. That was enough.

He was surprised to see so much open, green space along the river: parks, trees, a nature preserve, an area for biking called Rails to Trails. The water was brown. But the skyline of downtown Toledo just across the river was as lovely as any he had ever seen. Its tall red, blue, orange, white, yellow, black and silver buildings shimmered in the noonday sun. Its brick smokestacks, now dormant, looked like an art deco homage to the city's industrial past.

A few miles up the river, Nick spotted several restaurants in a tidy green space, trimmed with dogwood trees and rose bushes,

along the eastern bank. He pulled into the parking lot of the first
one, a place called Forrester's on the River.   •

There was a patio on the backside of the restaurant, facing the
river. On such a gorgeous day, Nick knew he'd want to have lunch
out there. So he reached for his Cubs hat. But then he hesitated,
remembering he was now in Indians territory. What the hell, he
thought, grabbing it and putting it on. We're even worse than
they are this year.

Nick pulled open the large, wooden front door and stepped
inside. The place was cavernous. White, paper globe lamps hung
from the metal girding of an exposed ceiling, which made him
think this had once been a factory. Small, white lights were
draped along the wrought-iron railing of a second-floor balcony.
Big Band Era music played in the background. Several older couples dined at round tables. Two old men, wearing hats with military emblems, drank beer at a bar in the corner. A large American
flag hung on a wall. The place seemed more like a VFW hall than
a restaurant.

"Good afternoon, sir," said the hostess, a middle-aged woman
wearing cat-eye glasses and her hair in a bun. "Will you be joining
us for lunch?"

"Yes. Just one. Do you have a table outside?"

"Yes, of course. Right this way."

The stone patio was nearly full, with a younger crowd. Most
people were sitting at round, glass-topped tables under big, red
umbrellas that said "Buckeye Beer." A college-aged guy, perched
on a stool at the end of the patio, was playing acoustic guitar.

"This is great," Nick said to the hostess.

"Would you like a seat in the shade?"

"No, thanks. The sun feels good."

"Your waitress will be out in a moment. Or if you like, I can
take your drink order now."

Nick still had a slight headache.

"I think I'll have a glass of iced tea."

"Very good. We'll get that right out."

Nick sat down at a tall table facing the river. The water was high, just a few feet below the crest of the bank. It had been a wet spring. Nick wondered if the water was always so muddy. Then he spotted a couple of "Toledo Mud Hens" jerseys and figured he was in mud city.

A few minutes later, his waitress appeared. She was younger than the hostess. She wore her hair in a ponytail. But she too was wearing cat-eye glasses. Nick wondered if they were a thing in Toledo. If so, he hoped they wouldn't catch on anywhere else. They reminded him of Sister Henry Marie, his grade school principal. He shuddered at the thought of the old nun.

"Iced tea?" asked his waitress.

"Yes."

She sat the glass down and placed a menu in front of him.

"I'll be back in a minute to take your order."

"Thanks."

Nick looked down at his tea, which was the same color as the river.

"Miss!" he called to his waitress.

"Yes, sir," she said, circling back. "Ready to order?"

"Not quite yet. But I've changed my mind on the iced tea. Could you bring me a Buckeye Beer instead?"

"Of course," she said, picking up his glass. "I'll be right back."

The guy on the guitar was pretty good. He was playing "Where Are You Going?" by Dave Matthews. His guitar work was adequate by Nick's high standards. But his voice was exceptional. It was strong, but soft and soulful too. His clear enunciation made Nick pay closer attention to the words.

> *I am no Superman*
> *I have no answers for you*
> *I am no hero, oh that's for sure*

Yeah, that's for sure, Nick thought.

His waitress brought his beer.

"Are you ready to order?"

"To be honest, I haven't even looked at the menu. Do you have any recommendations?"

"Well, if you're hungry, the cod sandwich and fries are a great choice."

Nick was ravenous, and he loved seafood. He was just about to go with the fish sandwich. But then he looked at the muddy river again.

"Do you have a Cobb salad?"

"Yes, sir."

"Great. I'll have that."

Sipping his beer, which smelled a little like cabbage, he pulled out his phone and plugged Cleveland into Google Maps. He was less than two hours away.

An ad popped up for the Indians game that afternoon. They were playing the Red Sox at 3:05. Tickets were still available.

Nick loved baseball. It was a gorgeous day. If he left soon, he figured, he could make the opening pitch. It felt strange to have this kind of flexibility.

"I'm on sabbatical," he murmured aloud, as if he needed to talk the idea into reality. It helped. He booked a ticket online.

A few minutes later, his waitress was back with his salad. Between bites, he booked a room at the Radisson, just two blocks from the Indians' ballpark, Progressive Field.

He waited for his waitress to look over and, when she did, he made a scribbling motion with his hand in the air. She nodded.

A woman at the next table was biting into a big piece of carrot cake. It reminded Nick of Elgin, which made him think of Jennifer.

He wondered how Lou had told her. He wondered how much pressure she was feeling right now. He wondered what she would say to his organization tomorrow morning.

He was tempted to check his email. He imagined a swirling mess in his absence back at the office.

Nick knew that information is power, and he had no interest in sharing his power. He went to great lengths to restrict information about his business. He shared little, even with his leadership team. He was careful to meet with department heads individually. He created a matrix of organization structures, systems and rules which ensured only he made the most important decisions about his business. He even controlled Lou's access to information.

As a result, when it came to Elgin's snack cake business, only Nick saw the big picture, and he called the shots.

He suspected that eventually Jennifer might be able to put it all together. But it would take her months, if not years.

Of course, that's if she stayed. Nick liked Jennifer, but he had a hard time imagining her trying to do his job. He smiled thinking about how quickly Lou would see this. He imagined Lou would be calling him soon to beg him to come back.

By the end of the week, he'd probably send the corporate jet to whisk Nick back to Chicago and save everything.

Chapter Seven

October 1966

Nick awoke to the sound of his father, yelling in another room.

"I told you I don't want you seeing him any more!"

His mother was saying something, but he couldn't make it out.

"No!" his father shouted. "I said no!"

"Shhhh! You'll wake the kids."

"Don't try to pull that crap!"

Nick's parents seemed to argue all the time any more. But he had never gotten used to it.

Nick turned over on his stomach. He put his pillow over his head and pulled it down tight over his ears. But he could still hear his father yelling.

When he heard him call his mother a bitch, he couldn't stand it any longer. He got up, careful not to wake his little brother, and quietly closed their bedroom door behind him.

He stepped into the hallway and peeked around the corner into the family room. His father was sitting in his armchair, his mother on the sofa. Nick must have made a small sound because both of his parents looked over at him.

"See?" his mother said. "I told you you'd wake the kids. Go back to bed, Nick."

"What's going on?" the boy asked, squinting in the lamplight.

"It's none of your business!" his father bellowed. "Now get back to bed."

His father was slurring his words. Nick had heard him this way before. He looked at his mother. Her eyes were red. She was wiping her nose with a white, lace handkerchief.

"Mom, are you OK?"

"What do you mean, is she okay? Go back to bed, Nick."

The boy didn't move.

"Nick, I said go back to bed!"

"No."

"Nick, don't ever defy me!"

Grabbing the arms of his chair, his father pushed himself up, teetering for a moment before balancing himself. Then, with an intimidating scowl on his face, he began staggering toward the boy.

"No, Jim!" his mother cried, standing up and stepping toward him to block his way.

Nick watched in horror as his father swiped his arm through the air and, with the back of his hand, struck his mother on the side of her head, knocking her to the floor.

"Ohhh!" she cried, landing hard on the carpet.

"Now get back to bed," his father growled at Nick, "before I do the same thing to you."

The boy looked down at his mother. She was on her hands and knees, moaning.

"Go back to bed, Nick," she pleaded.

"Mom, are you okay?"

"I'll be okay," she whimpered.

Nick looked up at his father. He was standing in the middle of the room, his hands hanging at his sides. His face was red. There was something wrong with his eyes. He was looking in Nick's direction, but his eyes were crazy. Nick had seen that look before.

His mother was struggling to get up. Nick went over to help her. But before he could, his father grabbed him from behind and threw him across the room. The boy tumbled across the carpet.

"I said go back to bed!" his father yelled.

Nick skidded to a stop and sat up on the floor. His father was just a few feet away. The old man towered over him. Nick had never been so frightened. He wasn't sure what do to. But something told him he should stand his ground. So he got up and just stood there, facing his father, not budging.

His mother managed to stand. She shuffled over to Nick, wedging herself between her husband and her son. She wrapped her arms around the boy and kissed him on the forehead.

"Good night, Nick," she said. "I love you."

Nick looked up at her. Tears were running down her cheeks. But somehow she managed a faint smile.

"Good night, Mom."

His father stumbled away, back toward his chair, mumbling something.

Nick went back to his room. He lay in his bed, listening through the wall as his parents resumed their fighting.

He lay there, confused. He was confused about why his parents fought so much. But he was even more confused about his father.

He couldn't figure him out. Sometimes, like tonight, he was angry. At other times, he was quiet. But there were also times when he could be kind.

Mostly, though, he seemed sad. Nick never saw him happy, and he never knew why.

To Nick, his father was a mystery. He never knew where he was coming from or which version of his father to expect at any given moment.

It would be years before he could begin to understand that these traits, of bipolar behavior and keeping people guessing, were in his own blood.

Chapter Eight

Nick rolled into downtown Cleveland about 2:45. He wasn't sure he would make the first pitch. But he'd try.

He pulled into the garage below the Radisson and took the elevator to the lobby. He checked in, went up to his room, changed into shorts and a golf shirt, grabbed his Cubs hat and headed to the ballpark on foot.

He walked fast. Progressive Field was only two blocks away, and he made it just in time to grab a hot dog and a beer before the first pitch.

The park was crowded. Even Nick's section, just above the left field wall, was packed. He had to squeeze past five or six people in his row to get to his seat. One man didn't stand up, and Nick accidentally splashed a little beer on his knee.

"Sorry, buddy."

"No problem," said the man, wiping his bare knee with a napkin.

That'll teach you to stand up when someone's passing, Nick thought.

He sat down between a younger woman and an older man. Next to the woman were two kids and the guy on whom Nick had spilled his beer. All four of them wore Indians jerseys. On his other side, the older man was sitting next to an older woman, whom Nick assumed was his wife.

No sooner had Nick sat down than everyone stood up for the

national anthem. Some took off their hats, put their hands over their hearts and began singing. Nick just stood there with his Cubs hat still on, sipping his beer.

It was a hot and cloudless afternoon. Nick knew he would be in the sun for much, if not all, of the game. Nevertheless, he flipped his hat around, with the bill in the back, in a vain and futile attempt to look cool.

"Beautiful day," he said to the woman next to him.

"Yes, it is."

"Rooting for the Tribe today?" Looking at her jersey, Nick realized it was a stupid question.

"Yeah."

Looking at his hat, she asked, "You?"

"Oh, yeah," he smiled. "I'm a Cubs fan only at National League games."

"That's good," she smiled.

"Your family?"

"Yes."

"Great day for a family outing."

"How about you? You from Chicago?"

"Yeah. I'm just passing through and thought I'd catch the game."

"I see."

She sipped on her soft drink.

"You have kids?"

She caught him between bites of his hot dog.

"Yeah, two," he mumbled. "But they're grown."

"Boy? Girl?"

"One of each. The boy is now—"

He couldn't remember how old his son was.

"Don't worry," she chuckled. "That happens to me all the time. I always have to think of the years they were born. My son is seven, and my daughter is five."

"My daughter is twenty-seven, and my son is twenty-five. My wife and I are twenty years ahead of you and your husband."

"Well, you don't look it."

Hey, she's flirting with me, Nick thought. And right in front of her husband, the guy I spilled beer on!

The sun was strong. Nick wished he'd put on some sunscreen. Not that he'd packed any. His arms and legs were not used to such direct sun exposure. His skin was already beginning to turn pink.

"Cold beer here!" a vendor sang out.

Nick raised his hand, quickly downing the rest of his beer as the sweaty vendor made his way up the steps.

He stopped, set his cooler down at the end of Nick's aisle and wiped the side of his face on his shoulder. He raised his index finger and mouthed "One?"

Nick nodded.

"Four fifty!"

Nick got out his wallet and pulled out a ten.

"Would you please pass that down?"

"Sure," said the woman next to him.

The vendor poured a beer into a plastic cup and sent it down Nick's way. When he saw the ten, he looked at Nick and rubbed the tips of his thumb and index finger together. Nick shook his head and waved him off. The vendor smiled and shouted, "Thanks!"

Out of the corner of his eye, Nick could see the woman next to him raise her eyebrows. He could tell she was surprised by his generous tip. He smiled.

She handed him the beer.

"Thanks."

He took a long drink. The beer was cold and refreshing. He licked the thick, sweet foam off his upper lip. Maybe this sabbatical wasn't such a bad idea after all, he thought.

Each side was retired three in a row. The second inning was about to begin. Nick remembered a trip to Wrigley with his friends the summer after his junior year in high school. They challenged each other to drink a beer an inning that game. Nick was the only one who could do it, although he didn't remember anything after the seventh inning stretch.

He was seventeen. Now he was fifty-three, old enough to know better. But what the hell, he thought. It was a gorgeous day. Thanks to Lou, he had nowhere to go. He was two blocks from his hotel, and he might not even be around in a few days. A beer an inning, he vowed to himself.

The older man next to him was chatting with his wife. Nick noticed that they laughed a lot. They were holding hands, her arm resting on his between their seats. They seemed to be so happy together. Nick wondered what that felt like.

"So where do your kids live?" the woman next to him asked.

"My son's in San Francisco, and my daughter's in Denver."

"Wow. They're pretty far away."

"Yeah."

"Any grandkids yet?"

"No, not yet. Neither one is married."

"Well, then, that's good, I guess."

"Yeah."

"It's hard to imagine my kids being all grown-up. But I know it'll happen. That's why I'm grateful for days like this."

"Yeah," he said, feeling guilty and sad. "Hold on to these days."

#

By the seventh inning, Nick had gotten up to either pee or get another beer half a dozen times. He'd become a nuisance to the people in his aisle.

But he was no longer bothering either the young family or the older couple who'd been sitting next to him. They'd left after the fifth inning, when they couldn't take any more of Nick's loud boo-ing and swearing.

Nick knew the ballpark stopped selling beer after the seventh inning. So at the seventh-inning stretch, he got up again and came back with two beers. By the end of the game, he had finished them both, for an even nine beers in all.

The Indians got beat, 7-2. By the eighth inning, most of the fans had left. But Nick sat there until the end. He was too drunk, too bloated and too sunburned to move.

He was the only person left in the whole section. An usher climbed the steps and stopped at the end of his aisle.

"You okay, buddy?"

"Yeah. Just fine," Nick said, slurring his words badly.

He tried to stand up, then fell back into his seat.

"You need a hand?"

"Go to hell," Nick snarled.

"Do I need to call security?"

"No, officer. I'll go peacefully."

The usher just stood there and watched as Nick baby-stepped his way down the aisle.

"A little over-served?" he asked as Nick reached the concrete steps.

"Why don't you mind your own business?"

"All right. I'm going to have to call security."

He unfastened a walkie talkie from his belt.

"Go ahead!" Nick yelled, grabbing the railing and wobbling down the steps.

"I've got a drunk in 181," he could hear the usher saying. But Nick made his way past the concession stands without interference, tripped down two flights of steps to the gate and slipped out onto the plaza. Somehow, at six-two, stumbling, wearing a Cubs hat and having consumed nine beers, he had eluded the fuzz.

And to think, at age seventeen, his friends had to carry him out of Wrigley.

I am the man, Nick thought.

#

On his way back to the hotel, Nick had to stop several people to ask directions.

Finally, he found it and stumbled into the lobby. He could barely stand up.

A family was checking in at the reception desk. Several young people were sitting in chairs near a stone fireplace. One of them was wearing a hat with the Cleveland Indians logo.

"Go, Tribe!" Nick whooped, pumping his fist in the air.

Everyone knew he was drunk. They tried to ignore him.

"Whatsa matter?" Nick yelled, demanding attention. "Everybody here a Red Sox fan?"

Nobody knew what to say.

"I root for the Cubs," said one of the guys sitting near the fireplace. His friends laughed.

Nick turned toward him and took a step.

"Suck up!"

A little girl at the counter was staring at Nick as she clutched her mother's leg. He turned towards her, almost losing his balance.

"Whatsa matter, kid? You ain't never seen a drunk?"

Her father turned around. He narrowed his eyes and took a step toward Nick.

"Hey, buddy," he said.

Two of the young guys got up.

"Hey, pops," said the one in the Indians hat. "Stay cool."

Nick was hammered, but he knew he was outnumbered.

"Pops?" he said indignantly, stutter-stepping toward the elevator. "I'm not your father!"

He jabbed at the button, missing it at first. Finally, the doors opened, and he stumbled in. He reached to push the button for his floor but missed it and lost his footing. He fell to floor, hitting his left shoulder hard against the elevator wall, the same shoulder he had hurt the night before.

"Crap!" he cried out.

Everyone in the lobby could hear him. But no one made a move to help.

When the elevator doors opened, Nick crawled out. He stayed motionless on all fours in the hallway for a minute. He was tempted to fall asleep right there. But he got up and leaned against the wall. He hugged the wall all the way to his room.

When he got to his door, he fumbled with his plastic key card, putting it into the metal slot backwards, then upside down. When he finally put it in right, he kept pulling it out too soon, causing a red light to blink.

"God damn it!" he yelled.

Finally, he saw a green light and heard a click, and the handle gave way. He pushed the door open and tripped into his room. This time, somehow, he steered clear of the door as it slammed shut.

He staggered over to his bed, plopped down and fell backwards. The room was spinning. He felt sick. He swung his legs over the edge of the bed. He knew he couldn't make it to the bathroom. He spotted a square, plastic garbage can under the desk. He stumbled over to it, dropped to his knees and threw up.

He made his way back to the bed, not even bothering to wash up. He lay there, looking up at the ceiling. He thought about his father when he was a kid, coming home drunk at night and yelling at his mother.

He remembered staring at his father, trying to make sense of it and feeling so helpless and afraid. He remembered his father glaring at him, bellowing, "What are you lookin' at, kid?"

Shivering, Nick wrapped the bedspread around himself and passed out.

Chapter Nine

June 1968

The school year was almost over. Like all fourth graders, Nick couldn't wait for school to end and summer to begin.

The days were getting hot. There was no air conditioning at St. Pius X. By mid-morning, Sister Bonita would ask for volunteers to open the windows. Nick, who always liked sitting near the windows, would hop up and help crank them open.

The fresh air felt great. Unfortunately, it was also a tease. It was good and bad.

Nick's tenth year was like that.

On one hand, it was a good year.

It was the year he began to learn how to play the guitar.

It was the year he read his first novel, *The Adventures of Huckleberry Finn*. It lit a passion in him to read and write.

It was the year of the first Apollo mission to make it into space. That was an important event. It lifted everyone's spirits after three astronauts had died in a fire aboard the first Apollo mission the year before.

But on the other hand, it was a bad year.

It was the year of violent protests over the Vietnam War.

It was the year of race riots, with U.S. cities on fire.

It was the year of assassinations of great men.

One morning, Sister Bonita told Nick's class that, the night before, Bobby Kennedy had been shot.

"Who's Bobby Kennedy?" someone asked.

"He's President Kennedy's little brother," Sister said. "He's running for President."

Oh, everyone murmured. Everyone at St. Pius X, in every Catholic school and in every Catholic home knew who President Kennedy was. His Mass card was taped to the wall of Nick's kitchen and pinned up on the bulletin board in his classroom.

President Kennedy's assassination was one of Nick's earliest memories. He was five years old. That afternoon, he was playing outside. His mother called him in. All the mothers in the neighborhood called their kids in. When Nick came inside, he saw his mother crying.

"What's wrong, Mom?"

"President Kennedy's been shot."

Nick didn't understand the concept of a President. Nor did he fully understand the concept of death. No one he knew in his young life had ever died. But he'd heard the words "President Kennedy" many times. In fact, he didn't know they were separate words. He'd only ever heard them uttered together.

His mother was sitting on the sofa, watching TV. She made Nick and his little brother, David, sit on the floor and watch too. Nick never knew why she did that. But he supposed it was because she was afraid and wanted to keep her sons close.

He remembered when, that afternoon, his mother heard something a man said on TV and shrieked.

"Oh, my God! They've killed him! They've killed the President!"

Nick wasn't sure what was happening. He only knew that his mother was very upset. He started crying. This made David cry too. The two boys climbed up on their mother's lap. Nick was getting too big to sit on his mother's lap. But that day, it felt like the only thing to do.

And now President Kennedy's baby brother had been shot too.

"We're going to Mass to pray for Senator Kennedy," Sister Bonita announced.

The class lined up, filed out of the classroom and marched up the stairs to the church. It reminded Nick of the same drill just two months earlier, the morning after Martin Luther King was shot.

Before that, Nick had never heard of Martin Luther King. But that morning, Nick and all the students at St. Pius X prayed for the repose of his soul. Now, they were all in church again, asking God to save the life of President Kennedy's little brother.

Later that day, Nick learned that Bobby Kennedy had died.

That's the kind of year it was for Nick. It was a jumbled, jarring, frightening time.

Some of his friends said all boys would eventually have to join the Army and fight in Vietnam. Nick didn't know where Vietnam was. But he'd seen the images on TV of soldiers who were wearing bandages over their eyes and villages on fire. He was scared to death that he might have to fight in such a place someday.

But he also knew that violence was not so far away. On TV, he could see American cities burning too, cities as close as Chicago. And he began to think that all famous men were sitting ducks.

Of course, in 1968, Nick was not the only ten-year-old boy surrounded by terrible events. But unlike other boys, he had no one to help him put them in perspective. His mother and father didn't talk about these issues. And Nick was always afraid of saying something that would set his father off.

Nick began to see the world as a dangerous place. But with no one to talk with, he kept his worries inside. They gnawed at him. He began biting his fingernails. In time, he would learn to control that nervous habit, but not before the other kids made fun of him.

Chapter Ten

Nick opened his eyes and looked at the clock on his bed stand. 10:03. At first, he wondered if that was AM or PM. Then it registered that the sun was shining.

He rolled over. Damn! A sharp pain shot down his arm. The surface of the bedspread, in which he was wrapped like a caterpillar in a cocoon, was rough and prickly against the skin of his sunburned arms and legs. He started to pull back the cover. Moving his arm, he felt a stabbing pain in his shoulder.

For a moment, he lay there, wondering where he was. Oh, yeah. Cleveland. It could be worse, he thought. He could be in Cincinnati. He'd spent a week there on business one day.

He peeled back the bedspread with his good arm and sat up on the bed. He had a dull headache. He was surprised it wasn't much worse. I should stick with beer more often, he thought.

The morning was almost shot, and he had no idea where he was going today. He hadn't given any thought to the next leg of his trip.

He stepped into the bathroom, flipped on the light, looked in the mirror and grimaced. His face was bright pink up to a straight line across his forehead, where the rim of his hat had stopped. His head looked like an Easter egg.

He turned on the water and stepped into the shower. The hot water stung every sunburned inch of his skin. He twisted the faucet to turn the temperature down, but the water immediately turned cold. He turned the dial back only to be scalded again. There didn't seem to be a warm setting at all. So, without even unwrapping a bar of soap, he got out.

He gently toweled off and grabbed the small, free bottle of lotion on the sink. He squeezed it out and slathered it on his arms, legs, face and neck. It made his skin burn even more, but he hoped it would help keep it from peeling.

He got dressed and looked at himself in the mirror on the wall. Between his sunburn and stubble, he looked like a beach bum.

He was famished. He decided to get some suggestions on a place to eat at the front desk and, since he hadn't planned his next stop, despite the crappy shower faucet, reserve his room for another night.

A pretty, young, Latino-looking woman was standing behind the desk.

"Good morning," he said.

"Good morning, sir. I hope you slept well."

He wondered what she meant by that. Did he look hung over? Had the desk clerk from last night warned her about him? Had the family with the little girl lodged a complaint?

"Yes, I slept like a baby."

"Wonderful."

"I've decided to stay in town a little longer. Can I reserve my room for another night?"

"Of course. What is your name?"

Whew, he thought. Maybe she's not on to me after all.

"Reynolds. Room 312."

"Thank you," she said, tapping away at a keyboard behind the desk. "I've got you down for another night with us. Anything else I can do for you?"

"Yes. I do have two requests."

"Certainly," she said, looking up and smiling.

"First, could someone fix the faucet in my shower? It sticks on either hot or cold. There's nothing in between."

"I'm sorry," she said, scribbling a note. "I'll send someone up this morning."

"Thank you."

She looked back up at him. Her eyes were the darkest shade of brown, almost black. She spoke with an accent as light as an early morning breeze. The combination drew Nick in.

"And your second request?"

"Pardon me?"

"You said you had two requests."

"Oh, yeah," he said. "What's the best place around here for a good burger."

"The Winking Lizard Tavern," she said, smiling. "It's only a block away."

Nick knew he was probably imagining things. But for a moment, he thought that, when she said "winking lizard," she actually winked at him. Maybe it was code, he thought.

Nick had never been with a Latino woman. But he was fairly certain Latino women had the hots for him. At any rate, this young lady was clearly checking him out.

But then he realized she was looking at his head. Damn! He had forgotten his hat. She wasn't winking. She was probably shielding her eyes from the Easter egg that was his head.

"Will there be anything else, Mr. Reynolds?"

"No," Nick said, feeling humbled and pink. "Thank you."

#

He ordered the Bo-Man's Bacon Cheeseburger and a Dirty Bastard ale. Between what he could remember about last night and his irrational thoughts about Latino women, Nick felt like a dirty bastard.

Waiting for his beer, he opened his laptop. He didn't really know Cleveland. He typed in "things to do in Cleveland."

The list was longer than he expected. It started with The Rock and Roll Hall of Fame. Cool. He'd always wanted to go there but never had the time. Now he had all the time in the world.

He clicked on Google Maps to check out his remaining route to Bar Harbor. The next big city was Buffalo, a little more than three hours away. He didn't see a larger city beyond that for quite a while. So he decided Buffalo would be his next stop.

It felt strange to have the flexibility to make such a decision. He'd grown used to the notion of not being in charge of his schedule or even his life. There was always someone with a question, an issue or a proposal. And there was always someone, like Jean, who was eager to tell him what to do.

After years of spending most of his days reacting to what others wanted, Nick no longer thought much about what he really wanted. He had become an amalgamation of others' interests. He was like a machine that had been cobbled together by a thousand tinkerers, all of them seeing him not for who he was, but for who they needed him to be.

But now these people were all gone. Nick was alone, in a strange city, without a plan. There was no one telling him what to do. "Do whatever you need to do to sort yourself out," Lou had said. That was it.

On one hand, this lack of being directed felt odd and off-putting to Nick. But on the other hand, it was beginning to feel like an opening to figure out who he really was and what he really wanted.

Maybe he would figure that out on his way to Bar Harbor. Maybe he could still figure that out in time. And if he couldn't, maybe there was no opening after all, only a closing. Maybe he'd strayed so far from his true self that he was hopelessly lost and there was no sense in going on.

But that was too much to think about right now. Nick was hungry and thirsty, and all he wanted was a good burger and a cold beer.

#

Nick loved rock and roll. He loved the sound of it, the look of it, the feel of it. But most of all, he loved the rebels behind it. And of all the rebels, the guitarists were his favorites.

And today he would spend all afternoon with them: Clapton, Harrison, Vaughn, Berry, Page, Van Halen, Beck, Richards, Santana, Allman, Knopfler and, of course, Hendrix. Today he got to listen to their music, watch them play on video, see their guitars up close. He was awed by their mastery and struck by how relatively clean all these guys looked. They might have been high. But on most, he didn't see even one tattoo.

There was even a booth where he could put on headphones and play along. For $50, he could even cut his own CD, accompanying his idols. He decided to play "Stairway to Heaven" with Jimmy Page. He knew he couldn't come close to keeping up, but the very idea of playing with Page gave him such a rush. He had to try.

He did his best, right down to picking the last few notes as Robert Plant crooned, "And she's buy-ing the stairway to heaven." He was sure the final product was a mess. But he was still lit up by the experience.

"You're good, man," said the young guy in the sound booth, handing Nick his CD. His arm was covered with a sleeve of tattoos featuring the logos of various bands. On the back of his left hand was the Rolling Stones' iconic red tongue.

"Thanks. I've played that song a few times."

"Well, it shows, man. You stayed with Page pretty well."

"I wish," Nick said grinning. "Right now, my fingertips are killing me. I haven't played much lately, and my callouses are gone."

"Ouch! Well, keep playing, man. Maybe one day you'll be back here as an inductee."

It was the kind of smart-aleck remark that normally would have set Nick off, especially from a guy with tattoos. But today, a day when he was free to do something he loved and freed from anyone who thought they knew better, he accepted the comment as the compliment it was and simply said thanks.

\#

It was early evening when Nick got back to his hotel. The Latino woman was gone. Bummer.

A young guy was now behind the desk. He looked familiar. Nick realized he had been on duty last night, when he had caused such a scene in the lobby.

"Good evening," Nick said.

"Good evening, sir."

Either he's being gracious or he doesn't remember me, Nick thought.

"How are you feeling today?"

Son of a bitch, Nick thought. He does remember.

"I'm doing okay."

Then he stopped and looked the guy in the eye. He looked so young and earnest. He reminded Nick of Josh, his son.

"I'm sorry," Nick said.

"For what?"

"For the way I behaved last night. I behaved badly, and I don't have a good excuse."

"It's okay. I'm just glad you're all right."

#

Nick went up to his room. He decided to take a shower, then grab dinner.

To his great relief, the hotel had fixed the faucet in his shower. He twisted the faucet until the water was between lukewarm and cool, then stepped in.

The cooler water felt good. But he still wasn't sure about using soap for fear it might be too harsh for his tender skin. So he just stood there, under the water, with his eyes closed, great music from the afternoon playing in his head.

Then it hit him. He remembered going online that morning and what was listed just below the Rock and Roll Hall of Fame: the Hard Rock Cafe. What a perfect place for dinner!

He got out, gently toweled himself dry, got dressed and went down to the lobby.

"Is the Hard Rock Cafe within walking distance?" he asked the desk clerk.

"Sure. It's an easy walk. Less than ten minutes."

"Great. Which way?"

"Turn left out of the hotel and head west on Prospect Avenue."

"Thanks."

Stepping out into the warm, early-evening air, for a reason he didn't understand, Nick made a vow to himself not to get loaded tonight.

#

"Welcome to the Hard Rock Cafe," said the hostess, who was dressed in black leather. She bore a striking resemblance to Joan Jett.

"Have you been here before?"

"I've been to a lot of Hard Rock Cafes, but not this one."

"Well, you're in for a treat."

"Oh, yeah? How so?"

For a moment, Nick thought Joan might be hitting on him.

"It's battle of the garage bands night. You made it just in time."

Nick had played in a garage band as a teenager. He well remembered how terrible they sounded. He imagined this could be a short dinner.

But Joan was right. No sooner did Nick sit down when the first band started performing a killer version of "Rock and Roll" by Led Zeppelin.

A waitress approached his table. She had frizzy hair and looked a little like Janis Joplin.

"So, it's battle of the bands night!" yelled Nick over the loud, but respectable, guitar solo.

"Not only that," Janis said, leaning in. "It's five by five night."

"What's that?"

"Five local bands each play a five-song set."

"That's a lot of music!"

"And a lot of beer," she rasped. "What can I get you, darlin'?"

Jesus. She even sounded like Janis.

"Bring me a bottle of the best and coldest beer you've got."

"My kind of man."

After his bacon cheeseburger for lunch but still leery of any fish from Lake Erie, Nick ordered a chicken sandwich and, as a nutritional bonus, sweet potato fries.

Then he kicked back and listened to the best garage band music he'd ever heard. It was so polished that he wondered if any of these guys had ever cut an album. Was "album" even a word any more?

Janis came back with his beer and took his food order. Nick sat back and took a big swig of beer. It was a hell of a lot tastier than that ballpark beer last night.

But he was mindful of the vow he'd made to himself. He would have only one beer per set, he decided. He wanted to avoid a repeat of last night.

Nick nursed his beer but devoured his food. By the end of the first set, the place had filled up. He was glad he had gotten there early.

#

Nick loved music. He had grown up with music. His mother played the piano. His uncle played the accordion. And his cousin, Mark, played the guitar. Going to family gatherings was like going to a concert.

Nick idolized Mark. He was about ten years older than Nick. Some of Nick's earliest memories were of watching Mark play his electric guitar. It was a Fender Stratocaster. It was sunburst, with waves of gold, red and black emanating from the center, double cutaways and a white pick guard that covered nearly half of the body. It was a badass guitar, and it had to be sunburst because Mark played it like he was on fire.

He played at every family get-together. Eventually, for most of Nick's cousins, the novelty wore off. But not for Nick. He loved listening to Mark play. He sat there, sometimes by himself, listening to every song, every chord, every note.

Nick's father noticed. One day, when he was ten, he was shocked when his father brought home a little Yamaha acoustic guitar and handed it to him. Nick was ecstatic, even though he had no idea how to play it.

That Christmas, he brought it with him to his grandparents' house. All his cousins were there. Nick couldn't wait to show Mark.

"Will you teach me how to play?" he asked.

Mark smiled and said, "Come with me, Nicky."

He brought Nick out to his car, which was parked on the street, and opened his trunk. There it was: his cool-as-hell Stratocaster.

"Think you can handle it?"

"What?"

"Carry it into Grandma and Grandpa's for me," he said, grinning. "I'll grab the amp. We'll have a little jam session in the basement."

That day, Mark taught Nick how to hold a guitar, where to put his fingers on the frets, how to strum and how to play half a dozen chords. Nick picked it up fast.

"You're a natural," Mark told him. "Of course, it's in your blood."

Nick went home and practiced that night until his fingertips were raw and throbbing. Before breakfast the next morning, he was back at it. From then on, he practiced every day. Soon, callouses formed on his fingertips. He began memorizing chords and learning songs. Every night after dinner, he would play in his room. Sometimes, he would play loudly, and his mother would ask him to keep it down. But his father never said a word. He didn't seem to mind.

That summer, his father entered Nick in a children's guitar competition sponsored by The Music Loft, a local music store. The competition took place on a Saturday morning in the middle of the store. The contestants sat in a semi-circle of folding chairs.

Their parents stood behind them among the guitars and ukuleles suspended from plastic-coated hooks along the walls.

When it was his turn, Nick stepped to the center of the floor, where the owner had marked an X with masking tape. He'd never played in public or been the center of attention. As he looked around the room, he realized every eye was on him. His knees were shaking. He looked around for his parents. His mother had a worried look on her face. His father simply smiled and nodded.

He slung the strap of his little guitar over his head, fished his pick out of his pocket and began to play "Wichita Lineman." It was a song he had played dozens of times. But he hadn't brought his sheet music, and he was so nervous that he forgot the chords. Less than a minute in, he stopped playing. He couldn't go on. Flustered and embarrassed, he took off his guitar and sat back down. Everyone clapped politely.

On the way home, his mother tried to console him.

"It's okay, Nicky. That happens to everybody. You'll do better next time."

But his father took a different tack.

"I think you're ready for a bigger guitar," he said.

It was the very thing Nick needed to hear because, between the time he had sat down, feeling ashamed, until that moment, he had decided to give up the guitar. But that simple comment by his father helped him to see his situation differently. It gave him hope. That night, after dinner, he practiced twice as long as usual.

His father was right. Nick was growing fast, and his little guitar was now too small for him. It had begun to feel like a toy in his hands. And it was cheap. It sounded like a toy.

What's more, music was changing. Folk music was out, and hard rock was in. Nick began talking about how much he wanted an electric guitar. He knew it was a long shot but figured it couldn't hurt to talk about it.

One Saturday, his father surprised him once again by bringing home a used, no-name electric guitar and a little amplifier. Nick was thrilled.

He played that guitar all through high school. He even formed a garage band, which performed at bars, the Linn County fair and a few wedding receptions.

On the day Nick graduated from high school, his father surprised him yet again with a new Fender Stratocaster. With the possible exception of his mother's wedding ring, it was the most expensive thing his father had ever given anyone.

Nick knew how much money meant to his father. He never felt closer to his father than he did that day.

He took his new electric guitar with him to college. For four years, he played it just about every day. But once he graduated and got a job, his guitar began to sit idle.

#

Tonight, all Nick could think about was playing again. He watched the lead guitarists tearing it up, set after set, and imagined himself up there playing.

As the fifth band was setting up, after only his third beer, Nick thought: what the hell? He approached the guy who was holding an electric guitar. He was wearing a black T-shirt. His arms were covered with tattoos.

"Hi, there," Nick said.

"Hey."

"I have a crazy question."

"Shoot."

"I play guitar. I was just wondering if you guys might have room for an extra guitar player during one of the songs in your set tonight."

The rocker leaned his guitar up against an amplifier. He rubbed his hands together, folded his arms and faced Nick, narrowing his eyes.

"So what do you play?"

"I like hard rock."

"So do we. That's all we play."

The rocker unfolded his arms and stuck his hands into his back pockets. He gave Nick a hard look.

"Don't take this wrong way, man. But are you any good?"

"Well, I've been playing for more than forty years, and I cut a CD today over at the Rock and Roll Hall of Fame."

Nick sounded a lot more confident than he felt. But, as an English major, he had learned long ago how to fake confidence.

"Oh, yeah?" said the rocker. "You got a song you'd like to play tonight?"

"How about 'All Along the Watchtower'?"

The rocker squinted his eyes and smiled.

"Mason, Matthews or Hendrix?"

"Hendrix."

"And you can play the lead?"

"Yeah."

"Well, there's a little problem. We've only got one guitar. I can handle the vocals, but you'd have to carry the guitar all by yourself."

"No problem."

"Are you sure? I mean you've never played with us before."

"Yeah, I'm sure. And if I fall short, I'll buy you guys all the beer you can drink."

"Deal. By the way, I don't think I caught your name."

"I'm Nick," he said, extending his hand.

"I'm Mark. Good to meet you, Nick. We'll play 'Watchtower' as our third song. Robbie will hit the first few chords on his acoustic. Pete will come in with him on the drums. Then you come in. I'll be singing lead."

"Sounds good."

"Be ready, man."

"I'll be ready."

"I know."

Nick sat through the first two songs, nervous as a kid on the first day of school.

"We've got a special guest on lead guitar on this next song," Mark announced. "Nick, come on up."

"Yeah!" someone shouted. A few people clapped. Somebody made a loud whistle.

Nick got up and made his way through the tables of curious customers. Mark took off his guitar and handed it to him. Then he handed him his pick. Nick slung the heavy guitar over his head. He looked at Mark, then out at the crowd. Every eye in the place was on him. No doubt they were all wondering what this old guy was doing up there.

But it was a song Nick had played hundreds of times, including at The Rock and Roll Hall of Fame that afternoon. I can do this, he thought.

Nick nodded, his pick at the ready. Robbie started strumming, and Pete started drumming. A few chords in, Nick hit the high notes Hendrix had made famous. He played the best he could. Having been away from the guitar for so long, he missed some notes and forgot a few parts. But the band carried him, he played well enough and, when the song was over, the crowd applauded loudly.

Mark was smiling.

"That was great, Nick," he said.

"Thanks," Nick said, as he handed back his guitar.

"Do you want to play another?"

"No, thanks," Nick said, grinning and patting him on the shoulder. "Take us home, Mark."

Nick made his way back to his table. One guy gave him fist bump. A woman gave him a smile. He sat down and leaned back in his chair. Relaxed and content, he sipped his beer as he listened to the last two songs of the night.

It was far from a professional or even a polished amateur performance. But Nick certainly hadn't fallen short. Still, he bought a round for Mark and all the guys in the band. He didn't stick around, though. He'd had three beers. That was enough. He wanted to keep his vow.

He settled up with Janis and walked back to his hotel. The young guy was still working behind the desk.

"Good evening," he said to Nick.

"Good evening to you."

Nick strode through the lobby which, last night, he had stumbled through. He went up to his room. He changed into a T-shirt, took off his jeans, brushed his teeth and slipped under the covers.

He lay on his back with his hands behind his head. He looked up at the blinking red light of the smoke detector in the middle of the ceiling. In his mind, he replayed his performance tonight. He could see the faces of the people in the crowd, how surprised and happy they looked.

It reminded him of the look on Jean's face the first time she saw him play the guitar. That was so long ago.

He wished he could make her happy again.

Chapter Eleven

Every kid has a dream. Nick's was to play professional base-ball.

The only problem was: he wasn't very good at baseball, at least not right away. Not that he didn't try.

When he was nine, he tried out for the Farm League. In Cedar Rapids, that's where all kids playing organized baseball got their start.

Tryouts were the first step. They were a big deal. Nick had to go to the city building with his dad a week beforehand to sign up. He waited in a long line of boys. Some brought their gloves, even though this would be a morning of pure paperwork. Some wore the caps of their older brothers who had played on the Farm League teams. One kid was even carrying a bat.

When Nick got to the front of the line and it was his turn to fill out the registration form, he looked up at his dad, who nodded and said, "Go ahead."

Nick had never filled out a form. He needed his dad's help with a few things. But for the most part, he managed it on his own.

"Good job," his dad said, as they handed the form to one of the baseball moms.

Nick felt so proud and grown up.

Tryouts were held at the city's ball diamonds the following Saturday morning. It was early April. It was cold, and the ground was wet. Dozens of boys streamed out of cars, their fathers close behind.

The boys lined up for their turns to hit, throw, field and run. The dads all sat in the bleachers, shivering, drinking coffee, smoking cigarettes, watching anxiously and shouting words of encouragement to their sons.

There were eight Farm League teams. Managers and coaches stood around, holding clipboards, watching every boy carefully and making marks next to his name.

Nick was nervous. He hadn't slept much the night before, and his stomach was so queasy that morning that he couldn't eat breakfast. But he was still glad to be there and eager to do his best.

He'd played baseball for years with kids in an empty lot in the neighborhood. But until that day, he'd never stepped foot on a real baseball field, with dirt, chalk baselines and real bases, not Frisbees. The other boys seemed to revel in it. But to Nick, it was all so intimidating.

One of the coaches handed him a bat. It felt heavy in his hands. "You're up, son," he said.

Nick stepped up to the plate. Another coach was lobbing in slow pitches. Nick made contact with a few balls but missed most of them. The bat was too heavy, and it was cold. So when he hit the ball, the bat stung his hands.

Next, he moved to another diamond, where he stood in a line to throw balls from third base to first. All his throws fell short.

He then moved to a third diamond, where he fielded fly balls in the outfield and grounders in the infield. He caught a few flies, but missed everything else.

Finally, he went back to the first diamond, where he ran the bases. Another coach was marking time with a stopwatch. Nick had no idea how well he did, but he ran as fast as he could.

When he finished running the bases, one of the coaches said,

"Thanks for coming out, young man. We'll be following up over the next few days."

"How did you feel out there?" his dad asked as they walked to the car.

"Good."

He was hoping his dad would offer words of encouragement or some sort of feedback. But he said nothing the whole way home.

That afternoon, the managers and coaches were supposed to get together to compare notes and make their picks. The next day, the managers were supposed to begin calling the boys they'd chosen. Nick waited by the phone. It never rang.

But he held out hope because there was always a second round, and he knew the managers always made a few final phone calls on Monday night. It was common knowledge that these were the second-string players.

At school on Monday, the boys were abuzz with who had been called on Sunday and what teams they were on. Nick felt bad about not being able to say which team he was on yet. But he hoped to be able to share good news the next day.

That night, he waited by the phone again. But once again, it never rang.

Nick still played pick-up baseball games in the neighborhood that summer. He still loved baseball.

He never talked about not making a Farm League team. His dad never mentioned it either.

But every night for weeks, Nick cried into his pillow.

#

Farm League in Cedar Rapids was for nine-year-old boys. A career in Farm League, therefore, lasted only one year.

Little League, by contrast, lasted three years. It was for boys ages ten to twelve. Tryouts were held every spring. But once you made a team, you could stay on it until you turned thirteen.

Despite his setback the year before, at ten, Nick decided to try out for Little League. Once again, he went to the city building with his dad to register. Once again, his performance at tryouts was mediocre. And once again, the phone call from a manager never came.

Nick was disappointed but undeterred. He still loved baseball. He knew he wasn't great at it. But he knew he could play and that he was improving.

So he tried out again at age eleven. Same result.

He tried out yet again at age twelve. Same result.

Nick still loved baseball. But as far as making a team, he'd given up.

Then one evening in early June when he was twelve, when he was tossing ball with his brother in the backyard, he heard the phone ring. His mother yelled out to Nick that he had a phone call.

"Hello?"

"Nick, this is Jim Davis. I coach Cunningham Construction. We're a little lean this year, and our right fielder just broke his leg. I see that you tried out this spring but didn't get picked up. We still have fifteen games to play this season. If you're still interested in playing, I'd love to have you on our team."

Nick could not believe what he was hearing. He felt weak in his knees. He sat down hard on a kitchen chair in stunned silence.

"Yes," he finally managed to say. "Yes, Mr. Davis. I'll be glad to play for you."

That summer, Nick grew four inches. He had always been strong. But he'd begun lifting weights and could now bench press one-hundred pounds. He was still lean, but he was getting muscular. He even began wearing his dad's T-shirts.

He began practicing with his new teammates every morning. Afterwards, he went to a batting cage, where he hit balls for half an hour. Every afternoon, he had his brother, David, throw him grounders and fly balls in their back yard.

"You're getting really good at this, Nick," David said.

"Thanks."

"You're wearing me out."

"If I paid you a penny for every ball you throw me, would that help?"

"You mean it?"

"Yep."

"Yeah!"

He's so young, Nick thought. One day, he'll understand the concept of slave labor.

Nick's hard work payed off. By the end of that summer, he'd hit five home runs and was named the MVP of his team.

That fall, he played in the Little League All-Star game. He started in right field.

It was the first Little League game in Cedar Rapids played at night. It was packed. Nick's parents and his brother and sister were there. Even the local radio station, WMT, was there, broadcasting the game live.

The manager of each of the all-star teams was the manager of the best team in his respective league. The coaches were an assortment from all the teams. Most of them didn't know Nick, and he didn't know them. But he remembered their faces. They were the faces of the men jotting notes on clipboards during the four years of his baseball tryouts.

That night, Nick hit a home run and a double and had five RBIs. He was named the game MVP.

Late the next winter, the managers of the next-level-up Babe Ruth League teams came calling. Each wanted Nick on his team.

Nick took satisfaction in knowing that some of the same men who had rejected him in Little League now wanted him in Babe Ruth. He took their calls and said he'd think about it.

The managers had a deadline for recruiting "select" players for their teams, before tryouts. Nick knew exactly what that deadline was. He waited until the very last minute to call Mr. Hostler, who coached Cedar Rapids Pharmacy, to tell him he would join his team. Mr. Hostler was delighted.

But Nick chose not to call the other managers back. And when they called him, he refused to take their calls. They had left him hanging in Little League. Now it was his turn.

Nick would play one more year of organized baseball. That year, he led the league in home runs. But despite his success, he lost interest in the game. He had seen how it worked. He had been wounded by the indifference of the men who could have chosen him but didn't. And when the tables had turned, and he had the upper hand, he chose to gloat and walk away.

At thirteen, Nick was beginning to develop a mean streak.

Chapter Twelve

The Latino woman was back at the front desk in the morning.

"Good morning, Mr. Reynolds."

"Good morning."

"I hope you slept well."

"Yes, very well. Thank you."

"How was the Winking Lizard?"

"Pardon me?"

"Your lunch yesterday."

"Oh. It was great. You were right. They have great burgers."

"I'm glad you liked it."

"I do have one more request."

"Only one today?" she smiled.

She remembered. Maybe she's hitting on me, Nick thought. Her eyes seemed even darker, her accent even more intriguing, than yesterday. Her silky brown hair, which had been pulled back yesterday, now fell loose over her shoulders. Suddenly, Nick's mind went blank.

"So what is it this morning?"

"What?"

"Your one request?"

"Oh, yeah. Can you recommend a good place nearby for breakfast?"

"Certainly. Try the HotSpot Cafe. It's just a few blocks away, over on Carnegie. They have great pancakes. I think you'll like it."

"The HotSpot Cafe. Thanks."

"Will you be staying with us another night?"

"No. I'll be checking out when I get back from breakfast. Thanks again for the tip."

"You're welcome," she smiled. "Enjoy your pancakes."

#

Over a tall stack of blueberry pancakes, Nick went online and booked a room at the Best Western in downtown Buffalo. He probably should have waited until he was finished eating because his laptop keyboard was now sticky with maple syrup.

Still feeling the music, he also purchased a ticket to see a concert by *Further*, a band formed by Bob Weir and Phil Lesh, two of the founding members of the *Grateful Dead*. They were both great guitarists. The band would be playing at an outdoor venue just north of Buffalo that evening. Another night of great music.

When Nick got back to the Radisson, the Latino woman was no longer at the front desk. Bummer.

He went up to his room and grabbed his gear. Then he checked out and took off for Buffalo.

#

He could see Lake Erie from the time he started. He caught glimpses of it all along the way. It reminded him of Lake Michigan.

He remembered the first time he'd seen Lake Michigan. He was a teenager. His family was spending a few days in Chicago. It was the only real family vacation he could remember.

Every summer, he and his little brother David would stay with their grandparents in Des Moines for a week. By car, it was less than two hours from Cedar Rapids. But his family had only one car, and his father needed it for work.

So the old man dropped his sons at the Greyhound station on his way to work. With stops in all the small towns along the way, it took them half a day to get to their grandparents' house. Now, such a ride would seem tedious. Then, it was an adventure.

Des Moines is hardly a metropolis. But it was twice the size of Cedar Rapids. Until he was in high school, it was the biggest city Nick had ever seen, and going there was his idea of a big vacation.

The summer after his freshman year in high school, his father surprised his family by taking them to Chicago. Some of Nick's friends had been there and told him it was huge. But nothing they said could have prepared him for the grand scale and majesty of the City on the Lake.

He was astonished when they began seeing suburbs an hour west of the city, some of them bigger than Cedar Rapids. His father, ever the tightwad, had booked a single room for all five of them at an inexpensive hotel far north of the city. But on the way, he decided to drive into downtown and spring for lunch.

Standing on the sidewalk on South Wacker Drive, Nick had stared up at the Sears Tower, which had just been completed. It was heralded as the tallest building in the world. Nick had seen pictures of it in school. But pictures didn't do justice to the structure's true enormity. Nick couldn't have imagined a building so large.

As impressive as it was, though, Nick was not intimidated. He sensed this building was designed to make a statement. It exuded power. For some reason, standing in its shadow, he too felt powerful. This is where I belong, he thought. One day, I'll work here. One day, I'll make a statement too.

After lunch, his family took a walk to Lake Michigan. Until then, the biggest body of water Nick had ever seen was Cedar Lake. It was less than ten feet deep. The entire lake was visible from any point along the bank.

To Nick, Lake Michigan looked like the ocean or at least how he had always imagined the ocean. It had whitecaps and freighters and stretched beyond the horizon. He had no idea a lake could be so vast.

Within the span of a couple of hours, Nick's world had expanded. He knew that in just a few days, he would be returning to Cedar Rapids. But he also knew he wouldn't be there for long. He knew he had glimpsed his future and that he was destined to live on a grander scale.

#

Now, he had lived in Chicago for more than thirty-five years and seen Lake Michigan countless times. But he'd mainly seen the lake from his office or his boat. He hadn't driven much along its shores.

This morning, driving along Lake Erie, the water had a different feel. It didn't feel endless like the ocean. Maybe it was because he could follow his progress on his iPhone and count down the miles to Buffalo.

He could see that the lake ended there, at the northeast tip. There, it became a river. It flowed on, but in a very different form.

Nick thought about Bar Harbor. He wondered if his life must really end there or if, like the water, it might flow on in some new way.

Chapter Thirteen

February 1972

At fourteen, Nick stood six feet tall and weighed one-hundred and forty pounds. He could bench press his body weight. And yet he was never a physical kid.

Except once.

Nick had just come home from school. He, his brother David and his sister Susan normally rode the bus together, both to and from St. Pius X. Today, though, Nick had stayed after school to practice with a few friends for the eighth grade variety show. They were playing "A Horse with No Name."

So it wasn't surprising that his brother and sister were already home. But as soon as Nick stepped in the door, he knew something was wrong.

David was lying on the sofa in the living room with his mother sitting at the end of the sofa, rubbing his feet. His brother had a bandage wrapped around his head and a black eye.

"What happened?" Nick asked.

"David had a bad fall at school," his mother said.

"What?"

His brother titled his head back and peeked out at Nick from under the bandage.

"I'm okay."

His brother was twelve. But he was small for his age. Lying there, he looked like a little boy.

"Your brother slipped on the ice at recess. He's lucky he didn't break any bones."

"Holy crap!" Nick exclaimed. "Sorry, Mom."

"It's okay, honey. I was pretty upset too."

"When did this happen?"

"Right after lunch," his mother said. "The school nurse bandaged David up and called me. Mrs. Harris gave me a ride to St. Pius to pick him up. We got home a couple of hours ago."

"I'm sorry," Nick said. "I had no idea. I would have come home."

"It's okay, Nick. He'll be okay."

"Yeah," David said. "I'll be more careful next time."

#

When Nick's father got home, David was still lying on the sofa. His mother was in the kitchen, making dinner.

"What happened to you?" he asked.

"I fell on the ice at school," the boy said. "But I'm okay."

"He'll be okay, Jim," his mother said, stepping into the family room. "No broken bones. He was lucky."

"Let me see that," his father said, stepping over to the sofa.

"I'm okay, Dad," David said anxiously.

Nick's father stared down at his son's face. He squinted, then reached down and pulled back the bandage covering the boy's left eye.

"How in the hell did you get a shiner like that from falling on the ice?"

"Jim! He had a bad fall. That's all. You should be a little more sympathetic. And watch your language."

"Do we have a steak?"

"Yes, but it's frozen."

"Then thaw it out! In the meantime, put a bag of frozen peas on that eye."

His mother headed for the kitchen.

"You sure you got that falling down?"

"Yeah, Dad. I'm sure."

His father looked over at Nick and Susan, who were both standing in the family room.

"Did you see it happen?"

"No, Daddy," Susan said, shaking her head.

"No, Dad," Nick said. "I didn't even know about it until I got home."

A few minutes later, dinner was ready. They all ate together. David was quiet. His father kept checking out his black eye.

#

That night, as Nick and David lay in their beds with their door closed, Nick said, "Okay. So what happened today?"

"Promise not to tell Mom and Dad?"

"Yeah."

"The Straus kid slugged me."

"David Straus?"

"Yeah."

"That bastard. Why?"

"I don't know. You know Straus. He's mean. He likes to pick on smaller kids. I guess I was just in the wrong place."

"Did he say anything to you?"

"Yeah. He said, 'Hey, Reynolds.' Then he cold cocked me."

"He cold cocked you?"

"Yeah. I never saw it coming. I didn't even see him hit me."

"How do you know it was him?"

"I heard his voice. Then I saw him standing over me."

"Did anybody else see it?"

"No, I don't think so. I was almost in the building at the end of recess. Everybody else was already inside."

"Son of a bitch."

"Don't tell Mom or Dad. Dad would go berserk."

"Yeah, he probably would."

"Thanks."

"I'm glad you're okay, David."

"I'm fine. I just wish I was bigger, like you."

"You will be. Don't worry. This won't happen again."

"Good night."

"Good night."

#

The next day, Nick was sitting with his friends in the cafeteria. He spotted the Straus kid eating with his seventh-grade buddies. He watched him get up and head to the bathroom. Nick followed him inside.

The Straus kid was standing at a sink. The only other boy in there was peeing at a urinal.

Nick grabbed the bully from behind and spun him around. He was a good-sized kid. But Nick was bigger and a lot stronger. Nick grabbed his shirt with both hands and threw him against the wall.

"What the hell?" Straus cried out, his back now against the wall.

"Yeah," Nick said. "What the hell, Straus? Why don't you pick on somebody your own size next time?"

Nick made a fist and hit him in the jaw as hard as he could. He'd never hit anyone before. Straus' head jerked sideways. Blood spurted from his mouth, spraying Nick's shirt.

Nick hit him hard in the chest, then the stomach. The image of Muhammed Ali flashed into his mind. He started hitting Straus hard and fast, like he'd seen Ali punching Joe Frazier.

Straus was a live punching bag. All he could do was stand there and take it. Finally, he slid down the wall, half sitting, half lying on the floor, moaning.

Nick stood over him.

"If you ever touch my brother again, I'll kill you."

By now, the kid at the urinal had finished his business and was watching the whole thing. Nick shot him a domineering look as he walked out.

#

A few minutes into math class after lunch, there was a sharp knock on Nick's classroom door. His teacher, Sister Helen, stepped over to the door and opened it. She said something to someone in the hallway, then looked over at Nick.

"Nick," she said. "May I see you?"

A few minutes later, Nick was sitting in a wooden chair across from Sister Henry Marie's desk. She was the principal.

Nick had always thought Sister Henry Marie was about eighty years old. Now, up close, he could see he had underestimated.

"Mr. Reynolds, did you hit Mr. Straus?"

"Yes, Sister."

"Why?"

Nick thought about it for a minute. Should he tell her the truth and risk blowing his brother's cover story? He decided to risk it, knowing Straus would get in trouble too.

"He slugged my brother yesterday for no reason at all."

"Well, that is no excuse for what you did today, Mr. Reynolds! Do you realize you may have seriously hurt that boy?"

"How seriously?"

"Don't test me, Mr. Reynolds. I don't know how seriously. All I know is that they just took him away in an ambulance."

It took all Nick's strength not to smile.

"You know that fighting is not permitted in our school. What you did today is a flagrant violation of our values and our rules. I am suspending you for three days, Mr. Reynolds. Now go out to Ms. Blakely's desk and call your mother to come pick you up."

#

Nick's mother gave him hell all the way home.

When they got home, it got even worse. Mrs. Straus called from the hospital to tell his mother that Nick had knocked out one of her son's teeth and cracked a rib.

"I am so sorry, Mrs. Straus," his mother said. "We'll cover all medical expenses. Nick is a good boy. I don't know what got into him."

Figuring she would find out anyway, Nick told his mother everything: that the Straus kid attacked David yesterday, that David had made up the story about falling on the ice because he knew his father would lose it, that Nick decided, on his own, to "teach that bully a lesson."

"What you did was wrong, Nick," his mother said. "It's always wrong to fight. Now I want you to go to your room for the rest of the night. And I want you to write that Straus boy an apology."

"But I don't owe him an apology."

"Nick! You're not listening to me. You did a terrible thing today. You hurt someone, and you created a stain on your reputation you'll have to live with the rest of your life. Now go to your room and write that apology. You should be thankful I'm not making this any harder on you. God help you, though, when your father gets home."

#

Nick was in his room, with David, writing his letter of apology, when he heard the garage door go up.

"Crap," Nick said. "Dad's home."

He heard his parents talking in the family room. He could mainly hear his mother's voice. Then his bedroom door opened. His father stepped inside.

"David, can you give us a minute?" he said.

"Sure, Dad," his brother said, giving Nick a worried look as he left.

Nick's father closed the door behind him, turned around and crossed his arms.

"Is it all true?"

"Yes, Dad."

His father looked over at the letter he was writing.

"What's that?"

"Mom told me to write a letter of apology to the Straus kid."

His father stepped over to his desk.

"Let me see that."

Nick handed him the sheet of paper. Without reading it, and looking Nick straight in the eye, his father tore it up and stuffed the pieces into his pocket.

Nick didn't know what to say.

"How tall are you, Nick?"

"Six feet."

"How much do you weigh?"

"One forty."

"You're going to be big, like me. Do you know what that means?"

"No."

"That means that sometimes you're going to have to protect the little guys."

Nick looked up, waiting for his father to say something else. But he simply turned around, walked to the door and opened it.

"Don't be late for dinner," he said on his way out.

Chapter Fourteen

Nick had never been to Buffalo. In his mind, he equated it with blizzards and cars buried in gigantic snowdrifts. He was glad it was June.

He parked behind the Best Western "On The Avenue" downtown. The hotel was a block long and five stories tall. It looked wafer-thin, more like a movie prop than a real hotel.

He went inside to check in. The young woman behind the desk was pretty and petite, with black hair pulled back into a tight pony tail.

"May I help you, sir?" she asked with a slight French accent.

Good lord, Nick thought. Two exotic women in one day.

"Good afternoon," he said. "How are you?"

Nick had no interest in how she was. He just wanted to hear her speak.

"Very well, sir. And you?"

"I'm good."

Just as he had made eye contact, he could see her gaze ascending to his forehead. Damn! He had left his hat in the car.

"I have a reservation for Reynolds," he said, relieved when she looked down and started typing.

"Yes, Mr. Reynolds. I have you staying with us for one night. Is that correct?"

"Yes."

"Very good. May I put that on a credit card for you?"

"Yes," he said, pulling out his wallet and handing her his Visa card.

"Platinum. I see you are well traveled, Mr. Reynolds."

"Yes, I travel a lot."

"Have you been to Quebec?"

"Yes. Several times."

"Then you have been to my birthplace," she smiled.

Nick loved being in the company of women, especially beautiful women, with foreign accents. He considered it one of the perks of overseeing a global organization.

When he traveled domestically, he met with his employees as little as possible. Instead, he usually met with customers. However, when he traveled abroad, he always made a point of meeting with his local employees. He knew the majority of them were women.

He would ask them lots of questions. Not because he was eager to hear what they had to say. But because he liked hearing how they said it. He never really listened to these women. He never got to know them. They were simply pretty faces, names in boxes on his organization charts.

Nick cared only about whether the leader of a given part of his organization was making his or her numbers. Who they hired was their business. He was just grateful for the chorus of lovely accents that made his business trips so enjoyable.

Nick noticed the desk clerk was now looking behind him. There was someone else in line. Bummer. He'd just asked what brought her to Buffalo. But she no longer seemed interested in small talk and handed him his room key.

"Any recommendations for lunch?" he asked.

"The Templeton Landing Restaurant is very nice. It's right on the Erie Basin Marina."

"Could I walk there?"

"Well, it's less than two miles."

Then she glanced down at his big belly.

"You might want to drive."

"Thanks," Nick said, sucking in his gut.

#

Nick parked at the marina. There was a well-manicured park along the waterfront. A stone path snaked through beds of roses, irises, orchids, petunias and marigolds.

It was a gorgeous, warm, sunny afternoon. He saw several people jogging, including a trim young woman wearing very short neon pink running shorts and a neon green sports bra. I've got to get back in shape, he thought.

The restaurant was at the south end of the basin. Nick asked the hostess for a table outside. She showed him to a green table with a blue umbrella on the red brick patio overlooking the marina. He could see Lake Erie just beyond it.

"Your waitress will be right with you," she said.

Less than a minute later, a middle-aged woman approached his table. She was built like a fireplug and dressed completely in black. It was not slimming.

"Can I start you with a drink?" she asked, setting down a menu.

"I'll have a light beer."

"Any specific brand?"

"Anything in a bottle," he said, eyeing the lake.

"Do you need a minute to look at the menu?"

She seemed to be in a hurry.

"Any recommendations?"

"The beef on weck."

"Pardon me?"

"The beef on weck."

"Whack?"

"Weck."

"What?"

"*Weck*," she said, sounding irritated. "It's roast beef on a kummelweck roll."

"A kummelweck roll?"

"It's a thin roll topped with salt and caraway seeds."

"With roast beef?"

"Yeah. It's rare and cut thin and topped with horseradish."

"I've never heard of it."

"It's a local favorite," she said, tapping her pen on her order pad.

"Okay. I'll try it."

"I'll be right back with your beer," she said, snapping her order pad closed and darting away.

Some people have no manners, Nick thought.

He wondered what day it was. Without work, he was completely losing track of time.

A boat puttered out of its slip into the marina. It was a bass boat, so small that the guy driving it and his sole passenger were practically sitting on top of each other.

When it came to boats, as with so many things, Nick was a snob. For many years, he had made a point of buying ever-bigger and more luxurious new boats every couple of years. During the summer, he and Jean would host friends for day cruises on Lake Michigan.

But those parties stopped about ten years ago, after a particularly awkward day when Nick got wasted.

He had dropped anchor about a mile out and proceeded to drink the afternoon away. That day, Woodford Reserve was his beverage of choice. He drank the whole bottle himself.

By early evening, when everyone was ready to head in, Nick could barely stand up. He was certainly in no condition to drive. Jean offered to take the wheel. He got defensive and called her a bitch. Everyone heard him, but no one was sure what to do.

Ted, one of Nick and Jean's neighbors, approached him.

"Nick, I'd be glad to take us in," he said.

"This is my boat, Ted," Nick said, drawing himself up to his full height. "You're my guest. Sit down."

Ted obliged. Nobody said anything the whole way in. They were all concerned for their safety, of course. But they were too intimidated to say anything else to Nick.

Not surprisingly, Nick came in too fast. He slammed the boat into the dock, jolting several people out of their seats. One of Jean's good friends, Marge, fell hard onto the deck. They later learned she'd broken her wrist.

When the boat finally came to a full stop, Ted jumped out and tethered it to the dock. Everyone got off fast, murmuring thank yous to Jean and taking off.

"Thank God we're alive," someone whispered.

When all their guests were gone, Jean grabbed Nick by his shirt and pulled him below.

"What in the hell are you doing?" she screamed.

"What do you mean?"

"We invite friends out for a cruise, and you get so loaded that you can't even drive the boat?"

"There's nothing wrong with my driving. I just came in a little hard."

"Nick, you're an ass."

"It's my boat. I can do anything I want."

"Nick," she said, shaking her head. "You'll never learn. Sometimes you have to think of others."

"I do, Jean! Why do you think I let you invite all these people out here today?"

"You let me invite them?"

"Yeah."

"That's how you see it?"

"Well, I never would have invited them myself."

"Well, Nick, you won't have to worry about that any more."

After that, no one, including Jean, ever went boating with Nick again.

Still, he kept buying expensive new boats. Eventually, though, they became smaller, and he spent less and less time on the water.

Now he had a 29—foot Rinker Bowrider. It was far more boat than he needed, and he took it out only once or twice a year. But it was one of the sleekest boats in the marina, white with a black hull. It turned heads.

To his knowledge, none of the other Chicago Yacht Club members had heard about the incident on his boat years before. In fact, most members had never met Nick. To them, he was just a rich business executive with a really cool boat.

And to Nick, that's what mattered most. "People judge us by what they see," his mother had told him. "Always look good."

Chapter Fifteen

April 1974

Nick was so tired of trying on clothes. He was sixteen, but his mother still treated him like a kid.

The run-up to Easter was the worst because it meant she would take Nick, David and Susan shopping for "Easter outfits," as she called them. Finding just the right clothes could take hours, even days.

Nick had better things to do on Saturdays. But now he was penned up in a dressing room in Killian's department store, trying on yet another shirt. How many different versions of blue shirts did his mother need to see?

He tucked in a light blue, button-down, all-cotton shirt with a muted white plaid pattern and stepped outside the dressing room for inspection. His mother seemed even more interested than usual. Standing beside her was a woman Nick didn't recognize.

"Nick," his mother said, "this is Mrs. Williamson. She works here in the advertising department. She has a question for you."

"Hi, Nick," Mrs. Williamson said, smiling and extending her hand. "One of my sales associates just called me and suggested you might be a good candidate for some print ads we'll be creating for our new clothing line for young men this fall."

"I'm not sure I understand," Nick said, looking at his mother.

"Mrs. Williamson wants to know if you'd be open to doing some modeling."

"Modeling?" he asked.

"Well, yes," Mrs. Williamson said, looking Nick up and down. "But just for our fall line-up."

The idea of modeling seemed so strange to Nick, and the word itself seemed so, well, feminine. He wasn't sure about this.

"What would that involve?" he asked.

"Well, it would probably mean you would need to spend a few days this summer at a photography studio we use downtown. It would mean trying on lots of cool clothes. And, oh, we would pay you one hundred dollars a day."

"A day?" Nick asked, incredulous.

His mother was beaming and nodding her head.

"Yes," Mrs. Williamson said. "A day."

Holy crap, he thought. That's $300. Any reservations he had about modeling vanished.

"I'll do it!"

#

In June, Nick spent three days modeling, two in a studio downtown and one in a nearby park. He modeled dozens of clothing combinations against dozens of backdrops. An art director taught him how to pose, and a photographer snapped hundreds of pictures.

They were full days. It was hard work, much harder than he'd expected. But he made more money in those three days than he otherwise could have by working all summer.

Nick loved the money. He spent half of it on a new Schwinn Varsity, ten-speed bike. He put the other half in the bank.

But the money wasn't even the best part.

The best part began in early August. That's when the ads hit.

Overnight, Nick's image was everywhere: in the newspapers, on billboards, at bus stops and, of course, all over Killian's. Everywhere people looked, there was Nick wearing the newest fall fashions: a corduroy jacket, geometric-patterned sports shirts, flare-bottom pants, wide leather belts, platform shoes.

By the time school started just after Labor Day, Nick had become a local celebrity, at least among the 1730 students at Regis Jesuit High School.

But even without the ads, Nick would have been hard to miss. He'd grown even more over the summer. Now he stood six feet, two inches tall. He had broad shoulders, long dark hair, a square jaw and a broad smile.

He had begun to catch some of the girls' eyes before. But now every girl in the school wanted to get a good look at Nick. One star-struck sophomore even approached him in the hallway with one of his ads taped to the front of her notebook and asked him to autograph it. Flashing a winsome smile, he gladly obliged.

Nick reveled in all the attention. For the first time in his life, it felt good to be in the limelight. He'd come a long way since his awkward moment at the guitar recital.

It was his first real exposure to business, too.

"Killian's paid you $300," his father grumbled. "Imagine how much money they made off of you."

Nick hadn't thought about it that way. He began to realize the power of advertising and how much money there is to be made by creating interest in products people might otherwise not know they want. Nick began to understand that Killian's featuring him in ads for these particular fashion lines, where and when those ads showed up and when he had done his photo shoots was no accident. It was part of a carefully planned, well timed campaign.

And he learned that a little notoriety can do some wonderful things for you. Once the ads broke, some of the hottest girls in the school, the ones he'd seen but hadn't met, suddenly wanted to date him.

Of course, his mother had always stressed how much his looks mattered. It's not that he didn't believe her. But at sixteen, when a "fast" girl asks you out and wants to make out in her back seat, you get religion.

Chapter Sixteen

After washing down his beef on weck with a couple of Bud Lights in the early afternoon sun, Nick was wiped out. He drove back to his hotel, went up to his room and fell into a deep sleep.

When he woke up, it was after five. He showered but decided against shaving when he imagined all the Dead Heads he'd see at the concert. Clean-shaven, he might look like a freak.

He checked the weather forecast. Clear with a low of sixty tonight. He pulled on jeans and a khaki shirt and grabbed a sweater.

He noticed the plastic garbage bag he was using for his dirty clothes was nearly full already. He wished he had packed more clothes. He decided to see if he could get his laundry done. He called the front desk. The guy on duty said yes. If he could drop his clothes off now, they would be ready for him in the morning. Nick grabbed his bag of dirty laundry and headed downstairs.

When he got to the front desk, he was relieved to see the girl from Quebec was gone. The prospect of handing her a bag filled with his dirty underwear creeped him out. Much better, he thought, to hand them to this guy.

He got in his car and headed to the Artpark, an outdoor concert venue in Lewiston, thirty minutes north of downtown. He saw signs for Niagara Falls. He had time to stop. He'd never seen the falls. But he remembered his parents had spent their honeymoon there, and he knew he couldn't go there without thinking of his parents' troubled marriage or his own. So he kept driving.

When he got to the Artpark, it was still sunny. But a cool breeze was blowing in from the Niagara River behind the stage. He was glad he'd brought a sweater.

The amphitheater seats were nearly full. People were putting down blankets and settling in on the grassy hillside beyond the seats. Damn. He'd forgotten to bring a blanket. That's the kind of thing Jean would have remembered.

Thinking about Jean that way made Nick miss her, at least for a moment.

Further was on in about an hour. Now a trio of aging hippies was onstage, singing folk songs. They reminded him of Peter, Paul and Mary. He felt old even remembering Peter, Paul and Mary. But then he looked around and realized he might be on the younger side tonight. What a bunch of geezers, he thought.

The hearty aroma of hot dogs and hamburgers on a grill made his stomach rumble. He followed white smoke to a concession stand, got in line and bought a hot dog and a beer. Fifteen bucks. Jerry Garcia, he thought, would be rolling in his grave.

Nick headed up the gentle hill and made his way through blankets and lawn chairs until he found an open spot. He crouched down, his knees cracking, and set his hot dog and beer down on the warm, dry grass. He extended his left arm slightly behind him, put his palm down on the grass and tried to lower himself to the ground slowly. But his arm buckled under his great weight, and he landed hard on his side.

"Ooof!" he gasped.

"You okay, man?" asked a guy with a gray pony tail sitting in a lawn chair a few feet away.

"Yeah, I'm fine."

Freaky old bastard, Nick thought.

He tried to sit up cross-legged. But he was no longer limber enough. So he leaned back and propped himself up on his elbow and forearm, using his sweater as a cushion.

Biting into his hot dog, Nick sensed someone was watching

him. He looked up and saw a woman with long, wiry, gray hair sitting next to Old Man Pony Tail. She was staring at his head. When she realized he'd caught her staring, she looked away.

"Do you mind if I sit here?"

It was a woman's voice from his other side. He looked up, expecting to see yet another grizzled folkie. Instead, it was a refined-looking woman, probably about forty. She was wearing blue jeans and a tan sweater. The tails of her white shirt peeked out from underneath her sweater. Her hair was brown and short. She was wearing sunglasses with black and gold frames and grey lenses. She had a blanket tucked under her arm.

"Not at all," Nick said, sitting up.

"Thank you."

She unfolded the blanket, unfurled it over the grass in front of her, only a foot or so from Nick. She sat down, effortlessly, cross-legged.

Without saying a word, she took off her sunglasses, laid them on the blanket, closed her eyes and started gently bobbing her head to the beat of the music.

She had a faint smile on her face. After a wispy rendition of "Where Have All the Flowers Gone?", she opened her eyes, looked around and stood up.

"I'm going to get something to drink," she announced, looking down at Nick. "Can I get you anything?"

"No, thanks," he said. "But I'll walk with you and grab another beer."

"Cool," she said. "I guess our stuff will be okay here."

Nick got up on one knee and pressed his palms down hard on his thigh to pry himself up. He hoped he didn't look like a "geezer."

He looked down at the space where he'd been sitting. The only thing there was his XXL sweater. He doubted any of the skinny old hippies would swipe that.

"After you," he said, nodding and extending his hand.

He followed her down to the concession stand. Across the

river, the sun was beginning to set, and the air was getting cooler. He caught a whiff of pot.

It was just before eight o'clock, when Further was scheduled to start playing. The lines at the concession stand were twenty people deep. Nick doubted he would make it back to his place in time for the first song.

He stood behind his new concert buddy in line. She turned around, smiled and extended her hand.

"Hi. I'm Tina."

"Hi, Tina. I'm Nick. It's nice to meet you."

As they inched forward, they began to chat. Nick learned that Tina lived in Buffalo and had been a Dead fan all her life.

"Me too," he said. "I think I've still got their 'Live/Dead' album around somewhere."

"Me too!" she said.

"You've got to be kidding."

"No, my father gave it to me. It's a classic."

Crap, Nick thought. It was one of the first albums he'd ever owned. She probably thinks I'm as old as her dad.

"So where are you from, Nick?"

"Chicago. Cedar Rapids, originally."

"I love Chicago. What brings you here?"

"Well, I'm on a sabbatical."

Just uttering those words made Nick feel weak. He felt the need to explain. He started thinking about what kind of a story he might spin to make Tina think well of him.

But then he thought: what the hell. I'll never see this woman again. Why not tell her the truth?

"I've been having trouble with people at work. My boss asked me to take the summer off and get my act together."

Nick couldn't believe he was being so open, especially with a complete stranger. He could hardly admit the truth to himself. He wasn't sure how Tina would react.

"Well, then," she said. "We have something in common."

"Oh, yeah?"

"Yeah. I'm taking some time off too. But not from my work. From my marriage."

Uh-oh, Nick thought.

They'd reached the front of the line.

"What kind of beer would you like?" she asked.

"You don't have to get that."

"My pleasure," she said.

"Well, thank you. Light. Anything light."

Again, Nick surprised himself. He never let anybody buy his beer. What in the hell was happening to him?

He followed Tina back up the hill. By then, Further had begun playing. They'd led off with "Truckin'."

"Truckin', off to Buffalo," crooned Bob Weir, sounding as strong and pitch-perfect as ever.

The hippies went wild. Pot now filled the air.

Nick and Tina got back to their spot. It was getting dark and definitely cool enough now for a sweater.

"Would you like to share my blanket?" she asked.

"Sure," Nick said as he put his sweater on. "Thank you."

He wasn't used to such kindness.

He sat down beside her, careful not to get too close. Tina sat cross-legged again. He didn't even try. Instead, he drew one knee up and folded his hands around it.

"So, Tina," Nick said, sipping his beer. "If you don't mind my asking, why are you taking time off from your marriage?"

"Not at all. I'm glad to talk about it. And I'd like to hear more about your sabbatical too."

"Sure."

"I've been married for eighteen years," she said, sipping her beer.

"And you're still married?" Nick didn't see a ring.

"Yeah, technically."

"And you're taking a time out."

"Yeah. You could say that."

"How long has it been?"

"Three or four months."

They sat there in silence for a moment, sipping their beers. Nick had just met this woman. He wasn't sure how much she really wanted to share.

"What happened?" he asked, hoping he wasn't asking too many questions.

"Are you sure you want to know?"

"Yeah. But let me ask you something first."

"Sure."

"Have you seen the Grateful Dead in concert?"

"Yeah."

"Me too. I just got these tickets yesterday so I'd have something to do tonight. This might sound crazy. But do you want to take off and continue this conversation someplace where we can sit at a table?"

She smiled.

"Sure."

"I've never been to Buffalo. What would you recommend?"

"There's a place called the Brickyard Pub, right around the corner."

"Sounds good."

"Nick," she said, just as he was about to get up.

"Yeah?"

"I'm still married. This is just for a drink, right?"

Normally, he would have taken umbrage. He knew his intentions were pure. He didn't like being challenged, especially by someone younger.

But he was not put off. Instead, he smiled and said, "Of course. I'm still married too."

Nick seldom mentioned his marriage any more. But for the moment, he stopped holding back, and the truth simply rolled off his tongue. This surprised him and felt strange.

"Thanks," Tina said, looking a little sheepish for having asked.

#

Nick walked Tina to her car, a Honda Civic, then followed her out of the parking lot. The pub was only two minutes away. They walked in together. The place was nearly empty.

"Hey, Tina," said the bartender, eyeballing Nick.

"Hey, Henry," she said.

She turned to Nick and said, "I come here a lot after concerts."

"I see."

"What'll you have, folks?"

"Another light beer?" she asked Nick.

"Sure. But I'm paying this time."

"Okay."

"Two Coors Light and two glasses," Nick said as Tina walked over to a tall table next to the wall. "Open a tab, would you?"

"Sure, buddy."

Nick brought their beers and glasses over and set them down on the table.

"So you were saying," he said, pouring her beer.

"What was I saying?" Tina asked.

"You were about to tell me what happened."

"Oh, yeah. How much time do you have?"

"All night."

Then he caught himself and added, "You know what I mean."

She laughed and said, "Don't worry. I'll let you go soon."

"Take your time," he said, raising his bottle to her glass. "To new friends."

"To new friends," she said, touching her glass to his bottle.

#

They talked for two hours. Actually, Tina did most of the talking. She told Nick about meeting her husband, Robert. They were in their early twenties. He was so romantic. By their second date, she'd fallen in love. Six months later, he proposed. Within a year, they were married.

Early on, they were happy. But Robert had a tough time keeping jobs, and he began to drink. Eventually, he took a job as a sales rep for a car parts company. He did well but didn't stop drinking. In fact, he drank even more.

This was frustrating to Tina, in part because she wanted to start a family. Her father had been a heavy drinker, and she was dead-set against exposing her own children to that. She begged Robert to moderate his drinking. His response was to start traveling more. That way, he could drink without Tina harping at him. Sometimes, he would be away for weeks.

Tina felt alone. She didn't know what to do. Then she met and fell in love with another man. Robert was gone so much he never knew. Tina felt guilty but told herself she was simply filling a gap which Robert had created.

Despite Robert's long absences and heavy drinking and the fact there was now another man in her life, Tina wanted to have children with her husband. He might have become a disappointment to her. But he was still her husband, and she wanted her children to grow up with a father, imperfect as he might be.

Tina and Robert rarely had sex any more. But she went off the pill thinking she would eventually get pregnant. But it never happened, and Tina and Robert grew even more distant.

They talked about getting divorced but somehow learned to live with the distance. Then one day Robert came home early from a business trip and found Tina in their bed with her lover.

Tina told Robert she was sorry and begged his forgiveness. He asked her why she'd done it. She told him it was because he was never around and, even when he was there, he didn't seem to care about her ... or himself for that matter.

He asked if she still loved him. She said she did. But the hurt was too great for Robert, and he moved out.

After a few months, they were both surprised by how much they missed each other. Now they were beginning to see other again, going on dates every couple of weeks.

"How's that going?" Nick asked.

"You know," she said, "I'm beginning to feel hopeful."

"Why?"

"Just recently, we've actually begun listening to each other again. For years, I didn't feel Robert was listening to me. I resented him for that. But what I'm beginning to realize is that I wasn't listening much either. And now when we get together, especially knowing it's only for a short time, I listen. It's amazing, isn't it? How much you can learn about someone just by listening to them and how good it feels to be listened to."

"Yeah."

"Oh, my," Tina said, looking at her watch. "It's getting late, and I've been talking all night. What about you, Nick? What about your sabbatical?"

The place had begun to fill up with aging hippies, floating in, high as kites, from the concert.

"You know, I'm just taking a little time off. There's really not much more to it. But you've given me a lot to think about tonight."

"Oh? How so?"

"Well, I've not been doing much listening lately either. I think that's probably an area for improvement in my marriage."

"Can I help you?"

"You already have," he said, smiling.

"Really?"

"Yeah. Ready to go?"

"If you are."

"I am. Let me take care of this for us. I'll be right back."

Nick stepped over to the bar and asked for the bill. They had only four beers. It was fourteen dollars. Nick said thanks and laid down a twenty.

The two of them walked to their cars. They were parked next to each other. She pressed a button to unlock her door, and he came around and opened it for her. He hadn't opened a car door for anyone in a long time.

"It was wonderful to meet you, Nick."

"It was great meeting you, Tina."

"Thank you for listening. I hope your sabbatical turns out to be everything you need it to be."

"Thank you. And I hope everything works out with Robert."

She stood on her tiptoes, put her arms around his neck and kissed him on the cheek. He gave her a hug and kissed her on the cheek too.

She got in, and he gently closed her door. He pulled out of the parking lot behind her. He followed her for a while as they both made their way back to Buffalo but lost track of her on the highway.

Chapter Seventeen

July 1976

Nick gripped the handle of the large, ice-cold, glass mug in his left hand and pulled back the creme-colored, ceramic handle on the spigot with his right. He tilted the mug so that the root beer splashed against the inside, forming just the right amount of foam on top.

This was Nick's second summer working at the root beer stand. He could draw root beer in his sleep. Without even looking at the mug, he knew when it was nearly full, when it was time to push back the spigot. Right now, it was good that Nick didn't need to pay close attention to what he was doing because he was distracted by Brenda, the new carhop.

She was going into her senior year at Washington High School, one of two public high schools in town. That alone piqued Nick's interest. He had attended Catholic schools all his life, and he had the impression that the girls in public schools were more "interesting." He had never dated anyone from a public school to find out. But he was pretty sure, based mainly on his friends who had, that it was true.

Now Brenda had her back to Nick. She was standing next to a car, taking a customer's order. Nick was admiring how snugly her white uniform fit her. Then he heard root beer splashing. He looked down and saw it spilling over the top of the mug and down the grooves of the stainless steel drain at the base of the root beer dispenser.

"Nick!" someone yelled. "Watch what you're doing!"

It was his friend Dave, who was working the cash register.

"Damn," said Nick, wiping the excess root beer from the sides of the mug with a damp cotton towel, then placing the mug on a tray on the orange, laminated countertop that rimmed the front and sides of the root beer stand.

His eyes were still fixed on Brenda, who had by now turned around and was heading toward Nick. He smiled as she sashayed his way, tearing the top sheet from her order pad. She smiled back. Maybe I'll ask her out, Nick thought.

The phone rang from inside the restaurant. Nick didn't hear it because he was so focused on Brenda. She had long brown hair and big brown eyes. She was tall. Nick had heard she was a swimmer. She certainly had a swimmer's build. Her upper body was especially well defined. And she had a rhythm to her walk, like a swimmer gliding through the water.

"Here you go, Nick," she said, sliding her order across the counter and still smiling.

This is my moment, he thought. I'll ask her out. Hell, I'll ask her out for tonight. But just then his boss, Greg, came to the screen door that led to the kitchen.

"Nick," he said dryly. "You have a phone call."

"I'll be right there, Greg," trying to put him off so he could pop the question.

"Nick, I think you need to take this call now."

"Okay," he said, wiping his hands on his apron. "I'll be right back," he said to Brenda.

He opened the screen door. His friend Tom was "slinging weenies" in the kitchen. That's what everyone who worked there called making hot dogs. Tom had placed four hot dogs in buns up his forearm and was spooning chili onto them. Nick marveled at his balance and precision. Tom never spilled a drop.

Greg was standing just outside the alcove that served as his office. The top half of the front wall was open, so that, sitting at his desk, Greg could keep an eye on those working in the kitchen and an ear on what was happening out front.

Nick had only seen Greg's office through the top half of the front wall. Now Greg asked him to take the call from inside his office.

Nick walked around to the doorway. Stepping inside, he was astonished by all the papers scattered everywhere: order forms, pay stubs and balance sheets. In an instant, Nick got a sense of all the work associated with running a small business, something he hadn't thought about before. To him, working there was about drawing root beer, slinging weenies and flirting with carhops. It was a teenager's world. But in that moment, he got a glimpse into a different world, a more serious and grown-up world, and he felt something inside him begin to shift.

"The phone's right there," said Greg, pointing to the black receiver on top of a stack of papers on his desk.

"Thanks," Nick said.

"Hello," he said. He could hear someone crying.

"Nick," said the sobbing voice. "Oh, Nick."

It was his mother's voice.

"Mom? What's wrong?"

"Oh, Nick. It's your father."

"What? Is Dad okay?"

"No, Nick," she said, sobbing. "He's dead."

"Dead? How?"

"Come home, Nick. Come home. I'll tell you when you get here."

"Okay, Mom. I'll be right there."

#

Nick tore home on his bike. He saw a police car pulling away from his house and another car, which he didn't recognize, parked in the driveway.

He pulled his bike into the garage and went into the house. His mother was sitting at the end of the sofa in the family room. Susan was sitting next to her, and David was sitting next to Susan. In a straight chair next to his mother was Father Bettner, their parish pastor.

"Oh, Nick," his mother said, stepping toward him.

"Mom," he said, embracing her. "Are you okay?"

"Yes," she lied. "Let's go into the living and talk for a minute."

Then turning to the priest, she said, "Father, please excuse us for a moment."

"Certainly," he said. "Nick, I'm sorry."

Nick followed his mother into the living room and sat next to her on the sofa. He was shocked when she told him his father had killed himself while he was on his mail route that afternoon.

"He shot himself, Nick. He shot himself in the heart."

"Why?"

"I don't know," his mother said, wiping her eyes with a handkerchief. "Your father could get very down at times."

Then she turned and looked Nick in the eyes.

"We all get down at times, Nick. Your father wasn't well. He needed help. But he wouldn't get it."

"Mom, I'm so sorry. What can I do for you?"

"I need to talk with Father Bettner privately for a few minutes. Could you take David and Susan outside until we're finished?"

"Sure. We'll be on the patio."

Nick took his brother and sister out on the patio. Susan was crying. Nick sat beside her on the glider and put his arm around her. David sat in a chair by himself. No one said a word.

It was hot, and the glass patio door was open. Through the screen door, Nick could hear bits of his mother's conversation with the priest. They were talking about the funeral.

Then it dawned on Nick that the Church does not usually offer funeral rites for Catholics who have committed suicide because it's considered a mortal sin.

He could hear his mother pleading with the priest. Then he heard Father Bettner say something about making an exception. Then he heard his mother blurt out, "Oh, thank you, Father."

#

After the funeral Mass at St. Pius and the burial at St. Joseph's Cemetery, everyone went to VFW Post 788 for a reception.

It was a dark and cavernous place, with a bar in the middle and flags, patriotic posters and framed war photographs hanging on cinderblock walls. Nick had been there for Christmas parties when he was a boy. His dad spent nearly every Friday night there.

After getting a plate of food for his mother, Nick got back in the buffet line for himself. He was right behind his Uncle Bob and Aunt Ruth. Uncle Bob was his father's older brother. He and Aunt Ruth lived in Omaha. Nick had never been there to visit. His father wasn't close with his siblings. Nick had seen Uncle Bob and Aunt Ruth only a few times in his life. He didn't know their children at all. None of them had come to the funeral.

Uncle Bob asked Nick to join them, and so he followed his aunt and uncle to their table.

"Sit right here, Nick," Uncle Bob said, motioning to the chair next to him.

Nick sat down. Not knowing Uncle Bob well, he wasn't sure what to say. No doubt feeling the same way, his uncle broke the ice.

"Nick, I haven't seen you since you were a little boy. Now look at you. All grown up. You look so much like your dad did when he was your age."

"Really? I haven't seen many pictures of him when he was young."

"He was a handsome guy. He was never hurting for a date. That's for sure. So, Nick, what are you up to these days?"

"Well, I just graduated from high school, and I'll be leaving for college in early September."

"Wow! I can't believe you're already heading off to college. Where?"

"Loyola in Chicago."

"Fantastic! What a great school — and a great city. What will you study?"

"I'm not sure. I'm going to start with English and declare a major later."

"Good plan. So, Nick, what are your interests?"

"Well, I like to play guitar."

"Ah! A chip off the old block."

Nick gave him a quizzical look.

"What do you mean?"

"Your dad. Your dad loved playing guitar."

"He did? When?"

"Are you kidding? He played beautifully. Picked it up when he was a little kid. He was a natural. He was playing in recitals by the time he was eight. We used to go to watch him. He blew everybody away."

"I didn't know Dad played the guitar."

"Well, in a way, if he hadn't, you might not have been here," Aunt Ruth chimed in.

"What do you mean?" asked Nick.

"That's how he met your mom. He was playing in a band at a dance at her high school. She saw him and thought he was cute."

"You're kidding."

"No," she continued. "And when they started dating, your father serenaded her. He was so romantic. She loved that."

Nick looked stunned.

"Why did he give it up? Playing guitar, I mean."

"I don't know," Uncle Bob said. "You'll need to ask your mom. Not now, of course. But when things settle down, you should ask her."

He took a drink of beer from his plastic cup.

"Nick," he said. "I suspect there are a lot of things you don't know about your father, that you'll be learning in the days and years ahead. He was no saint. And he had his demons. But I can tell you that, deep down, he was a good man, and I know he loved you."

"Thanks, Uncle Bob," Nick said. "Thanks for telling me these things."

Nick looked up and saw his mom sitting a couple of tables over. She was sitting next to her sister, Aunt Rita. The plate of food that Nick had fixed for her sat before her untouched. Aunt Rita was saying something to his mother. But she wasn't looking at Aunt Rita. She was staring off into the distance. She had a strange look on her face, a look, it seemed to Nick, of both sadness and relief.

His mother and father had had a contentious relationship for as long as Nick could remember. At that moment, he thought of his own difficult relationship with his father. He knew he would miss him. But just then, looking at his mother, Nick also felt an unexpected sense of relief.

Chapter Eighteen

Nick got up early, showered and, for the first time in nearly a week, shaved. Over breakfast in the lobby, he went online and decided his next stop would be Albany, four and half hours away. He booked a room at the Holiday Inn Express in downtown Albany. Then he picked up his clean laundry at the front desk, checked out and took off.

As he was making his way to the highway, he passed a grade school. Kids were playing on the blacktop behind a chain link fence. He was surprised to see school still in session. In Chicago, the kids were already beginning summer vacation. He supposed they got a lot more snow days in Buffalo.

Seeing all the kids made him think of Ashley and Josh. Now Ashley was a teacher in Denver, and Josh managed investments in San Francisco. Nick hadn't been to either city to visit them.

There was a time when being so far away from his children and not seeing them for so long would have been hard for Nick to imagine. He remembered holding Jean's hand and putting Ashley on a school bus on her first day of kindergarten. They stood there together, Jean holding Josh's hand too, waving at their little girl, as she smiled and waved back through the window. Nick did not cry easily. But as the bus pulled away, his eyes welled with tears.

The same thing happened two years later, when Nick and Jean put Josh on a bus for his first day of kindergarten.

When his children were little, Nick was a doting father. He

would indulge them, taking them to a store to buy toys whenever Jean was out. He would take them to movies. He would take them to parks to feed the ducks.

Even then, as much as he loved his children, it was sometimes hard for Nick to spend as much time as he wanted with them. As his career took off, work pressed in on him. He spent more and more time at the office, and he began to travel. He saw his children less and less. He missed their soccer games. He missed sending them off to dances. He almost missed Ashley's high school graduation.

As his children grew up, Nick became detached from their everyday lives. Sometimes, it was as if Jean were a single parent. Nick felt his children slipping away. He knew it was his fault, and his feelings of guilt gnawed at him. But he never did anything about it. He was too focused on himself.

Now he spotted a sign for a rest area. He pulled off the highway and parked his car. He walked over to a concrete picnic table under a big pin oak tree and sat down.

People were hurrying into a white building with restrooms and ambling out. Some were strolling around under the shade of sugar maples, birches and oaks on grass made sparse by too much foot traffic and too little sunlight. Some were walking dogs on leashes. Some, like Nick, were sitting at picnic tables. A family was eating lunch at one about twenty feet away.

Nick closed his eyes. He listened to the family members talking as they ate together. He couldn't hear what they were saying. But he could hear the tone of their voices. They sounded happy.

He opened his eyes, pulled out his phone and sent a text message to each of his children.

How are you?

About a minute later, he got a response from Ashley.

I'm fine, dad. And you?

And then he got a response from Josh.

OK. U?

He sent them each the same message.

I'm fine. On my way to Bar Harbor. Thinking of you. Hope to see you again soon. Love, Dad

Chapter Nineteen

September 1976

Nick had just moved into Campion Hall, a freshman dorm at Loyola, with his good friend, Jim Monroe.

They'd grown up together in Cedar Rapids and, three months ago, graduated together from Regis Jesuit. Both wanted to move to Chicago. Both applied to Loyola. Their grades were good enough for admission.

But the Jesuits at Regis took no chances with their students. They maintained strong connections with all the big Jesuit universities, and they didn't hesitate to use those connections to ensure a place for their students.

Just to make sure Nick and Jim's applications were given careful review at Loyola, Brother Leo at Regis made a few phone calls on their behalf. A few days later, the boys got their letters of acceptance.

#

The Jesuits were organizers. Father Jack, who lived in Campion, walked up and down the hallways as students were moving in, inviting everyone to a reception the Jesuits were hosting for all incoming freshmen the next night. It would be held at the Jesuit Residence, also known as the Jez Rez.

This helped put Nick's mother's mind at ease.

"How nice," she said.

Nick's mom had driven him the two hundred and fifty miles from Cedar Rapids and was helping him unpack.

"It's so good to know you'll be in such good hands here," she smiled.

Little did she know the freshmen reception would actually be a keg party.

*

Nick and Jim had enjoyed plenty of beer in high school. But they'd always had to sneak it. Now the beer was not only flowing freely but being served by priests. How nice indeed.

All the freshmen were given name tags at the door. Nick and Jim knew no one. They stuck together, not so much out of friendship but insecurity. For two boys from Cedar Rapids, it was a pretty sophisticated crowd.

Making quick work of his second beer, Nick noticed a girl across the room. She was slender and petite with long blond hair. She had the face of an angel. She was standing in a small group of girls, holding a glass of Coke.

She wasn't saying much. Instead, she seemed to be paying attention to what the other girls were saying and laughing a lot. She laughed with her whole body, then took a step back as if to revel in whatever she was finding so amusing. She had the laugh of a child, pure and uninhibited.

Nick could not take his eyes off her. He was drawn to her like he had never been drawn to anyone.

"I have to meet that girl," he told Jim.

"Which one?"

"The blond."

"Which blond?"

"That one."

Jim had no idea who Nick meant. But whoever she was, he knew from Nick's dumbstruck look that something was up.

"Okay," he said. "Let's go over and say hello."

"Don't let me say anything stupid," Nick said.

"No guarantees," Jim said smiling. "Come on. You'll be fine."

As they made their way across the room, Nick could see her name tag. Jean. Yes. It was a perfect name. And he could now see her eyes. They were sapphire, like he had always imagined the color of the sea.

"I don't think I can do this," Nick said to Jim, grabbing his arm.

"Why?"

"I'm too nervous."

"What? I've never known you to be nervous about anything. Come on, Nick. It's just a girl. You've never had any trouble with girls before."

"This one is different."

"How?"

"I don't know. I just don't want to screw this up."

"Hey, this was your idea."

"I know."

"Nick, I won't let you screw this up. Now, come on. She's just a girl, a freshman, just like us. Let's just say hello."

Jim is a good friend, Nick thought, but he doesn't understand. This was not just a girl. Somehow, without having even met her, Nick knew she was the one.

"Hi, I'm Jim," his wingman said, extending his hand to a girl named Sarah. When he did, he noticed Nick wasn't paying attention to Sarah at all and figured she wasn't that blond.

Sarah was standing next to Jean. Nick was staring at her. This, Jim finally realized, was that blond.

"Hi, I'm Jim," he said. "And this is my friend, Nick."

"Hello," Jean said, smiling and extending her hand. But Nick didn't offer his hand. He didn't do anything. He was frozen, staring at her face. He expected her to laugh. But she didn't laugh. Instead, she just smiled and said, "Where are you from, Nick?"

But he couldn't speak.

"Cedar Rapids," Jim said, slapping his tall friend on the back. "He's from Cedar Rapids."

"I've never been there," Jean said. Her voice was soft, like her face. "What's it like?"

"Tell her what it's like, Nick," Jim said. "I'm going to grab a beer."

Then he left, and the other girls Jean was with began to move on too, leaving Nick and Jean standing there alone.

"It's nice," he finally said. "You'll like it."

"I will?" she laughed.

"I mean you would like it if you ever visited."

"I'm sure I would."

"What are you studying, Nick?"

He had to think about it.

"English," he finally said. "I'm an English major."

"Me too! I want to teach. How about you?"

"I don't know yet. I picked English because I'm not sure what I want to do yet. I figured it's a good place to start."

"That's interesting. I'll bet we're in some of the same classes."

"English Comp at eight-thirty, Monday, Wednesday and Friday?" he asked hopefully.

"Yep," she smiled.

Nick and Jean stood there, talking until the reception was over. Then he walked her to her dorm. It was an all-women's dorm. He stood at the front door as she fished her key out of her purse.

"You know," he said, "when we met tonight, I don't think I shook your hand."

Nick extended his hand. He had big hands, and they were rough from all the yard work he'd done that summer. Jean put her right hand in his. To Nick, her hand felt so small and soft. Then she wrapped the fingers of her left hand over both of their right hands, creating a kind of bond. She looked up at Nick and smiled.

"It was so nice to meet you, Nick. I'll see you in class on Monday."

Then she stood on her toes and reached up and gave him a kiss on the cheek.

"Good night," she whispered.

Nick was so enchanted that he didn't kiss her back or even give her a hug. His arms hung limp at his sides.

She unlocked the door and, as she disappeared through it, looked back, her ocean eyes open wide and sparkling in the moonlight.

He stood there, looking at the door, not moving, saying nothing. He'd met a lot of girls and kissed more than a few. But he had never met anyone like Jean, and no girl had ever kissed him so gently or whispered good night or looked at him that way.

Finally, he turned around and began walking. He made his way toward his dorm, several blocks away. It was Saturday night. There were a lot of students milling about. He wandered past them, oblivious, like a zombie.

When he got back to his room, Jim was watching TV and drinking a beer.

"How'd it go?"

"It was unbelievable, Jimmy,"

"Grab a beer and tell me about it, big man."

"Okay," he said, still hearing her voice. "I'll try."

#

On Monday, Nick got to English Comp class early and stood outside the door, waiting for Jean. He spotted her coming down the hall. She was wearing khaki pants and a blue and green striped rugby shirt with a white collar. Two nights before, at the party, Nick had been so focused on her face that he really hadn't checked out her body. She was very fit. She must be an athlete, he thought.

As she got closer, he could see her eyes. Those lovely, piercing blue eyes! She was looking at him just as she had in the moonlight two nights before, the last time he'd seen her. Looking at her face this morning, he hoped he would never go that long without seeing her again.

"Good morning," he stammered.

"Good morning, Nick."

He loved hearing her say his name. He loved hearing her speak at all. She was from Michigan. He loved how fast she spoke and how she smashed her words together, like saying she was from "aeh Narbor" instead of Ann Arbor.

They walked into the classroom together. Nick waited for Jean to find a seat, then sat next to her. During class, he scooted his desk back ever so slightly so that he could watch her as their professor droned on about topic sentences and transitions.

He loved her face. She had high cheekbones and a small, perfect nose. Her skin was light and flawless. Her straight blond hair was parted in the middle and cascaded down the sides of her face, over her shoulders and down her back.

Most of all, he loved her eyes. He noticed she carried a pair of wire-rimmed glasses and, whenever their professor would write on the chalkboard, she would slip them on. This guy wore out the chalkboard, and she took copious notes, so she wore her glasses for much of the class. But even through the glare of her lenses, her eyes looked just as blue.

When class was over, Nick walked out with her.

"When is your next class?" he asked.

"In ten minutes. I've got three in a row on Monday mornings."

"Do you have poetry at eleven?"

"Yeah. You?"

"Yeah," he smiled. "I'll see you then."

"Okay. I'll see you then."

Just before eleven, he was waiting in the hallway, just outside their classroom door.

"Hello again, Nick."

Oh, the way she said his name!

He sat next to her again and once again moved his desk back slightly so that he could watch her the whole time. Afterwards, he asked if she wanted to have lunch in the cafeteria.

"I'd love to. How about twelve-thirty?"

"Perfect. See you then."

They had lunch, then spent the afternoon together, walking around campus. They talked about where they were from and their families and why they'd chosen to go to school in Chicago.

For Jean, it was a chance to live in the big city and get a degree that she could use to teach. Her dream was to teach English in high school. She'd looked at several colleges in Michigan. But she had long loved Chicago, having spent time there with her cousins as a kid. She loved the hustle and bustle of downtown, the big buildings, the river, the lake, the art, the food and even the Loop. And, of course, the shopping.

For Nick, Chicago was a place where he could learn how to make a lot of money. He was a child of the sixties, but all the talk about peace and love left him cold. He wanted to be rich and powerful. He wasn't sure how he was going to do that. But he was pretty sure that, in Chicago, he could find a way.

But the sixties and early seventies had one decidedly lasting effect on Nick. He had rock and roll in his soul.

"I play a pretty mean guitar," he told Jean that afternoon.

It's not that she didn't believe him. But Nick was six-two, a strapping young man who looked like he just rolled in off the farm. She had a tough time imagining him playing guitar or any musical instrument for that matter.

But Nick liked surprising people.

He smiled as he saw a look of surprise in Jean's eyes that weekend. They'd gone uptown with a group of other freshmen to a bar where a local band called "Jailbreak" was playing. They were good, covering the top rock groups of the day: America, Eagles, Boston, Queen.

At a break, Nick got up and talked with the lead singer. Jean watched him listening to Nick, then nodding, then pointing to his guitar, which was resting on a stand on the small stage at the end of the bar. Nick came back to the table, with a little bounce in his step, smiling.

"What's up?" Jean asked.

Nick just grinned and said, "You'll see. I hope you like it."

She gave him a playful smile.

As the band members finished their drinks at the bar and re-grouped, Nick patted Jean's hand, got up and walked up onto the stage.

The lead singer switched on his microphone.

"Ladies and gentlemen," he said, "we're going to start this next set with a song made famous by Jimi Hendrix, performed by one of your very own, Nick Reynolds, a freshman here at Loyola, on the guitar."

The crowd started hooting and hollering. Jean just sat there, looking incredulous.

Nick slung the guitar strap over his head, took the pick from between the strings and pivoted to take his cue from the lead singer, who nodded. With that, Nick strummed the first few chords of "All Along the Watchtower," and the band joined in.

He played it masterfully, with power and finesse. He didn't miss a lick. The lead singer could barely contain himself, waving him arms and whipping the crowd into a frenzy after each of Nick's impressive guitar solos.

Jean sat there stunned. During Nick's virtuoso performance, a couple of the girls at her table leaned over and said something to her, giggling. Nick was watching.

He played just that one song. He'd made his point. And Jean never looked at him the same way again. Before she had found him pleasant and cute. Now she began to find him irresistible.

And as Jean soon learned, playing guitar wasn't Nick's only hidden talent. He had a gift for writing too. There was a creativity, a cadence, a power about his writing.

Nick looked like a farm boy. He talked like one too. He talked slowly. And he didn't say much.

But express himself he did — in writing.

One Tuesday afternoon, Jean came back to her dorm after class. She opened her door and was surprised to see an envelope had been slipped underneath. It was the size of a greeting card. It was addressed to Ms. Jean Carlson in neat handwriting that was unfamiliar to her. There was no name in the upper left corner, only "120 Campion Hall."

It could be only one person, she thought. But what was it? Her heart raced. She closed her door, put her books on her desk and sat down on her bed. She'd never received a card from a boy.

As she rested the envelope on her knees, she realized it was flexible. It was not a card, but a letter. Her hands were shaking as she pushed the seal of the envelope open with her index finger, careful not to tear its contents.

Inside were two sheets of plain, white paper, folded three times and then again at the end to fit. She unfolded the pages. It was a poem, handwritten in blue ink.

Angel

It was Saturday night
I knew no one
I looked around the crowded room
And saw you.

You looked like an angel
I watched you laugh like I imagine angels laugh
With all their spirit
Holding nothing back.

Then you turned to me and said hello
That's all
Hello
And you extended your hand
But I didn't take it
Because I had never seen an angel
And I did not know how to act.

But now I do.
I know what it's like to hold an angel's hand, to walk with
an angel, to be kissed by an angel.
I know these things because I have held your hand, walked
with you, been kissed by you.

And I will forever divide my life between the time before
and after I met you.

It has all been good.
But this will be the better part
The happier part
The part filled with grace
Because I now know an angel.

I love an angel
And that angel
Is you.

Nick

Jean stared at the words and gasped when a teardrop hit the paper. Reflexively, she tried to wipe it away. But this only made the ink run. So she pulled the paper close to her mouth and blew it dry.

It was the most precious gift she had ever received. She thought it was the most beautiful thing she had ever read. She had an urge to run up and down the hall, sharing it with everyone. She wanted to tack it up on the bulletin board above her desk so she could read it every day and the other girls, seeing it, would jealously wish their boyfriends would write them something so lovely.

Boyfriend, she thought. Was Nick now her boyfriend? She'd never had a serious boyfriend. The very idea took her breath away.

She looked down at the poem. She wanted to read it again. But she decided to save it for later. She put the sheets of paper back together, folded them and put them back in the envelope.

Then she looked around the room for a special place she might keep this most special gift. She looked down at her bed pillow and slipped the envelope underneath.

She planned to keep it under her pillow, without ever telling a soul, for the rest of her life.

Chapter Twenty

About an hour east of Buffalo, Nick decided to stop for coffee and a bathroom break. He pulled off I-90 at a place called Henrietta, just south of Rochester.

A sign for the Rochester Institute of Technology reminded Nick that Elgin had recruited there. They'd hired engineering students to help design new, lighter and less expensive packaging materials for the company's snack cakes.

Designing lighter, but still sturdy, packaging for a product designed to crumble on your tongue was a tall order. The idea itself emerged from a product supply review, where Nick had found out Elgin was at a cost disadvantage of up to five cents a case versus its leading competitors. The cause was more expensive and heavier packaging materials.

When he learned this, Nick came unglued.

"What? You're telling me we're paying a premium for the part of our product people can't even taste?"

Nick had a way of succinctly and memorably expressing the heart of an issue.

"But our products are softer, Nick," said Jerry, his head of product supply. "They require stronger packaging."

Nick did not look amused.

"Jerry, how many cases did we ship last year?"

"In the U.S.?"

Nick rolled his eyes.

"Yeah, Jerry. Let's start with the U.S."

"About twenty million."

"Okay. Now let's say we're losing a nickel on every case we ship. How much is that?"

"But Nick. We're not losing money on every case."

"Bullshit!" Nick roared. "Just a minute ago, your guy told me we're at a five-cents-a-case cost disadvantage versus our competitors."

"But we've found ways to offset that gap."

Nick clenched his jaw and loosened his tie.

"So you're telling me that there are other people in my organization who are making up for your deficiencies?"

"Nick ..."

"Look, Jerry," Nick fumed. "Let me give you the number. It's $1 million. That's how much money you're costing us every year by being complacent about this. Guess what? That's your new cost savings target for the year. Now go out and find a way to pack and ship our products for five cents a case less. And if you can't do it, let me know in six weeks so I can find a new product supply director who will."

Now Nick knew that, in terms of total profit for his division, $1 million amounted to a rounding error. But to him, that wasn't the point. He wanted to use this as an example of the mindset he expected all his leaders to adopt.

To cut costs fast, Jerry hired a local package design firm to come up with a short-term fix. To build the capability he would need longer term, he stepped up recruiting at the best engineering schools to bring in the right talent. One of these schools was the Rochester Institute of Technology, where Jerry had recently hired several very impressive new players.

In six weeks, Jerry was back in Nick's office, telling him how he was going to deliver on his new cost savings target for the year. He also told him he planned to recruit a select team of engineers for the sole purpose of finding and exploiting ways to save ten cents per case in material costs moving forward, without trading off quality.

Nick leaned back in his chair, put his hands behind his head and smiled.

"I scared the hell out of you in that meeting last month, didn't I, Jerry?"

"It wasn't the most pleasant day of my career."

"Well, it worked. You've not only given me what I've asked for — you've gone beyond it and taken the long view. Finally, somebody's listening to me when I talk about strategy!"

"Thanks," he said. "I appreciated the push."

About six months later, when Nick began to see real cost savings from Jerry and his team, he promoted Jerry to VP and made a big deal out of it with his leadership team.

"Improving our numbers, folks," he said. "That's why we're here."

Nick believed that deeply. But in his heart, he also knew that his best employees, like Jerry, could deliver better results without all his bullying and histrionics. He knew that from watching people like Lou.

But no one was afraid of Lou either. And at that point in his career, when Nick was still gunning for CEO, he believed that instilling fear in others gave him a competitive edge.

Chapter Twenty-one

February 1981

Nick had started at Elgin Foods in June of 1980, right out of college. He spent the first three months in brand management training at the home office in Chicago. He learned about the company, its values and how it operated. He spent the next three months in sales training in Indianapolis, working with retail customers.

He got his first marketing assignment just before Christmas. Right after the holiday, he would be an assistant brand manager for a "new product concept" in the snack cakes division.

Nick was excited when he learned that the new product concept was to introduce a line of specialty cakes, but only in bakeries, and then, after a year, to expand distribution to grocery stores and exploit the "professional bakers" credential.

The company's research showed this idea was so appealing to about twenty percent of snack cake consumers that they would be willing to pay more for such specialty cakes. Based on these findings, Finance made the case for why this two-step approach could generate significantly more profit than launching directly into grocery stores. Management, hungry for fatter margins, bought it.

By the time Nick joined the project, the basic business plan was set. His job was to flesh out the marketing plan for bakeries.

He dove in, working closely with Leo Burnett, Elgin's advertising agency, to prepare print ads and promotional materials. He met with Elgin's sales people. He even visited bakeries in the Chicago area to better understand their businesses and how they operated.

The brand team needed to present the marketing plan to management in February in order to secure the budget needed for launch. This gave Nick less than six weeks to get up to speed, develop advertising and get ready for his first management presentation. He worked fourteen-hour days.

In the meantime, at Christmas, Nick had proposed to Jean. Their wedding was set for early May. This didn't leave much time to plan and get ready. But in those days, weddings were simpler, and five months was time enough. Of course, even in those days, the grooms didn't play an active role in planning a wedding. But Nick set a new low.

It's not that he didn't want to get married. He was thrilled by the prospect. But consumed by his new job, he simply had little time to give.

He and Jean were living in their own apartments in Chicago. With his busy schedule, days would go by without them seeing each other. Jean would call Nick every night, though, to keep him up-to-speed. He knew she was working hard on the arrangements for their wedding — in addition to managing her own new job as a kindergarten teacher.

Nick knew he should be pitching in. But he also knew he wouldn't have another chance to prove himself early at Elgin. So he chose to devote himself to his new job, even though he knew his choice disappointed Jean. It was the beginning of years of disappointing his family, of feeling conflicted, of learning to live a life where he was sacrificing too much.

And Jean got the first glimpses into Nick's workaholic behavior. Even before his presence as her husband, she began to know his absence.

To compound this unease in his personal life, Nick began to have some misgivings about his new project at work.

The more he talked with bakers, the more he realized that Elgin would risk a backlash at the time of the broader retail launch unless it shared the whole plan with bakers from the start. Most bakers loved the idea of selling something that wasn't available to consumers broadly, something people had to come into their bakeries to buy. However, they didn't know those same products would soon be sold in grocery stores.

And Nick couldn't tell them because Elgin considered that information confidential. The company reasoned that, if the unconventional launch was known too early, competitors could undermine it or try to replicate it with their own brands.

Nick mentioned his concern to his brand manager, whose name was Phil.

"You've got to be kidding me," Phil said.

"No, I'm serious."

"Look, Nick. The company has done a lot of research to prove this model out, and it's betting on this project big time. It's a little late for second guessing."

"Yeah, but that research was done with consumers, not bakers."

"Listen, Nick. Are you on board here or not?"

"I'm on board, Phil."

"Good. Now get back to work. And whatever you do, don't mention anything negative during the management presentation."

Nick was taken aback. How could Phil not see the logic in what Nick was saying? How could he not see that the model was flawed?

"Got it?" Phil asked.

"Got it," Nick said, even though he was starting to wonder what he'd gotten himself into.

He didn't share his concerns with anybody else, including Jean. He was tempted to talk with her and ask for her advice. But she was so busy with the wedding plans and her own job. Plus he thought she might either not understand his challenge or see his struggle as a sign of weakness.

And so he kept his problem to himself. It would be years before he would fully understand the downsides of going it alone and the irony of believing anyone is ever really alone.

#

Nick's role in the management presentation was relatively small. He was there only to share a few print ads that would run in trade magazines as well as counter and window displays for bakeries. It was pretty straightforward, but he rehearsed with the team a dozen times.

Every business proposal at Elgin ends with a short list of the "key issues." Most of these issues are not really key issues at all, but rather carefully crafted questions, whose answers are carefully crafted too. Some are even shared with management in advance, to avoid any surprises.

In the case of Nick's project, the key issue flagged at the end of the team's presentation had to do with the availability of some of the raw ingredients if the product took off faster than expected. Having noted this potential issue, Phil proceeded to share the plan being developed with the purchasing department to line up alternate sources of supply, as a precaution.

Normally, at this point in a budget meeting for a major new initiative, management would be giving its go-ahead. But today, the division manager, a man named Jim Edwards, the ranking person in the room, decided to ask one more question.

"How do you think bakers are going to react to this plan?"

Phil jumped in.

"Well, Mr. Edwards, our research shows they're very favorable toward our new product line."

"Have you told them that, in a year, these products will be sold in Jewel?"

"No," Phil said, looking over at Nick. "We haven't."

"What do you think their reaction will be when they realize that?" Edwards asked.

"We think they'll be fine," Phil said.

"Why?" Edwards pressed.

"Well, there are two reasons," Phil said, glancing down at some notes he'd made for himself. "First, they're likely to see an overall increase in their business in the first year. And second, we'll be telling them we want to work with them to bring them even more innovative products in the future."

"What innovative products?" Edwards asked.

"R&D is working on those now," Phil said.

"Don't you think it would be a good idea to know what those products look like now and be able to talk about them with bakers sooner rather than later?" Edwards asked.

"But we consider that information proprietary," Phil said.

"I understand that," Edwards said, raising his voice. "But don't you think it's at least a good idea to let bakers have the big picture from the start?"

Phil said nothing. No one said anything.

So Nick jumped in.

"I do," he said.

Everyone in the room looked at Nick.

"You do?" Edwards asked. "Why?"

"So we can make them our full partners," Nick replied.

Edwards leaned forward and smiled.

"Bingo," he said. "Phil, I think you need to begin listening to the junior member of your team. Now I want you guys to go back to the drawing board and develop a plan that brings bakers in under the tent. Either that or scratch this plan and come up with one to launch this new product line in grocery stores from the start, with the same project economics. You can delay the launch if you need to. But I want to see your plan in two weeks."

"Mr. Edwards——" Phil stammered.

"Two weeks, Phil," Edwards said, standing up. "I'll see you back here in two weeks."

On his way out, Edwards looked at Nick and smiled.

#

"Shut the door," Phil said as he pulled Nick into his office.

But before Nick could even swing it closed, Phil yelled, "What the hell was that?"

"What do you mean?" Nick asked.

"Why did you have to say anything?"

"Edwards asked a question, and nobody was answering him. So I did."

"You have got to be shitting me, Nick. I told you not to say anything negative in that meeting. Now look what you've done! This whole project probably just got shot down, and I'll take the hit. What in the hell were you thinking?"

"I was just telling the truth."

"What?"

"The truth. I was just telling the truth, Phil."

Phil's face was bright red. He leaned forward across his desk.

"All right, Nick!" he snarled, jabbing his index finger into the air. "You want the truth? Here's the truth. I never wanted you on my team in the first place, and I think you're doing a lousy job. I don't think you belong here. And as your boss, I'm telling you to either find another position in the company or get out."

"Phil, I believe in this project," Nick said, his voice trembling. "We just need to adjust the plan. Edwards said he wants to see our new plan in two weeks."

Phil laughed, a sneering, derisive laugh.

"Man, you don't have a clue. There's no adjusting this plan. The whole thing's a bust. We're screwed. We're screwed because you couldn't keep your damn mouth shut. Now get out of my office, Nick. Call HR. Maybe they need an English major somewhere."

"Phil——"

"Get out, Nick. Now. Leave all your files with Sherry. And don't ever come back here again."

Chapter Twenty-two

It was almost noon, and Nick was getting hungry. Time for lunch, he decided.

He was just north of Syracuse, still a couple of hours from Albany. He saw signs for the Village of Liverpool and decided to stop there because it reminded him of the Beatles.

As he pulled off the highway, he saw half a dozen signs for places to eat. "Heid's of Liverpool" jumped out at him because the "i" in the logo was a hot dog on a bun and he had a hankering for a good hot dog.

Heid's was less than a mile off the New York State Thruway. As he got close, he couldn't miss it. "HEID'S" was spelled out in giant, red, neon letters across the top of what looked like a super-sized chimney above the entrance to the restaurant. The edge of the chimney was trimmed with blue neon tubes. The restaurant itself was rectangular, made of yellow and red bricks, with oblong windows. It looked like an old-time diner and a drive-in theater marquee mashed up. Just above the windows, a sign read: "Food You'll Like."

The parking lot out front was full. Nick pulled around back, where there was much more room. He parked there and walked back around the building to the front door.

Just inside, he realized he was already standing in a long line, which flowed from right to left, cafeteria style. He wasn't counting on a wait. But the line seemed to be moving pretty well.

"May I help you?" asked a young woman in a white uniform behind the stainless steel counter. She looked like a nurse.

"I'd like a hot dog, I think."

"They'll take your hot dog order at the end," said the nurse. "I'll take your drink order and any sides that you'd like."

Complicated, Nick thought. He looked up at the menu board. There was a long list of drink and side options.

"I'll have a birch beer and an order of fries."

"Very good," said the nurse. "We'll have that ready for you at the end of counter. You can order your hot dog and pay for your food there too."

Nick grabbed a plastic tray and shuffled down to the end of the counter. Near the end hung another menu board, with lots of "hot dog" options, from Italian sausage to something called a Texas Hot.

But as Nick looked around, it seemed just about everybody was ordering what looked like bratwurst. He figured that was the safe play. But he didn't see bratwurst on the menu.

"May I help you?" asked a pleasant-looking woman, also dressed in a white uniform, as Nick moved to the end of the counter.

"Yeah. I was wondering if I could get a bratwurst."

She smiled.

"You mean a coney."

Nick was confused. He knew what a coney was. It was a chili dog. But as he looked around, he didn't see anybody eating chili dogs.

"I'm sorry," he said. "I'm talking about one of those big, white hot dogs. Isn't that a bratwurst?"

"No. That's what we call a coney."

"Really? What's it made of?"

"Well, our coneys *are* unique. They're made with pork, veal and egg whites. It's the egg whites that give them their color."

"I see," Nick said. "That sounds good. I'll take two."

"Very good. And what would you like on your coneys?"

"What do you recommend?"

"The brown mustard."

"Sold."

"Anything else?"

"No, that'll do it."

"Is this for here or to go?"

"For here."

"That'll be $6.99."

Wow, Nick thought. What a deal. Nick handed her a ten.

"Keep it," he said.

"Thank you, sir," she said, sliding his food and drink across the counter. "I hope you enjoy those coneys. Come back and see us again."

"Thanks. I will."

Nick made his way into the dining room. He spotted only one open table. He took small steps over to it, careful not spill his drink or bump into anyone. He set his tray down on the red, laminated tabletop and slipped onto the curved, high-backed bench.

He pulled a paper napkin from the chrome dispenser on the table and unfolded it across his lap. The gesture seemed a bit formal for a hot dog joint, but it was a habit. He took a sip of birch beer. It tasted like root beer, but with a hint of wintergreen and vanilla. He liked it.

Nick picked up a coney and took a big bite. It was mild and tender. He could taste the veal. The brown mustard added a certain spicy sweetness. It was unlike any hot dog he'd ever eaten and nothing like what he would have called a coney.

Nick looked over at the table to his right. Two guys who looked like construction workers were each chowing down on three coneys with sauerkraut heaped on top and cheese fries on the side. Nick felt like a wimp.

At the table to his left sat an older couple. He guessed they were in their seventies. In front of the man was a half-eaten coney. In front of the woman was a paper basket of chicken fingers.

He was reading a newspaper and seemed oblivious to her presence. She sat quietly, looking around and occasionally taking a small bite of her chicken fingers and a sip of coffee.

Nick wondered how long they'd been together and for how long they'd shared meals without exchanging a word. He assumed they were not always this way. He imagined there was a time when they talked and held hands and gazed into each other's eyes.

Nick remembered such a time in his own life, when he and Jean were inseparable. How long ago it now seemed.

He wondered how Jean was right now. Maybe he should check in, he thought. He knew she was tracking him on her iPhone. But maybe she'd like to know he was okay.

He pulled out his phone and typed in "Jean." Her number popped up. The cursor blinked in the text message box. His thumbs were poised above the keyboard.

But what should he say? That he was okay? He knew that saying anything less would cause her concern. But how could he tell her he was okay when he was not?

He cancelled the text and put his phone away. Tracking Nick on her phone would have to suffice.

#

After lunch, Nick decided to stop for gas. He pulled into a Sunoco station on Oswego Street, a two-lane road which runs through Liverpool and back to the turnpike.

Nick leaned back against his car as the gas filled his tank. He noticed the small houses along Oswego. They all had small front yards. They reminded him of the house where he grew up in Cedar Rapids.

He saw a man cutting grass. He was a big guy. He wore a white v-neck T-shirt, plaid shorts and dark socks and shoes. He reminded Nick of his father.

Nick's yard in Cedar Rapids was immaculate. His father cut the grass at least once a week and kept the bushes neatly trimmed. He was in charge of everything in the yard except for the flowers.

His mother was in charge of those. His father never touched her flowers, and his mother never cut the grass. Nick always assumed they'd made some sort of arrangement.

When he was about ten, like most boys that age, Nick wanted to cut the grass. He asked his father.

"No," he replied, without explanation.

His father often ended conversations abruptly, and Nick didn't press. But later, he asked his mother why.

"Your father is very particular about his yard," she said.

#

After breakfast one Friday morning that summer, when Nick would normally go outside and play, his mother said, "Nicky, dad's been struggling with a really bad cold. I don't think he's going to feel up to cutting the grass this weekend. Would you like to cut it?"

"Yeah!"

"Well, let me show you how to start the mower," she said.

They went out to the garage. His mother wheeled his father's red Craftsman lawnmower out onto the driveway. She filled the gas tank and pulled back a lever on the handle.

"Push this lever all the way down if you want to turn it off," she told Nick.

"Okay."

Nick was so excited he was shaking.

"Put your left foot up here," she said, pointing to the base of the mower. "Then pull the cord hard."

Nick put his foot on the mower, grabbed the hard-rubber handle of the cord and pulled it with all his might. He nearly fell backwards. The handle slipped out of his hand, and the cord quickly recoiled. The engine chugged and sputtered, then settled into a strong, steady, low growl.

His mother pulled the lever on the handle all the way back. The engine revved higher and louder.

"Good luck!" his mother yelled, smiling.

"Thanks!"

Nick had never cut grass. No one had ever taught him how. So he simply tried to do what he'd seen his father do many times: first cut the borders of the yard, then go back and forth, in straight lines.

It was early summer, and the grass was thick. The mower stalled out several times. The first time it happened, Nick was tempted to go get his mother. But he decided to try to restart it himself. He pulled the lever back on the handle and yanked the cord hard. The engine sputtered but died. This happened twice. On the third try, though, it started.

It took him more than an hour to finish. The sun was high in the sky, and his mother was waiting with a tall glass of cold lemonade.

"Good job," she smiled.

"Thanks," he said, drenched in sweat.

Nick couldn't wait until his father got home from work. He knew he'd told him he couldn't cut the grass. But he hoped he would be glad he wouldn't need to cut it himself, at least not this weekend.

It was just after five o'clock, the time his father always got home. Nick watched through the living room window as his father's blue Ford Fairlane pulled into the driveway. His father was looking out his open window at the yard. He was frowning.

The garage door was up. But his father didn't pull into the garage, as he normally did. Instead, he parked in the driveway.

Nick heard his car door open, then slam shut. He heard his father's footsteps in the garage. He heard the wooden screen door between the garage and the dining room creak open.

Nick had a bad feeling. He hunkered down on the living room sofa, out of sight.

"Who cut my grass?" the old man bellowed.

"Jim," his mother said, stepping into the dining room from the kitchen. "I asked Nick to cut it."

"Why?"

"Well, it was getting long, and I know you're not feeling well. I thought you might appreciate not having to cut it this weekend."

"It's a mess! The rows are all crooked, and he missed big patches. I told that boy not to cut my grass. Now I'm going to have to go out there and cut it all over again."

"Jim, it looks fine."

"Maureen, don't tell me how my yard should look. By the way, I thought we had an agreement."

"What do you mean?"

"You told me you were never going to touch the lawn."

"But I didn't, Jim."

"Right! You had Nick do it for you! What a cheap shot! Don't ever do that again."

Nick heard the screen door slam and the lawnmower rolling out of the garage. He heard the engine roar to a start on the first pull.

Nick sat there, looking out the window. He watched as his father, still dressed in his mail uniform, trudged back and forth, with a scowl on his face, across the front yard.

His mother poked her head into the living room.

"There you are," she said.

Her face was red. She looked like she'd been crying.

"I'm sorry, Nick," she said, stepping over to the sofa and sitting down next to him. "You did a good job today. I'm sorry your father has chosen to act this way."

"It's okay, Mom," he said.

But she could see the hurt in his face.

"Nick, I'm going to the nursery in the morning to buy flowers. Would you go with me and help me plant them in the back yard along the fence?"

"Sure," he said.

The next morning, while his father was still sleeping, Nick went to the nursery with his mother. They bought rose bushes, Morning Glories and Black-eyed Susans. When they got home, his mother showed him how to plant them.

After that, every spring and summer until he graduated from college and moved away, Nick helped his mother tend her flowers in the yard. Her flower gardens were the envy of the neighborhood.

He started cutting the grass again too, but not for another eight years, after his father was gone.

Chapter Twenty-three

June 1984

Jean had been in labor for nearly fourteen hours. She was moaning and sucking on ice chips. So was Nick.

Doctor Salter said Jean was five centimeters dilated "and holding." Nick had missed their childbirth education classes, but he knew that wasn't good.

"What should we do?" he asked the doctor.

"Well, we have three options."

Good lord, Nick thought. You're a doctor. Just tell us what to do.

"Option one. I can let her go like this a while longer and see what happens."

"You mean in this kind of pain?" Nick asked.

"Yes."

"What's option two?"

"An epidural. It will take her pain away. But it might slow down her contractions."

"Ahhh!" Jean shrieked, grabbing the sides of the bed.

All his life, Nick had nearly fainted at the sight of a needle. The very idea of an epidural made him light-headed.

"What's option three?" he whimpered.

"A C-section."

Nick began seeing stars.

"Mr. Reynolds!" exclaimed the nurse. Fortunately, she was quick on her feet and managed to help Nick to a chair.

"Put your head between your knees," she said. "Take deep breaths."

She pressed a button on her pager. Moments later, another nurse entered the room.

"I need a hand here, Peggy," the first nurse said.

Peggy hurried over, stood next to Nick and started rubbing his back.

"I'll take the epidural," Jean moaned.

When he heard the word epidural again, Nick began to teeter in his chair. But the nurses closed in on him, like a vise, and kept him steady.

"Hang in there, Mr. Reynolds," the first one said. "Peggy, hold onto him while I get a cold washcloth for his forehead."

"He'll be okay," she said as she walked by Jean, whose face was contorted from the pain of giving birth to one baby while being married to another.

#

"It's a girl," Doctor Salter said.

"Oh!" Jean cried. "Is she okay?"

"Yes, it appears everything is just fine," Dr. Salter said, as she lay the baby on Jean's chest.

Nick was still sitting in his chair across the room. He wanted to see the baby, but he knew the doctor wasn't finished with Jean. He knew she was doing things he had heard about but never wanted to see. But he had to see his new daughter.

He got up and stepped over to the bed, careful not to look down, where the doctor was still working. Jean was crying and smiling — and holding the most beautiful thing Nick had ever seen.

"Say hello to Ashley, Nick."

"Hello, Ashley," he said, bending down to kiss her on the head. Tears were streaming down his face.

Looking up at Jean, he said, "I love you."

"I love you too."

They took turns holding Ashley in the delivery room for the next hour. When the nurses took the baby away to clean and wrap her, Nick followed them, not letting his daughter out of his sight.

Later, Jean told Nick it was the only time she had ever seen him walking on his toes.

#

By nine o'clock that evening, Ashley was in her crib in the nursery with the other newborns, and Jean was exhausted. Nick decided to go home and let them both get some rest.

"I'll be back in the morning," he said, kissing Jean goodbye. "Just call me at home if you need anything."

#

Nick was exhausted too. But he was also wired. So he decided to stop at a bar near his house for a nightcap.

"What'll you have?" asked the bartender.

"Your best bourbon, on the rocks."

"Special occasion?"

"Yeah. My first child was born tonight."

"Congratulations! Boy or girl?"

"A girl, named Ashley. The most beautiful little girl in the world."

"No doubt," the bartender said, sliding Nick's drink across the bar. "This one's on the house."

"Thanks."

"To Ashley," the bartender said, raising his glass.

"To Ashley," Nick toasted.

Nick threw back his drink and ordered another. A few minutes later, out of nowhere, he began ripping into his father.

"My old man was lazy," he told the bartender. "It's not like he had a lot to do. He was around a lot. I was too. Hell, we lived under the same roof for eighteen years. But he never even tried to get to know me. You know, he never once asked me, 'Nick, how are you?' I don't think he really cared."

"I'm sorry," said the bartender.

"I'll never be like that with my kids," Nick said. "I'm going to be there for them, every day."

Nick continued laying into his father. The bartender listened patiently. But after Nick's fourth glass of bourbon, he had to cut him off.

#

Nick stumbled into his house about two in the morning and passed out on the sofa.

He was in such a deep sleep when Jean called at seven that he didn't even hear the phone ring. She kept calling back. Finally, he answered. But he was still feeling the effects of the bourbon. He was slurring his words. Jean was all too familiar with his drunk voice.

"How could you do this to us, Nick?" she sobbed.

Then she hung up.

Nick fell back to sleep.

He finally got to the hospital about noon.

Chapter Twenty-four

When Nick left Liverpool, it was sunny. There wasn't a cloud in the sky. But about an hour east, he began to see gray storm clouds forming in the distance. Then the sky went dark. It reminded Nick of tornado season in Cedar Rapids when he was a boy. He wondered if there were tornadoes this late in the spring in central New York.

Tornado or not, Nick could see a wall of darkness coming toward him. Lightning flashed from the clouds. Thunder boomed and cracked. Fierce winds rocked his car. Hailstones rained down like bullets. Then the rain began. First it came in sheets, swaying wildly back and forth across the highway. But then the rain came down so hard that Nick could barely see the road ahead. It was like driving through a waterfall.

He had driven through storms, bad storms, many times. He actually liked the challenge. He prided himself on always plowing through them and took satisfaction in making fun of drivers who pulled off the road. "Wimps," he would sneer, as he drove past them, their emergency lights blinking. "Stupidest thing you can do in a storm," he would say to Jean and the kids. "Most of those guys are going to get hit from behind by other wimpy drivers pulling off. Serves them right."

But Nick had never faced a storm like this one. The sky was so dark, the rain so heavy and the wind so fierce that he knew he could not go on. He knew he had to pull off the road.

Just ahead, he saw a string of red, flashing lights. Then he saw the contour of an overpass. A few moments later, he was under a bridge, and he realized the flashing lights he had seen belonged to several cars and trucks that had taken cover and were parked on the side of the road.

For a moment, instinctively, Nick thought of the drivers with disdain. He thought he might pass them and keep going. But then he looked beyond the bridge. He could see only a deluge in the darkness. And he realized he would be foolish to head back into it. So he pulled off the road, in front of a semi.

Nick waited the storm out there. As he did, another car pulled off just ahead of him. In it, he could see children moving back and forth and jumping up and down in the back seat. They were smiling and waving at him. He waved back.

It made Nick think about the choice he had made through the years to never pull off the road during storms, to keep going. And for the first time, as he watched the children in front him, he realized the arrogance and selfishness of his choice.

He stepped on his brake, pressed the starter button in his dashboard and cut his engine. He sat there quietly, fairly amazed that he had at last made a different choice. He sat there until the storm passed.

Chapter Twenty-five

September 1989

"Are you sure you're up for this?" Jean asked, standing in the family room.

"Jean," Nick said, sitting in his recliner, "I'm the oldest of three kids. I did a lot of babysitting growing up."

"Nick, you don't babysit your own kids."

Good point, Nick thought.

"We'll be fine. You have fun. We'll see you tomorrow."

"All right," she said, not sounding convinced.

"Mommy," whined Ashley, hugging her mother's leg. "When will you be back?"

"I'll be back tomorrow afternoon, sweetie," said Jean, smoothing her daughter's silky blond hair.

"Mommy," whimpered Josh, hugging Jean's other leg. "Don't go, Mommy."

"Wow. You guys certainly aren't making this easy," Jean said.

She got down on her knees and put her arms around her two small children. She had never left them overnight. This was as hard for her as it was for them.

"Jean, you never get a break," Nick said. "You deserve an overnighter with your girlfriends. Have fun and don't worry about us. We'll be fine."

"Okay," she said, giving Ashley and Josh each a kiss on the cheek. "Mommy will miss you. Be good for Daddy."

She got up and walked over to Nick. She bent down and kissed him lightly on the lips.

"Thank you, Nick," she said. "If you need me for anything, I've left the number of the bed and breakfast on the kitchen counter. We'll probably go into the city this afternoon and have dinner there tonight. Otherwise, I'll be at the B&B, and I'll be home by early afternoon tomorrow."

"Have a great time," Nick said.

Jean fished her keys out of her purse, threw the kids a kiss goodbye and opened the door to the garage. She turned back toward Nick and said, "By the way, I'll leave the kids' car seats in the garage just in case you decide to go out."

"Okay."

"Don't take them out without their car seats."

"Okay."

#

As soon as Jean drove off, Nick took the kids upstairs. He had managed to sound gracious to Jean, and he really did feel she deserved this time away with her friends, and she had made these plans long ago. But it couldn't have come at a worse time for Nick.

Elgin was about to acquire Lone Star Cakes, the biggest and oldest snack cake company in the southwestern U.S., and Nick was on point. The acquisition had been his idea. He came up with it over a beer after work with a colleague, Ted, who worked in sales for Elgin. He told Nick that, no matter how hard Elgin tried to compete with Lone Star, it couldn't beat them, especially in Texas and southern California.

"Why don't we buy them?" asked Nick.

"Fat chance," said Ted.

"Why?"

"Well, first of all, it would cost a bundle. Second, it's privately held. We'd need to convince the family to sell."

"Everything's available at a price," Nick said.

The next day, Nick mentioned the idea to his manager, a middle-aged guy named Sam. He had worked all over the company, including the mergers and acquisitions, or M&A, group. Sam listened to Nick's idea and suggested he talk with one of his former colleagues in M&A.

The M&A guy, named Brad, was intrigued. He told Nick the company had looked at acquiring Lone Star years ago, but the family wasn't interested in selling. So it was no longer on the priority list.

"We're swamped right now," Brad said. "But if you want to go for it and your boss will give you some time and you line up a sponsor, I could give you about twenty-five percent of one of our junior manager's time."

Nick talked with Ted, who was supportive. Then he made an appointment with his friend Lou Bradford to see if he would serve as his sponsor. Lou agreed on the spot.

Three months later, Nick had developed a rough proposal, which included how Elgin might discretely approach the owners of Lone Star through a powerful third party: the Governor of Texas. Elgin had a plant in Austin. It was small but a good, steady source of jobs and taxes. Nick shared his plan with Lou, who was impressed. He told Nick he was going to ask Ted to put Nick on a special assignment so he could focus full-time on developing a recommendation for the acquisition. Ted didn't want to lose Nick but agreed, recognizing the importance of the project and the stripe on Lou's sleeve.

Nick spent the next six months fleshing out his proposal, which he then personally presented to senior management, with Lou at his side.

Senior management agreed with Nick's proposal.

"Who's going to lead this project?" asked Jim Edwards.

"Nick," Lou said. "This was Nick's idea. He's owned it. I think he should lead it until we announce the acquisition."

"I agree," said Edwards, smiling at Nick. "Congratulations,

young man."

Nick's plan to use the Texas Governor to approach the family worked. Six months later, the acquisition was now set to be announced next Wednesday. The deal had been agreed in principle. But there were still final contract details to be resolved, and all the communication materials needed to be finalized. A six-inch binder filled with contract and communication materials was nestled in a soft leather briefcase on the floor of Nick's bedroom. M&A had given it to him just before he left the office yesterday. He knew it couldn't wait until Monday. That would be cutting it too close. He knew he had to spend quality time on it this weekend, when he was supposed to be watching his kids. He never mentioned it to Jean because the acquisition was confidential and he didn't have the heart to ask her to cancel her little getaway.

Upstairs, he brought Ashley and Josh into Ashley's room and turned on her TV.

"You guys watch a little TV while dad gets a little work done. Okay?"

"Okay, Daddy," Ashley said, grabbing the remote.

"Okay," Josh said, sitting on the floor in front of the TV.

With the kids squared away for the moment, Nick went into his bedroom, where he had a small desk. He pulled the heavy binder out of his briefcase and began to skim it. He hadn't looked at it last evening. As he leafed through the pages of the contract, he was struck by how many times he spotted "TBD" in brackets. And as he looked at the communication materials, he saw big chunks still missing, from plans for covering retail customers to key points in the news release.

"Holy crap," Nick thought.

Within minutes, he knew he needed access to his files in his office in order to begin to fill in the blanks. He would have to take the kids to his office for a while.

He slid the binder back into his briefcase, which he grabbed and carried with him down the hall.

Ashley and Josh had just begun watching Pee-wee's Playhouse.

"Kids, we're going to go bye-bye."

"Where are we going, Daddy?" Ashley asked.

"We're going to Daddy's office for a while."

"Oh, boy!" exclaimed Ashley, jumping up.

"Oh, boy!" exclaimed Josh, jumping up too but not really understanding why.

The kids followed Nick out to the garage. Just inside the garage, Nick saw their car seats.

"Damn," he muttered.

"What did you say, Daddy?" Ashley asked.

"Nothing," Nick replied. "Let's put your car seats in my back seat."

He threw his briefcase on his front passenger seat and proceeded to wrestle with the kids' car seats in the back. Ashley kept asking him about the strange words he kept muttering.

When he finally got the car seats in place and the kids situated, Nick realized it was lunch time.

"You guys hungry?" he asked, as he pulled out of the driveway.

"Yeah!" they answered in unison.

"How about driving through McDonald's?"

"Yeah!" Ashley squealed. "A Happy Meal!"

"Happy Meal!" Josh shouted. He knew what that meant.

#

Elgin's office was closed on Saturdays. But Nick went into the office enough on the weekends and stayed late enough at night to know all the receptionists and security guards at the front desk.

"Hey, Charley," he said as he approached an older man sitting behind a large, semi-circular desk in the lobby.

"Hello, Mr. Reynolds," Charley said. "I see you brought your helpers with you today."

"Yep. Charley, these are my kids, Ashley and Josh. Kids, say hello to Mr. Harris."

"Hello," Ashley said.

"Hello," said Josh.

Their cheeks were covered with mustard and ketchup from their hamburgers.

"I'll be here for an hour or two," Nick said. "Maybe I'll see you a bit later."

"Probably so. I'll be working all afternoon."

Nick brought the kids up to his office. His office was relatively small, with a desk and a small pedestal table with two chairs. Nick wondered how to keep his kids occupied. Then he remembered Pam kept candy in a bowl on her desk.

"Wait here," he said. "I'll be right back."

He stepped into Pam's cubicle, grabbed the candy bowl off her desk and brought it into his office.

"All right! Candy!" Ashley cried.

"Candy!" shouted Josh.

Nick set it down on the pedestal table. Ashley climbed up on one of the chairs. Nick lifted Josh and sat him down on the other.

"Would you guys like to color?" Nick asked.

"Yeah," said Ashley, as Josh stood up on his chair and stuck his hand into the candy bowl.

Nick went to his desk and pulled out a dozen or so sheets of white paper. Then he grabbed all his pens, pencils and markets from his top drawer and a cup on his desk. He put a small stack of paper in front of each of his kids and sat the pens, pencils and markers in a pile on the table.

"Here you go," Nick said. "Why don't you draw some pretty pictures for Mommy?"

With his kids focused on drawing and eating candy, Nick pulled the binder out of his briefcase, set it on his desk and sat down to work.

The three of them were there the rest of the afternoon. Nick accessed his files, made some phone calls and got as much done on the contract and communication materials as he could. He kept getting interrupted by his kids, who wanted something to drink or to go to the bathroom. Several times they escaped, and he had to chase them down the halls. Once, when they were being especially quiet, he looked over to find them coloring on his wall with magic markers. He tried to clean it off with a wet, soapy paper towel from the bathroom. But it didn't work. He would ask Pam to call the building maintenance people on Monday.

Nick noticed it was beginning to get dark and realized he needed to get his kids home. He packed up his binder, stuffed all his kids' drawings in his briefcase and headed out. When they got to the lobby, Charley was gone.

#

They drove through the McDonald's in Elmhurst for dinner. Happy Meals again.

When they got home, Nick knew he needed to spend some more time on the acquisition materials. He went upstairs with the kids and put his briefcase in his bedroom. He helped the kids put their pajamas on. He set Josh up to watch *Teenage Mutant Ninja Turtles* on the TV in his room and let Ashley play video games in her room. Then he went to his bedroom to resume his work.

As darkness fell, he realized it was bedtime for his kids. He went to Josh's room and found him asleep on the floor in front of the TV. He turned off the TV, picked Josh up and put him to bed.

He could hear Ashley playing *DuckTales* in her room. She looked up as he stepped inside.

"Ready for bed, sweetie?"

"Almost, Daddy."

"Almost?"

"Will you read to me?"

"Sure. What would you like to read?"

"Where the Sidewalk Ends."

She got up, turned off the TV, walked over to her bookshelf and pulled out her favorite book. She climbed up on her bed, and Nick sat down next to her.

He wondered how long this would take. He was thinking about his work.

"What should we read?" he asked.

She opened the book with a certainty that told Nick she knew exactly which poem she wanted to read.

"This one," she said. "Reginald Clark."

Nick smiled. He knew that poem. He hadn't read it himself, but he had heard Jean reading it plenty of times with Ashley and Josh at night.

"All right," Nick said, taking the book and setting it on his lap.

"Afraid of the Dark," Nick began. Ashley smiled up at him.

"I'm Reginald Clark, I'm afraid of the dark, so I always insist on the light on ..."

Nick looked down. Ashley was frowning.

"What's wrong?"

"Your voice," she said. "You don't sound like Mommy."

"What do you mean?"

"I mean you sound scary. The way you read makes me afraid."

"Afraid? Oh, sweetie, I'm sorry. I'll try to read softer."

But it was no use. His deep voice, maybe combined with a poem about being afraid of the dark and no doubt the impatience Ashley could sense, made his daughter close the book. She seemed anxious and disinterested.

"Do you want to read something else?" Nick asked.

"No, Daddy. I want to go to bed. Can I leave the light on tonight?"

"Sure, sweetie," he said, putting her to bed and kissing her on the head.

"Good night, Daddy."

Nick left and went back to his den. He worked well into the night, periodically checking on his kids.

Then he went downstairs, poured a glass of bourbon in the kitchen and took it out on his patio. It was a crisp, early fall night. Nick was wearing jeans and a T-shirt. It was cool enough for a jacket, but he was already embedded in his Adirondack chair and didn't have the energy to go back in the house.

He sat back and took a long drink and looked up at the second level of his house, at the windows of his children's rooms. They were both asleep, less than thirty feet away. Yet he felt so very distant from them, like a stranger in his own house.

Maybe Jean was wrong. Maybe you can babysit your own kids.

Chapter Twenty-six

Nick arrived in Albany by mid-afternoon. As he pulled into downtown, he could see the Hudson River, just to the east.

He'd seen the Hudson from Manhattan many times. But he hadn't been to Albany. The river is a lot more picturesque in Manhattan, he thought.

"Good afternoon, sir," said a soft-spoken young man wearing horn-rimmed glasses behind the desk. "Checking in?"

"Yes, I am."

"Your name, please?"

"Reynolds. Nick Reynolds."

"Ah, Mr. Reynolds," he said, his fingers tapping rapid-fire across a keyboard behind the counter. "Yes, I have you staying with us for one night," he said in a low, monotonous voice. "Is that correct?"

For a moment, Nick wondered if this guy was actually a robot.

"Yes."

"Would you like to put that on a credit card?"

"Sure," Nick said, handing him his Visa card.

"I see you are well-traveled, Mr. Reynolds."

Nick wondered if these hotel clerks all got the same training.

"Yes, although I've not been to Albany."

"Ah," he said, finally smiling and speaking in a voice that sounded human. "Welcome to our city."

"Thank you. Any suggestions on what to see around town?"

"You're leaving tomorrow?"

"Yes, in the morning."

"Well, in that case, you might consider touring the capitol building before it closes this evening."

"What time is that?"

"Seven o'clock."

"The capitol building, huh?"

"Oh, yes. It's an architectural marvel."

"How far away is it?"

"It's a ten-minute walk. Would you like me to mark the route for you on this map?"

"Sure."

The clerk pulled the cap off a Sharpie, pushed his glasses up on his nose with his index finger and, upside down, traced the streets from the hotel to the capitol building. He's either done this before or he really is a robot, Nick thought.

"Here you go, Mr. Reynolds," he said, tearing the top page off a pad of maps and handing it to him."

"Thanks very much."

"You're welcome. Enjoy your stay."

#

As he approached the capitol building, Nick realized why the clerk had recommended checking it out. It was magnificent: a five-story structure made of white granite and marble with pyramidal red roofs at each end. It reminded Nick of La Grand Place in Brussels.

The inside was even more impressive. A massive, lavishly carved sandstone staircase swept up toward tiled walls beneath vaulted ceilings adorned with murals and crowned with skylights.

Nick usually thought of himself as the most powerful man in any room. He was certainly often the biggest. Yet standing there in that colossal atrium, looking up, he felt small.

He was eager to learn all about it. He stepped over to the information desk. Fortunately, the last guided tour of the day was just about to begin.

The tour guide explained that construction on the building had begun just after the Civil War. It took more than three decades to build, under the direction of five architects. The western staircase alone took fourteen years and cost more than a million dollars.

At last, in 1899, Theodore Roosevelt, then the Governor of New York, declared the building complete. At the time, it was the most expensive building in America.

The whole thing was built by hand. The floors and huge columns were made of marble quarried in nearby Westchester County and cut by state prisoners at Sing Sing. The faces of every major figure of the day were intricately carved into the staircases by a battalion of stonecutters — five hundred and thirty-six in all, many of them from Scotland and Italy.

Every hallway, every archway, every door was impressive. But even Nick, who had seen palaces and castles all over the world, was astonished by the assembly chamber, the largest room in the building.

The vaulted ceiling rose to a height of more than fifty feet. Sweeping sandstone arches were painted in tones of greenish-blue, red and black and highlighted with gold. They were anchored by four enormous pillars of polished granite. Sunlight streamed in through large windows of both clear and stained glass. Semi-circular rows of desks faced a wide, raised rostrum in the front of the room. All the wood was mahogany. All the chairs were upholstered with red leather. It was a noble, even regal room.

The tour guide pointed out that the offices of the current members of the state legislature were on the second floor. But they were off-limits to the public. Nick saw lots of well-dressed people walking briskly up and down the hallways of the second floor. He wondered if they were staffers or lobbyists. He was drawn to power, and he could almost feel it in the air.

When the tour was over, Nick was still curious, especially about where the government officials worked. He wondered if the governor himself might be there today. As the tour group disbanded, Nick took off up the so-called "Million Dollar Staircase."

A security guard was sitting at a small desk on the landing at the top of the stairs.

"May I help you, sir?"

"Good evening, officer," Nick said, hoping to ingratiate himself. "I was wondering if I might see where the governor works."

"I'm sorry, sir. But that office is off-limits."

"I understand," Nick said, trying to sneak a peak down the hallway. All he could see were heavy wooden doors.

He turned around and slowly descended the stairs. How strange, he thought, that the offices of public officials would be off-limits to the people they're charged with serving.

But then he thought of his own office and how few people he hosted there any more. There was no sign outside of Nick's office declaring it off-limits. But it had become a fortress, and Nick realized that he too had become detached from the people he was supposed to be serving.

#

Descending the steps to the lobby, Nick spotted a familiar face etched in the stone cornice at the top of a granite column. It was the soft, bearded face of Walt Whitman, whose poetry had inspired him so long ago.

Nick loved Whitman. He remembered reciting a favorite stanza from "Song of Myself" to Jean when they were in college.

> *I celebrate myself, and sing myself,*
> *And what I assume you shall assume,*
> *For every atom belonging to me as good belongs to you.*

Jean would tear up, and sometimes Nick would too. He read poetry to Jean because he loved her. He read her this particular stanza by Whitman because he believed it.

Nick had felt close to Jean and, in those days, to others too.

\#

Nick decided to leave the building through the eastern exit because he wanted to go down the seventy-seven steps leading up to it.

On the tour, Nick had learned the capitol building has seventeen steps approaching its western entrance, where he had come in, and seventy-seven steps approaching its eastern entrance — in honor of 1777, when New York replaced its colonial government with state government. Nick was a sucker for history.

As he neared the bottom, Nick saw a man sitting on the second step. He had long, grey hair and a bushy beard. On the stone walkway in front of him was a little basket with a piece of cardboard sticking out of it.

Nick looked straight ahead, trying to avoid eye contact, as he descended the last few steps. He'd just passed the man and was about to step out onto the plaza when he heard a voice.

"Sir, can you help me?"

Nick hesitated but kept walking.

"Sir," the man called after him. "Can you help me?"

Nick was accustomed to seeing bag men and beggars in downtown Chicago. He stopped giving them change years ago, when he convinced himself they were only buying booze with it.

This evening, though, something inside told him to stop. He turned around and faced the man.

"How can I help you?"

"Can you spare a few dollars so I can get something to eat?"

"No. But I'll buy you a meal."

Nick smiled to himself at his own cleverness, calling the man's bluff. He figured he'd thrown him off his trail, and now this guy would leave him alone.

Instead, he said, "Okay."

Then he leaned forward, picked up the basket and stuffed it into a black, plastic bag sitting on the step next to him. He stood up and threw the bag over his shoulder.

Realizing the man had called his bluff, Nick pulled out his wallet and plucked out a few dollars.

"No disrespect, sir," the man said. "But you said you were going to buy me a meal."

"You're right. I did say that," Nick said, putting his wallet back in his pocket. "Where to?"

"There's a diner around the corner."

"Okay. After you."

As the man walked by, Nick expected him to stink. But he smelled no worse than Nick himself did after a long day.

Nick had seen hundreds, maybe thousands of homeless people over the years. Their clothes always seemed baggy. But this man's clothes seem to fit pretty well. Not only that, they were in good shape. He wore a dark blue jacket. It looked similar to the one Nick had bought at Dick's last Saturday, the one he was wearing right now.

"What's the name of the place?" Nick asked, not because he wanted to know but to test the man's intentions.

"Cafe One Eleven."

Well, that sounds pretty specific, Nick thought.

He walked a few steps behind the bag man. People were strolling around. Nick knew no one. But he didn't want even strangers to think he and this guy were together.

A few minutes later, they'd arrived at Cafe One Eleven. It was for real.

The man stopped at the front door. He turned around to face Nick.

"Shall we go in?"

"What?"

"So I can order my food."

"Yeah," Nick said. "Sure."

The man opened the door and held it for Nick.

"Thank you," Nick said, as he stepped past him.

It was a small place, a sandwich shop, with a lunch counter, tables and booths. Several people were sitting at the counter.

The hostess, a plump, middle-aged woman with short, bright orange hair, greeted them at the door.

"Good evening, gentlemen. Two for dinner?"

This gone on long enough, Nick thought. He reached for his wallet so could give this guy ten bucks and get the hell out of there. But the man turned to him and surprised him by asking, "Care to join me?"

Impossible. This whole situation, Nick thought, was impossible. He never even gave street people a dime any more. Now he was about to have dinner with this guy?

But having gone this far, how could he say no?

"Okay," Nick said.

The man smiled, turned to the hostess and said, "Yes, two for dinner. We'd like a booth."

"Is that okay with you?" he asked, turning to Nick.

"Yeah. That's fine."

The hostess walked them to an open booth.

"Your server will be right with you. Can I get either of you something to drink?"

Nick looked at the man, who nodded, signaling him to go first.

"Yes," Nick said. "Coffee. Black."

"Same, please."

Nick's dinner companion gently tossed his plastic bag onto the padded bench. He sat down and slid over, pushing his bag against the wall. The bag had holes in it. Nick caught a whiff of dirty socks.

This isn't happening, Nick thought. He looked around to see if anyone was watching him. No one was. He sat down.

"I didn't really expect you to buy me dinner," said the man.

"To be honest," said Nick, "neither did I."

"I know. Thank you."

Sitting across from him, under a light suspended from the ceiling, Nick finally got a good look at the man. He was thin, but his face was full and round. His beard and hair were long, grey and wiry, his beard slightly whiter than the thinning, combed-back hair on his head. His nose was broad, his eyebrows arched. His skin was dark and deeply wrinkled. His deep-set eyes were light blue and small. They reminded Nick of the cat's eye marbles he used to play with as a boy.

"My name is Paul," he said, extending his hand across the table.

"I'm Nick," he said, shaking it. He felt ashamed that this bag man's manners were better than his own.

"I'm glad to meet you, Nick," he said, smiling. He was missing some teeth.

The waitress brought their coffees and handed them menus.

"Any recommendations?" Nick asked, half kidding.

"Do you like roast beef?"

"Yeah."

"Then I'd recommend the Big Stan."

"What's that?"

"Grilled roast beef with caramelized onions, provolone cheese and horseradish mayo on any type of bread you like."

Wow, Nick thought. Pretty sophisticated for a bum.

"That does sound good," Nick said.

A minute later, the waitress came back.

"Do youse know what you'd like?"

"Go ahead," Nick said, remembering his manners.

"I'd like the Big Stan."

"Would you like fries with that?"

Paul looked at Nick, as if to ask permission. Nick nodded.

"Yes, please."

"I'll have the same," Nick said, handing the waitress his menu.

Both men sipped their coffee.

"You thought I was going to buy booze with your money, didn't you?"

"The thought crossed my mind."

"I understand. I don't blame you. But I want you to know I don't drink."

"Not at all?"

"Not any more. I haven't had a drink in twenty years."

"Why did you give it up?"

"I was an alcoholic, and my wife left me. She kicked me out and took everything. I stopped drinking because I couldn't afford it."

Nick glanced away as he sipped his coffee. Then he looked at Paul.

"Are you homeless?"

"Yes."

"How long?"

"Years."

"What happened?"

"Do you really want to know?"

"Yes, I do."

For the next hour, Paul shared his story.

He was born in New York City. He grew up there and went to college at Fordham. He majored in finance and went to work for an investment firm right out of school.

Like Nick, Paul had met his wife in college. And like Nick and Jean, Paul and his wife got married in their early twenties and started a family a few years later.

Paul was happy at home, but he struggled at work. He was good with numbers. But he was shy and had a tough time working with people. For a while, he was able to get by on his financial skills. But over time, his firm changed. Everyone was expected to work in teams and even directly with clients. But Paul was strictly a number cruncher. He had a hard time keeping up.

One day, his manager called Paul into his office.

"Paul, there's no easy way to say this. So I'll cut to the chase. We're letting you go."

"What?"

"You're good with numbers, Paul. But you're a solo act. We need everyone around here to be a team player. We think you'd be a better fit somewhere else."

Paul never saw it coming. He was devastated.

That's when he started drinking. He took a series of accounting jobs but managed to lose them all. His response was to drink more. But that made it all the harder to hold down a job. Finally, his wife had had enough. She took the kids and left.

His spirit broken, Paul went after low-paying, unskilled jobs. He even washed dishes. He could find odd jobs. But he had lost his self confidence.

One day, he simply couldn't get out of bed. He stayed in his apartment for weeks. His shyness had morphed into an overwhelming fear of interacting with others.

Unable to work, he could no longer pay his rent. When he was evicted, he had nowhere to go. For a while, he lived in his car. But soon he had to sell even that. He moved to emergency shelters. But they turned him out when the weather got warmer. So now he lived on the streets, usually sleeping in parks or homeless camps.

"I'm sorry," Nick said.

"Thank you."

"Paul, I know something about feeling beat up at work. And drinking too much."

Paul looked into Nick's eyes. Just then, Paul looked so familiar to Nick. But he couldn't place him.

"Where are you from, Nick?"

"Chicago. Cedar Rapids, originally."

"What brings you here?"

"I'm taking a little break. I'm on my way to Bar Harbor."

"Bar Harbor. I hear it's beautiful up there."

"Me too. I've never been there."

"So why Bar Harbor?"

"Well, at first it was simple. It was one of the few places in the country I haven't been."

Nick paused and looked away.

"And now?" Paul asked.

"Now," Nick said, looking back at him, "I'm beginning to think it's not really about Bar Harbor at all."

"What do you mean?"

"I think it's about what's happening on the way."

"And what's happening?"

"I'm not sure. But I feel like I'm waking up."

"Will there be anything else, gentlemen?" their waitress asked.

"Would you like anything else?" Nick asked. "Something to take with you?"

"No, thanks."

"Just the check," Nick said.

"Here you go, sweetie."

They got up, and Nick paid at the register. Paul held the door and followed Nick outside. It was getting dark.

"Where will you stay tonight?" Nick asked.

"I have a place."

"Are you sure?"

"Yeah, thanks."

"Okay."

Nick didn't know if Paul was telling the truth. But he wasn't going to press.

"It was good to meet you, Paul," Nick said, extending his hand.

"It was good to meet you too, Nick," Paul said, taking it. "That was the best meal I've had in a long time. I can't thank you enough."

Nick looked down and folded his hands in front of him.

"Paul," he said, looking up.

"Yeah?"

"No one can really see us, I mean on the inside. We're bigger than anyone can know. No one can see all we are on the inside."

Paul smiled. Nick wondered if Paul understood what he was trying to say.

"Yes," Paul said. "We contain multitudes."

Nick took one last look at Paul's face.

"I feel like we've met before," he said.
"Me too."

#

Walking back to his hotel, Nick shook his head at the whole unlikely experience.

As he passed by the capitol building, he thought about the famous faces he'd seen carved into the sandstone inside.

Then it dawned on him.

He'd been dining with Walt Whitman.

Chapter Twenty-seven

May 1991

Nick should have known better than to try to squeeze in a breakfast meeting on a Saturday. He should have come home the night before. He should never have cut it so close.

Severe storms in New York kept every plane grounded at La-Guardia.

He booked the next available flight. But it was too late.

He landed at O'Hare as Ashley was receiving her First Communion.

Chapter Twenty-eight

Nick woke up early. He was hungry, as usual. But for once, he decided he would exercise before breakfast.

He'd walked more in the past few days than he had in years. His legs were sore. It was the type of muscle soreness he hadn't felt in a long time. It felt good.

In high school, Nick played baseball, football and basketball. He liked all three, especially baseball. But he really loved running. He wasn't fast, and he couldn't run far — two miles tops. He thought about joining the track team but knew he couldn't compete. So he ran alone.

He kept running in college and even after he started working. But then he got busy, and he ran only on weekends. That's when he began to gain weight. When he hit thirty, his knees began to hurt, and he stopped running altogether.

His weight ballooned. In college, he weighed about 190. Now he was pushing 270. His doctor had told him he was obese and that he needed to lose at least fifty pounds. Nick stopped seeing him.

But he knew his doctor was right. And now, on sabbatical, with time for himself, Nick had no excuses not to exercise.

Except one. If he was going to end his life in Bar Harbor, what was the point of doing anything to improve his health now?

But what if he wasn't able to go through with it? He might as well make an effort to get a little healthier, just in case.

He was certainly in no condition to run. But he knew he could walk. So he put on his tennis shoes, shorts and a T-shirt and went down to the hotel fitness center to walk on the treadmill before breakfast.

He walked for only ten minutes at three miles per hour. But that was ten more minutes than he'd spent on a treadmill in twenty years. It was a start.

He spotted an exercise mat rolled up in the corner and thought about doing some sit-ups. He grabbed the mat and unrolled it. He knelt down, leaned back and, with some straining and grunting, managed to do five sit-ups. Nothing to brag about. But again, it was a start.

He wasn't sweating enough to need a shower before breakfast. So he walked down to the dining area off the lobby.

Nick knew that if he really wanted to lose weight, exercise alone wasn't going to cut it. He'd also need to change his diet. He scanned the breakfast buffet. At one end were cereal, yogurt and fruit. At the other, bacon, eggs and pancakes. His stomach growled. It wasn't even close. He'd start his diet tomorrow.

He loaded up his plate and opened his laptop. The next big city was Boston, two and a half hours away. At last, a city he was familiar with.

He loved Fenway Park and wondered if the Red Sox were in town. Click. Jackpot! They were playing Detroit at Fenway at 1:35 that afternoon. He bought a ticket online, then booked a room at the Park Plaza downtown for only ninety bucks. He wondered if travel agents got such good deals.

Nick glanced at the buffet and thought about Paul. He wondered where he'd slept last night and if he would have anything to eat this morning.

#

As Nick pulled out of Albany, he noticed all the maple trees along the highway. There were lots of other hardwood trees and evergreens, too. But maples predominated.

For a while, they held his interest. But then they all began to blend together. They became seamless, like an endless cloak over the gently rolling hills.

By the time Nick reached the Massachusetts state line, he no longer even saw the maples. They had become merely a backdrop against which his eyes picked out occasional hemlocks, birches and spruces.

When Nick was a child, a single maple leaf was a thing of wonder. Now whole forests of maples had become invisible to him.

#

What day is this, he wondered. He was losing track of time. He played the days of his trip back in his head and realized it was Friday. It had been nearly a week since his meeting with Lou.

He thought about what Paul had told him about being let go. He thought about his own rough meeting with Phil early in his career.

That day back in 1981, it was clear to Nick that Phil disliked him. But in the months and years after, he had been surprised to discover that Phil was actually working behind the scenes to stunt his career, whispering to his peers that Nick was not a guy they really wanted on their teams.

But unlike Paul, Nick's spirit remained unbroken. After Phil told him to consult with HR to find a new job, he did. He wasn't happy about it, but he kept going. He took one less desirable job after another at Elgin and toiled away at them for longer than he wanted. But he tackled his assignments with vigor. He did good work, and people noticed. Then he got that shot at managing the Long Star Cakes acquisition, and he had handled it masterfully. That really put him on the map. After that, he was seen as a rising star in the company.

What Nick never knew, though, was that he hadn't done it alone. He had had quiet advocates, people like Lou Bradford and Jim Edwards. Not that they carried him. But they'd kept an eye on him. They had his back and made sure he didn't fall through the cracks.

That was a role Nick had never learned to play or even fully appreciate. He still felt that people like Lou and Jennifer were too soft.

But he also knew that Lou had every right to let him go, and didn't. He wondered where he'd be right now if, last Friday, Lou had made a different choice.

Chapter Twenty-nine

July 1996

"You boys ready for your big game?" Jean asked, as she stepped into the family room.

"Ready for action," Nick answered.

Josh said nothing. He was watching a soccer match on ESPN.

"Ready to roll, big guy?" Nick asked.

"I guess," said the boy, looking indifferent. "I'll be in the car."

And with that, he clicked off the TV, slid the remote on to the coffee table, grabbed his Game Boy and headed to the garage.

"You know, you'll never get that out of his hands," Jean said.

"What?"

"That Game Boy."

"Well, boys are into video games these days."

"He's addicted."

"Oh, come on, Jean. He's not addicted."

"Have you seen him put it down since Christmas?"

Nick had no comeback.

"I rest my case."

When Ashley was born, Jean shifted from teaching grade school full-time to filling in as a substitute when needed. This gave her much more time for the kids. She got to watch them grow up. Unlike Nick, she saw them every day. Unlike Nick, she knew what their kids liked and disliked. And she knew that when it came to things like Game Boy and baseball, Nick didn't have a clue.

"He'll forget all about that stupid game when he gets inside the ballpark," Nick said.

"How much do you want to bet?" Jean challenged.

"Give me a break. The Cubs versus the Cards on a Saturday afternoon in July. What's not to like?"

"I know that sounds like a great afternoon to you, Nick. But have you noticed that Josh really isn't into baseball?"

"Not into baseball? How could a ten-year-old boy not be into baseball? He watches ESPN non-stop."

"Yeah, but he watches soccer."

"Soccer?"

"Yeah, Nick. You know, the sport he plays."

"It's a fad."

"Nick, Josh has been playing soccer since he was five."

"I know. But that's not a real sport."

"Have you ever played catch with him in the back yard?"

"No. But I've tried."

"And why do you think he's said no?"

"I don't know."

"Nick, I'm trying to tell you that Josh just isn't into baseball. He's not you."

"Well, thank God for that, huh?"

"You know what I mean. He has different interests."

"I think he'll get interested in baseball in a hurry when he sees Sammy Sosa smack one out of the park."

"Nick, I'm sorry to tell you this. But Josh probably doesn't even know who Sammy Sosa is."

"All right, Jean," Nick said, standing up and twisting his Cubs hat onto his big head. "We'll see how many baseball fans there are in this house by the end of the day."

"Have fun, Nick."

"We will."

#

As they walked into Wrigley, Nick remembered his first time there, when he was seventeen. Bill "Mad Dog" Madlock was the Cubs' star that year. Madlock had a hot bat and an even hotter temper. Fans never knew when Mad Dog might start fighting with the ump or even charge the mound.

Nick thought about mentioning Mad Dog to Josh. But he figured if he really didn't know who Sammy Sosa was, he wouldn't have a clue about Mad Dog.

"Want a hot dog?" Nick asked.

"No."

"Hamburger?"

"No."

"Peanuts?"

"No."

"Popcorn?"

"Nope."

"Anything at all?"

"Well, I could go for some nachos."

"Nachos?"

"Yeah."

Holy crap, Nick thought. Who is this kid? All that soccer's warped his brain.

#

When they got to their seats, the Cubs were still taking batting practice.

"When does the game start?" Josh asked.

"One twenty."

"What time is it?"

"Just before noon. Why? Do you need to be somewhere?"

"No," said the boy, not catching Nick's sarcasm, as he dipped a nacho into hot, gooey cheese and pulled out his Game Boy.

#

"So how was it?" Jean asked, as Nick and Josh walked into the family room from the garage.

"Fine," Josh said, shrugging his shoulders. He walked by his mother and disappeared up the stairs.

Nick trudged over to his recliner, took off his hat and plopped down. He looked worn out.

"So, how did it go?" Jean asked.

Nick shook his head and made a tight-lipped smile.

"You were right. He hated it."

"Hated it?"

"Yeah, and now he hates me."

"Oh, Nick!"

"It's true."

"Why would you say that?"

"He kept playing that damn Game Boy. About the third inning, I made him put it away. That pissed him off. He didn't talk to me for the rest of the game or the whole way home."

"I'm sorry, Nick."

"Well, I'm sorry too, Jean. I'm sorry I took him to the game."

"You shouldn't be sorry about that. You love baseball. There's nothing wrong with wanting to share that with your son."

Nick looked sad, as if he could cry.

"Oh, Nick," Jean frowned.

She got up, walked over to him and took his left hand in both of hers.

"What's wrong?"

"I just spent an entire afternoon with my son, and he hardly said a word to me."

"Oh, Nick. You know how ten year old boys can be."

"You think that's it?"

"Yes," she said, stepping back over to the sofa. "Yes, I do."

"Well, I think there's more to it."

"Like what?"

"I don't know. I just feel like there's no real connection between us."

"He'll outgrow it, Nick."

"I don't know, Jean. I never did with my father."

Nick thought of his father coming home when he was ten, fuming about the way he had tried to mow the lawn, how upset his father had been, and how things were never the same between them after that.

"That was different," said Jean.

"Not really," said Nick. "And I think that's what bothering me."

Chapter Thirty

Nick was an hour and a half outside of Albany, about halfway to Boston, when he saw a sign for the Botanic Garden of Smith College. It was about thirty minutes north, in Northampton.

Nick hadn't been to Smith College. But he was familiar with the garden there. He'd seen dozens of photographs of it in a coffee table book his mother used to read to him as a kid. It was called *New England's Glorious Gardens*.

The Botanic Garden of Smith College was one of his mother's favorites. She loved showing Nick the yellow lilies and lavender orchids being cultivated in the greenhouses, the purple irises and orange asters rimming the ponds, and the blue phlox and white alyssum bordering the winding rock paths.

Through books like this, and by working with him in the yard, Nick's mother taught Nick so much about flowers. She taught him their names. She taught him when and where they should be planted. She taught him which types of flowers would look good where, how to arrange them by size, color and texture, how to create a landscape.

Nick loved learning about flowers. He loved designing new flower beds. He loved helping his mother build stone walls and create river rock paths. He loved seeing the bulbs he planted in the fall sprout and blossom in the spring.

But what he loved most was being in touch with the earth. There was something about digging in the soil that made Nick feel alive. He spent hours in the yard. It was hard work. But it filled him up.

As he approached the exit for Smith College, Nick was tempted to pull off and spend the afternoon touring the gardens there. But then he remembered he'd bought a ticket for the Red Sox game that afternoon. So he decided to keep going.

But Nick now had flowers on his mind. For some reason, he thought of the flowers he'd planted thirty years before, when he and Jean moved into their first house, in Buffalo Grove, north of Chicago.

The house was old and small, and the yard was tiny. But Nick was thrilled to have a yard and, at last, some grass to cut.

Nick and Jean worked together to get the yard in shape. They trimmed trees, reshaped mulch beds, planted new shrubs, created stone pathways — and planted dozens of different types of flowers.

When it came to yard work, in that first house, Nick and Jean did everything together.

"This is our yard," Nick said when they moved in. "It belongs to both of us."

A few years later, Nick and Jean had two small children, and they needed a larger house. Fortunately, Nick had finally gotten a promotion, and they could afford to upgrade. They bought a three-bedroom split level in Elmhurst.

At first, Nick and Jean again tackled the yard work together. But as Nick spent more time at Elgin and Jean spent more time with the kids, they had less and less time for the yard.

So Nick hired a neighbor kid to cut his grass, and he began to let the flowers go. They took too much time.

Four years and two promotions later, Nick and Jean decided to buy their dream house in Winnetka, on the North Shore. They bought a four-bedroom place on a two-acre, wooded lot.

The yard was in pristine condition. Nick was now working eighty-hour weeks and traveling a ton. He knew he'd have no time for yard work. As soon as they moved in, he asked Jean to hire a lawn service.

And so Nick passed the exit for Smith College and kept driving toward Boston.

It's probably just as well, he thought. Touring that garden might only have reminded him that he'd lost touch with the earth and the work that had once filled him up.

Chapter Thirty-one

December 1997

It was Friday afternoon, just a short week before Christmas. Everyone in the office was in a holiday mood and hoping to go home early.

Nick wasn't sure what to make of his secretary telling him that Lou Bradford wanted to see him.

"What does he want?"

"I don't know," Pam said. "Helen didn't say."

"Crap. That can't be good."

Grabbing his suit coat, Nick said, "Why don't you go home early, Pam? I might be a while."

"Thank you, Mr. Reynolds. Have a good weekend."

#

"Go right in, Mr. Reynolds," Helen said. She didn't look happy. A day like any other.

"Come in, Nick," Bradford said, sitting behind his desk. "Please close the door. Have a seat."

"How are you, Lou?"

"I'm doing great, Nick. In fact, really great."

"Oh, yeah?"

"Yeah. I've just approved this news release, which we're going to issue on Monday."

"Good news?"

"I think so. Here," he said, handing Nick a sheet of paper on Elgin letterhead. "Read it for yourself."

Elgin Foods announced today it has appointed Nicholas G. Reynolds to the newly established position of Vice President-North America. Mr. Reynolds will have responsibility for all of the company's business operations in the United States and Canada. The move will be effective January 1, 1998.

It went on, but Nick had read enough.

"Lou!"

"Congratulations, Nick."

Lou stood up and walked around his desk. He gave Nick a firm handshake, clasping his right hand with both of his.

"You are so deserving of this."

"Thank you, Lou. I could not be more pleased."

"Well," Lou smiled, "you might be when I go over your new salary information."

Lou sat back down. He slipped on his reading glasses, opened a folder and pulled out a sheet of paper.

"You know the drill," he said, peaking over his glasses. "I can't give you this quite yet. But let me read you a few numbers. Do you have a pen handy?"

Lou relished moments like this. As good as he was with the business, he was even better with people. He loved motivating his employees. And today Nick was feeling very motivated.

After he shared the key numbers, Lou told Nick a few things about the new job. It was all so exciting. But Nick was particularly happy to learn he would continue reporting to Lou.

"I know it's Friday, and everybody's eager to get out of here," Lou said. "But would you have a few extra minutes?"

"Sure."

"Great. I'd like you to talk with Jim."

"Jim?"

"Yeah. Jim Edwards."

"Sure. Right now?"

"Yeah."

Nick smiled. Lou was so damn good at this.

"I've got to tell you, Lou," Nick said as he got up. "There was a long time when I wasn't sure this would happen."

"You had a slow start, Nick. That's all. Lots of people start slowly. The important thing is that you hung in there."

"I appreciate all you've done for me, Lou."

"You've made your own breaks, Nick. Have a good talk with Jim. Enjoy your weekend."

#

At that point, Nick had been to the CEO's office only a few times, mainly to negotiate budgets. He suspected this time would be a lot more pleasant.

"Go right in, Mr. Reynolds," Jim Edwards' secretary Phyllis said. She was smiling.

Everybody seems to know everything up here, he thought.

"Come in, Nick," Edwards said. "I understand Lou has just shared our good news."

"Yes. I'm thrilled."

"I am too, Nick," he said, extending his hand across his desk. "Congratulations. I know you'll do a great job leading our North American businesses."

"Thank you, Mr. Edwards. I know the bar is high. I won't let you down."

"I know you won't. Have a seat, Nick."

Nick had a feeling the old man was about to impart some words of wisdom.

"I have no doubt that, in this new role, your business results will be impressive, just as they have been for years. Our North American business could not be in better hands."

"Thank you, Mr. Edwards."

"I would only ask that you take good care of your organization too. It's important to take care of the people who deliver your numbers."

"I'll do my best, sir."

"You're going to have a much larger organization than you've ever had. Get to know your people, Nick. Make sure you know who your stars are and keep them growing. Don't hesitate to get rid of poor performers. And keep watch for people who have a lot of potential but might need more time, and help, to grow. Be their advocate. Don't lose sight of them. In time, they could be your most important players."

"Yes, sir. That's very good advice."

Edwards smiled.

"Do you remember the first time we met, Nick?"

"I'll never forget it. It was in a meeting to present our plan for that bakery-first idea."

"It was a bad idea."

"Yeah, it was."

"And you said so in the meeting."

"Yes, I did."

"You were the only one. I knew that day you had a lot of potential, and I've never lost sight of you."

"Thank you, Mr. Edwards."

"You're welcome, Nick. And please call me Jim."

"Thanks, Jim."

#

Nick's announcement was made the following Monday. On Tuesday, he called together his new leadership team. He shared his expectations and went over the key financials for every business in North America.

On Wednesday, the last day in the office before the holiday break, Nick called Phil, his first manager with Elgin, to his office.

Phil's career had plateaued, even as Nick's had taken off. After Nick's first assignment, nearly eighteen years ago, they'd almost always worked in different parts of the business. Now, though, everyone working in North America would be reporting to Nick, directly or indirectly. That included Phil.

"You wanted to see me, Nick?" Phil said, standing in his doorway.

"Come in, Phil. Sit down."

"Congratulations, Nick."

"Thanks. You know I don't officially begin my new job until January. But Jim Edwards has suggested that I make getting my organization right my first order of business."

"That sounds like a good idea."

"I think so. Phil, you've been in the candy business a long time. Based on the numbers I just reviewed, that business has lost a lot of money over the past few years. I think we're going to need to make some changes."

Phil shifted uneasily in his chair.

"What do you have in mind?"

"I think you need to either find something else in the company or move on."

Phil seemed shocked.

"Are you letting me go?"

"No, Phil. I'm sure you've got skills and experience we can use somewhere. I just don't think you'll make a good fit on my team. So I suggest you talk with HR. I'm sure they'll find something for you, maybe in corporate."

"Nick, can't we talk about this?"

"There's nothing more to talk about, Phil. Now get out of my office."

Chapter Thirty-two

Nick arrived at the Boston Park Plaza just before 12:30. He decided to valet park, check in, leave his bag at the front desk and take a cab to Fenway so he could make the first pitch.

As he was passing through Gate B, he glanced at his watch. It was just after one. If he moved fast, he could still grab a hot dog and a beer and get to his seat before the national anthem.

"Sorry 'bout yer luck, buddy," said the guy working the concession stand. He had a thick Boston accent.

"Pardon me?"

"The Cubs," he grinned. "Maybe next year."

Nick had forgotten he was wearing his hat.

He was glad he was. It was sunny and hot, and his seat was in right field.

But then he thought about his arms, his legs and his neck. His skin was no longer pink from his sunburn at the Cleveland game. But it was still sensitive.

He decided to duck into a Red Sox gift shop and see if they sold sunscreen. Fortunately, they had a few tubes at the checkout.

Nick bought one. He stepped over to the T-shirt section, set his beer and hot dog down on the floor and slathered sunscreen all over his exposed skin. A young mother, who had been shopping for T-shirts with her two kids, looked a little freaked out. She grabbed her children and took off.

Nick didn't mind. But he felt funny taking care of himself. He wondered what Jean would think. First walking on the treadmill and now protecting his skin. What's next? Watercress and carrot juice?

Shuddering at the notion, Nick grabbed his hot dog and beer and headed to his seat.

Today his section was nearly empty. He got to his seat just in time for the national anthem.

This time, though, Nick stood up. Not only that, he took off his hat and held it over his heart.

He remembered going with his father to watch the Cedar Rapids Cardinals, a Class A minor league team, play in Veterans Memorial Stadium as a kid. Nick was wearing a Cardinals cap. His father insisted he take it off and place it over his heart during the national anthem.

Nick was amused as his father, who seemed to shun protocol, stood at attention, snapped his right hand to his forehead, stared out at the flag and sang the anthem loudly.

Later he learned his father had served in Korea. He never talked about it, and Nick never knew the details. All he knew was, that during the national anthem, his father changed.

Nick never served in the military. He grew up during the Vietnam War. But it ended when he was only fourteen. All his friends were against the war, even though they didn't know much about it. And Nick couldn't care less about politics.

But it didn't stop him from spouting off and repeating slogans he had heard at school. Once at dinner, he called American soldiers "baby killers." His father exploded.

"Nick! If I ever hear you say anything like that again, I'll throw you out of my house, and you'll be sleeping on the street!"

His father didn't speak to him again for weeks. This is how he dealt with conflict.

Nick learned a lot from watching his father.

#

By the third inning, Nick's section was filling up. Nick was still sipping on his first beer. He made a bet with himself that he wouldn't drink more than two beers the whole game. He wasn't exactly sure why. But a fleeting memory of his drunken episode in the hotel lobby in Cleveland made him feel a rare modicum of restraint.

A couple of young guys, probably in their twenties, were sitting a few seats away, near the end of the aisle, one row below Nick.

Nick noticed them because they were so loud, yelling at Tigers players, cussing at the ump, even giving the Sox hell. They kept getting up to buy beer. Nick could tell they were loaded.

An older couple was sitting in front of them. The woman was wearing a straw hat with a wide brim. Around the fifth inning, the bad boys decided to start dropping their peanut shells into the brim of the woman's hat. Neither she nor her husband noticed. This only made the bad boys laugh harder.

At the seventh inning stretch, the older couple got up. As the woman leaned forward, peanut shells cascaded over the brim of her hat and fell all over her dress. She screamed, not realizing what was happening. The bad boys roared and gave each other high fives, laughing so hard that they spit out their beer.

When his wife screamed, her husband reflexively put his arm around her. Then he realized she was okay, just covered in peanut shells.

"It's okay, dear," he assured her. "You're okay."

He took off her hat, turned it upside down and shook out the remaining shells. She brushed off her dress. Her husband brushed off her seat. The two of them sat back down.

The bad boys were still chuckling.

The old man turned around and looked up.

"Did you guys do that?"

"Yeah, man. Just a little clean fun."

"Well, I don't think it's very funny. You scared my wife to death. I think you owe her an apology."

"Get over it, man."

"Yeah, man. It was just a joke."

"I don't think you boys heard what the gentlemen said," Nick said in a booming voice. He was standing behind the bad boys with his arms crossed. "Now apologize to this nice lady."

They turned around in their seats and looked up.

"Who are you?" one of them sneered.

"Son, I don't think you really want to find out. Now apologize. Then either get your act together or get the hell out of here."

"Says who?"

Nick stepped the rest of the way along his aisle and took a step down. He was now standing right next to the bad boys, staring down at them. He looked like Andre the Giant in a Cubs hat.

"Now!" he growled.

"Okay," said the one on the end. He leaned forward and said, "I'm sorry."

"And you?"

The other one murmured, "I'm sorry."

"What was that?" Nick asked, leaning in.

"I'm sorry!"

"Now I think you boys have a decision to make."

They grabbed their beers and stood up.

"We were just leaving."

They skedaddled down the steps, spilling beer on themselves on the way. When they got to the bottom, they turned and looked up. One of them made a face and gave Nick the finger.

Nick grabbed the handrail and lurched forward. But they both scrammed.

"Thank you," said the man, looking up at Nick and extending his hand.

"You're welcome, sir," said Nick, shaking it.

"Yes, thank you, young man," said the woman.

"You're welcome, ma'am. Enjoy the rest of the game."

Nick went back to his seat and sat down. Having someone's back was a role he was not used to playing.

It reminded him of giving the Straus kid what he had coming to him. It felt good.

The Sox won, 7-3. Nick sat through the whole game and slowly made his way to the exit with the crowd. He had only had one beer. Like having someone's back, it made him feel good.

#

"Where to, boss?" asked the cabbie.

"Cheers," Nick said.

They arrived from the ballpark in less than ten minutes. It looked exactly like the bar in the old TV show, including the iconic sign with "Cheers" in fancy script above "EST. 1895" and an old-fashioned hand with a finger pointing downward.

Nick walked down the stairs. He opened the door, half expecting to see Sam and Woody behind the bar and Karla waiting tables. But the place looked nothing like the bar in the TV show. It was much smaller. Still, it was warm and inviting.

"Welcome to Cheers," said the hostess. "Just one?"

"Yes."

"For dinner?"

"Yes. Would it be possible to eat at the bar?"

"Of course."

Norm had been Nick's favorite character on the show. He bellied up to the bar, just like he'd seen Norm do dozens of times. The hostess followed him and handed him a menu.

"Enjoy your dinner."

"Thank you."

"What'll you have?" asked the bartender. He looked a little like Cliff, but nothing like Sam or Woody.

"Sam Adams."

When in Boston, Nick thought.

"Pint?"

"Why not?"

Nick glanced at the menu. Holy crap, he thought. The high price of fame.

The bartender drew his beer and sat it down on the bar. At least the big glass mug looked like Norm's.

"Dinner?"

"Yeah, I'll have a cheeseburger and fries, please."

For a moment, Nick thought about ordering something healthier. Instead, he decided he'd walk on the treadmill at his hotel for fifteen minutes in the morning. Besides, this was only his second beer today, and he'd already decided it would be his last.

Only two beers. Again, he wondered what Jean would think. She'd been trying to get him to cut back on his drinking for years. It had become a huge source of conflict in their relationship: both his heavy drinking itself and her nagging him about it.

Nick had never liked anyone telling him what to do. Jean knew this when she met him. Nick was a young man who knew what he wanted.

But if Nick knew what he wanted, he never gave much thought to what getting it would take. Nor did he ever imagine how achieving it would change him.

He'd become rich and powerful. But in the process, he'd become a beast.

Over the years, Jean had watched as the man she fell in love with changed into someone she sometimes barely recognized. He was no longer the man who wrote her poetry or the father who read bedtime stories to his children. That man was gone. In his place, there emerged a selfish, quick-tempered, insensitive, overweight, drunken brute.

For years, their children had created a sort of buffer between them. But when they left home, Jean saw nothing but Nick, and she didn't like what she saw.

One night in 2008, it all boiled over. Nick had driven home drunk.

"I've had it with you, Nick!" Jean screamed. "I don't even know who you are any more. You're sick. You need help. You really need help. You could've killed somebody tonight! But you don't care about that. All you care about is you. You're the center of your world. And you treat everyone else like crap. Well, I'm sick of it, Nick. I'm sick of being treated like crap and watching you destroy yourself."

Nick just stood there, in the family room, teetering. He wanted to sit down. But he knew if he did, Jean would just lay into him even more. He was so tired. He didn't feel like fighting. All he wanted to do was go to bed. He stumbled to the stairs and took the first step.

"Don't even think about sleeping in our bed tonight, Nick," Jean called after him. "I don't want to sleep with you any more."

And so that night, Nick slept in the guest room. And the next night. And the next.

Not only did Nick and Jean stop sleeping together, most days they barely spoke to one another. They were like planets in different orbits.

They remained married. Sometimes Nick thought it was a miracle that Jean didn't leave him.

But over time, as he ate his meals, watched TV and went to bed alone, he began to feel that Jean had left him.

#

Nick got no love at Elgin either.

There, he was increasingly known as a son of a bitch. It was a reputation that was well-deserved, and Nick was its primary architect.

For example, when someone in his organization screwed up, he used it as an opportunity to teach everyone a lesson.

Once one of his finance managers made an error in a monthly statement. When Nick found out about it, he called the manager and his whole team into his office. There, he lambasted the poor guy and fired him on the spot.

At a sales meeting for a major new snack cake initiative, Nick rode a small steamroller, the size of a riding lawnmower, onto the stage in the ballroom. He was wearing a hard hat. People were looking around, wondering what was going on. Nick was famous for his stunts, but they'd never seen one quite like this. When Nick got to the center of the stage, he got off and stepped over to the podium.

"What's our share in the U.S.?" he asked, leaning down to the microphone.

"Number one!" someone yelled.

"That's right," Nick said. "And do you know what being number one in a market entitles you to?"

Before anyone could respond, Nick raised his hands and said, "Hold on. Do we have any lawyers in the room?"

No hands went up.

"Good because I'm going to use the D-word. Being number one in a market entitles you to dominate it. Now there are a lot of opinions about what dominating a market really means. Let me show you what I believe it means."

Nick stepped back over to the steamroller and straddled it. A heavy metal song began blasting. Colored lights bounced off a disco ball hanging from the ceiling. Several young women in short, tight, sequined dresses brought out trays of competitors' snack cake products. They set them down on the stage. The audience sensed what was coming and began clapping to the beat of the music.

Nick threw the steamroller into gear and slowly drove it over the trays of products, smashing them into a giant pancake. Then he backed over them. He did this several times, back and forth, until the snack cakes became a slurry and he had literally crushed the competition.

Nick pumped his fists in the air. Everyone in the front few rows, the ones who knew Nick would do something outrageous and were good with that, went crazy. But most employees just stood there. They had grown weary of Nick's bizarre, immature, machismo antics and didn't want to encourage him. But in the glare of the footlights, Nick couldn't see those people.

When Nick said dominate, he meant it. When a leading European snack cake company announced it would be opening a test market in Peoria, Nick had his team flood the market with coupons, each of them good for one free Elgin snack cake. He did this for thirteen weeks in a row. By week fourteen, every man, woman and child in Peoria had enough coupons for free Elgin snack cakes for a year. The European company's test never got off the ground. They packed up and went home.

Within Elgin, Nick wasn't known as tough. He was known as a bully. Nobody wanted to work for him. Turnover in his organization was twice that of any other business unit in the company.

But he consistently posted the company's best business results. And over time, senior management decided to give Nick a pass, to look the other way, to occasionally slap him on the wrist, even as he became, as Lou had said, "a human wrecking ball."

This was Nick's persona. After years of working so hard to create such a reputation, how could he now not live up to it? After all this time, how could he possibly change?

#

Nick took the last sip of his beer and settled up.

"Can I call you a cab, buddy?"

"How far is the Park Plaza hotel from here?"

"Less than a mile."

"No, thanks. I'll walk."

Again, he wondered what Jean would think.

Nick looked around one last time. The inside of this place really did bear little resemblance to the bar in the TV show. And yet the outside was the real thing.

How much better it would be if the inside and the outside matched, Nick thought.

#

The sun was beginning to set, and the air was getting cool. Nick slipped his jacket on and began walking.

He walked through Boston Common, a 50-acre park in the center of downtown. He'd driven past it on business trips but never been inside.

Paved paths wove through grassy stretches painted with flowers and dotted with statues. Nick was surprised to see so many different types of trees: maples, crab apples, cherries, lilacs, honey locusts, river birches, chestnuts, sweet gums, oaks, elms and weeping willows. He remembered these trees from his childhood. He'd seen many of them around Cedar Lake.

Nick had always been drawn to the water. Now he walked past a small lake, its edges rimmed with a ribbon of concrete. He sat down on a bench, under a weeping willow.

A week ago, he'd been sitting in Lou's office. Before that meeting, he would never have imagined he'd now be sitting on a park bench in Boston.

He remembered how angry he felt that night, how he'd driven home drunk and thrown up. He remembered avoiding Jean at Parker's the next evening and not telling her goodbye before he left in the morning. He remembered harassing the waitress at the Over Easy and yelling at that little girl in the hotel lobby in Cleveland.

What the hell had become of him?

No wonder Jean hated him.

No wonder he hated himself.

"Sort yourself out," Lou had said.

He wanted to do that. But how? Where would he begin? And was it too late? Was it even worth trying?

Maybe Jean was right. Maybe this was all a ploy to get Nick to retire. Maybe he was done.

Chapter Thirty-three

June 2000

"Come on, Dad," said Ashley, standing in the doorway of Nick's den. "I only need five more hours of driving practice, and you haven't taken me out once."

"I'm in the middle of a big project right now, sweetie," Nick said, staring at his computer monitor. "Can't your mother take you out this afternoon?"

"She's gone, Dad. Remember? She'll be gone all afternoon. Just one hour. Can't you take a break for just an hour?"

Nick really was in the middle of a big project. But it wasn't urgent. The truth was he had been avoiding taking Ashley out to practice driving because he didn't think he could take it. Just the other day, Jean had told him Ashley had run into their mailbox. Nick knew he had a short fuse these days, and he didn't want to risk blowing up at his daughter.

"How about tomorrow? Can't Mom take you out tomorrow?"

"I'll be gone tomorrow, Dad. Please?"

Nick looked up at Ashley. At sixteen, she was looking grown-up. She had Jean's lean, athletic build, pretty face and blond hair. But she had Nick's height. She was nearly six feet tall, taller than any of the other sophomore girls and half the sophomore boys. But it didn't seem to bother Ashley.

And it certainly didn't stop boys from asking her out. The

very idea of his daughter dating was still a source of anxiety for Nick, even though he'd grudgingly agreed she could date when she turned fifteen. He had been holding out for eighteen, but Jean and Ashley wore him down.

Nick knew that Ashley would get her driver's license soon, with or without his help. He saw his daughter so little these days, and he knew that once she began driving, he would see her even less. He looked at her and thought of all the things he'd missed when she was growing up and felt guilty as hell.

"All right," he said. "Give me an hour. I'll take you out then."

"Yes!" she shouted, pumping her fists in the air. "Thank you, Daddy! I'll see you downstairs in an hour."

Then she was gone.

Daddy? She hadn't called Nick Daddy in a long time. He wished she was a little girl again. He wished he could do it over again.

#

Ashley was waiting by the door to the garage when Nick got downstairs.

"Ready?" she asked with a smile.

"Yep. Let's go."

"Can I have your keys?"

Nick reached into his pocket, pulled out the keys to his Mercedes and handed them to Ashley. He was starting to feel anxious already.

As he sat down in the front passenger's seat, Nick realized he'd never sat anywhere in his car except the driver's seat. It felt strange and only added to his unease.

Nick stiffened in his seat as he watched his daughter back out of the garage. Her rearview mirror seemed to just miss the frame of the garage. She started backing down the driveway fast.

"Easy," Nick said. He couldn't resist.

Ashley slammed on the brake.

"What?" she asked.

"Huh?"

"Why did you say 'easy'"?

"I thought you were going a little fast. There's a slight curve at the end of the driveway, you know."

"I know, Dad. I've lived here a long time."

She sighed loudly.

"Is this how you're going to be the whole time? Because if it is ..."

Jesus, Nick thought. She sounds just like Jean.

"No," he answered. "I'll try keep quiet."

"Thank you," she said, taking her foot off the brake and backing down the driveway.

Halfway down the street, Ashley slammed her brake on again.

"Dad! I thought you said you were going to behave!"

"What?" he asked, acting hurt. "I didn't say a word."

"Why are you pumping your foot on the floor? There's no brake over there."

"Sorry," he answered sheepishly. "I'll stop."

As Ashley drove through the streets of Winnetka, narrowly missing parked cars and almost running a red light, miraculously, Nick held his tongue and kept his feet still. But he began sweating and digging his fingernails into his armrest. When Ashley cut a corner a little close, Nick let out a muffled grunt, which he assumed Ashley heard but chose to allow.

But when she announced that she was going to "get a little highway driving in," Nick couldn't stand it any longer.

"Highway driving?" he blurted out. "Ashley, you've got to be kidding! You're not ready to drive on the highway."

"Guess what, Dad? I already have. And I'm going to do it again!"

"Not in my car, you're not! Now, Ashley, let's stay here in town."

"Oh, Dad!" she exclaimed. Then she pulled over to the curb, slammed on the brake and burst into tears. "See? That's why I never go driving with you! I knew you'd be this way. Mom said you'd be this way. I thought I'd give you a chance, but I was wrong. I was wrong," she sobbed, pressing her forehead against her hands on the steering wheel.

Nick felt terrible. His daughter asks to practice driving with him for one hour, and he brings her to tears? What kind of father was he?

"Ashley, sweetie, I'm sorry. Yes, you can get a little highway driving in. Let's go down ninety-four for a couple of exits. I just don't want you to go all the way to the city because it can be such a mess."

"Thanks, Dad," she said, sniffling.

Nick looked over at her. She was wiping her eyes with the back of her hand, but he didn't see any tears. And she was smiling. As she put the car in gear and headed toward the highway, Nick realized he'd been played.

#

By one exit down I-94, Nick was pumping the floor almost constantly with his foot. He told Ashley to stop following other cars so close. And he insisted she stay in the right lane.

"How am I ever going to get any experience passing anyone if I stay in the right lane?" she huffed.

"With your mother," he shot back.

By the time they got off the highway at the second exit to turn around, Nick told Ashley he thought it was time he took over.

"Oh no, you don't!" she said, punching it on the bridge over the highway and taking a hard left turn onto the northern entrance ramp.

"Hey, young lady!" Nick barked, as Ashley pulled back out onto the highway, crossing over into the middle, then the left, lane. "I said stay in the right lane!"

"Dad, be quiet!" Ashley snapped. "I'll have us home in ten minutes. Then you'll never have to do this again."

Nick couldn't believe this was happening. So much for his sweet, little daughter. And so much for thinking he could still tell her what to do. And in his car. In his car!

"Watch out!" Nick cried as another driver began to pull into the left lane in front of Ashley.

She slowed down and laid on the horn, and the other guy got back in his lane.

"I saw the whole thing, Dad," she said calmly. "That guy's an idiot. Good thing I've got skills. Good thing you're with me."

Fifteen minutes later, Ashley was pulling into their driveway. Pulling into the garage, she went a little too far and lightly bumped Nick's bicycle, which he hadn't ridden in about ten years, causing it to fall over.

"Sorry, Dad."

Before Nick could say anything, Ashley turned off the car, pulled out his keys and dropped them into his left hand.

"Thanks, Daddy," she said, patting his arm. "That was fun."

Then she got out and disappeared into the house. Nick couldn't move. He sat there, shaking, sweating and wondering what had just happened. For the past hour, he, a man who commanded thousands of people every day, had just given up total control to a sixteen-year-old. And not just any sixteen-year-old. Someone he thought he knew.

Where did she learn to manipulate people like that? When did she become so arrogant? When did she stop listening to me? How did she become so headstrong?

Finally, Nick extricated himself from his car. Standing up, he felt a bit dizzy. Slowly, he made his way into the house. He went into the kitchen, poured himself a glass of bourbon and wondered again what had happened to his little girl.

Chapter Thirty-four

Nick woke up early. Having only two beers the entire day before made for a very light sedative, and he wasn't hung over. Feels good, he thought. I could get used to this.

Nick remembered his pledge to himself to walk fifteen minutes on the treadmill this morning. He got dressed and headed to the Park Plaza's fitness center.

It was unlike any fitness center he'd ever seen. For starters, it bore a person's name. It was called the David Barton Gym.

It was cavernous, with an impressive array of weights and exercise equipment in both contemporary and art deco styles, including stationary bikes that looked like 1940s motorcycles. Colorful lights, up-tempo music, celebrity posters and even an upscale lounge gave it a nightclub feel. It didn't make Nick feel any fitter. But it sure made him feel a lot hipper.

A dozen or so people were working out. Some were running on treadmills or pedaling the motorbikes. Some were using the nautilus machines. Some were lying on mats, doing what he assumed were Pilates. All were young women wearing spandex. Naturally, Nick was convinced they were all watching him.

After walking fifteen minutes on the treadmill, Nick was feeling so good and enjoying the scenery so much that he decided to walk another fifteen. It was his longest workout in years.

Still convinced the ladies were eyeballing him, he strutted over to one of the nautilus machines and did a few bench presses.

He hoped no one noticed that he was lifting only twenty-five pounds.

He thought about attempting a few sit-ups. But he was afraid that after all his walking and lifting, if he got down, he might not be able to get back up. So he decided to take off.

On his way out, he made a complete sweep of the place, sucking in his gut and saying goodbye to every woman who would make eye contact.

He went up to his room. He shaved and showered. Then he came back down to the hotel restaurant, called Off the Common, for breakfast.

He chose the buffet. Feeling a little healthier because of his workout, he bypassed the eggs, bacon and pastries and opted for raisin bran, Greek yogurt and fresh fruit. He even had green tea instead of coffee. Once again, he wondered what Jean would think.

He opened his laptop. He wondered how far it was to Bar Harbor and whether he could make it in a day. He learned it was still nearly three hundred miles away, much farther than he wanted to drive today.

What was in the middle? Portland, Maine. He decided that would be his next stop.

On the map he noticed that, from now on, he would be traveling along the water. As he scanned the coastline, his eye caught a sprinkling of islands off the coast of Portland. He made a mental note.

He was surprised to see so many kids in the restaurant this morning. Then he remembered it was Saturday.

He watched a family of four at the next table. The little boy and little girl were coloring on paper placemats.

Their mother was paying close attention to them. She was coloring with them, handing them crayons and telling them what a good job they were doing.

Their father was typing on his iPhone with his head down. His wife said something to him, but he didn't respond. He seemed to be in a world of his own.

Color with your kids, Nick thought. Talk to your wife.

Chapter Thirty-five

May 2006

Nick was in the middle of an annual review of his business in developing markets. He had a tension headache, brought on by his frustration with the numbers he had just been presented.

Developing markets made up only about a quarter of Elgin's snack cakes business globally. But sales and profits in these lower-income markets were now off for two years in a row, and this was creating a drag on the growth of Nick's business overall. He knew that if his results in developing markets didn't improve soon, his status as the leading business in the company would be at risk, and that was a prospect Nick was not willing to accept.

"I thought you said we'd be seeing real improvement by now," he said to Amit, his vice president for developing markets.

"We thought that would indeed be the case," said Amit. "But we were counting on stronger income growth and a larger consumer base in the BRIC countries."

"So, Amit," Nick said, sitting back in his chair, his head pounding, "you're telling me that your numbers are low because of slower-than-expected income growth rates in markets like China?"

"That's right."

"Amit," Nick said, rubbing his temples, "what was income growth in China last year?"

"The whole country?"

"Yes."

"On average, about two percent."

"Now what was the income growth in Beijing?"

"Beijing?"

"Yes, you know, the capital of China."

"I'd need to look that up, Nick."

"Go ahead. I've got time."

Amit reached for one of several binders he'd brought to the meeting and slipped on his reading glasses. He flipped through the tabs until he found the section he was after and ran his index finger down the page.

"Eight percent," he said.

"Eight percent," said Nick. "So income in Beijing is growing four times faster than in China overall?"

"That's right."

"So I assume your marketing spending in Beijing is four times greater than it is in most of China?"

"No," Amit said. "It's not."

"It's not?"

"No, it's consistent with what we're spending in the rest of China."

"Amit," Nick said, leaning forward and putting his palms down on the conference table, "a few minutes ago, I was beginning to conclude it was time to begin cutting our investments in developing markets and increasing them in developed markets in order to deliver the sales and profit growth we all know the company is expecting of us. But based on this conversation, I realize that would have been a mistake. Do you know why?"

"No, I don't."

"Because," Nick said, his eyes narrowing, "we'd lose customers in Beijing and Bangalore and Moscow and Sao Paulo, and our competitors would move in and we'd never get our customers back! Your numbers suck, Amit, not because of slower income growth in the BRIC countries but because you're spreading your investments across fifty countries like a baker spreading a paper-thin layer of icing on a sheet cake. Eight percent income growth? Our folks in Madrid and Frankfurt and right here in Chicago would kill for an opportunity like that. Now, I want to you to go away and rethink and recalibrate your marketing plan. I want you to step up your investment in the cities where you see the biggest growth and pull back everywhere else, at least for the next few years. I want you to deliver four percent sales growth and six percent profit growth next fiscal year. Not a penny less. And I want your recommendations in two weeks."

"Two weeks?"

"I've already given you a head start on China, Amit," Nick said, rubbing his temples again and looking pained. "Do you really need more time?"

"No, Nick. We'll be back to you in two weeks."

"Good. Meeting adjourned."

As Amit and his team were clearing out, Pam appeared at the conference room door. She looked serious.

"Hello, Pam," Nick said. "What is it?"

She made her way into the room, past the people filing out, and over to her boss.

"You have a phone call, Mr. Reynolds."

"Who is it?"

"It's your sister."

"My sister?"

"Yes."

"Did she say what it's about?"

"It's about your mother."

"My mother? Is everything all right?"

Pam looked somber.

"You need to talk with Susan, Mr. Reynolds."

#

Susan, who lived just three miles from Nick's mother in Cedar Rapids, told him she had died suddenly and unexpectedly of a massive heart attack early that afternoon. She had been waiting on a customer in the dress shop where she worked. She was only seventy.

Both of Elgin's corporate planes were away. So Nick had Pam book flights out of O'Hare for him and Jean for first thing in the morning. That way, Nick could get home and pack.

Ashley was a senior at Northwestern, just about to graduate. Josh was a sophomore at Stanford. Jean arranged flights to Cedar Rapids for both of them.

The visitation for his mother was held two evenings later at Westbrook Funeral Home, where his father's visitation had been thirty years before. His father's casket had been closed. His mother's was open. To Nick, she looked in death just as she had looked in life: lovely. Her hair, her skin, her dress, her jewelry — they were all perfect.

The funeral Mass was at St. Pius. Father Baker, the parish pastor, had asked Nick, David and Susan if they would like to say a few words. Susan, an introvert, and David, who tended to stutter when he got nervous, declined.

Nick considered it but ultimately he declined too. He knew there would be many people attending the funeral whom he had not seen in many years, friends of his parents, his relatives and even his own childhood friends. At work, he didn't think much about his appearance. Most of his employees had only known him as an overweight, balding, middle-aged man. Besides, he was the boss, and everyone deferred. But back in his home town, where many people had known him as a handsome young man, he had an image to uphold. He loved his mother. But he hated the idea of all those people staring at him in church.

So no one other than Father Baker spoke at the funeral. Fortunately, he had grown to know Nick's mother quite well over the years. She was an active member of the parish, including taking care of the flowers on the church grounds.

"Maureen was one of the most beautiful women I have ever known," he said in his sermon. "She was a beautiful person through and through. And everything she touched became more beautiful. We have to look no farther than the grounds of this church. Maureen envisioned, planted and took care of every flower that adorns this sacred space. She told me once that things of great beauty made her feel the presence of God. Well, today I think I can say with certainty that Maureen is with God, no doubt reveling in the beauty of his divine garden."

The burial was at St. Joseph's Cemetery. Her gravesite was next to his father's. Nick had not been there since his father was buried thirty years earlier.

After the ceremony, Nick told Jean and the kids to go on to the reception. Through an old friend who had stayed in Cedar Rapids, Nick had reserved a banquet room at Elmcrest Country Club. To his knowledge, his mother had never been there. But they had driven past it countless times when he was boy, and his mother always commented on the beauty of the flowers on the front lawn.

"I'll be along shortly," Nick told Jean and the kids, who secured rides to the reception with relatives.

When everyone had gone, Nick got into his mother's car and watched two workers take down the canopy over the casket and remove the chairs around it, then lower the casket into the ground and cover it with dirt, leaving a slightly raised bed of dirt over the grave.

Once the workers had gone, Nick got out of the car. He took off his suit coat and laid it on the back seat. Then he stepped around to the back of the car and opened the trunk. He reached in and pulled out a shallow cardboard box containing pots of daffodils, tulips, hyacinths and primrose. In the box were also a garden shovel and a pair of gloves. He had bought all of it at a nursery the afternoon before.

Nick closed the trunk and carried the box to his mother's grave. He figured the fresh dirt would eventually settle and be covered with grass. So he stepped back from the grave to try to envision where, in the existing grass, he should plant the flowers. At first, he looked only at his mother's gravesite. But then he looked at his father's too. And he decided to plant the flowers in front of both of their headstones and between them too.

He planted about two dozen flowers in all. When he was finished, he was kneeling on a strip of grass between his parents' graves. The knees of his suit pants were matted with grass and dirt. He took off his gloves and reached down and ran his hands over the low mound of loose dirt. It felt good to get his hands dirty again, to be close to the earth again, to be close to his parents again.

Nick knelt there and thought about his parents. They were each so complex and so profoundly different from one another. Generous and selfish, gentle and brutal, strong and weak. They were a mix of all these traits.

He looked at the flowers he had planted. And the thought occurred to him: who will water all these flowers? When he planted flowers with his mother as a boy, there was always an agreement that the two of them would take turns watering them. It was this very time of the year when they would plant flowers together. How he missed those days. How he missed creating something beautiful with his mother. How he missed his mother.

Nick folded his hands and bent down to say a prayer for his mother and tell her goodbye. As he did, he began crying, his tears gently falling on the yellow daffodils.

Chapter Thirty-six

Nick was about twenty miles north of Boston when he saw the first sign for the Plum Island Lighthouse. It was a little more than an hour away, about halfway to Portland.

He'd seen lighthouses from a distance but never been inside one. I might as well check it out, he thought. I'm in no hurry.

On the highway, Nick routinely drove ten to fifteen miles per hour over the speed limit. It wasn't that he was short on time. He was never late for appointments. He drove fast because he saw driving as a competition. He was convinced his driving skills were superior to those of anyone else on the road. He believed, therefore, he'd earned the right to drive faster than anybody else. He believed that speed limits simply didn't apply to him.

Nick normally drove in the left lane like a high-speed plow. He was constantly pressuring some poor driver from behind to force him to make way. Sometimes, the car ahead wouldn't budge. This infuriated Nick. In those cases, he would find a way around, slip in front of the other car and tap his brakes. Nick took special pleasure in watching in his rear view mirror as the driver now behind him had to brake, sometimes even skidding. Serves him right, he said to himself. Then he'd step on it just in case the guy decided to go after him.

This morning, though, Nick stayed in the right lane and drove *under* the speed limit for a change. Cars and trucks whisked by him. Some had even pressed impatiently behind him before sling-shotting around.

But Nick didn't care. This morning, he had no urge to drive fast or compete. Instead, he was thinking of the family in the hotel restaurant. He was thinking of his own children and how he had always been in such as hurry as they were growing up. He was thinking of what he would give to be driving here, or anywhere, with his small children in the back seat and his young wife by his side once again.

He sighed, a remorseful sigh, and slowed down even more, as if, by slowing down and letting others pass, he might get another shot.

#

Nick turned off I-95 at a town called Newburyport. He drove southeast along a river and crossed a bridge onto Plum Island. There, he followed the main road, called Northern Boulevard, to the lighthouse at the north end of the island.

The lighthouse was easy to spot. It stood about forty feet tall, much taller than any other building around. It was wooden, white and slightly tapered. At the top was a circular platform, rimmed by a thin railing. It looked like a crow's nest on a ship. Within it was a round room and, within that, an emerald cylinder. A black cupola capped it off.

As he drove toward it, Nick couldn't take his eyes off the lighthouse. There was something about it. He was surrounded by other beautiful buildings. But only the lighthouse commanded his attention.

Nick knew why. The lighthouse was the most important thing on the island. It saved lives. It had a higher purpose, a broader responsibility. It might be weathered and even old-fashioned, but there it stood, lighting the way.

Nick saw himself that way. At least he used to. Nowadays, though, he wasn't so sure.

#

Nick parked in a small lot and walked up a red brick pathway, which wound past a small, two-story, white house. He assumed this was where the lighthouse keeper lived. Did lighthouses still have keepers? He knocked on the door. No one answered.

So he kept walking up the brick path toward the lighthouse. He came to a small, gray door and knocked on it. Again, no one answered. He twisted the knob. It turned easily, and the warped door popped open. He peeked inside. No one was there, only a spiral, wooden staircase.

Nick squeezed through the door frame, which had obviously been built when men were smaller. In Nick's case, much smaller. He ducked inside and pulled the door shut behind him.

The place smelled musty, like an old cellar. Nick grabbed the railing and started climbing the stairs. They were narrow and creaked under his weight. It was a tight, steep climb. Nick's quads burned, and he had to stop three times on his way up to catch his breath.

When he got to the top, Nick walked through an open door onto a small, circular, wooden observation deck. In the center was the emerald cylinder he'd seen driving up. It was probably six feet tall. Inside the bright green glass was a single light bulb, surrounded by dozens of squarish lenses arranged in the shape of a giant egg. He supposed the lenses reflected the light. He imagined that, burning brightly at night, the whole thing must look like a big, green lantern.

The round deck was open to the air. Metal plates formed a rim around both the bottom and the top, with metal bars crisscrossing, like lattice, in between. Standing there, he could see a bay to the east and a river to the north and west.

The bayside of the island was a sandy beach, which extended as far as he could see. The beach was wide. There was a natural shelf — in some spots, a cliff — along the inner edge. Rows of wooden houses stood right along this edge. Several were so close that they'd actually collapsed over the side, onto the beach. One was even partially submerged in the water. What a way to live,

Nick thought.

He was just beginning to survey the waters when he saw a car pull into the parking lot below. He watched a young man, dressed in business clothes, get out. He walked to the brick path leading to the lighthouse and followed it without hesitating or looking around. He seemed to know where he was going.

A minute later, Nick heard the door down below open, then close. He heard footsteps on the staircase. For a moment, Nick became anxious. Could this man be coming for him? The scene with Jimmy Stewart hanging from the gutter in *Vertigo* flashed through his mind.

But then he realized how ridiculous that was. How in the world would anyone know he was there, in the top of a lighthouse on Plum Island? Besides, Nick was a big man. In a worst-case, Hitchcockian scenario, he could take care of himself.

Through the open doorway stepped a man in his early thirties. Nick was standing across from him, his back against the metal lattice. He figured the man would be surprised by his presence, so Nick said "Hello" as a heads-up.

"Hello," he replied, still looking startled. "Sorry. I wasn't expecting anyone to be here."

"Neither was I," Nick said. "Welcome."

The young man smiled, then looked past Nick toward the bay.

"Beautiful day," he said. "You can see for miles this morning."

"That's for sure," Nick said, turning around, his hands gripping the metal bars.

"What brings you up here today?" the young man asked.

"Well, I'm just passing through on my way to Portland. I saw signs for this place on the highway. I'd never been inside a lighthouse, so I thought I'd check it out."

"Pretty cool, huh?"

"Yeah. Very cool."

The young man stepped around the emerald cylinder. He stopped about ten feet from Nick and also turned toward the bay.

"What brings you here?" Nick asked.

"I'm on my way home to Boston. I had a business trip in Portland. I stop here whenever I get the chance."

"You've been here before?"

"Many times. My father used to take us here when I was a kid. I've been out there, on the water, many times too."

"I've never been here," Nick said. "What's beyond the bay? The ocean?"

"Well, eventually. But not right away. The bay flows into the Gulf of Maine. The gulf flows into the ocean."

"I see. The gulf must be huge."

"It is. It stretches from Cape Cod to Nova Scotia."

"You sound like you know a lot about this part of the world, young man," Nick said, turning and extending his hand. "Nick Reynolds."

"Hi, Nick," he said, shaking hands. "I'm Tony Vecellio."

"Tony Vecellio," Nick repeated, grinning. "What a great name."

"Thanks. It's Irish."

Nick chuckled. Both men turned back toward the bay.

"Where are you from, Tony?"

"Originally, Kennebunkport. Now I live in Boston."

"And you used to come here as a kid?"

"Yeah. My dad had a boat. He used to take us down here, from Kennebunkport. We'd put in at a marina over there on the Merrimac," he said, pointing at the river. "Then we'd walk to this lighthouse and climb up here and look out."

"Sounds like fun."

"Actually, getting here took some doing. But my dad was an ex-Navy guy. He was up for it."

"Was it dangerous?"

"The water's always dangerous. But the trickiest part of the trip was right down there, where the river flows into the bay."

"Tough headwaters?"

"Yep. Sounds like you know a bit about boating too."

"I've got a small boat on Lake Michigan. But I'm hardly an expert like your dad."

"I've seen Lake Michigan. It's a lot like the ocean. I'm sure you can hold your own on the water. Are you from Chicago?"

"Yeah. Cedar Rapids, originally. But I've lived in Chicago since college."

"Where'd you go to school?"

"Loyola."

"That's funny. I went to Boston College. I thought you might be a Jebbie," he said, using the name students of Jesuit-run schools sometimes call themselves.

"I'll take that as a compliment."

"It is," he said with a smile. "What brings you here, Nick?"

"Well, I'm on a sabbatical."

It was still hard for Nick to say the word.

"Cool. Where are you heading?"

"Bar Harbor."

"Bah Habah. Have you been there?"

"No."

"Well, you're in for a treat."

"So does your father still have his boat?" Nick asked, wanting to change the subject.

"No, he died a few years ago."

"I'm sorry."

"It's okay. He's really the reason I'm here."

"What do you mean?"

"My dad loved the water. And he loved coming up here. He used to come up here, right where we're standing, and stare out at the water for the longest time. In fact, as kids, it used to bore us to tears. My dad would be looking out at the bay, and my sister and I would get so frustrated that we would go back downstairs with mom and wait for dad outside. He would come down eventually, and we'd be so anxious to leave. Once, when I was a teenager, I asked him, 'Dad, what are looking at?' He told me, 'Tony, if you look out at the water long enough and let everything else go, you'll find the truth.' Now, I know that sounds a little wacky. I asked my dad what he meant by that. He said he couldn't tell me, that I'd have to find the truth on my own. For him, it was in the water. He found it in the water."

"That's a beautiful story," Nick said.

"Yeah. He was an amazing man. He taught me how to operate a boat. And he asked me to sprinkle his ashes out there. So when he died, I took his boat, with my mom and sister, from Kennebunkport down here. We sprinkled his ashes out there, in the bay. And whenever I'm traveling this way, I stop and come up here and look out. And do you want to know something? Sometimes, when I look at the water long enough, I can see him. I can see his face in the waves."

Nick didn't know what to say. He just stood there, like Tony, looking out at the bay.

"What about you, Nick? Is your father still living?"

"No, he's been gone for some time."

"I'm sorry."

"It's okay. Thanks for sharing your story about your dad. He would be very proud of you."

"Well, I hope so. Speaking of fathers, I need to get going. My son will be getting out of school in a couple of hours, and I want to be there to pick him up today."

"Well, then, I'll say goodbye," Nick said, extending his hand. "It was good to meet you, Tony."

"You too, Nick. Enjoy Bar Harbor. Enjoy your sabbatical."

"Thank you."

Nick listened to Tony's footsteps all the way down the staircase, then watched as he walked along the brick path to his car. He opened his door, looked up and waved. Nick waved back. Tony got in and drove away.

Nick stood there, his hands still gripping the metal bars, looking out at the bay. He thought about what Tony's father had told his son. He looked out at the waves and wondered if he too could find the truth.

Chapter Thirty-seven

July 2008

Nick had grown to love Saturday mornings. He loved the solitude and peace. He loved being able to run errands at his own pace before going into the office in the afternoon. It was a respite from his hectic life, a life packed with projects, paperwork and people.

He had these mornings to himself lately because, by the time he got up, Jean was gone. She usually had appointments on Saturday morning. That was fine by Nick.

This Saturday morning, he was at Lakeside Foods, picking up a few things he normally wouldn't ask Jean to buy — personal care products like deodorant and indulgences like ice cream. He'd stopped asking Jean to buy ice cream when she kept telling him he didn't need it.

As always, he took extra time to check out the snack cakes section. Wherever he shopped, Nick wanted to make sure Elgin's products were positioned just right and that nothing was out of stock. If he noticed any issues, he'd pull out his phone and send a testy message to his VP of sales, telling him to get on it. Nick did store checks whenever he traveled. His sales VP had grown accustomed to dispatching members of his team to stores all over the world, night and day.

Today Nick stood in the front of the snack cakes section and was shocked to see Elgin's most popular SKU completely missing. He was just pulling his phone out when someone called his name.

It was one of his neighbors, a guy named Jeff.

"Hey, Nick!"

"Good morning, Jeff."

Jeff was a busybody. Nick kept his phone out, hoping he would take the hint and move on.

"Wow! It's my lucky day. I've now seen you and Jean, and it's not even noon yet."

"Oh, yeah? Where'd you see Jean?"

"Saw her at Peet's. She was having coffee with Bob Perkins. Carol said she saw them there just a few days ago too. I guess they've become an item. You'd better watch out, Nick."

Nick slipped his phone back into his pocket and picked up the plastic shopping basket he'd set on the floor when he was inspecting the shelves.

"Well, you know Jean and Bob work together. I think they're working on a project for the new school year."

"Yeah," Jeff said with a grin. "That's probably it. Well, it's good seeing you, Nick. Have a good day. And tell Jean hi."

Nick hurried to the check out. He could feel his blood pressure rising.

#

It was early afternoon. Nick was sitting in his recliner, reading the *New York Times*, when he heard the garage door go up.

"Nick," Jean said, as she walked into the kitchen with a bag of groceries. "What are you doing home?"

"I decided to go into the office a little later today."

"Oh? Things slowing down at work?"

"Not really. But I'll catch up tomorrow."

Nick could see Jean through the doorway. She was standing at the island in the kitchen, beginning to unpack groceries.

"So I ran into Jeff Adams at Lakeside this morning."

"Oh? How's Jeff?"

"He's fine. He said he saw you having coffee with Bob Perkins this morning."

Jean was pulling a can of baked beans out of the grocery bag. She stopped and put it down on the counter top. Her eyes got wide, and her mouth dropped open a little. Then she picked up the can and started moving again, like a mannequin coming to life.

"Yeah," she said, sounding anxious. "I ran into him at Peet's."

Nick said nothing. Jean continued unpacking groceries.

"Are you screwing Bob Perkins?" Nick asked in a loud voice.

Jean walked to the doorway of the kitchen and looked across the family room at Nick.

"What did you say?"

"I asked if you're screwing Bob Perkins."

"What in the hell are you talking about, Nick?"

"I thought you weren't seeing Bob any more."

"Nick, that was years ago. We've been over this. I'm not seeing Bob Perkins."

"Well, Jeff told me that Carol saw you with him at Peet's just a few days ago."

Jean looked like a rabbit caught in a trap.

"Well, I think she has me mistaken for somebody else," she said, turning around and stepping back into the kitchen. "You know, to some people, all blonds look alike."

"You're lying," Nick said, folding the paper and dropping it on the floor.

"What?"

"I think you're lying."

"Oh, really? Why would I be lying to you, Nick?"

"Were you with Bob Perkins this morning?"

"Yes! Yes, I was."

Nick got up and walked into the kitchen. He stepped over to the sink and leaned back against the counter, on the other side of the island from Jean. He folded his arms and tilted his head, as if he were expecting her to say something.

"What? I ran into Bob at Peet's. We were both grabbing coffee. We decided to sit down and chat for a minute."

"Really? What were you chatting about?"

"Nick Reynolds! That's none of your business."

"Well, guess what, Jean? When my wife starts hanging out with another man, I think that is my business."

"Nick, stop this. I'm not hanging out with anybody."

"Jean, let me ask you something."

"What?"

"Why are you wearing perfume?"

"What?"

"Do you always wear perfume on Saturday mornings?"

Jean closed her eyes and shook her head.

"Look, Nick. I don't know what you think is going on here. But whether I choose to wear perfume on any given day is none of your damn business!"

"Are you screwing Bob Perkins?"

Nick really knew how to get under Jean's skin.

"No! Now stopping asking me that."

"So what are you two doing together? Jean, I'm not a fool. I know you're seeing Bob."

Nick did not actually know that. But he sensed he was gaining the upper hand, and he was not about to give it up.

Jean leaned back against the pantry door and looked Nick in the eye.

"Yes, in a way, I am seeing Bob."

Nick knew that Jean would come clean. She always did. But he was still surprised.

"What?"

"I've been seeing Bob for coffee."

"Why?"

"I enjoy talking with him. That's all. We have a lot in common."

"Like what?"

"We're working on some projects together at school."

"How often are you seeing him?"

"I don't know."

"How often?"

"Nick, why are you grilling me like this?"

"How often!"

"I don't know. Maybe once a week. Nick, there's nothing going on."

Nick shifted his weight, uncrossed his arms and put his palms down on the edge of the counter behind him.

"You've been seeing Bob once a week? For how long?"

"I don't know."

"How long, Jean? How long has this been going on?"

"Nick, nothing is going on."

"How long!"

"Weeks. Months. I'm not sure."

"Years?"

"Yes, but only in the summers — and only for coffee."

Nick looked away, then back at Jean.

"Why?" he asked.

"Why what?"

"Why have you been seeing him? And why haven't you told me?"

"Maybe we should sit down."

Crap, Nick thought. This can't be good.

They moved into the family room and sat down at opposite ends of the sofa.

"I don't know where to begin," Jean said.

"How about the truth? Why don't you begin by telling me the truth?"

"Okay, Nick," she said, her voice rising. "Here's the truth. I have coffee with Bob because he listens to me. He asks me questions and actually wants to hear my answers. He cares about me."

"He cares about you?"

"Yeah, Nick. He cares."

"How do you know that, Jean? How well do you know this guy?"

"I've gotten to know him pretty well."

"Have you slept with him?"

"No, Nick! I haven't. Not everything's about sex."

"Tell me about it," Nick said, rolling his eyes. "So why haven't you told me any of this before now?"

"Nick," she said, leaning toward him. "For starters, when would I tell you? You're never around. And even when you're here, you're someplace else. The kids are gone. You're gone. I'm lonely, Nick."

"And so why haven't you told me?"

"Because I knew you would react just this way, that you would be defensive, that you would never understand."

"Well, Jean. Maybe you're right. Maybe I'm an idiot because, until Jeff said something to me this morning, I was oblivious to all of this."

"Nick, you're not an idiot."

"I'm not?" Nick said sarcastically.

"No, you're just not around. You just don't know me any more."

"Jean, I'm your god damned husband!"

"And I'm still your wife, Nick. We're still living here together."

"But?"

"But we're living separate lives. You haven't heard a thing I've said for years."

"Unlike Bob?"

"That's right, Nick. Unlike Bob."

"I'll tell you what, Jean. Why don't we get a divorce? Bob's married. At least I think he's still married. He can get a divorce too, and the two of you can run away and be happy living in some little apartment on a couple of teachers' salaries. Then you can listen to each other and work on projects together and not have to sneak around having coffee any more."

"Nick, that's not what I want."

"It's not? Well, what in the hell do you want, Jean?"

"I want you, Nick. I want you. I don't want a big house. I don't want to be married to an executive who's in love with his work and hates his employees. I don't want to be married to a man who no longer takes care of himself. I want to be married to the man I married, the man who used to write me poetry. That's what I want, Nick. That's all I want. I don't want Bob. I want you."

Nick got up and began pacing around the room.

"It's because I'm fat, isn't it?"

"What?"

"It's because I'm fat and Bob's in good shape. That's why you're attracted to him."

"Nick, you've got to be kidding me. You haven't heard a word I've said."

"I repulse you, don't I, Jean?"

"What?"

"You hate the way I look."

"Nick, to be honest, you do repulse me at times. But it has nothing to do with the way you look. Sometimes, I hardly recognize you. You've become mean. I've heard the way you talk to people at work. You never used to treat people like that. And when you're drunk, I can't stand you. You're a mean drunk, Nick. No, that's not attractive."

"My drinking. I knew it. That's what this is about. You just can't let it go. I'll bet you complain to Bob about my drinking."

"Nick, this is not just about your drinking. And I don't talk to Bob about that. In fact, we don't talk about you at all."

"Well, that's reassuring."

Jean buried her face in her hands. Then she looked up, with fear in her eyes, and said, "Do you want a divorce, Nick?"

He stopped pacing and turned toward her.

"No."

"What do you want then?"

"You really want to know?"

"Yes."

"Okay. I'll tell you want I want, Jean. I want a wife who isn't so needy. From the minute I wake up to the minute I fall asleep, I've got people asking me for things. Everyone wants something from me. But never once does anyone ask what they can do for me. All they do is complain. And then I come home. I'm exhausted, and you expect me to sit here and listen as you drone on about some poor kid at school. Well, guess what, Jean? I don't care. I just don't care. What do I want? I'd like to come home once, just once, and hear you say, 'Nick, you're amazing,' and then have you leave me alone."

If he'd looked at Jean, Nick would have seen the pain and sadness in her face. But he didn't look at her. Instead, he walked away and said, "I'm going into the office."

"Nick, please don't go."

"I have nothing more to say, Jean."

After that, neither Nick nor Jean ever mentioned Bob again. When Nick came home at night, Jean no longer shared things about her day. She knew he didn't care.

But she didn't have to say a word. Every few days, her perfume said it all.

Chapter Thirty-eight

Nick drove into downtown Portland on a red bridge over a wide river. It was just before noon.

He could tell it was an old town, with its tree-lined, cobblestone streets, its monuments, and its dark red brick buildings with arched doorways, stone fronts and dormers. But it looked new too, with townhouses and upscale restaurants and shops.

It was a harbor town. Coming in off the bridge, Nick could see dozens of sailboats and fishing boats on the water and an island with a lighthouse in the distance. He could see seagulls circling overhead.

He hadn't booked a hotel room. He spotted a Residence Inn at the intersection of two streets that came together in a V. The hotel was built to fit. It was shaped like a wedge. Nick pulled into the parking lot behind it.

"Good morning, sir," said the desk clerk. She was tall, thin and blond, with blue eyes.

"May I help you?" she smiled.

"Yes, I'd like a room. If possible, overlooking the water."

"Certainly. Let me check."

She looked down, and her fingers danced across her computer keys.

"Well, we're in luck. I have a room on the fourth floor, overlooking the bay. Shall I book that?"

"Yes, please."

"Very good. How long will you be staying with us?"

"Just one night."

Nick handed her his Visa card.

"I see you are well-traveled, Mr. Reynolds."

"Yes, and yet somehow I've managed to miss Portland until now."

"Well, we're glad you finally made it."

After his workout and light breakfast that morning, Nick was ravenous.

"Can you recommend a good place for lunch on the water?"

"DiMillo's. Great seafood and a great view of the bay."

"This is my first time to Portland. Please excuse my ignorance. What's the name of the bay?"

"Casco Bay. It goes out into the Gulf of Maine."

"From the bridge, I could see some islands out there."

"Oh, yes. There are many islands in the bay."

"How many?"

"Well, they used to be called the Calendar Islands because some people thought there were three hundred sixty-five of them. But the real number is closer to two hundred."

"Wow. If I wanted to visit one this afternoon, which would you recommend?"

"That depends on what you're after."

"One with a sandy beach."

"Then I'd recommend Peaks Island. It's only a few miles out, and there are some really nice beaches there."

"Is there a ferry?"

"Yes. In fact, it takes off from the pier right next to DiMillo's."

"Thanks a lot. You've been very helpful."

"You're welcome, Mr. Reynolds. Enjoy your visit."

#

DiMillo's was a floating restaurant, part of a marina on the bay. It was clearly a seafood place. Even the logo, with a lobster across the "o," said so.

But the name also said Italian. And the combination made Nick crave a seafood pasta dish for lunch.

"I'm sorry, sir," said his waitress, an older woman whose name tag said Rose. "We don't begin serving pasta until dinner."

Nick looked into her eyes and smiled.

"Excuse me, miss. Are you Italian?"

"Why, yes, I am," she said, blushing.

"I thought so. Such a natural beauty."

Nick had the seafood alfredo.

He would start eating healthier the next day.

#

There were about twenty people and a handful of cars on the ferry to Peaks Island. Nick asked the captain how long the trip would take.

"Seventeen minutes," he said.

Now here was a man who knew his job.

It was sunny, but the air was cool. Nick was glad he was wearing his jacket and hat. He leaned over the rail and looked out across the water. He could see countless islands in the distance and at least a dozen freighters and barges crisscrossing the bay. Funny, he thought. He hadn't noticed all these islands and ships from the shore.

As the ferry pulled into dock, Nick could see why there were so few cars onboard. Everyone on the little road up ahead was either riding a bike or driving a golf cart.

It reminded Nick of Mackinac Island, a tiny island in Lake Huron between Michigan's Upper and Lower Peninsulas. There were no cars there either, only bikes and horse-drawn carriages.

Jean used to go there with her family as a girl. It was her favorite place in the world. Nick and Jean went there on their honeymoon. They stayed at the Grand Hotel, a wedding gift from Jean's rich Aunt Mildred. Jean told Nick that being there with him was "a dream come true."

She took Ashley and Josh to Mackinac Island several times when they were kids. Nick had planned to go too. They were supposed to be family vacations. But he never made it. Some crisis or big project at work always kept him away.

Now Nick stepped off the ferry and onto the Peaks Island dock. He headed down the boardwalk, toward the beach.

He passed Forest City Seafood, with plastic bins of fresh lobsters out front; Down Front, an ice cream shop; the Cockeyed Gull, a restaurant; and Hannigan's Island Market, a small grocery store whose sign read, "If we don't have it, you don't need it."

At the end of the boardwalk, Nick descended a long, wooden ramp to the beach. There were dozens of people there: kids building sandcastles, adults reading books or snoozing in low-slung beach chairs, teenagers tossing frisbees, an older couple reading magazines under an umbrella. A family was eating lunch on a red-and-white checkered tablecloth with a picnic basket in the middle. A woman in a sunhat sat alone on a boulder at the rocky, grassy edge of the beach. A young man was maneuvering a kite, making it dart, dive and dance in the breeze. A man and a small boy were building a rock tower. Two teenage girls were lying face down on beach towels with the unfastened straps of their bathing suits hanging loose at their sides. Two teenage boys with sunglasses lay on beach towels nearby, no doubt hoping for the girls to make some sudden movement. Hip hop music was playing on a boom box. A mother was scolding her kids for throwing cheese curls to the seagulls, which were swooping in closer and closer, snagging them in mid-air. A man and a woman were paddling kayaks several hundred feet from shore. No one was swimming. The water's still too cold, Nick guessed.

Nick's legs and back were a little sore from his workout that morning. He needed to sit down. Of course, he hadn't thought about bringing a beach towel or a chair. He looked around for a place to sit. He spotted some flat rocks nestled among boulders at the upper edge of the beach, shielded by pine trees. He shuffled up and sat down on a big, flat rock, his legs dangling over the edge.

He looked out over the whole scene. So this is what it's like, he thought. This is what a vacation looks like.

It's not that he never took his family on vacation. Over the years, they'd gone to some great places, even Hawaii. But every vacation turned out the same. Jean and the kids would end up doing things together, without Nick, who was always working.

His absence used to infuriate Jean.

"Why did you even come with us?" she would say. "You're never around."

"What are you talking about? We all went to dinner last night."

"Yeah, and you spent most of the time on your BlackBerry."

"Jean, I told you we've got a big deal going down. The company needs me right now."

"Well, guess what, Nick? We need you too. But you're never there for us any more. And even when you're with us, you're somewhere else."

Jean would never understand, he had thought. She could not possibly understand Nick's situation. Her world was so different. It was so much simpler. She was a grade school teacher. She might be back to working full-time. But all she had to do was prepare lesson plans, teach and grade homework and tests. And she got summers off.

By contrast, every minute of Nick's day was booked. He had imagined that getting to the top would give him more freedom. He could delegate tasks and choose what he worked on.

But instead, with so much responsibility, and so many people now looking to him for direction or permission, his to-do list only grew. He felt like a man walking uphill whose pack was always getting heavier.

And along the way, he began seeing people as an intrusion, a distraction from the task at hand. At some point, he had even begun to see his family as an intrusion. And he had begun avoiding them.

But it wasn't always that way. He remembered making time

for his young family. He remembered taking his kids to the zoo, maybe twenty years ago. That day, Jean snapped a picture of Nick holding Ashley, who was probably about seven, and Josh, who was probably about five, as a giraffe bent down over the bars of its cage, sticking out its long, black tongue. The kids were looking up in wonder, and Nick was smiling, looking like a big kid himself. It was one of Nick's favorite pictures. He framed it and kept it in his den.

It reminded him that he hadn't always been an absent father. But he knew Jean was right. At some point, his work became the focus of his life. He began going into the office early, staying late and bringing work home, even on weekends. He became obsessed with work, with little time for anything, and anyone, else.

At work, he had changed too. He was viewing projects in terms of how they could advance his career, and people in terms of how they could help him sell more stuff. Those who delivered were in. Those who didn't were out.

Nick realized that he had become all about Nick. Everything else had become secondary, if he paid it any mind at all. And it had worked. He kept getting promoted, making more money, gaining more power.

But look where it had gotten him, he now thought. He'd lost his family and friends and alienated his employees. He'd become a bully and a lonely man.

And now he was sitting on a rock on an island on a sabbatical he was being forced to take and which was probably his boss's diplomatic way of letting him go.

His life had been so promising. But he had screwed it up so badly.

Nick looked out, past the beach. He stared at a buoy swaying in the water. He'd always been drawn to the water. Maybe that was his truth. Maybe that's why he was heading to Bar Harbor. Maybe that was his final destination.

Why not? What was the point of going on? Had he not fulfilled his destiny? Had he not amassed power and wealth? Had he not exceeded anything his father had expected of him? Had he not become the center of much attention, just as his mother had wished for him?

Why go any farther? There were only risks. The risk of trying to change and failing. The risk of continuing to disappoint those around him. The risk of the humiliation of being let go and replaced.

But what about the risks of taking his own life?

Would his family miss him? Maybe at first. But he knew he was already a husband and father who had gone missing. His wife and children might have loved him once. But not anymore. Why should they? Yes, they might miss him for a moment. But then they would probably feel relieved.

Would Elgin miss him? No. In fact, he would probably be doing Lou a favor, sparing him the awkwardness of announcing his retirement. Jennifer would feel liberated. And the organization would probably rejoice.

Would God punish him? Who knows? But how could God's wrath be any worse than the emptiness he was feeling right now?

Strange, Nick thought. People will no doubt think it's strange that a man who seemed to have it all, a man who seemed so confident, would take his own life.

But they won't understand. They won't understand the loneliness of living on an island that you yourself built. They won't understand the despair of discovering that reaching your goals has only diminished you. They won't understand the pain of hurting those you love the most, of hurting them so deeply that they no longer want anything to do with you.

Nick looked down at the rocks all around him. A big rock, he thought. When I get to Bar Harbor, I'll tie a rope around my waist and a big rock to the other end and walk out into the harbor until the water is over my head. I'll let the water wash over me. Then I'll drop it. I can do that.

Nick slid down off the rock, trudged across the beach and lumbered up the long, wooden ramp to the boardwalk. He went to

Hannigan's, the grocery store that sells anything you need, and bought what he thought he needed: a twelve-foot rope.

He carried the neatly wound rope in a white, plastic grocery bag to the Cockeyed Gull, where he sat at a table on the deck over-looking the bay. He sat there, drinking beer, the rest of the after-noon and into the evening. As darkness fell, he watched the lights of Portland glow and sparkle in the distance.

How had he gotten it so wrong? When had he changed? When had he stopped caring about people? When had he started ignor-ing his children? When had he become so cold and distant toward Jean? How in the world could he not have told her goodbye?

"Last ride into Portland tonight!" the captain called from the ferry below.

Nick got up and stumbled onto the boat, holding tight to the railing. When the vessel lurched forward, he felt sick. He leaned over the rail and threw up. As he bent down, his hat fell off. He reached for it in vain and watched it fall into the dark, churning water.

"You okay?" asked a woman who was standing nearby.

"Yeah," Nick said, wiping his mouth with the back of his hand. "Just a little seasick."

As he wobbled off the boat, the captain asked him if he needed a cab.

"No, thanks. I'll be fine."

Most nights when he was drunk, someone asking if he needed a cab would have set Nick off. But not tonight. He had given up. He no longer felt like fighting.

Chapter Thirty-nine

February 2010

At Elgin, February meant budget season.

Nick hated budget season. He wasn't a numbers guy. But it wasn't the numbers he hated about budget season. It was the people.

Nick insisted on zero-based budgeting, where all expenses must be justified for every new period. Everyone who worked for him knew this. Yet many tried to make a case for why the bulk of last year's budget was essential this year — and why they needed even more.

It drove Nick crazy. So crazy that he began insisting that anyone proposing an increase must also propose an offsetting cut.

"The heart of strategy is sacrifice!" he would roar. "Unless you're giving something up, you're not being strategic!"

After being cowed, those making these proposals would reluctantly find the savings somewhere, getting Nick off their backs for another year.

But what bothered Nick most were costly proposals for new ideas. And what he hated most about these proposals was the arrogance and tunnel vision of the people making them.

There were always some who were convinced that their new idea was so big and so important that Elgin could not afford not to fund it.

Nick couldn't blame his employees for giving it their all. He'd done the same many times on his way up. But it was their provincialism that drove him nuts.

Everyone pitching a new idea acted as if it was the "next big thing" for the company. Nick knew better. In fact, he knew that, in some years, none of the initiatives in his part of the business was a top priority for Elgin. But of course, not letting anyone in his organization see the big picture, Nick was the only person in the room who knew this.

But that didn't keep him from cutting anyone too full of himself off at the knees.

Once a guy named Brian was foolish enough to begin his presentation this way: "Nick, we believe this could be the biggest thing for Elgin this year and, over the next hour, we're going to show you why."

In that single sentence, in Nick's book, Brian had committed two cardinal sins. First, he was boastful. Second, he had called his boss's boss's boss by his first name.

Nick angrily dismissed Brian and his team after spotting a typo on their first slide. Later, after he'd read the team's proposal, he sent a blistering note to Brian and copied his whole team.

For Nick, budget season was a blood sport. Over the course of several weeks, he'd hear dozens of presentations. Every team knew its chances of making it through were slim. In fact, Nick prided himself on funding less than ten percent of all proposals for new ideas.

For most of the people in his organization, then, budget season was the equivalent of a one-man firing squad.

Of course, Lou heard the stories. Periodically, he would voice his concerns to Nick privately.

This morning, he had called Nick to his office once again.

"You're demoralizing your organization," he said.

"They know the drill."

"What do you mean?"

"They know my track record. They know only one in ten new

ideas is going to get funded."

"That seems low."

"Low? Really, Lou? What was our corporate growth rate last year?"

"Nick, you know it was five percent."

"How about without my division?"

"Three percent," Lou said, averting his gaze. "All right, Nick. Just try to go a little easier on people."

"I will, Lou," Nick lied. "Thanks."

Nick got up and walked out. Not because the CEO had dismissed him. But because Nick knew that, as long as he was enabling Lou to hit his corporate targets, Lou would stay out of his shorts.

Nick hated budget season.

But not really.

Chapter Forty

Nick was dreaming about a big rock. He was standing on the bottom of Frenchman Bay. He had tied a rope around the rock and dropped it. It sank, but it kept floating back up. He kept pushing it back down, but it kept floating up and hitting him in the head. It knocked off his baseball cap. Nick looked up and watched it spiraling toward the surface of the water.

His father was standing next to him. He told Nick to swim up and get his hat and put it over his heart. But before he could move, the rock hit him in the head again.

Nick woke up to the sound of rain hitting the window. Everything was dark. He was shaking and sweating. His heart was pounding hard. His head was pounding even harder.

It was just a dream. There is no water, he said to himself, only rain. There is no rock, only this throbbing pain in my head.

The details of his dream were already fading away. But he still remembered he had been underwater, in Frenchman Bay.

Nick now imagined walking out into that bay. He imagined his arms straining to bear the heavy rock. He imagined the waves lapping at his chest, then his chin, then covering him completely.

Gusts of wind slammed the rain against his window. Nick pulled the covers up to his neck.

He remembered the rope he'd bought yesterday and how he had thought it all through. He knew there was no turning back.

But he wasn't ready.

#

When he woke up again, it was morning. But his room was still dimly lit. It was still raining.

Where am I, he wondered. Oh, yeah. Portland, almost to Bar Harbor. I might get there yet today, he thought. This could be my last day on earth.

Even so, he was hungry. He got dressed and went downstairs for breakfast.

Over bacon and eggs, he opened his laptop. Bar Harbor was still three hours away. What's the rush, he thought. Maybe he'd spend another day in Portland. He'd never liked driving in the rain.

He looked up places to see in Portland. The Portland Museum of Art popped up. That sounded like a good place to hang out on a rainy day.

He stopped at the desk and reserved his room for another night. He asked the clerk, a young guy with a pony tail, how far away the museum was.

"Less than a mile. Would you like directions?"

"Sure."

"Let me show you."

He pulled out a map of downtown Portland and drew circles around the hotel and the museum and a slightly zigzagged line between them.

"Is it walkable?"

"Yeah, but you'll get wet."

"Do you have an umbrella I can borrow?"

"Sure," said the clerk, pulling one from behind the counter. "Just bring it back when you check out."

#

On his way to the museum, Nick passed the Wadsworth-Long-fellow House, an impressive, three-story, red brick structure. A sign out front said it was Longfellow's boyhood home.

Nick liked Longfellow's poetry but hadn't read him for a long time. Maybe I'll catch this place on the way back, he thought.

He got to the museum just after it opened.

"Good morning," said a lady at the information desk. Her grey hair was fashioned into a bun behind her head. She wore a dark blue cardigan sweater, with the thin collar of a white blouse peeking out, and black, horn-rimmed glasses. Her lips were pursed. She looked like a living representative of Victorian repression.

"Good morning," Nick said, closing his umbrella and looking around for a place to put it.

"Just set your umbrella in the coat room," said Queen Victoria, pointing to a doorway to his left. "You can open it up there and let it dry out, if you like."

"Thanks."

Normally, Nick wouldn't bother opening his umbrella to let it dry out. But this wasn't his umbrella. He popped it open and set it on the floor in the back corner of the coat room.

He kept his jacket on, though. It was a chilly morning.

"Welcome to the Portland Museum of Art," said the queen as Nick stepped into the lobby. "Have you been with us before?"

"No, this is my first time."

"I see. Well, you've certainly picked a good day to be indoors!"

"Amen," Nick said, stuffing his hands into his jacket pockets to warm them. "Any exhibits you would recommend?"

In a sleepy, old New England town like this, the home of Henry Wadsworth Longfellow, Nick envisioned galleries of oil paintings of serene, pastoral landscapes.

"Oh, yes. We're hosting a wonderful exhibition that's just opened. It's called 'The Selfie Show.' It's an extraordinary collection of self portraits."

"Self portraits?"

"Yes. Did you know, for example, that the Mona Lisa is actually a self-portrait of Leonardo da Vinci?"

"No, I didn't. Sounds interesting."

"I think you'll enjoy it. It's on the second floor."

"Great. Do you charge admission?"

"Oh, yes. I almost forgot. It's fifteen dollars. Thirteen if you're a senior."

"What do you consider a senior?"

"Sixty-five."

Then she quickly added, "Looks like you'll be paying full price. By a long shot."

Nick smiled. She's flirting with me, he thought. He noticed a little, black bow at the bottom of her collar in the front. Suddenly, she looked like a package, waiting to be unwrapped.

He pulled out his wallet and handed her a twenty. As he looked up, he caught her staring at his head.

She looked down, took his twenty and handed him a five.

"Enjoy," she said, without looking back up.

#

The exhibition was divided into two parts.

The first was smaller, a collection of photographs of famous self-portrait paintings. Most were framed. Some were on easels. A few were hanging on the walls.

The second part took up the bulk of the floor: dozens of blown-up "selfies," most of them mounted in acrylic frames on the walls.

Nick read the description at the start of the exhibit:

> *Self-portraiture has been a staple of artistic practice for centuries. But is the selfie a new and legitimate art form or just the latest form of narcissism? The reality of our personal identity is that it is not only fluid but self-assigned. Here is a look at how we see ourselves, how we express ourselves, how we recreate ourselves.*

Nick began with the smaller, older section.

He saw images of artists at work in ancient Egyptian paintings and sculpture and on Greek vases. Even Zen Buddhist monks, he learned, created self-portraits.

In some paintings, the artist appeared as a face in the crowd. Rubens' *The Four Philosophers* was like that. In Jan van Eyck's famous *Arnofini Portrait*, the artist was shown in a mirror.

Nick found this older work instructive, like reading a history book, but not very interesting.

He moved on to the new section.

It began with a photo of Buzz Aldrin. The caption said that, in 1966, he took the first selfie in space. Now this, Nick thought, is more like it.

From there, the exhibition was all selfies, all contemporary photos. They were all arresting and intriguing. Many were disturbing.

A stream of water poured in and out of the open mouth of a woman named Pilar in Spain. The ghostly eyeball of a man named Nate in Melbourne stared away from his camera. A man named Keever in Michigan sat a table in a purple suit pointing a gun to his head. A young woman named Valentina in Germany was made up as a sad clown. A man named Richard in New Mexico stood in front of a line of urinals, looking puzzled. The surprised, bespectacled face of Evan in Los Angeles was lit up by his iPhone. Tears rolled down the cheeks of an older woman named Li in Beijing. Charles in Cleveland lay in a hospital bed. A topless woman named Asja in Berlin squatted in front of a brick wall, lighting a cigarette. Double exposure made a young woman named Aylin in Istanbul appear to have four eyes and two mouths. A man named Colin in Arizona wore a skull mask. The face of a woman named Marie in Paris looked bruised.

Who were all these people, Nick wondered. And why did they all look so sad? Is this how they saw themselves? Is this how they wanted to be seen? He wondered how they really looked, when they weren't mugging or wearing costumes.

He meandered through the selfies, feeling more and more on-edge. Finally, he came to the end of the exhibit. There, a solitary, framed picture rested on an easel.

But on closer inspection, he realized it was not a picture. It was a tinted mirror. Beneath it was the word "Selfie."

Nick looked into it. He looked at himself closely. His eyes were deep-set with dark circles underneath. His hair was thin and mostly grey. An overhead spotlight shone off his scalp. His nose was red. His jawline was gone, replaced by fleshy jowls that sagged into his tree trunk of a neck. His forehead was deeply creased, and the edges of his mouth were turned down. His body had grown so wide that most of it stretched beyond the frame of the mirror.

He longed to see himself as the lean, handsome teenager in the Killian's ads. But now he could see he bore little resemblance to that younger version of himself. He looked a lot more like the people in the selfies.

Am I so different from all these people, he asked himself. "For every atom belonging to me as good belongs to you."

His dark dream, the cold rain and now this. It was too much. He left the gallery and descended the stairs to the lobby.

"Finished so soon?" asked the lady behind the desk.

"It's all I could take," Nick said, retrieving his umbrella.

It was still raining, a cold, hard, noisy rain. He opened his umbrella and started walking, trying to remember the way back to his hotel.

#

Two blocks away, he came upon a diner called Nosh. He ducked inside to get out of the rain.

He squeezed into a booth next to the window. Feeling obliged to buy something and craving warmth, Nick ordered a bowl of tomato soup and a cup of coffee.

He looked at his watch. It was just before noon. What else would he do all day, he wondered.

He remembered the Wadsworth-Longfellow House. Maybe he would tour it. He pulled out his iPhone to look it up and see if it was open.

He discovered the old house was now a museum, restored to look as it did when Longfellow lived there in the 1800s. It was now full of Maine artifacts too.

But there was no mention of any of Longfellow's actual work. Nick was interested in reading Longfellow's poems, not seeing the old desk where he wrote them.

He typed in "poems by Longfellow" and scrolled randomly. The first one that caught his eye was called "The Rainy Day." How fitting, Nick thought.

> *The day is cold, and dark, and dreary;*
> *It rains, and the wind is never weary;*
> *The vine still clings to the mouldering wall,*
> *But at every gust the dead leaves fall,*
> *And the day is dark and dreary.*
>
> *My life is cold, and dark, and dreary;*
> *It rains, and the wind is never weary;*
> *My thoughts still cling to the mouldering past,*
> *But the hopes of youth fall thick in the blast,*
> *And the days are dark and dreary.*
>
> *Be still, sad heart, and cease repining;*
> *Behind the clouds is the sun still shining;*
> *Thy fate is the common fate of all,*
> *Into each life some rain must fall,*
> *Some days must be dark and dreary.*

Exactly, Nick thought. Dark and dreary. He supposed Longfellow was right: that behind the clouds, the sun is still shining.

But as he looked out the window at the driving rain, he could see no sign of the sun. In the glass, Nick could see only the reflection of his own face.

He wondered if anyone would miss it.

\#

When Nick got back to his hotel, he felt drained. He was cold, wet and shivering. He went up to his room, took a hot shower, got into bed and fell into a deep sleep.

When he awoke, it was so dark that Nick thought he might have slept right into the night. But it was only five o'clock. It was still raining.

Nick was hungry. On such a dreary night, he thought about staying put and eating in the hotel restaurant. But if this was truly going to be his last night on earth, he thought he might go someplace a little more interesting, especially in a harbor town.

As he grabbed his jacket, he spotted the rope. It was lying on the floor. He could hardly look at it. He picked it up and stuffed it in his duffel bag.

He stopped at the front desk. The tall blond from the day before was back on duty. He thought about buying the rope at Hannigan's. If she only knew where her recommendation had led him.

"Good evening, Mr. Reynolds."

"Good evening. How are you?"

"I'm fine. Thank you. How was Peak's Island?"

"The beaches were beautiful. And DiMillo's was great too. Thank you again for the recommendations."

"My pleasure."

"Now I have one more request."

"Yes?"

"Could you recommend another restaurant for dinner, somewhere with a great view of the harbor, within walking distance?"

"Boone's Fish House. Great seafood. Right on the harbor. Two blocks away."

"Thank you. If you don't mind, I'll borrow your umbrella a little longer."

"Not at all."

#

Nick got a table next to a window upstairs, overlooking the harbor. He ordered a baked, stuffed lobster and a beer.

Through the veil of rain and fog, he could barely see anything past the boats docked in the marina below. He couldn't even see the water. He could see only the blinking lights of a few boats brave or foolish enough to be untethered in the inky mist.

Raindrops streamed down the outside of the window. They reminded Nick of the tears he'd seen running down the face of the old Chinese woman in the selfie.

He thought of Jean, Ashley and Josh. He missed them all so much. Thinking about the prospect of never seeing them again, he began to cry.

Nick considered crying a sign of weakness. But now he wept openly, even as his waitress brought his food. He didn't even try to hide his tears. His waitress said nothing. She simply set his food down and walked away.

When she came back to check in, Nick was still crying.

"Are you okay, sir?" she asked softly.

"Yes," he sobbed.

"Would you like another beer?"

"Yes," he whimpered.

Nick had heard about guys crying in their beer, but he had never done it himself.

At last, he stopped crying. He dried his eyes, wiped his face with his napkin and motioned to the waitress for his check. She looked relieved.

He reached for his wallet, but it wasn't there. Crap, he thought. He must have left it in his room. He'd probably been distracted by the rope.

He felt stupid and started crying again.

A few minutes later, he would talk to the manager, who would call the young lady at the front desk at his hotel. She would vouch for him, and he would be able to swing by the restaurant the next morning and settle up.

But right now, Nick Reynolds, a man for whom power and wealth meant everything, sat weeping, penniless and alone.

He tried to look out the window. But the rain was coming

down hard. Now he couldn't even see the lights of the boats in the harbor. He could see only his own reflection.

He was tempted to look away. But he didn't. Instead, he looked deeply into his own face. There he saw the faces of Jean, Ashley and Josh; of his mother and father; of David and Susan; of Lou, Jennifer and Phil; of the waitress in Chicago and the little girl in Cleveland; of Marian and Paul; of priests and nuns; of the men with clipboards at Little League tryouts.

In his own face, Nick saw the face of every person he had ever known. They were all there. Every one.

There is no such thing as a selfie, he thought.

At last, he had begun to see the truth.

Chapter Forty-one

That morning, as Nick was walking from his hotel to the Portland Museum of Art, Jean, who hadn't heard from her husband in nearly a week, was sending a text message to Bob Perkins.

She knew it was probably not a good idea. But she was only inviting him over for coffee. They'd had coffee dozens of times over the years.

But it had always been at Peet's. What if someone were to spot Bob's car in the driveway or see him coming in or leaving the house? The neighborhood was filled with busybodies.

So what, Jean thought. It was a risk she was willing to take. Bob was a colleague and friend. We're working together on a project. That's the truth. If asked, she could explain.

Besides, Nick had left her. He was now probably a thousand miles away. That was his choice. He could have asked her to go along or at least said goodbye. She was married to the most inconsiderate man in the world. She was lonely, and she would now be alone all summer. Was it too much to invite a good friend to her house for a cup of coffee?

A few minutes after Jean sent her text, Bob responded.

I'd love to. What time?

How about 3:00?

Sounds great. See you then.

#

Jean had met Bob five years earlier at a faculty meeting. He was just joining the staff at St. Mary's. There were only two other male teachers at the school. One was fresh out of college. The other was in his mid-fifties, about to retire.

Bob was somewhere in the middle. Jean guessed he was in his late thirties. In that first faculty meeting, he stood and introduced himself. He said he and his family had just moved to the area from Detroit, that his wife had been transferred to Chicago. With a smile, he called himself a "trailing spouse." He said they had two kids. Both of them would be enrolling at St. Mary's.

Any man in a mainly female work environment is probably going to get attention. But that was never in question with Bob. He was very good-looking. He had thick brown hair, an athletic build and an easy smile.

What stood out for Jean, though, was his voice. He was soft-spoken, and his way of speaking had an unusual cadence. It sounded lyrical. And as soon as he spoke, she could tell he was from Michigan. His accent reminded Jean of home. She found it comforting.

After that faculty meeting, Jean introduced herself to Bob and welcomed him to St. Mary's. They chatted about Michigan. He told her he'd never lived anywhere else. She said he would like Chicago and offered to share her insights, based on her own experience as a transplant from Michigan.

"I'd like that," Bob said. "Maybe you'd be open to having coffee sometime?"

"Sure."

She was flattered.

#

Bob taught English to the younger kids. Jean taught it to the older ones. They soon found themselves working together to co-ordinate curriculum and compare notes on students.

Jean enjoyed working with Bob. Maybe it was her teaching tenure or that she was ten years his senior or just that he was new. But he listened to her, and he really seemed to value her opinion. Nick had become so domineering. It was refreshing to Jean to be around a man who actually listened to her. She looked forward to seeing Bob at school every day. She even began to miss him on the weekends.

Jean was always mindful that both of them were married. But at times, watching the curve of his jawline as he talked or listening to the rhythm of his voice, she allowed herself to think of him as more than a colleague.

One day at lunch, just before the school year ended, Bob approached Jean in the cafeteria.

"Jean, when we met, I asked if you'd be open to getting coffee sometime."

"I remember," Jean smiled. "I said yes."

"How about next Tuesday?"

"Sure. Where would you like to meet?"

"How about Peet's?"

"Great."

"Would ten o'clock work for you?"

"Perfect. I'll see you then."

Jean knew it was all wrong. But that whole weekend, she felt like a teenager getting ready for a date. She bought a new pair of tight-fitting jeans and a new sweater. She had her hair colored and got a new, youthful-looking cut. The change was so dramatic that even Nick noticed.

"Going somewhere?" he asked.

"Not really. Just decided to freshen up my look."

It was a white lie, the first of many.

Jean chose not to tell Nick she was having coffee with Bob. He would be needlessly jealous. Besides, he would be working, as usual, and never know.

On Tuesday, Jean and Bob met at Peet's. They talked for several hours. Until then, they'd known each other only professionally. But that day, they began to share their personal stories. And they enjoyed being together so much that they agreed to do it again.

They ended up meeting at Peet's for coffee two more times that summer. Jean was tempted to tell Nick but decided against it. At the same time, sensitive to the way things might look, she asked Bob if his wife was okay with them meeting like this. He said yes.

That fall, Jean and Bob began having lunch in the faculty lounge whenever they weren't on cafeteria duty. This turned out to be about three days a week. The following summer, they resumed having coffee about once a month at Peet's. The summer after that, they met every other week. The summer after that, every week.

Sometimes, Jean worried they might be getting too close. But she told herself they were just friends. She told herself they had good reason to be together. She told herself that, at last, she had a man in her life who listened to her, who cared about her, who enjoyed being with her.

It wasn't a physical relationship. But Jean appreciated the way he looked at her. She was nearly fifty when they met. It was nice to have a man, let alone a younger man, notice her for a change.

Over time, she found herself confiding just about everything in Bob, even the details of her relationship with Nick. He confided in her too. He told her that, not unlike Nick, his wife had become obsessed with work.

After coffee one summer morning, Bob walked Jean to her car. They hugged goodbye, as they always did. This time, though, Bob pulled Jean close and kissed her on the cheek. She was surprised and, instinctively, pulled away. She left without saying goodbye.

Jean and Bob continued having coffee that summer and eating lunch together at school that fall. Neither of them ever mentioned the incident in the parking lot. But when they said goodbye, they no longer hugged.

#

Jean was a little nervous when she saw Bob pull into the drive-way. She wasn't used to inviting men into her house, let alone when her husband was away.

She watched him through the window. He got out of his car and just stood there, looking around. Sometimes Jean forgot how large and impressive her house was.

She greeted him at the front door.

"Hi, Bob! Welcome."

"Hi, Jean. What a beautiful home you have."

"Thank you. I thought it might be a nice change of pace from Peet's."

"Yeah," he smiled. "I guess we have fallen into a bit of a rou-tine."

"Please come in."

He stepped inside. She closed the door behind him.

"I've made some coffee for us. I thought you might like to sit out on the deck. It's such a pleasant afternoon."

"Sounds great."

He followed her into the kitchen. The aroma of freshly brewed coffee with a hint of vanilla filled the air. Jean stepped over to the counter and poured two cups of coffee.

"You take two scoops of sugar ..."

Just then, she felt two hands on her shoulders. Bob was right behind her. He startled her, and she spilled a little sugar on the counter. He pressed the front of his body against her backside and kissed the back of her head. She gasped and dropped her spoon.

"Bob? What are you doing?"

She turned around, facing him, her rear end against the counter. He smiled, put his hands on the sides of her face and began to lean forward.

"Bob! Stop!" she cried, pushing him away.

"What are you talking about, Jean? Isn't this what you had in mind?"

"No! Not at all. I invited you over for coffee."

"And I'm glad you did. Jean, I know what you need. Let me give you what you need."

"No, Bob," she said. "I think you should leave."

He grasped her shoulders. "Are you sure?"

"Yes," she said, pushing his hands away. "I'm sorry, Bob. I'm sorry if I gave you the wrong idea."

"I'm sorry too, Jean."

He turned and walked to the front door. She trailed him by a few steps, not wanting to get too close. Without turning around to face her, he said, "Goodbye, Jean."

"Goodbye."

She locked the door behind him, then stepped into the living room. Through the sheer curtains, she watched Bob get into his car and drive away.

Jean sat down on the sofa. Her hands were trembling. Her whole body was shaking. Maybe she had been naive, she thought. Maybe she had led Bob on. Not just today. But for years.

Thinking about all she had shared with him, she began to feel sick to her stomach. She began to wonder about his intentions all along. Bob had become her friend. But now she knew their friendship was over.

The very idea made her sad because it meant the one man who had begun to fill the gap in her life would no longer be there for her. Her husband was gone and now this man too. She felt so alone.

She thought about Nick. She wondered where he was right now. She had an urge to call him, to reach out to him, to hear his voice.

She was worried about Nick. He had been so angry when he left. Calling him, just to make sure he's okay, would be such a simple thing to do.

But she couldn't bring herself to do it. Her relationship with Nick had a hard edge to it. Calling or even texting him now, just to see how he was doing, felt too soft.

Jean went back into the kitchen, turned off the coffee maker and poured herself a glass of chardonnay. She stepped out on the deck, slid down into Nick's Adirondack chair in the shade of a big elm tree and began to cry.

She sat there, drinking wine and crying, for the rest of the afternoon and into the evening. For the first time in years, she truly missed her husband.

Where are you, Nick, she thought. Where are you? We've been apart too long. I need you. I want to be with you again.

She had no idea where her husband was or how to get him back. She didn't know that, at that very moment, in a restaurant overlooking the Portland Harbor, Nick sat crying and missing her too.

Chapter Forty-two

Nick awoke early, with the sun. His room felt like an oven. When he got in last night, he was so cold he'd cranked the thermostat all the way up. Now he peeled himself out of bed, turned off the heat and opened the window.

After a shower, and with a cool breeze now blowing through the window, he felt refreshed. Then he glimpsed the rope through the open flap of his duffel bag. It reminded him of what day it was. All of a sudden, he felt light-headed.

He sat down on the bed, closed his eyes and took a deep breath. He imagined wading into Frenchman Bay. He wondered if the bottom dropped off gradually. He wondered if his body would be numb by the time the water covered his head. He wondered if he could really go through with this.

He decided to put it out of his head and get moving. He packed up and headed down to the lobby. He returned the umbrella at the front desk and grabbed a cup of coffee and a bagel from the breakfast bar on his way out.

He swung by Boone's to pay his tab from last night, then headed north on I-295.

Bar Harbor was three hours away. But it was still early. If he drove straight through, he might get there by noon.

What day was it, he wondered. Then he remembered it was Sunday. The Lord's Day. As his mother often reminded him, Nick was born on a Sunday.

"Sunday's child is full of grace," she used to tell him.

His mother used to talk about grace a lot. She told Nick it would be his salvation.

Nick never heard his father talk about grace. On the contrary, one of his favorite sayings was: "You get what you deserve."

Growing up, Nick was never sure who was right. So he hedged his bets. He worked hard. But once in a while, usually when he was in trouble, he also prayed for grace.

He never knew if his prayers were answered. But the more he achieved, and the closer he got to reaching his goals, the less he thought about grace and the more certain he became that he'd done it all himself.

Now, though, driving through the sugar-mapled, red-spruced rolling mountains of eastern Maine on a sunny Sunday morning, knowing this might be his last day on earth, Nick said a little prayer for grace.

Maybe his mother was right. Not that he was full of grace. But that, somehow, it might still save him.

He could still hear her singing. "'Tis grace has brought me safe thus far, and grace will lead me home."

#

It came from his right side, just as he was checking his left rear view mirror to see if he could pass a truck.

The big deer was bounding, moving so fast that Nick barely saw it before it hit his car. His window was open. He could hear the animal's bones break against his front bumper.

Nick slammed on his brakes. His airbag exploded, slamming him back against his seat. He lost his grip on the steering wheel, and his foot slipped off the brake pedal. The front of the car jerked to the right, and the back fishtailed to the left. The whole car shook violently as it spun around.

Nick thought for sure it was going to roll over. But it kept spinning until the rear wheels caught the edge of a shallow ditch and the car rolled backwards into it. There, it came to an abrupt stop. The back bumper was wedged into the base of the ditch, and the front of the car extended over the edge at a forty-five-degree angle.

Nick sat motionless, as the airbag began to automatically deflate. He saw his face in the rear view mirror. He could see no blood. His left shoulder and arm hurt from being thrown against the door when the car was spinning. His chest hurt from the airbag, and his back and neck hurt from the jolt when the back end of the car hit the bottom of the ditch.

But he was okay, even though he could barely move. He managed to pull his phone out of his pants pocket and dial 911.

As he waited for the police, Nick looked around, best he could. Blood and fur were plastered on the right side of his windshield. There were cracks in the glass, like a big spiderweb, but it hadn't shattered. Through his open window, Nick could see trees along the side of the road. Through his windshield, he could see the hood of his car and, beyond it, a cloudless sky.

Nick felt helpless. For some strange reason, as he sat there, he thought of Jim Edwards. He thought of Jim smiling at him at the end of that meeting thirty years ago, where Nick had spoken up. He thought of Jim calling him up to his office when he made vice president and still remembering that incident. He'd seen Jim only a handful of times over the course of his career. But he'd always felt his presence.

Maybe this was grace. Maybe he hadn't done it all himself. When he hit that deer and the airbag went off, his hands popped off the steering wheel and his foot slipped off the brake. If he'd managed to hold on, the car might have flipped.

Maybe this was what his mother was talking about.

#

Nick watched as the officer approached.

"Are you okay?"

"Yeah, I think so. Just stuck."

"What's your name, sir?"

"Reynolds. Nick Reynolds."

"I'm Lieutenant McKenzie," he said, looking at the car wobble in the ditch. "I think I might be able to open your door. But I don't know if I can hold it open. With this angle, I'm not sure it's safe for you to try to get out on your own."

"What are our options?"

"Well, we could wait for a tow truck to pull you out, but that could take a while, and I doubt you're very comfortable in there."

"You got that right," said Nick, bunching up the airbag. His neck was beginning to hurt pretty badly.

"Well, in that case, I'm going to call for an EMT unit. They can help you get out and get you to the hospital."

"That sounds good."

Two paramedics arrived a few minutes later. In the meantime, Nick called AAA.

The paramedics and the police officer huddled and came up with a plan.

"Mr. Reynolds," said McKenzie, "I'm going to try to hold your door open while these guys help you get out of your car."

"Okay," Nick said. "I'm ready."

McKenzie opened the door and wedged his shoulder under it to give Nick enough room to get out. The paramedics reached in and grabbed Nick under his arms. His seat was several feet above the ground, and he began to slip. He was so heavy that the paramedics fell backwards under his weight. But it was a soft landing, in the tall grass, and they broke his fall.

The paramedics got up right away. They helped Nick up.

"Can you stand, Mr. Reynolds?" one of them asked.

"Yeah, I think so," Nick said.

But as they let go of his arms, he felt weak and collapsed in the grass.

"Let's get you on a stretcher," the other paramedic said.

"Okay," Nick said, feeling dazed.

Just then, a tow truck arrived. The driver hopped out and walked over to the car.

"You okay?" he asked Nick, as the paramedics strained to lift him onto the stretcher.

"Yeah," Nick said.

"We're heading to Mid Coast," one of the paramedics said.

"Mr. Reynolds," said the tow truck driver. "I can see your car is going to need some serious repair work. If it's okay by you, I'll tow it to a shop in town. It's called Roland's. They'll give you a call. I've got your number."

"Okay," Nick said, grimacing.

He reached into his pants pocket.

"Here," he said, handing his car key to the driver. "I guess you'll need this."

#

Nick had been on the road for only thirty minutes when he hit the deer. It happened a few miles from the town of Brunswick. The paramedics took him to the emergency room of Mid Coast Hospital.

The ER doctor, a petite young lady, examined Nick and took an X-ray of his neck and back.

"Well, Mr. Reynolds," she said, fifteen minutes later. "You're a bit bruised. But you're lucky. No broken bones or serious injuries. I'm a little concerned about your neck, though. It looks okay right now. But I know it's sore, and sometimes it takes whiplash days or even weeks to show up. So we need to pay close attention to your pain level, especially over the next few days. I'm going to give you an OTC pain medication now. You can take two of these every eight hours. But if your pain gets much worse, I want you to either call me or see your primary care doctor."

"Okay. In the meantime, will I be okay to drive?"

"Where are you going?"

"Bar Harbor."

"That's two and half hours from here."

"I know."

"Well, if it was me, I'd rest for a day or two."

"Well, I'm on my own, and my car's in the shop, so it looks like I'll be staying put for a little while."

"That's good. So if your pain level gets worse while you're still here, definitely give me a call."

"I will."

"Is there anything else I can do for you today, Mr. Reynolds?"

"I guess I'm going to need a hotel room and a cab. Can someone help me with that?"

"Of course. Our receptionist out front can help you with all of that."

"Thank you."

Slowly, Nick made his way down the hallway. Instinctively, he felt his pants pocket for his key. But his pocket was empty. For an instant, he panicked. Then he remembered his car was gone.

Nick stopped walking and stood still. He felt so weak. Not just from the accident. He felt he had lost his bearings. He was alone, in a strange town, more than a thousand miles from home, with no car, no gear, no place to stay and no plan. He felt so helpless.

And yet, at that very moment, once again, he began to think about grace.

#

The receptionist suggested he stay at the Fairfield Inn. Nick called to book a room while she called a cab.

As he was waiting for his ride, his phone rang.

"Hello?"

"Mr. Reynolds?"

"Yes."

"It's Leon from Roland's Auto Body. Do you have a moment to talk?"

"Yes, I do. Thanks for calling."

"Sure."

"Have you had time to check out my car?"

"Yes, we have."

"Shoot."

"Well, the good news is that we should be able to fix everything right here in the shop."

"That is good news. What's the bad news?"

"It going to cost about $15,000 and take us at least a week."

Nick wasn't worried about the money.

"A week?"

"Yeah, we're going to need to order some parts, like the front and back bumpers. We can probably get everything in a few days, but then we'll need time for the repairs. I'd say a week to be safe."

"Wow," Nick said, rubbing his neck. "I guess you've got me. Go ahead. I'll let my insurance company know."

"We're glad to get started. But we'll need a credit card number and your signature."

"Can we handle it over the phone?"

"I can take your credit card number. But you'll need to come in to sign because it's going to be over ten grand."

"Okay. How far are you from the Fairfield Inn?"

"Just a few miles."

"Okay. I'm just about to leave the hospital. I'll stop by on my way to the hotel. I should be there soon. By the way, is there a way I can get a loaner car?"

"Unfortunately, we don't have loaners. But there's a car rental place in town. We can hook you up."

"Hold off on that. I'll let you know when I get there."

"Fair enough. We'll see you soon, Mr. Reynolds."

#

In the cab, Nick considered his options.

It was early afternoon. He could go ahead, rent a car and drive to Bar Harbor whenever he was feeling better.

He could stay in Brunswick for a week while his car was being fixed. But as he passed a place called Frosty's Donuts, with a gigantic, sprinkled donut for a sign, he imagined he might go stir crazy there.

He could fly. But he wasn't sure of the nearest airport. And then, when he got to Bar Harbor, he'd have to rent a car for the summer.

It was too much to think about right now. The cab was pulling into Roland's. He would sign for the work, go to the hotel and develop his game plan later.

#

"Can you wait here for a few minutes?" Nick asked the cab driver as they pulled in.

"Sure, buddy. I'll wait as long as you want."

Nick could hear the meter clicking.

"I'll be right back."

Nick spotted his car in the parking lot. The front bumper was crumpled, the hood was creased and the right headlight was smashed. He couldn't see the back but imagined it was in bad shape too.

The garage doors were closed, so he went into the office. A large man stepped in from the garage.

"Hi, I'm Leon," he said, extending his hand. He was probably two inches taller than Nick but fifty pounds lighter and twenty years younger. He had short red hair and a bushy beard. He wore overalls and a white T-shirt that was covered with black smudges. He looked like a big time wrestler.

"Nick Reynolds," Nick said, shaking his hand.

Leon's hand was huge and leathery, even bigger than Nick's. It felt like a catcher's mitt.

"Let's go take a look at your car."

Nick followed him back out front.

"You can see the damage in the front," Leon said. "You'll need a new radiator too and maybe a few hoses. But that should be it for under the hood."

"That's good, I guess."

"Yeah. Let's take a look at the back."

Nick didn't like the way he said that.

"Your rear bumper and tail lights will need to be replaced," Leon said. "That's pretty simple. The bigger deal is that your transmission looks pretty torn up."

"How big a deal?"

"Depends on if we need to repair it or replace it. We'll know once we get it into one of the bays and can check it out from underneath."

"Let's say you need to replace it."

"Could run an additional $5,000. But if we do need to work on your transmission, Mr. Reynolds, I'll call you first."

Nick turned to Leon and looked him in the eye.

"No need to call me, Leon. I trust you."

"Okay, Mr. Reynolds," he smiled.

They walked back into the office.

Nick gave Leon his credit card and signed for both a twenty percent down payment and an estimate of up to $20,000.

"Thank you, Mr. Reynolds," Leon said, handing Nick the receipt. Then he pulled Nick's suitcase and duffel bag from behind the counter.

"We took your gear out of the trunk," he said, picking up his suitcase and slinging his duffel bag over his shoulder. "Do you need anything else out of your car?"

"No, thanks."

"Let me help you out to the cab."

In his work, Nick often used Ronald Reagan's old "trust but verify" line. As a practical matter, though, he trusted virtually no one. He was always second guessing people and micromanaging their work. That was one of the reasons no one liked working for Nick.

He'd met Leon thirty minutes ago, over the phone. He seemed like a straight shooter. Everyone today—Officer McKenzie, the paramedics, the tow truck driver, the ER doctor, the hospital receptionist and now Leon—had all taken good care of him. And he had put his trust in them.

Nick wondered what it would be like to live this way all the time. He hadn't known what it was like to really trust people for a very long time. He missed it.

#

Nick wasn't sure how long he'd be in Brunswick, and he figured he might as well be comfortable. So when he got to the Fairfield Inn, he booked the executive suite.

His backwas stiff, and his shoulder was throbbing. He dragged his bags into the living room area of his suite. He sat down on the sofa, took off his shoes, put his feet up on the coffee table and leaned back.

He was facing the window. The royal blue drapes were pulled back, and a sheer white curtain covered the window. It was late in the afternoon, and the sun was still fairly high in the sky.

Through the sheer curtain, he could see hardwood and fir trees out beyond the parking lot. They made him think of the deer he'd hit. Nick had never killed an animal. He hoped the deer's death had been quick, that it didn't suffer long.

Would his own death be quick, he wondered.

He called his insurance agent, Deborah. He knew she wouldn't answer. It was Sunday. But he left a message, letting her know about his accident and that he'd authorized the repair work.

Sitting in the hospital, he'd thought about calling Jean. He knew she was tracking the location of his cell phone. She might have even been able to see he was at a hospital. At a minimum, she would see that he'd be staying in Brunswick for a while. No doubt, she'd wonder what's going on.

Nick knew it was time to call his wife. Buthe was still reluctant to do so because, when he had accidents of any sort, she tended to get angry, and he always ended up feeling foolish.

As a result, he'd stopped telling Jean about his accidents. Instead, he tried to cover them up, like the broken glass last week on his deck. He knew, though, she'd eventually find out about this one.

So he decided to go ahead and make the call.

"Hello? Nick? Is that you?"

"Yeah. Hi, Jean."

"Where are you? Is everything okay?"

"Yes, I'm fine. I'm in a little town just north of Portland, Maine called Brunswick. I might be staying here for a few days, and I wanted to let you know."

"Brunswick? What are you doing there? Are you okay?"

"I'm fine, Jean. Don't worry."

"Nick, what's going on?"

"I hit a deer on the highway, and my car's in the shop. I've got a hotel room. I'll be staying here for a few days, maybe a week, until my car's repaired."

"You hit a deer? Are you okay?"

"I'm fine. I went to a hospital here, and they checked me out. My neck's a little sore. But there's nothing serious."

"Oh, Nick. That sounds so scary. I'm sorry. I'm glad you're okay."

"Thanks."

"How bad is the damage to your car?"

"Well, the front and back bumpers, the radiator and the windshield will need to be replaced, and I might need a new transmission. But our insurance will cover everything. I've left a message for Deborah."

"Good lord, Nick. Are you sure you're all right?"

"I'm fine, Jean. Really. I was going to let you know when I got to Bar Harbor. But now I'm going to stay here until my car's fixed. So I thought I'd let you know."

"I'm so glad you did. I've been worried about you."

"There's no need to worry, Jean."

"But I have been worried about you, Nick. You didn't say goodbye, and I haven't heard a word from you."

"I'm sorry, Jean."

"No, I'm sorry. I know I told you that you shouldn't go on this trip. I know this sabbatical wasn't your idea. You have every right to go wherever you want. I shouldn't have tried to stand in your way."

Nick expected a different reaction, at least a hint of "I told you so." But there was no trace of it or anything remotely edgy in Jean's voice.

"Thank you, Jean. It's been an interesting trip. I've had a lot of time to think about things, to think about my life."

He could hear a whimper, a sure sign that Jean was about to cry.

"Are you okay?"

"I'm okay, Nick," she whispered. "But I've missed you."

"I've missed you too, Jean."

Silence.

"Really?" she asked.

"Yeah."

"Where are you, Nick? Where are you staying?"

"I'm at the Fairfield Inn."

"Are you comfortable there?"

"Yeah. I figured I'll be here for a while, so I got the executive suite."

"Will you stay in touch with me?"

"Yes."

"Is there anything I can do for you? Is there anything you need?"

"I'm fine, Jean. Really. Just take care of yourself."

"I am so glad you called."

"Me too. It's good to hear your voice."

"Get some rest tonight, Nick. I'll see you soon."

"I will. You get some rest too."

"Good night."

"Good night."

"Nick?"

"Yeah?"

"I love you."

"I love you too."

#

Nick was stiff and sore but, as usual, also hungry. He decided to go out for dinner. He showered, then went down to the lobby to consult the desk clerk on his options.

The clerk was a hipster. He had a well-trimmed beard, with a little soul patch. His glasses were straight out of the 1950s, with horned rims on the top and wire rims on the bottom. He wore a small, round, black earring in his left ear lobe.

Nick had always been suspicious of hipsters. He considered them air heads, although he'd never actually met one. He would never hire anyone who looked like that. He even told his HR folks to screen them out.

Of course, HR hired them anyway. Nick would see them in the hallways and the elevators. But he shunned them. And whenever he saw Lenny, he would always give him hell for hiring such strange-looking people.

Tonight, though, Nick was feeling mellow and, given this guy looked like a beatnik, he figured he would know if there were any cool spots around town.

"There are lots of great places downtown," he said. "What are you after?"

"Well, it might be a tall order, especially on a Sunday night. But I'd love to find a place with Italian food and live music."

"Oh, man!" said the hipster. "You're in luck. There's a jazz quartet at the Frontier Cafe tonight. I was just there last night. They're fantastic. The Frontier has great Italian food too."

"Sounds great. How far away is it?"

"About two miles. You need a cab?"

"Yeah. Thanks."

While Nick waited for the cab, the hipster told him all about the Frontier. He told him it used to be a mill, that it now shows art films, displays work by local artists, and features live music, mainly jazz, almost every night.

"You need to get a table near a window so you can watch the river," said the hipster.

"Which river is that?"

"It's called the Androscoggin. It runs right past the restaurant. There's a little waterfall right there. Very cool at sunset."

Nick was impressed. He figured he was wrong about hipsters, at least this one.

"Thanks," he said as his cab arrived.

"You're welcome, man. Have a great evening."

#

By the time Nick got to the Frontier, the jazz band, called "Charlie's Diggers," was setting up. There was one table open near the windows. He took it.

The hipster was right. The river flowed right by the restaurant, and there was a little waterfall. Nick suspected it was caused by a low-level dam which ran diagonally across the river. The dam was so shallow that Nick could hardly see it. But he could see the water cascading over it and almost changing course before tumbling onto boulders below.

A waitress came to take Nick's drink order. He knew he'd be having Italian, so he ordered a bottle of a Tuscan red. When she came back to pour the wine and serve bread, he ordered the rigatoni Bolognese, just as the band began to play.

The hipster wasn't kidding about the music either. Charlie was on an acoustic/electric guitar and lead vocals. His diggers played the drums, a bass cello and a piano. They started with a slow, bluesy version of "Give Me One Reason." Nick had heard that song played dozens of times. Maybe it was the wine, but he thought this was the best cover he'd ever heard.

When it came to guitar playing, Nick tended to be very judgmental. No matter who was playing, he sized them up and always thought of something he'd do better. In thirty-five years, Nick hadn't heard a guitarist play who he didn't think he could one-up.

Charlie was pretty damn good, though. In fact, he was so impressive that, for the first time he could remember, Nick didn't listen for flaws: a complex chord compromised, a hurried riff, an off note or a missed fade. Instead, he simply sat there, eating his rigatoni, sipping his wine and enjoying the music without dissecting it.

For once, he didn't imagine himself going up, grabbing the guitar and showing the crowd how it's done. Tonight, he was quite satisfied not to be playing. He was content to simply listen.

Nick watched the setting sun cast gold and red hues across the smooth surface of the river above the dam. He felt calm.

And he thought of Jean.

#

The band finished at 9:30. Nick had enjoyed their music so much that he went over and thanked Charlie and his each of his diggers.

"Let me know if you ever get to Chicago," Nick said to Charlie. "I know a lot of people there who would love to hear you play."

"We will, man. You got a card?"

"Sure," Nick said, pulling his business card out of his wallet and handing it to him.

Charlie looked at it carefully.

"Wow!" he exclaimed. "We had a president with us here tonight, boys!"

It was the first time on this trip that Nick had shared his card with anyone. Normally, he took great pride in giving it out. It was a way of impressing people. But now he felt embarrassed, like he was trying to show off.

"I love good music, Charlie. You're always welcome in Chicago."

"Thank you, man."

Nick went back to his table and ordered a Knob Creek on the rocks. He looked out the window as he sipped it, allowing himself to be mesmerized by the shimmering reflection of the moon in the still water of the river above the dam.

His thoughts drifted back to Frenchman Bay. He couldn't re-member exactly where along the way he had decided to take his own life. But he was beginning to reconsider.

Not because he was sure he could make things right. But be-cause he was beginning to realize that to take his own life meant to give up, to be defeated. And there was something inside Nick that refused to be defeated.

It was the thing that kept him coming back every spring for baseball tryouts, the thing that made him keep playing the gui-tar after his awful performance at The Music Loft, the thing that made him stick it out at Elgin after Phil tried to scuttle his career.

But there was something else too: the idea that he was worth-while, and even lovable, quite apart from his own efforts and fail-ings, that there was something else at play in his life, something he had not earned, something, maybe the one thing, that could not be earned.

In his heart, not just his mind, Nick had begun to allow for grace.

#

When Nick got back to his hotel, the hipster was still at the front desk.

"How was it?"

"Fantastic. It was everything you said and then some."

"Wonderful. I'm glad you enjoyed it."

"By the way, I'm Nick."

"Nick, I'm Matt," said the hipster, shaking his hand. "It's been a pleasure to meet you."

"Thanks again for your good advice, Matt. Good night."

"Good night, Nick."

Nick went up to his room, put on his PJs and opened his closet. He reached in and pulled a plastic laundry bag from the metal clips of a clothes hanger.

He stepped into the living area, picked up his duffel bag and sat it on the sofa. He fished out the rope and slid it into the plastic bag. He opened his door, walked down the hall to a vending area and dropped the bag into a trash can.

He went back to his room, climbed into bed and fell into a deep and peaceful sleep.

Chapter Forty-three

Nick was awakened by a knock on his door. He opened his eyes and, for a moment, struggled to know where he was. He looked around and remembered he was at the Fairfield Inn but then forgot he had heard something.

Knock, knock.

Now it registered.

"Come back later," Nick growled, not even attempting to hide his irritation at housekeeping.

"Nick?"

That voice made him sit up.

"Nick, it's me, Jean."

Good lord, he thought.

"Jean!" he exclaimed, throwing back his covers and scampering to the door. He opened it. There she was, standing in the hallway, her hands folded in front of her, looking up at him. She looked tired.

"Oh, Nick," she said, embracing him. "Are you OK?"

"Jean."

He wrapped his arms around her.

"I'm fine."

He bent down, kissed her on the cheek and hugged her tightly. She hugged him tightly and kissed him on the cheek too.

"What are you doing here?" he asked.

"I left for the airport right after you called last night."

"What? You did?"

She smiled.

"Why don't I come in and tell you about it?"

"Oh, of course," he said, pushing the door open with his elbow. "Where are your bags?"

"I brought only one bag. It's in the car. We can get it later."

She stepped inside. He locked the door behind her.

"Come in," he said, feeling a little silly, given she was already in. "I have a living room. Maybe you'd like to sit down and rest."

"Thank you. I could use a little rest."

He walked ahead, showing her the way.

"Please, sit down," he said, gesturing toward the sofa.

She sat down, slipped off her loafers and tucked her feet under her.

"Can I make you some coffee?" Nick asked.

"No, thanks," she yawned. "I think I might like to take a little nap."

He sat down on the sofa next to her. There was just a little gap between them.

"Did you travel all night?"

"Almost. I left Chicago about nine and arrived in Newark a little after midnight. I had a long layover and got to Portland early this morning. I rented a car at the airport and drove straight here."

"My lord, Jean. I'm so surprised to see you. I mean I'm so glad to see you."

"And I'm glad to see you too, Nick. After you told me about your accident, I had to come here and make sure you're okay. I hope I'm not intruding."

"Intruding?" he smiled. "No. You're not intruding. I'm so glad you're here."

"And I'm so relieved you're okay."

"I'm fine. Just a little sore."

Her right hand was resting palm down on the sofa in the space between them. Nick covered it with his left hand. Jean turned her hand over. Their fingers intertwined. To most couples, this might not have been a big deal. But Nick and Jean hadn't held hands in years.

She smiled, leaned her head back and closed her eyes.

"Would you like to lie down?" Nick asked.

"I really want to talk with you, Nick. But, yes, I'd love to lie down right now. I could really use a nap."

"Would you like to lie down here? I can get you a pillow and a blanket."

"Actually, I think I'd be much more comfortable in bed."

"Okay."

Nick got up and, still holding her hand, led Jean to his king-sized bed.

"Make yourself comfortable," he said.

"Thank you."

Nick wanted to give her some space. He stepped back into the living room and sat down on the sofa. From there, he could see Jean taking out her earrings and setting them down on the nightstand. He watched her unbutton her red sweater, take it off and lay it on a chair. He watched her slip off her jeans and lay them on top of her sweater.

Jean worked out several times a week. Spinning, Pilates, weights. She had the body of a forty year old. Now wearing only a white T-shirt, pink underwear and white socks, she slipped under the covers.

She looked over at Nick.

"Are you coming back to bed?"

Nick hadn't slept with his wife in three years. He didn't need to be asked twice. He walked over to the bed and, still in his PJs, slipped under the covers too.

They moved close together, facing each other.

"Nick, please hold me and warm me up."

He moved in close. He slipped his left hand behind her neck. With his right, he rubbed her back, arms and legs to warm her up.

"Oh, that feels so good."

And she felt so good to him. Her back was firm. Her upper arms were toned. Her waist was lean. Her hair felt so soft and smooth against his rough, unshaven face. She was not wearing perfume, but her hair smelled like strawberries.

He leaned in and kissed her on the cheek. But she didn't reciprocate. She'd already fallen asleep. He eased away, but only slightly. He just lay there and looked at her.

The window was behind him, and the morning light shone on her face. It illuminated the grey in her blond hair, like silver threads woven into cornsilk, and the fine lines etched into her cheeks.

She too was fifty-three. But right now she didn't look so different from when he had met her, when he had first seen her face and thought she looked like an angel.

#

When Jean woke up, two hours later, Nick had shaved, showered and gotten dressed. He was sitting on the sofa. He was on his computer, exploring options for brunch. He'd found a place nearby he thought Jean would like called the Kopper Kettle. They served French toast, her favorite.

"Good morning," she said, stepping into the living room.

"Good morning, sleepy head."

He hadn't called her that in a very long time.

"Hungry?" he asked.

"Famished."

"I think I just found a great place for brunch."

"Great."

"It's a few miles away. I'll need a ride."

"Thankfully for you, I've got wheels," Jean said playfully. "Let me get a shower. Would you go down to the car and get my bag?"

"Glad to."

She handed him the keys and told him to look for a new, dark blue Nissan Altima in the parking lot. Then she gave him a hug and a kiss on the cheek and slipped into the bathroom.

On his way out to the car, Nick pondered what an unlikely morning it had been. He wasn't sure what was more surprising: Jean showing up or them treating each other with such civility. And the morning wasn't over. He smiled.

He pulled her small suitcase out of the back seat and wheeled it up to their room. Jean was still in the shower. He sat down on the sofa, got back online and started looking at options for dinner. He hoped Jean might decide to spend the night.

She stepped out of the bathroom with a towel wrapped around her. From where he was sitting, Nick had a clear view of the bedroom.

"I put your suitcase on the stand next to the bed."

"Thank you."

Through the doorway, he could see Jean from behind. Leaning over her suitcase, she let her towel drop to the floor. He hadn't seen her naked in a long time. Taking care of herself had certainly paid off. She looked fantastic.

As she bent over to put on her panties, she turned sideways. He could see her breasts. They were still firm.

Standing up, she looked up and caught him staring. She smiled.

"I'll be ready in a minute."

"No rush."

Nick decided he should give her some privacy. He looked down and resumed checking out options for dinner.

About ten minutes later, she stepped into the living room. She was wearing black jeans, a white chiffon blouse and a pink cardigan sweater. She looked like she'd just stepped off the cover of the Chico's catalogue.

"You look great," he said, standing up.

"Thank you. You look pretty good yourself."

It felt so strange and wonderful to be trading compliments.

"Ready to go?" he asked.

"Yep."

"If you drive, I'll navigate."

"Deal. I assume you know where you're going."

"Kind of," he said, as they walked into the hallway. "It's a restaurant called the Kopper Kettle. It's in a part of town called Topsham, which is just across the Androscoggin River."

"You sound like you really know your way around here."

"Not really. But I had dinner at a place overlooking the river last night. Brunswick is a nice little town."

"Okay, Mr. Reynolds. I'm in your capable hands."

She walked in front of him, sashaying a little. She still had such a lovely butt. For the first time in years, Nick thought he might have a shot at holding that in his capable hands.

In the parking lot, he wasn't watching for Jean's rental car. When she stopped to unlock it, he accidentally ran into her. Reflexively, he grabbed her waist.

"Sorry."

"No problem," she smiled.

He opened the door for her. Nick hadn't opened a car door for his wife in years.

"Why, thank you, Nick. Such a gentleman."

"You're welcome," he said, gently closing the door behind her.

He got in and typed the Kopper Kettle into his maps app. He pointed out the Frontier Cafe as they passed it and the Androscoggin as they crossed it.

It took them less than ten minutes to get there. At first, Nick wondered if it was the right place. Online, he'd seen only photos of the food and a few, positive customer reviews. Now he was looking at a plain, rectangular, cinderblock building.

He guessed the restaurant was originally a house. The "house" half was painted blue. The "garage" half was painted white. A long, blue awning covered a row of small windows on the garage side. An arched blue awning with a big copper kettle imprinted on it covered a glass door at the end. A few cars and a couple of pickups were parked out front. The place looked more like a warehouse than a restaurant.

"Jean, this doesn't look as nice as I had expected."

"It looks fine, Nick. I'm sure they have good food."

He really liked this new, more relaxed version of Jean.

They got out of the car and held hands walking up to the restaurant. Nick opened the door for her.

"Thank you."

It was a basic diner. Not fancy or modern, but clean.

"Is this okay?" Nick asked.

"It's perfect."

"You two can grab a table or a booth anywhere you like," a waitress called out from behind the counter. "I'll be right with you."

They slid into a booth near a window. Two minutes later, the waitress arrived with a pot of coffee and menus.

"Coffee?"

"Yes," they said in unison.

She handed them menus and filled their mugs.

"I'll be back in a minute to take your order."

Nick looked across the table at Jean. He couldn't remember the last time they'd been out to eat together alone.

They scanned their menus and slid them to the end of the table.

"What are you having?" Nick asked.

"The French toast."

"I thought so," he smiled.

"How about you?"

"I think I'll have a veggie omelet with some fruit."

"Nick Reynolds, you've changed!"

"Well, I'm trying to eat a little healthier."

Jean smiled and studied his face.

"No, I don't mean how you're eating. You seem different."

"Ready to order?" their waitress asked, pen in hand.

She took their orders, and Jean continued.

"You do seem different, Nick."

"How?"

"Well, for starters, you're not in a hurry. And I have to say you've been really nice to me this morning. It's wonderful."

"I've slowed down on this trip, Jean. And I've learned a lot about myself."

"Like what?" she asked, sipping her coffee.

Nick took a sip of his coffee too. Then he leaned forward, looked into Jean's eyes and spoke slowly.

"I'm a narcissist, Jean. I'm arrogant. I drink too much. I'm a bully. I'm a terrible boss. I'm an absent father and an inattentive husband. I'm rich and powerful. But I care only about my work. I've lost all my friends. I don't take care of myself. I'm obese and ugly. I'm angry, lonely and sad. This is what I've become, Jean. This is what I'm learning about myself."

Jean was stunned. She knew many of these things were true. But in thirty years of marriage, she'd almost never heard Nick say anything self-critical. She could hardly believe these words were coming out of his mouth.

"Nick ..."

Just then, their waitress returned with their food.

"Can I get you two anything else?"

"No, thanks," Nick said.

"Nick, I'm listening."

He leaned back in.

"I've been thinking a lot about my father. At his funeral, Uncle Bob told me Dad loved music and played the guitar when he was young. I was shocked. But I couldn't believe I was shocked. How could I have not known my own father, the guy who had bought me three guitars, had played the guitar himself? How could I not have had a clue? I asked Mother about it. She said that soon after they were married, Dad decided music was a waste of time, that he needed to make something of himself. So he joined the Army. He went to Korea. When he got home, he didn't know what to do. Somebody told him the post office was hiring. So he applied and got the job. But he never liked his work. Mother told me the only thing Dad ever really loved was music. He told her that one day, when he could afford it, he would quit his job and become a musician. He wanted to make a lot of money, but he didn't know how. He felt trapped. And so he drank, and he walled himself off from everyone, even my mother."

"Warm up your coffee?" their waitress asked.

"Sure," Nick said, sliding his cup toward her.

"Yes, please," said Jean.

"Is your food okay?" their waitress asked. Neither of them had touched a thing.

"Oh, yes," Jean said. "We're just a little slow this morning. I hope that's okay."

"Of course. Take your time. There's no rush."

"When Dad died," Nick continued, "the only thing I knew was that he always talked about making a lot of money. And so that's the baton I picked up and ran with. Dad never really had a shot at being rich. But I did, and I took it. And I made a lot of money. But the more money I made and the higher I rose in the company, the more I felt separated from the things I really loved, the more I felt separated from you and the kids and the more I thought only of myself. Just like Dad, I began to wall myself off and drink too much. And just like him, I began to think about taking my own life."

"Oh, Nick ..."

He reached across the table and held her hand.

"But I am *not* my father, Jean. And I'm not going to give up or destroy myself. I want to start over. When I took off on this trip, I was angry. I thought this sabbatical was about the worst thing that had ever happened to me. Now I believe it might be the best. It's given me new eyes. I want to spend the summer in Bar Harbor and start over. Will you go with me?"

"Oh, Nick," she said, squeezing his hand. "Yes. Yes. Let's start over together."

Nick held Jean's hands in his.

"There's one more thing I want to tell you, Jean."

"What's that?"

"I've never cheated on you."

"What?" she asked, giving him a quizzical look.

"I know you've probably wondered about that over the years."

"Well, yes, I have."

"I've had a few opportunities, you know."

"I'm sure you have," she smiled.

"And I've been tempted."

"But you've never given in?"

"Never. Not once."

The expression on Jean's face was a mixture of surprise, joy and relief.

"Why, Nick?" she asked, squeezing his hands. "Why?"

"It's simple really. I could never make love to a woman who I don't carry with me in my heart."

"Oh, Nick," she said, tears welling up in her eyes.

"Jean, you were always with me. Always."

#

They walked out into the parking lot, holding hands. It was a bright, warm morning.

"It's such a lovely day," Jean said. "Would you like to go for a walk?"

"I'd love to."

"You sure you're up for it? I mean, with the accident and all?"

"Yeah, I feel fine. A little sore, but fine. And believe it or not, I've been walking a bit lately, mainly on the treadmills in my hotels."

"You've got to be kidding! Nick, you are a new man!"

They strolled around the little town of Topsham, down the sidewalks, past the shops, cafes, churches, little houses and cabins. They discovered a trail which led into the woods. They followed it to a creek and sat down on a big rock overlooking it. Nick put his arm around Jean, and she rested her head on his shoulder.

"So tell me a little about your trip," she said. "Where did you go? What did you do? Who did you meet?"

"Well," he said with a grin. "I began by blowing a gasket on the Dan Ryan."

"Seriously?"

"Seriously!" he laughed.

Nick proceeded to tell Jean everything. Well, almost everything. He didn't mention Marian at Notre Dame, or getting drunk at the Indians game. Not yet. But he hit the highlights.

He told her about his experiences and what he was beginning to rediscover about himself. How playing the guitar at the Hard Rock Cafe made him remember how much he loved music. How Whitman's quote and having dinner with Paul made him realize how separate he had become from people. How Longfellow's poem made him realize how dreary his life had become. How the selfie exhibit made him realize how self-absorbed he'd become. How being alone made him realize how much he'd been missing his family.

"Oh, Nick," Jean said. "How amazing."

"It's been an amazing journey."

"There's something I want to share with you too."

"I'm listening."

Emboldened by Nick's openness, Jean told him that she'd felt a gap in her life, especially after the kids left home, and that she'd allowed Bob Perkins to fill that gap. She told him they'd been having coffee for years. She told him that she'd invited Bob to the house for coffee last Saturday and that, when he came on to her, she kicked him out. She told him she could never bring herself to say anything about Bob over the years because she knew Nick wouldn't understand.

"But that's no excuse," she said. "I'm sorry for what I've done, Nick, and I'm sorry for not telling you."

"Jean," he said, looking down, "I'm the one who owes you an apology."

"For what?"

"For not being there for you."

"You were busy."

"No. It's not because I was busy that I wasn't there for you.
I wasn't there for you because my life got so filled with me that
there was no room for anyone else. I don't blame you at all, Jean.
I wouldn't even blame you if you'd slept with Bob."

"Really?"

"Well, maybe just a little."

His arm around her shoulder, he gave it a squeeze.

"Did you really kick him out?"

"Yes. Right out the front door."

"Did you kick him in the ass?"

"Oh, Nick!" she half laughed and half cried. She wrapped her
arms around him. "You're back. I knew you'd come back. I've
missed you so much."

He held her close and began crying too. The two of them sat
there, on that big rock, crying. They held each other for a long
time.

Finally, Nick turned toward Jean. He wiped away her tears
with his fingertips.

"Will you be staying for dinner?"

"Yeah," she said, sniffling. "If you'll have me."

"I never want to go anywhere without you again."

"Oh, Nick. That's the most romantic thing you've ever said."

"Really? I think I've had much better lines than that."

"Okay," she smiled. "Maybe you are a little arrogant."

They laughed and got up. They stood there, facing each other,
holding hands and smiling.

"Are you ready to go?" she asked.

"Yes."

"Hang on," she said. "There's something else I have to tell you
right now."

"What's that?"

He hoped it was nothing else about Bob Perkins.

"You're not ugly, Nick. Far from it. In fact, I want you to know
I've never found you more attractive."

He blushed, something he seldom did.

"And you're even cuter when you blush."

"Let's go," he grinned.

They strolled back to the car, holding hands.

"Would you like to drive?" she asked.

"No, you go ahead. I'll be your navigator."

"That's funny. I have a thing for navigators."

"Cool," he said with a little swagger.

#

When they got back to hotel, Jean decided to take another nap. "I'm exhausted. I hope you don't mind."

"Not at all. Sleep as long as you like. I'll go online and find a place for us to have dinner. What are you in the mood for?"

"Surprise me," she said, kissing him on the cheek.

Jean stripped down to her underwear and T-shirt again and climbed back under the covers. Nick went into the living room and sat down on the sofa. But he didn't open his laptop. He would find a restaurant later.

Right now, he simply sat, closed his eyes and felt thankful for this day.

#

Nick made himself a cup of coffee. Filling the little coffee pot with water in the bathroom, he was careful not to wake Jean.

He sat back down on the sofa, went online and checked out dinner options. There were a surprising number of nice restaurants in Brunswick.

But he kept coming back to the Frontier Cafe. He'd liked everything about it last night and thought Jean would like it too. Plus, a jazz guitarist would be performing there tonight.

So he made a reservation for six-thirty. He requested a table near a window with a good view of the river.

#

Jean liked the look of the place even before she walked in.

"Nick, this is perfect," she said, as they pulled up.

He walked around the car and opened her door.

"Why do I feel like I'm on a first date?" she asked, smiling.

"I just hope you'll kiss me good night."

"Just wait."

Nick felt a warm buzz inside he hadn't felt in a long time.

They were seated at a table near a window with an even better view of the river than the one he had last night.

"This is beautiful," Jean said, looking around. "The whole thing. It's perfect, Nick. Thank you for bringing me here."

The waitress brought menus and a wine list and went over the specials.

"May I start you out with a drink?"

"Go ahead, Jean."

"I'll have a glass of your house chardonnay."

"Very good. And for you, sir?"

"I'll have the same."

"Very good. I'll be back with your wine and to take your order in a minute."

"Thank you," Jean said.

She looked at Nick.

"Just one glass? Not a bottle?"

"Would you like a bottle?"

"No. But you usually do."

"One glass will be plenty tonight."

"Wow, Nick. You really have changed. I'm impressed."

"Just wait," he said, smiling.

He looked out the window.

"That's the Androscoggin River," he said, pointing out the spot where the water falls off. Tonight a mist rose from the rocks below, backlit by the sun, which was now getting low in the sky.

"Look," Jean said. "I can see a rainbow in the spray. How beautiful."

Nick was no longer looking at the river. He was watching Jean.

"Yes," he said. "How beautiful."

#

"Any recommendations?" Jean asked.

"Well, I had the rigatoni here last night. It was excellent. But I think I'll try the seafood tonight."

Jean smiled, so amazed to see Nick eating so healthy.

"I heard you texted the kids."

"Yeah."

"Ashley called me right away."

"She did?"

"Yeah. She wanted to make sure everything was okay. Josh called too. I told them about your sabbatical, that you were on your way to Bar Harbor."

"Jean, I'm sorry I didn't text you too."

"That's okay, Nick. I'm glad you reached out to the kids. I was tracking your progress, and I figured you'd let me know when you got to Bar Harbor."

Their waitress returned with their wine. Jean ordered the rigatoni. Nick ordered scallops and risotto.

"To us," Nick said, raising his glass.

"To us," Jean said, smiling.

The guitarist was setting up. He was in his forties with a goatee and a pony tail. A week ago, he was the kind of guy Nick would have tried to avoid. Now, he was eager to hear him play.

Nick and Jean sipped their wine.

"Nick, I just want you to know how much I appreciate what you shared with me this afternoon."

"Thank you for listening. I was so glad to share it."

"Nick, I know you're feeling guilty about what's happened in our marriage."

"I feel awful about it."

"I understand. But I want you to know you're not the only one at fault. I told you I've needed someone to listen to me. But if I'm completely honest, I have to admit that I've not been a very good listener myself."

"Jean ..."

"Nick, you may not have always been there for me over the years, but I've not always been there for you either. And I've been hard on you. I'm sorry. If our marriage has been broken, I'm as much at fault as you are."

"Do you think our marriage has been broken?"

"Well, yes."

"Do you think we can fix it?"

"I do."

"Do you think that's going to take time?"

"I do."

"I do too."

"It's going to be challenging."

"I know."

"I'm up for it."

"Me too," said Nick. "And I accept your apology."

"Thank you," said Jean, squeezing his hand.

#

When they got back to the hotel, Jean said, "Let's get to bed early."

"Okay."

They brushed their teeth and slipped under the covers. Nick was lying on his back. Jean turned on the lamp on her nightstand.

"Nick, will you do something for me?"

"Sure."

She handed him two folded sheets of paper. They were yellowed, with tattered edges and small holes along the creases.

"Would you read this to me?"

She handed Nick the pieces of paper. He unfolded them and read aloud the words which he'd penned thirty-five years before.

"Angel," he began. "It was Saturday night ..."

By the time he finished the poem, both Nick and Jean were crying. They held each other and made love and fell asleep in one another's arms.

Chapter Forty-four

Nick was sitting on the sofa, drinking coffee, when he heard Jean get up.

"Good morning, sleepy head," he said, as she stepped into the living room. She was wearing only a night shirt.

"Good morning," she said with a smile.

She sat down next to him, pulled her knees up to her chest and tucked her heels into the cushion beneath her. She wrapped her arms around him and kissed him on the cheek.

"How did you sleep?" she asked.

"Like a baby."

"Thank you for last night," she said.

"Thank you."

"You're blushing," she said. "It's cute."

He put his arm around her and kissed her on the forehead.

"What would you like to do today?" he asked.

"I was thinking we might leave for Bar Harbor."

"Now there's somewhere I've never been," he smiled. "You hungry?"

"Yeah."

"You okay with the free breakfast off the lobby?"

"Sounds perfect."

Nick started to get up.

"Hang on a minute," Jean said, putting her hand on his chest. He leaned back.

"I just want to tell you something."

"What's that?"

"I just want to tell you how grateful I am for what you shared with me yesterday. I mean about your trip and your father and what you're learning about yourself. And I want you to know how grateful I am for you, Nick. I love you. I'm so glad you're here. I'm so glad we're here together."

"Thank you, Jean. I'm so glad we're here together too."

She smiled, pushed her feet out from underneath her and began to sit up.

"Hang on," Nick said. "Now I have something I want to ask you."

She sat back down.

"What's that?"

"Will you forgive me?"

"Forgive you. For what?"

"For all the awful things I've done and all the things I should have done but didn't over the years. I'm sorry for everything."

She looked up at him and smiled.

"Oh, Nick. I do forgive you. Now, can you forgive yourself?"

He thought about it for a moment.

"I don't know. I hope so."

#

It was an unseasonably warm morning. They rode with the windows down. The rush of warm air and sweet smell of pines made Nick feel connected to the world around him.

Jean was driving. "It's my charter," she'd said with a wink as they approached her rental car in the hotel parking lot. It was the first time in a long time Nick had ridden in the passenger seat. He liked being in charge.

This morning, though, he was happy that Jean was driving. He was happy to let go and enjoy the scenery.

When she drove, Jean liked to stop about every hour to go to the bathroom or just take a break. Normally, stopping so often would drive Nick crazy.

But about an hour outside of Portland, as Jean pulled into a rest area, it dawned on him that the pace of this whole trip would have normally driven him crazy. Ever since he'd blown that gasket in Chicago, he'd slowed down. And it felt good.

Jean parked, and they got out.

"Do you have to use the bathroom?" he asked.

"No. You?"

"No."

"Let's take a little walk," she said.

She slipped her hand into his, and they walked around a green space, under the shade of maple and oak trees.

"Do you mind if we sit for a minute?" she asked, as they came to a picnic table.

"Not at all. Would you like something to drink?"

"No, thanks," she said, smiling. "I just want to sit here with you."

Nick sat down next to Jean. He'd been on the road, by himself, for more than a week. But he'd felt he was on his own for years. And now, the idea of someone, let alone the woman he loved, wanting simply to sit with him for a moment made all his loneliness fall away.

#

They got to Bar Harbor a little after noon. Neither of them had been there. They were surprised to learn the town is located on an island, called Mount Storm Island.

Nick navigated through the wide streets of the little town to the rental office near their cabin in the northeast corner of the island.

The cabin Nick had rented was one of five, called Tide Watch Cabins. He'd requested one on the water. It was a one-bedroom place, overlooking Frenchman Bay.

"I have a reservation for Reynolds for a cabin for the summer," he said to the lady at the desk in the rental office.

"Oh, yes, Mr. Reynolds. We've been expecting you," she said, looking at Jean.

"My wife will be joining me. I hope that will be okay."

"Certainly."

"And we might have a couple of visitors for a few days," he said, smiling at Jean. "Will we have some other rental options nearby?"

"When would they be arriving?"

"At this point, we're not quite sure. But we hope it will be in either late June or early July."

"Let me see," she said, flipping the pages of a book on the counter. "Do you think it might be over a weekend?"

"Yes," Jean said. "Probably a long weekend."

"Well, if that's the case, I would have one other cabin available. It's not on the water, but it's right behind yours."

"Sounds great," said Jean. "Would it be possible to hold it for us for a day or two? We should be able to let you know very soon."

"That won't be a problem," she said, scribbling in the book.

Nick and Jean checked into their cabin. It was cozy and clean, with a broad front porch overlooking the water.

"Oh, Nick! This is perfect," Jean said, as they stood on the porch, looking out at islands and a lighthouse in the bay.

"It is pretty great, isn't it?" Nick said, grabbing Jean and pulling her close.

They stood there for a minute, embracing. They'd been married for thirty years. But Nick was rediscovering his wife: the curve of her lower back, the scent of her hair, the quiver of her lips.

As he held her close, Nick looked out over the water. This was the place, he thought. This is where I was going to end it all.

Now, instead, he felt like he was beginning again.

#

They drove into town for lunch. Nick noticed that just about every restaurant advertised its lobster. I'm going to have to pace myself, he thought.

After lunch, Nick and Jean picked up some groceries and drove around a bit to get their bearings. The downtown had a frontier feel, with lots of outfitter shops, a general store and, strangely, an abundance of Subaru Foresters. But there was a refined touch too, with art galleries, upscale restaurants and a tea house. Nick even spotted a music store.

He had picked Bar Harbor because he hadn't been there before. But there was something familiar about it.

On their way back to their cabin, Nick and Jean realized that their place bordered Acadia National Park. Nick remembered seeing pictures of the "wild gardens" there in his mother's coffee table book. He hadn't had time to tour the Botanic Garden of Smith College. But now he'd have all summer to meander through the wild gardens of Acadia. He was thrilled.

After they unpacked their groceries, Nick and Jean decided to take a walk. Holding hands, they strolled along a flat, crushed-stone trail called, fittingly, Shore Path, which wound along the bay. Just below them, on one side, lay the rocky shore. On the other side were trees, flowers and the open lawns of cottages and homes.

On the lawn of one home, a man was tossing a baseball with a young boy. He threw the ball high into the air. Looking up, the boy rocked back and forth and pounded his glove, keeping his eyes on the ball. It landed in the center of his glove.

"Good catch!" the man yelled.

"Thanks, Dad!" the boy called back with a smile.

It was an idyllic scene. But it reminded Nick of all the times he did not toss balls with his own son. It reminded him of all the times he wasn't there for both of his children. It made his heart ache. He stopped walking.

"Are you okay, Nick?" Jean asked.

He looked past her, at the man and his son tossing the ball.

The pain grew more intense.

"Nick, are you okay?" Jean asked again, this time with more concern in her voice.

He looked at her. She could see the pain in his eyes.

"Nick, what's wrong?"

"I've been an awful father, Jean."

She turned around and saw the man and the boy.

"No, Nick," she said. "You've not been an awful father. Ashley and Josh love you very much."

"Really? Then why don't they ever call? Why didn't they come home last Christmas?"

"Oh, Nick. They're busy. They're just busy. It has nothing to do with how they feel about you."

Nick looked at Jean. He knew his kids were busy. But he also knew Jean was not telling him the whole truth. He knew he was not a part of his children's lives and that he had not been a part of their lives for a long time. And he knew it was his fault. It made his heart hurt. It was a familiar pain, the pain of knowing he had fallen short. And he knew of only one way to assuage it: with a drink.

But that wasn't an option right now. So he told Jean he was okay, and they walked back to their cabin for the night, without Nick saying another word.

#

Jean was tired and decided to go to bed early.

"Are you sure you don't want to join me?" she asked.

"No. I'm going to stay up a little while and read."

"Okay," she said, kissing him on cheek. "Are you sure you're all right?"

"Yeah, I'm fine."

"Nick, you're a good father. And I know you're going to be an even better father in the days and years ahead."

"Yeah. Well, I hope you're right. Good night. I love you."

"Good night. I love you too."

Jean went to bed. But Nick was not fine. He kept thinking of the father and son tossing baseball, and his heart was still aching. With Jean gone, he stepped into the kitchen, uncorked a bottle of red wine and poured himself a glass.

He stood there and threw it back like it was water.

Then he poured himself a second glass and threw it back too. He felt the pain in his heart begin to dull.

He poured himself a third glass, drank it down slowly and felt the pain ease a little more.

Then he poured a fourth glass, emptying the bottle. He guzzled it and began to feel numb.

Just then, Jean emerged from the bedroom. She saw the empty wine glass in Nick's hand and the empty bottle on the counter. At first, she looked dumbfounded. Then she looked furious.

"Nick! Did you drink all that wine?"

He didn't know what to say.

"Oh, Nick!" she exclaimed. "You're drunk! I've been gone for thirty minutes, and you're already drunk! How could you do this? You haven't changed a bit."

"Jean," he said, setting his glass down on the counter. "I'm sorry."

"Don't tell me you're sorry, Nick. Don't ever tell me that again. And don't tell me you're going to change. You've got to show me. That's the only thing that matters, the only thing I can believe."

"Jean ..." he moaned, stepping towards her.

"No, Nick," she said, backing away. "No. You have got to stop this. You've got to change. I want to be with you. But you've got to want to change. So I suggest you go over to that sofa and sit down and think about whether you really want to change. Good night."

And with that, she turned, walked back into the bedroom and shut the door. Nick stood there for a minute, in a daze. Then he shuffled over to the sofa. He sat down and thought about what had just happened. Then he lay down and fell asleep.

#

The next morning, Nick was already sitting at the kitchen table, drinking coffee, when Jean woke up.

"Good morning," he said. He felt like getting up and giving her a hug, but he didn't want to push it.

"Good morning," she said. "How are you feeling?"

"Much better."

"No hangover?"

"No, but that's not why I'm feeling better."

"What do you mean?" Jean asked, pouring herself a cup of coffee.

"I mean I had some time to think last night, after you went back to bed. I was thinking about my father, who drank just about all the time. He was an alcoholic, no doubt. For years, I've thought I was an alcoholic too. But last night, I started thinking about the way I drink. I don't drink all the time, and I actually don't think I'm an alcoholic. I abuse alcohol. To me, it's like a drug. It dulls my pain. I drank that bottle of wine last night to dull the pain of feeling like a bad father. Sometimes I drink to dull the pain of all my problems at work. Sometimes I drink to dull the pain of being out of shape. Sometimes, to be honest, I drink to dull the pain of being at odds with you. I drink, Jean, to dull my pain. But I'm in pain every day, and I don't drink every day. There are times, including this past week, when I choose not to drink. I don't know if I can give up drinking altogether. But I don't know if I have to. I think I can learn to control my drinking. But I don't know how to do that. I think I need to get some help."

Jean sat down at the table across from Nick. She put her head in her hands and began to cry.

"What's wrong?" he said. "You don't believe me?"

"No," she said, looking up. "I do believe you, Nick. I believe everything you're saying is true. I'm crying because I realize now I was too hard on you last night. I'm always too hard on you. You do need to change, Nick. But so do I. We both need to change, and that's going to take time. And I want you to know you can count on me along the way. I'm sorry I blew up last night. I'm sorry I walked away."

They got up and held each other tight.

"I believe in you, Nick."

"Thank you, Jean. I feel it."

They grabbed their coffee, stepped into the living room and sat down beside each other on the sofa.

"Nick, if you're serious about getting help, I know of someone really great in Chicago."

"I am serious, Jean. I need help. I'll do what I can on my own this summer. But I know I'm going to need help. Just give me your person's number, and I'll set up an appointment for as soon as we get home."

#

After breakfast, Nick and Jean went for a walk along Shore Path. They were surprised to see enormous boulders along the shoreline which were wide at the top and narrow at the bottom. Nick was amazed that objects so large and upside down could be standing at all, especially with the waves slapping at their base.

"Why do you think they haven't fallen over?" he asked Jean, sitting next to her on a wooden bench.

"I don't know," she said. "Why do you think we're sitting here together, in Maine, looking out at the sea?"

"It's a bit of a mystery, isn't it?"

#

That evening, Jean called Ashley and Josh and invited them to spend a long weekend with her and Nick that summer. They were both delighted.

They quickly agreed on the Fourth of July holiday. Josh would fly in from San Francisco, Ashley from Denver. Ashley asked if she could bring her boyfriend.

"Of course, sweetheart," Jean said, smiling at Nick. "We'd be happy to host Michael too."

Nick raised his eyebrows. Meet the parents, he thought.

Jean walked to the rental office to reserve the cabin behind them for the holiday weekend. At last, she thought, a family vacation.

#

The next morning, Nick and Jean walked along Shore Path for an hour. For Jean, it was a way to keep up her exercise regimen. For Nick, it was the beginning of nothing less than total rehabilitation.

After that bottle of wine their first night in Bar Harbor, Nick was able to cut back his drinking. He kept eating healthier too, switching mainly to seafood. Between walking every day and eating right, in two months, he thought he'd lose about twenty pounds.

He also bought an acoustic guitar. It was a Yamaha, a full-sized version of the first guitar his father had bought him as a boy. Nick had played the electric guitar for so long that playing an acoustic was almost like starting over. He found he had to really think about what he was playing, even with songs he'd known how to play for decades. He had to slow down.

For Nick, it was a summer of slowing down.

#

About ten days after Nick and Jean arrived in Bar Harbor, Nick got a call from Leon at Roland's in Brunswick.

"Good morning, Leon. What's the good word?"

"Well, your car is completely fixed, good as new."

"That's great. Did it need a new transmission?"

"Yes, it did. I thought we might be able to repair your old one, but it was just too torn up."

"I understand. Well, is my car ready to be picked up?"

"Yes, it is."

"Good. My wife rented a car in Portland. We're in Bar Harbor. We drove the rental here. You'd mentioned a car rental place in Brunswick. Do you think I could return it there?"

"Well, you should give them a call. But I'm sure you could. They have a lot of cars going back and forth to Portland."

"Great. Then I'll plan to come in this afternoon."

"How will you get here from the car rental place?"

"How far away is it from your place?"

"Just a few miles."

"I'll take a cab."

"No worries, Mr. Reynolds. I'll come and pick you up. Just give me a call when you get there."

"Sounds good, Leon. Anything else?"

"Well, I guess we should talk about the final price."

"No need, Leon. We'll cover that when I get there. I trust you."

#

Ashley, Mike and Josh flew into the Bangor airport on Friday, the first of July. Their flights arrived within an hour of each other. Nick and Jean were waiting to greet them.

Nick hadn't seen his children in more than a year. Josh arrived first. He was wearing a Cubs hat.

When he spotted his parents, he quickened his step. Nick ran to him, arms wide open. The two men embraced. Nick kissed his son on his cheek.

"I've missed you, Josh."

"I've missed you too, Dad."

As soon as he saw Ashley walking down the terminal, Nick began to cry. Looking at her, Nick could see his daughter being born. It had been the happiest day of his life.

She ran to him, and he ran to her. They embraced. Tears flowed down Nick's face.

As they hugged, Ashley peeked at Jean over Nick's shoulder and gave her a quizzical look.

Is he okay? she mouthed.

Jean smiled and nodded her head.

After hugging her mother and brother, Ashley said, "Mom, Dad, Josh, I'd like you to meet Michael."

Nick hadn't even noticed him. Then he remembered that this guy might actually be The One. It was a moment he had dreaded.

"Hello, Mrs. Reynolds," Michael said, giving Jean a warm embrace.

"Hello, Mr. Reynolds," he said, turning to Nick and extending his hand. Ashley was beaming.

And what Nick felt was the opposite of dread. At that moment, he felt filled with grace.

#

The next day, the five of them rode bikes in Acadia National Park. They stopped to have lunch at the wild gardens. There, Nick took great pride in pointing out every type of flower.

"Wow, Mr. Reynolds," Michael said. "You certainly know a lot about flowers."

"I spent a lot of time with my mother in her garden as a boy," he said proudly.

That evening, they had dinner in town. Lobster, of course.

Afterwards, they all went back to Nick and Jean's cabin. Nick opened a bottle of wine and poured a glass for each of them.

"To our togetherness," Nick toasted.

Just as they were all sitting down, Jean turned to Nick and said, "I just remembered. It's garbage night."

"Oh, yeah," Nick said. "I'll be right back."

"Do you need a hand, Mr. Reynolds?" Michael asked.

"Sure."

Nick and Michael went out the back door. Nick grabbed the cabin's single garbage can. Michael grabbed the recycling bin. They carried them out to the end of the gravel driveway.

On their way back, Michael said, "I'd like to ask you something, Mr. Reynolds."

"Sure, Michael."

"I love Ashley very much," he said, his voice quavering. "I've never loved anyone so much. I'd like to spend the rest of my life with her, and I'd like to ask your blessing to ask her to marry me."

\#

After his kids left, Nick's days seemed to fall into a regular rhythm: walking with Jean in the morning; re-reading Hemingway and Faulkner, writing poetry and taking a nap in the afternoon; playing guitar in the evening.

He was unwinding, drawing a breath, stepping off a treadmill he'd been on, in one form or another, for thirty years.

Maybe I'll be around another thirty years, he thought. Or maybe thirty days. So what? What really matters? What's most important to me? What do I still need to do?

Nick asked himself these questions over and over. Until one morning, sitting next to Jean on a bench overlooking the bay, watching the sun rise, his path forward became clear.

Chapter Forty-five

Nick hadn't had any contact with Lou Bradford or anyone at Elgin since he left his office and took off on his sabbatical over two months ago.

But he'd been thinking a lot about what Bradford had said, about Nick needing to get his act together but also having a place on his leadership team if he could do that.

Nick wasn't willing to give up. But he also knew he couldn't simply come back to Elgin after three months off as if everything were the same.

What were his options? This is what he'd been thinking about so deeply. Now he had an idea. He shared it with Jean as they walked back to their cabin.

"Do you think I'm crazy?" he asked.

"Not at all. I think it's a terrific idea. But do you think Lou will go for it?"

"I don't know. But I'm going to try."

"Well, I'm proud of you, Nick. Go for it."

"I will, Jean. There's one other person I'd like to run this by first."

"Who's that?"

"Josh."

"Josh?"

"Yeah."

"Why?"

"When he was here, he asked me what I'm going to do next. I told him I wasn't sure. He invited me to use him as a sounding board. Pretty cool, huh? Well, I'm going to take him up on it. I'm going to call him and get his thoughts."

"Good for you, Nick. I know he'll be honored."

"You know something, Jean?"

"What's that?"

"My dad never asked for my opinion about anything."

"Oh, Nick," Jean said, putting her arms around him. "You're a wonderful father."

About an hour later, Nick called Josh. Nick was standing in the kitchen. Jean was sitting on the sofa, watching him as he explained his idea and listened to what Josh had to say.

"Really?" Nick said, smiling. "That's the same thing your mother said! Thank you, Josh. I'll let you know how it goes. Have a great day."

And then he paused and said, "I love you too."

Nick sat down next to Jean. He didn't say anything. But he had a big smile on his face.

"Nick, you look so happy."

"I am happy, Jean."

"Why?"

"I love being here with you. I love being able to pick up the phone and talk with my son. I love the idea that our daughter is going to marry a good man. I am blessed, Jean. I feel like the most blessed man on earth."

#

Nick sat down at the kitchen table, opened his laptop and wrote this letter to Lou.

Dear Lou,

I hope you are well.   •

First, I want to thank you for the opportunity to take time off this summer and suggesting this sabbatical. I really needed a break, much more than I realized. It has been a wonderful experience.

I am in Bar Harbor, Maine with Jean for the summer. We're renting a cabin on the bay. It's like a second honeymoon.

I've had a lot of time to think about things and where I'm going. I've reflected on the things I know now I need to change, especially how I treat people. I've been a jerk.

I want to apologize to you. You've always been in my corner, even when I've not deserved it. I am deeply grateful, and I am sorry I've behaved badly.

I've also reflected on your generous offer to come back to work after Labor Day. I would like very much to do that, but in a new and different role. Here is my proposal.

Assuming Jennifer is doing a great job and you agree she is ready for promotion, I think we should officially give her the title of president and let her run with my old job.

In turn, I would go on a special assignment for the rest of my career at Elgin. I'd like to report to you and be responsible for two things. First, helping you set our overall corporate strategy. Second, working with you to identify and prepare our next generation of leaders, across the company.

The first plays to my strength. The second is an opportunity, an opportunity to make a positive, lasting impact, not just on the business but the organization too. I know the idea of me helping others develop might seem like a stretch. But I'm up for it, and I really believe I can do it.

I would be happy to play such a role for as long as you see fit.

I would also be happy to retire, if you believe that is the best thing for the organization and the right move for me.

Please let me know what you think. If easiest, let's talk by phone.

Thank you for everything, Lou.

Best regards,

Nick

He re-read his letter several times. He suspected it was a long shot. But he knew he could do this job. Long shot or not, he had to propose it. It was the best way he could think of to make things right at Elgin.

He took a breath and pressed "send."

Lou was usually prompt on email. But Nick heard nothing back that day. When he woke up the next morning, there was still no response from Lou. Nor all the next day.

Maybe he didn't know what to say. Maybe he thought Nick was being presumptuous. Maybe he thought Nick had lost his mind.

But when he woke up the following morning, this message was waiting in his inbox.

Dear Nick,

I can't tell you how happy I was to get your letter, to know you are well and that you and Jean are enjoying your "second honeymoon" in Bar Harbor.

I am so gratified to hear you've had an opportunity to sort through things. This was my hope. I look forward to hearing more about your experience.

I love your idea about the special assignment. But I want to build on it.

I'd like you to serve in a new role, which we'll call Chief Operating Officer. In this role, you'll do exactly the two things you've proposed, and you'll report to me.

But I'd like to add two elements.

First, I'd like you to work closely with Jennifer to prepare her to succeed me as CEO in two or three years. At that time, you and I will both retire, and the role of COO will go away. It will no longer be needed because you will have set us up for success.

Second, I agree that the idea of putting you in charge of developing others is a stretch. I do think you can do it, Nick, but not without some training and, frankly, the opportunity to build some trust with the organization. Doing this is going to take time.

So I suggest you tackle corporate strategy as a first priority, even as you go through some organization development training. I have a great program in mind for you. I went through it myself years ago. Jim Edwards suggested it.

This way, people will see you're improving. You'll be ready to work with them, and they'll be receptive to you when you take on the leadership development role, in about six months.

What do you think? If this sounds good to you, I would like to announce your appointment the day after Labor Day, when you're back in the office. Please let me know.

I am in your corner, Nick. Let's finish strong together.

Your friend,

Lou

Wow! It was even better than he was hoping for.

Nick was sitting at the kitchen table. Jean was still asleep. Nick read Lou's letter again and began to cry.

A little while later, Jean stepped into the kitchen. She saw Nick crying. She saw his laptop open on the table.

"Nick, are you okay?" she asked, walking over to him and putting her hands on his shoulders.

"Yeah, I'm fine," he said, sniffling and wiping away his tears. "I heard back from Lou."

"Really? What did he say?"

"He said yes," Nick said, laughing.

"Yes? Well, then why were you crying?"

"Here," he said, handing her his laptop. "Read it."

Jean sat down and read Lou's message.

"Oh, Nick. It's wonderful! Are you going to do it?"

"What do you think? Do you think I should?"

"Yes! Nick, I think you'd do a fabulous job in that role. And staging it that way is brilliant. How are you feeling about it?"

"I'm thrilled, Jean. But I do have one concern."

"What's that?"

"I want to leave room for the other things that I now know are important to me."

"Like what?"

"Like you and the kids. Playing music. Reading. Writing poetry. Our walks in the morning. My health. These things are precious to me, and I never want to compromise them again."

"Nick, I'm so glad to hear you say that. I want those things for you too. And I have a feeling that, after this summer, you can find a way to do this job without trading off the important things. Whatever you decide, just know you have all my support."

"Do you really think I can do this, Jean?"

"I don't think there's anybody in the world more qualified to do this job than you, Nick. So do it for two or three years, and we'll retire together."

"I like that idea," Nick smiled. "Would you like some coffee?"

"I'd love some."

#

After breakfast, Nick took his laptop out on the front porch and wrote this to Lou.

> *Lou, I am thrilled and accept your wonderful offer. But I must add one thing. On this sabbatical, I've come to understand the importance of balance in my life. You will certainly get my best work as COO. But I will need quality time for my family and other interests too. Provided you're OK with that, I'm in. Best. Nick*

Lou responded within minutes.

> *I am very OK with that, Nick, and I too am thrilled. Thank you. I'll be in touch and look forward to seeing you on September 6. Best. Lou*
>
> *P.S. I'm also going to tell Jennifer. I think it's only fair that we clue her in. Of course, I'll ask her to keep everything in confidence. But you might be hearing from her.*

Nick came inside and shared the latest messages with Jean.

"Oh, Nick!" she cried, giving him a big hug. "I'm so happy for you! I'm so happy for us! Let's walk into town this morning and celebrate over lunch."

It was about a two-mile walk to downtown Bar Harbor, twice as long as Nick and Jean normally walked each morning. When he first arrived in Bar Harbor, Nick could not have made such a long walk. Now, he did it with ease.

#

When they got back to the cabin, Nick opened his laptop and checked his email. He had a message from Jennifer.

> *Hi Nick,*
>
> *Lou just shared the good news. Congratulations! I am thrilled for you.*
>
> *I also want to thank you for all you've done, and continue to do, for me and for the business. I can see now all the smart decisions you've made over the years on every part of the business, in every part of the world. I have a new and deeper appreciation for what you've built.*
>
> *Elgin is fortunate to have you. I am fortunate to have you. I look forward to working with you in your exciting new role.*
>
> *Enjoy the rest of your summer.*
>
> *My best.*
>
> *Jennifer*

Chapter Forty-six

Nick awoke early, as Jean slept. He went into the kitchen and made a pot of coffee. He poured himself a cup, stepped out on the front porch and slid into the Adirondack chair which had become like a friend that summer.

The sun was rising, burning off the fog over the bay. The air felt crisp. It was early August, and the Maine nights had already begun getting cooler. Soon summer would be winding down. Nick and Jean would be back in Chicago.

He thought about going home. Should he simply retrace the route he had taken or go a new way?

He wondered what Jean would want. Then he remembered her favorite place in the world.

Nick smiled, a big, broad smile. He jumped up, as excited as a kid on Christmas morning. He went back into the cabin and hurried to the bedroom.

Jean was still sleeping. Nick sat down on the bed beside her, bent down and kissed her on the cheek.

She opened her eyes.

"Good morning," he said.

"Good morning," she said, smiling and looking curious.

"Jean, I have an idea."

"What's that?"

"Let's leave today and stop at Mackinac Island on the way home."

Jean looked up at Nick and blinked.

"Really?"

"Yeah, really. We can stay at the Grand Hotel."

A smile broke out over her face, and she giggled like a little girl.

"Oh, Nick!" she cried, reaching up and putting her arms around his neck. "I'd love that!"

She held his face in her hands and kissed him on the lips, a long, soulful kiss.

#

They chatted about their new plan over breakfast. They decided to retrace much of Nick's route to Bar Harbor, heading west toward Michigan when they got to Buffalo.

After breakfast, Nick booked the honeymoon suite at the Grand Hotel, the same room where he and Jean had stayed thirty years earlier. Then they packed up, checked out and took off.

It took them five days to get to Mackinac Island. They could have made it in two. But they took their time, stopping whenever and wherever they liked.

They even stopped in Albany, where Nick gave Jean a tour of the state capitol building. They went in through the eastern entrance, climbing the seventy-seven steps. Nick thought he might see Paul. But he wasn't there.

#

When they got to Michigan, they dipped down to Ann Arbor to visit Jean's family. They had dinner with her parents and stayed with them overnight. It was the first time Nick had seen them in years.

Nick had never asked his father-in-law, Tom, for Jean's hand in marriage. Doing so had fallen out of fashion in those days. But that's not why Nick didn't ask. He'd thought he was above it.

Over dinner, Nick said, "Tom, there's something I've been meaning to ask you for thirty years."

"What's that, Nick?"

"May I have your daughter's hand in marriage?"

"Gladly," he answered with a smile.

"Whew!" Nick sighed, smiling at Jean and raising a toast.

Gladly, Nick thought. What a gracious response. He really wished he'd asked Tom thirty years ago. He felt even more grateful that Michael had asked him for Ashley's hand in Bar Harbor.

#

Nick and Jean arrived in Mackinaw City on a Thursday afternoon and took a ferry to the island. The captain had radioed ahead. A horse-drawn carriage, compliments of the Grand, was waiting for them at the dock.

Once they'd checked in, Nick told Jean he needed to run a quick errand.

"Where are you going?" she asked.

"You'll see," he said mischievously.

"Nick, tell me."

"Now, Jean," he smiled. "A man has to keep a few secrets."

"Okay. But don't be long. I'm looking forward to dinner with my charming husband."

"Dinner? Is that all?"

"We'll see. A woman has to keep a few secrets too."

Oh man, Nick thought.

He went out to the hotel's pool house and rented bikes for him and Jean for the next few days. He hopped on one and peddled it to St. Anne's Church, which was just a few minutes away.

There he made arrangements with the pastor, Father Finn, for him and Jean to renew their wedding vows the next morning. It would be a surprise.

As he was about to leave, Nick decided to stop for a minute to say a prayer. He slid into a pew, put down the kneeler and got on his knees. The cushion on the kneeler was generous. But Nick was not used to kneeling, and his knees ached.

He looked up at the altar. He wanted to say an Act of Contrition, but he couldn't remember the words. But he could remember begging Jean's forgiveness a few days earlier and her asking if he could forgive himself.

Nick still wasn't sure if he could. He closed his eyes. In the quiet of his mind, he imagined himself asleep, then waking up. He was standing in a cage. He looked around. The cage was resting on a vast, grassy plain.

He heard a low, deep growl behind him. He turned around. There stood an enormous lion. He was staring at Nick's right hand. Nick looked down and saw a keyring with a single key dangling from his fingers.

He turned back around and, without fear, stepped forward to the door of the cage. He inserted the key in the lock, turned it until he heard a click and pushed the door open.

He assumed the lion would rush by him to escape. But instead, he slowly stepped forward and stopped right beside Nick. He was looking out the open door, just inches from freedom. But he didn't move. It was as if he were waiting for Nick to grant him his release.

The lion's dark mane was nearly up to Nick's chest. He raised his left hand and gently placed it on the great beast's head, barely touching it. But with that, the lion sprang through the opening, bounded into the tall grass and disappeared.

Nick opened his eyes. He was still kneeling, but his knees no longer hurt. In fact, for the first time he could remember, he felt no pain at all.

#

The next morning, after breakfast, Nick surprised Jean with a carriage ride from the hotel to St. Anne's. On the seat of the carriage, a dozen red roses were waiting for Jean. The card read, "Marry me all over again."

Father Finn greeted them at the front door of the church.

"Good morning, Mrs. Reynolds," he said, extending his hand. "It's a lovely day to renew your wedding vows."

"Oh, Nick," Jean said, her voice trembling. "This is incredible. I don't know what to say."

Nick smiled. "Just say, 'I do.'"

"Okay."

"Follow me, kids," said Father Finn.

Nick extended his left arm. Jean took hold of it. They followed the priest down the aisle to the edge of the sanctuary, where they renewed their vows and pledged the rest of their lives to one another.

#

Nick and Jean stayed on Mackinac Island for three days, then took off for Chicago. They'd been on the road for about an hour when Jean fell asleep. She was facing Nick. She looked like an angel.

The leaves of the maples along the highway were beginning to turn red, orange and yellow. Whole cornfields lay bare once again. Summer was drawing to a close.

On his way to Bar Harbor, Nick had thought his life, too, was drawing to a close. He had felt alone and unloved. He'd wondered if anyone would even miss him.

But then he got spun around, and he began to understand that he was neither alone nor unloved. No one had left him or stopped loving him. They were simply waiting for him.

Rays of sunlight streamed through gaps in the clouds. They made Nick think of his mother and what she had told him about grace being his salvation.

Now, he felt filled with grace. And he chose not to think of his failings or even the exciting opportunities ahead, his past or his future, his exodus or his journey home.

Instead, Nick chose to pay attention to the road and simply drive.

About the Author

Don Tassone has a passion for the written word. He has a degree in English. After a long career in the corporate world, Don is returning to his creative writing roots. *Drive* is his debut novel. His debut short story collection, *Get Back*, was published in March, 2017. Don also teaches at Xavier University in Cincinnati. He and his wife Liz live in Loveland, Ohio. They have four children.

CPSIA information can be obtained
at www.ICGtesting.com
Printed in the USA
FFOW02n1757220917
40165FF